THE WITCH WHO CAME IN FROM THE COLD

[s e a s o n 1]

CREATED BY **LINDSAY SMITH, MAX GLADSTONE**

WRITTEN BY
LINDSAY SMITH, MAX GLADSTONE
CASSANDRA ROSE CLARKE, IAN TREGILLIS
MICHAEL SWANWICK

ILLUSTRATED BY **MARK WEAVER**

SAGA PRESS

LONDON SYDNEY **NEW YORK** TORONTO NEW DELHI

SERIAL BOX

SAGA PRESS

AN IMPRINT OF SIMON & SCHUSTER, INC.

1230 AVENUE OF THE AMERICAS, NEW YORK, NEW YORK 10020

LINDSAY:
For Emily and Katie,
and the Soviet-flavored magic we all weave.

MAX:
To the people of Prague, with love and apologies.

IAN:
For Sara.

MICHAEL:
To all my Russian friends.
May the Cold War never return.

CONTENTS

ГРИМОИРЭ

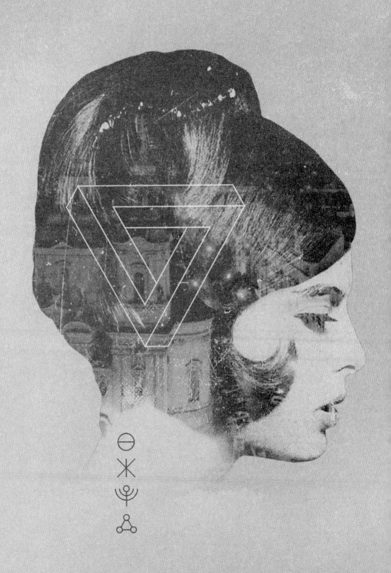

EPISODE 1

A LONG, COLD WINTER

Max Gladstone and Lindsay Smith

Prague, Czechoslovak Socialist Republic
January 18, 1970

1.

Tatiana Mikhailovna Morozova lay on her belly on the slate roof tiles, trying not to let the cold harden her muscles. She needed to stay limber for whatever came next—if it ever came next. The past few nights had proven fruitless, but she couldn't let down her guard. She listened to Prague's nightlife settle around her, from the distant mutter of drunks to the crunch of thin boot soles against snow to the heavy chill crackling in her numb ears, and tried to sift through them for any signs of her target.

But none of the street sounds were out of the ordinary; not a single person was out of place. Her entire operation, so carefully crafted, had been for nothing.

Tanya grabbed the binoculars from the rooftop ledge—KOMZ, dense metal and enviable optics, standard KGB issue—and surveyed Staré Město Square once more. A lone man crossed the square, kicking up a swirl of fog in his wake, but his frowning face was not that of her target. She swiveled her gaze across the night-stained square toward the streetlamp at the northwestern entrance, where a woman leaned against the post. Tanya couldn't hear the repetitive click of the lighter flicking open and snapping shut, but she could imagine it; she knew the sound too well. Nadezhda was just as bored as she was—knowing Nadia, probably more. If their target didn't show soon, it'd be another empty night. Another battle lost.

With a growing sense of desperation, Tanya checked each exit of the square once more. Their sources had hinted that their adversaries were working on a new, advanced scouting method, and this was just the sort of night for them to turn it loose. All their analysis indicated tonight was ideal—weather conditions, star alignment, magnetic pull, all those fiddly little calibration elements operators like her rarely had to take into consideration. That's what bureaucrats were for. But if Tanya let another target slip past, too many people would pay the price.

Several of their assets had already vanished, and they couldn't afford to lose even one more. She had a better chance out here, on the edge of the Iron Curtain, but then, so did the other side. It was difficult to get information when she was back in Moscow, spending her days in the dank basement of the Lubyanka headquarters, pretending she couldn't hear the screams from the interrogation cells. And her family was better connected than most, better skilled at greasing the ancient gossip machine that far predated the East-West divide.

The messages they did manage to pass on were always brief, vague, smuggled in via coded newspaper advertisements or a short radio broadcast on a signal strong enough to pierce the censors' static. *We have located one in Burma,* the message might read, or *One lost to them in Marrakesh.* Tanya didn't know which side was ahead but suspected the score was a little too even for anyone's comfort.

Something rattled on the roof ledge beside her.

Tanya dropped the binoculars and glanced toward the array of devices lined up on the stone. They weren't so much devices, really—the largest of them was scarcely wider than a ruble—as charms. Talismans. One was twitching like an electric wire starting to fray; another hummed with a barely visible glow. Some kind of detector slowly coming to life.

Tanya held her breath like a fist squeezing shut. There it was, just on the edge of her hearing: a shuffle and scrape, dry and rhythmic. So rhythmic it sounded mechanical. Close enough, anyway. Tanya raised the binoculars again, and sure enough, Nadia had flicked the lighter to life. Their target had arrived.

Nadia lit the cigarette, but held it aloft, uncertain. *Come on, Nadia. Give me a direction. Give me something to work with.* The bright cherry bobbed as Nadia scanned the square.

Finally, she jabbed it in the direction of a frothily ornate building tiered like a wedding cake of stone.

Tanya swiveled toward the old town hall. There it was, a dark figure, a blur behind the veils of fog. *Crunch. Crunch.* Each step in slushy snow a labored act. Was the target injured? Weak? Undercharged? They could only be so lucky.

She set the binoculars aside and bounded for the fire escape.

Drahomir was drunk. That was, after all, the plan.

He leaned over the table, clutching his beer with both hands. "And then I could see your friend Joshua to be holding the two pairs—I knew he had them, from his eyes, which are soft as pools. I am an excellent judge of character."

"You sure are, Drahomir." Gabe Pritchard raised his glass. "Here's to your success."

Smoke and jukebox jazz owned Bar Vodnář after dark. Candles flickered on tabletops. The lamps burned low, and conversation rumbled behind the music, Czech cut with jags of German and French. When the door opened, it drew eyes like filings to a magnet, but never held them long.

"I stayed in, to show him I was not afraid. I could turn the jack or the six, and his pairs would be as nothing against my straight. Through the, what is it—"

"The turn."

Drahomir grinned like a horse about to bite an apple. "The turn! But you turned no jack, and no six." He slapped the table once to emphasize each loss. "And he, what is it, re-raised. So all of my money, I push it into the center of the table. I will scare him away. And then, to find on the final card the jack, my friend!" He laughed and slapped Gabe hard on his bad shoulder. Gabe kept his own smile beaming and laughed along, though less harshly. "Gabriel! Poker is full of such strange words. Is there a word for this miracle?"

"It's called being a river rat, Drahomir."

"Rats," Drahomir observed, "are fantastic animals. They are hardy, and they live well in the most inhospitable corners of our earth. Wherever you find man, look beneath him and you will find a rat."

Gabe himself was neither a rat nor drunk, but he faked the latter well. Throughout the game at Josh's place, he'd steadily poured himself shots of iced tea from a whiskey bottle; after dragging the victorious Drahomir to drinks at the Vodnář, he'd switched to "gin and tonic." Jordan, who ran the bar, owed Gabe, and he owed her. She knew that when he ordered a gin and tonic with a twist, he meant hold the gin.

Plain tonic was perfect for this kind of work: Gabe had never acquired the taste for quinine, and damn if the stuff didn't make him squirm just as well as if it were fully loaded.

But that wasn't the only reason he wanted to squirm now.

This talk of rats and reading men might mean Drahomir had jumped a step or two ahead of Gabe's agenda. Gabe liked agendas: He liked conversations to move where and when he wanted under conditions he controlled. The plan had been to get Drahomir drunk and excitable—which Josh's sacrifice back at the poker table, and his sleight of hand, achieved neatly—but, flush with triumph, the man might be too drunk, too excitable, for the gentle work to come.

Gabe felt a sharp pain in the middle of his forehead and hoped it was only nerves. He leaned forward and lowered his voice. "I'm glad you enjoyed the game, Drahomir."

Drahomir mimicked him. "Enjoyed? I found it wonderful. Such talking, it feels like playing against *men*. I have, you know, played mostly chess—there we keep silent, we watch, we are like machines. I never liked much gambling, but this!"

"It's a game about friendship, really," Gabe offered. "It teaches you to know people. When you can trust them. When you can't."

"Will we play again?"

"Soon," Gabe said. The pain intensified. He grimaced.

"Are you well?"

"I'm fine, Drahomir. A headache."

"Ha. A few too many drinks, my friend?"

"No, nothing like that." He focused on Drahomir's dark eyes, willing the pain away. "Look, Drahomir, we've known each other for a while now. I'm glad my job at the embassy lets me work so closely with you at the Ministry of Economics. It's been a good partnership." Another wash of pain split his head in half between "good" and "partnership," but he kept his voice level. Drahomir looked concerned, but was it concern for Gabe, or concern at the subject of their talk? Jordan, at the bar, stared at him—at them. Had he made a sound without noticing?

Don't overthink it. Make the touch; make the call. You've strung this guy along, now show him the bait, and the hook. Gabe and Josh had figured Drahomir for an idealist and a patriot—a smart one, he'd have to be, the man had survived more purges than a cholera victim, but an idealist and a patriot still. Gabe had gone thirteen rounds with headquarters over the proper pitch. Don't offer money; that would make us seem venal and corrupt. Play into Russian narratives. Let him know money's around if he needs it, but don't think you can buy him. Don't offer asylum. If he wanted to run, he'd have run already.

Give Drahomir Milovic, assistant undersecretary of the Czech Ministry of Economics, a chance to be a hero. And let him take it.

Headquarters was doubtful.

"I especially value your friendship given everything your country's been through in the last few years," Gabe continued. Meaning, though he wouldn't say it out loud: the Prague Spring, Soviet tanks in the Staré Město, the end of their government's short-lived normalization. This was when Gabe needed the soft eyes, the earnest stare, the Marlboro Man jaw and the aw-shucks John Wayne calm: *You can trust me, sir. I'm Amurican; ah just want whut's right.* And he could have done it, had done it in a hundred gin joints all over the world, except for this damn *pounding* in his *head* like some furious dwarf burrowing inside his brain, mining for gold. It was all he could do to keep from wincing. *Pull it together, dammit. Make the pitch.* "We agree on a lot of things. You like freedom. You like being able to trust the people you sit next to. You like making your own choices, for your own reasons."

The dwarf hit a fresh vein of ore. Gabe raised a hand to his temple and tried not to scream.

"My friend," Drahomir said, worried—worried about Gabe because of this beautiful connection they shared that Gabe had spent the last six months building, block by painstaking block, "you seem unwell. We should find you perhaps a doctor."

I know people, Gabe could not say, because the words could not escape the ring of the dwarf's hammer, *who would give their lives to know what you know. To sit at the minister's ear and hear the poison the Soviets whisper there. To watch the little traces that matter: sudden shifts in spending patterns, interest in new industries in third-world nations, transfers of raw capital backed by Red guarantees.* And when Drahomir said, *Ah, but I have this knowledge, and I can do nothing to help my country, to help my people,* he, Gabe, would reply, *You can. Knowledge, Drahomir, is power. Like at the table, when you knew my buddy held two pairs. And if you help us—and I'm not talking anything major here, just little details, schedules, the answer to a question or two once in a while, so long as you feel safe—you can sleep at night, and know you've done your part to slide a knife between the ribs of those smiling bastards who step so tenderly onto your country's throat and bear down.*

That's what he would have said, but with kinder and more measured words, with the soft Iowa assurance he'd deployed so readily with assets in Cairo and Madrid and Bangkok and Milan, so that Drahomir, like all the men and women before, would listen, and look into his heart, and find that in that secret place he had forged, unwilling, unsuspecting, a tool to Gabe's own specs: a hammer, maybe, or wrench or screwdriver or pry bar or knife. A tool with a handle, waiting to be used.

That's what Gabe would have said, but the dwarf hit cerebellum pay dirt and what he said, instead, was sharp and four-lettered and of no use to anyone at all.

Tanya and Nadia crossed paths one block west of the square, ahead of their target. The street was a patchwork of shadow and light, everything reduced to hazy blobs that either melted into the darkness or blotted the lamplight. Having to rely on their own imperfect eyesight, the women were at a disadvantage.

Better to focus on what they could turn in their favor; better to minimize their shortcomings and leverage their strengths. Just as their forebears had stolen the secrets of the atom bomb rather than wasting money uncovering it for themselves. She and Nadia had three advantages over their target: One, they could be certain their target would take the most direct path available to its destination. Two, that it would move at a steady pace. Three, and perhaps the most crucial, it had no idea they were looking for it.

In truth, Tanya much preferred stalking this kind of prey over the usual drunken, paranoid diplomats the *rezidentura* chief frequently sent her to follow. Those men were always ready to throw a punch, looking for spies everywhere, a confusing mix of alcohol and counterintelligence training sending them looping halfway around Staré Město trying to shake tails real and imagined. But that's where the advantage ended. Diplomats, agriculture secretaries, cultural attachés, and the like—they rarely showed a fraction of the raw determination that tonight's prey surely would.

"Couldn't get a good look," Nadia said, voice pitched low so it wouldn't echo off the stone around them. "Still not sure who they're after."

"We're close to Bar Vodnář." Tanya pointed along the narrow, curving street ahead, through the hazy shapes of balconies and cherub statues jutting from the dark. "Everyone likes to make trouble there."

"Well, let's try to stop it before it gets too close. Last thing we need is to pick a fight with some supercharged construct." Nadia pitched her cigarette into a snow bank. "You have enough dampeners?"

Tanya's jaw stiffened. Between her grandfather's constant second-guessing and Nadia's chiding, it was hard not to feel like a child fumbling along. Hadn't she proven herself enough? But she nodded, huffing out a white cloud of breath before her. "I'm ready."

"Great." Nadia rolled her shoulders and her neck—the fighter in her limbering up for a brawl. "Since we don't know exactly what we're dealing with, let's keep it standard. You take the lead, find out who our target's after. See if you can't get that person to safety in a hurry. Use the Vodnář safe room if you have to, though try not to get that nosy bartender involved if you can avoid it. I'll circle back and try to delay or disable our target."

Tanya refrained from pointing out that this was exactly how *she'd* set up their operation last time, only with their roles reversed. That operation belonged to another world—a whole other set of problems. Their mundane daytime world of geopolitical struggle, scrabbling for scraps of information that could change the fate of governments, entire continents. How tiny it all seemed, comparatively.

No, Tanya thought as she glimpsed their target up ahead. Its limbs—definitely something stony, bound with metal and a host of other elements—shimmered in the dim streetlights a block away. A construct, a being assembled by powerful sorcerers and breathed to life with elemental energy. A creature fueled by a single purpose: to hunt down an elemental Host.

This world was something else entirely.

Gabe's dwarf wormed spineward. He grimaced and clutched the table's edge.

"My friend," Drahomir said. "You are not well. A doctor must be found."

"It's fine, Drahomir." Gabe ground the words between his teeth. "I have to ask you something." Hammers struck his temples. *Meet Drahomir's eyes. Be John Wayne.* "You probably know I don't—" He tightened his jaw through a spasm. Jordan set down her towel, watching him openly. He was attracting too much attention, dammit. "You won't be surprised to learn I don't work—" But he cut off for a rapidly indrawn breath as wires of pain shot up and down his spine.

Fine officers stroked out on assignment. People had heart attacks. But this didn't feel like a heart attack. Poison? He'd not left his drink unattended—that was a rookie mistake. Could Drahomir have—no. They'd watched the man. They knew him. He wasn't a killer.

Drahomir took his wrist. "Gabriel, let me take you to the hospital. Or at least your embassy. You are in pain. They will surely want to care for you."

And let Drahomir go down with him in public documents, let him be seen entering the American embassy—how much use would the man be then? Gabe tried to shake his head.

A shadow blocked out the light. "I'll take care of him. I've seen this before."

Jordan Rhemes set her hands against the booth tabletop and loomed over them. Silver strands in her dark hair caught the light.

Drahomir looked at her, astonished. So did the rest of the bar.

Too much, Gabe wanted to say to her. *You're attracting attention.* Not that Gabe himself wasn't, here and now.

"He is my friend," Drahomir repeated. "I will take him to hospital."

"You," Jordan replied, "should leave now. It's past your bedtime, Assistant Undersecretary. Your wife is no doubt anxious. I'll make sure he's safe."

"I cannot." He held on to Gabe—why? Maybe Drahomir knew what Gabe wanted to say; maybe he wanted to agree, if Gabe could just get the damn words out.

"You can," she said, and looked at him. The turning of her head left a trail of music, like soft bells, and her eyes were large. Drahomir paled. He tried to speak but found no voice. "Go."

Drahomir scooted from the booth and stood. He backed toward the door, eyes fixed on Gabe, and in his gaze Gabe saw the wreckage of months of planning. Groping behind himself, Drahomir found the door, opened it, and staggered out into twists of fog and snow.

Jordan nodded once when he was gone, as if she had settled everything, or anything. "I was worried he might follow through with that hospital idea. That wouldn't be good for any of us."

"Do you have any idea how long it took me to get him here?" Gabe whispered in Coptic.

"Won't matter one bit if you drop dead in my bar."

"You had no right—" But before he could finish his sentence, the world thinned and sped up at once, and the table rushed to meet his face.

Tanya sprinted back from the lead, just far enough that Nadia could see her, and met the other woman's eyes. *Confluence,* she mouthed. The intersection of two ley lines, those globe-spanning sources of energy, several of which cut through Prague. They could power everything from the tiniest charm to a massive ritual conducted by hundreds of sorcerers.

The particular confluence they were approaching happened to lie beneath Bar Vodnář, to the consternation of pretty much every sorcerer in central Eastern Europe. The bar's owner, Jordan Rhemes, wasn't exactly friendly to institutionalized witchcraft, no matter which institution it was. And for reasons Tanya found it best not to question, she was especially unfriendly to witches who happened to also be intelligence officers for the KGB.

Nadia held Tanya's gaze just long enough: Message received. They could use the energy from the ley lines to power some of their rituals—hopefully enough to stop the construct. Easy. Then all they had to do was corner a creature formed of elemental magic for a single-minded purpose—the pursuit and capture of a Host. A task it would continue for eternity until it either acquired its target or had been completely smashed into its base components. *Yes.* Tanya twisted her mouth into a scowl. *It's as simple as that.*

Nadia reached into her satchel and pulled out a small charm. Tanya couldn't see it from this distance, but she had a pretty good idea which one Nadia had chosen—two stones sandwiching a dried paste of dirt, bound with a thin copper wire in an elaborate design. Nadia puffed out a sharp breath onto the charm to supply the final component, then lobbed it over the construct's shoulder as hard as she could.

The charm plinked against the cobblestone street several feet ahead of the creature. For a moment, nothing happened. Tanya used the delay to dart forward one block, evening her path with the construct's once more. Then the creature's foot landed just short of the charm.

A dagger of rock and hard-packed earth shot up from between the cobblestones, sending the monster flying as it pierced two stories upward into the air. The crack of shifting earth ricocheted across the ornate facades that lined the street. Tanya cringed at the noise—but the time for subterfuge had passed. They could not allow this abomination to reach the Host. The construct crashed onto its back in the middle of the street, limbs whirring frantically, its mechanical drone shifting into a dizzying screech.

"*Poshli!*" Nadia shouted at Tanya as the stone dagger submerged itself back into the street. *Go.* "Find the Host!"

Tanya sprinted forward into the fog. Only a block to Bar Vodnář. If the Host was nearby, he or she might feel drawn toward the ley lines, whether they understood why or not. And depending what type of elemental they hosted . . .

Well, Tanya didn't want to think about what might happen to an unsuspecting Host if he or she tripped a ley line without proper training. Especially with a construct homing in—who knew what they might unknowingly unleash while trying to protect themselves? The power of two ley lines coursing through someone who didn't know enough to channel them properly— it'd make the cover-up for their last intelligence op look like a stroll in Gorky Park.

With the construct down, Tanya now had to rely on the

charms in her trench coat pockets to track down the Host. Not that they were much more reliable, this close to the ley lines, than any of her other field equipment—the static-snarled bug detectors, wonky signals scans, improperly ciphered codes that passed as standard issue. One charm vibrated the closer it got to anything powered by elemental magic, but unfortunately, that description applied to a surprising portion of Prague. Two things this city was lousy with: spies and witches. And more than a few, like Tanya and Nadia, who qualified as both.

The humming in her pocket grew fainter then stronger as she crossed the street. The confluence was only a few blocks away now, so accounting for its pull . . . Tanya took a deep breath and plunged around the corner of the next building. Right into a young woman.

"Oh! *Omluvte mě!*" the girl cried, reeling back. Her blond hair, only a little lighter than Tanya's own, was tucked into a knitted cap, and she wore a thick boiled-wool coat over flared trousers. A university student, if Tanya had to guess. Working class, probably a good little junior Communist who supported the Party and attended all the right rallies and didn't associate with those Prague Spring, Alexander Dubček types who only ever made trouble.

But the charm was vibrating madly, threatening to drill a hole in Tanya's thigh. This had to be the Host.

"Come with me. Quietly, please." Tanya's Czech was filed off at the edges, prickly with her Moscow accent. "Do not make a sound." She looped her arm through the girl's and ushered her toward the next block—the back alleyway and service entrance for Bar Vodnář.

Tanya knew she looked terrifying right now, her face flushed with exertion, blond wisps of hair snaking free of her braid, her lips pulled back in a painfully false grin. But sometimes fear was a necessity. Fear got people to comply.

The girl resisted for only a second before her limbs softened in resignation. "Who—who are you?" she whispered as they approached the alley's mouth. "No. Let me guess. *Státní bezpečnost?*" The Czech secret police. "KGB, with that accent."

"Quiet. I need you quiet for one minute." The darkened alley enveloped them, but now they were only yards from the confluence: Whether the Host girl could feel it or not, Tanya could sense every charm and talisman jammed in her pockets coming to life. "I can explain everything."

The touch of cold metal cleared Gabe's head and righted the spinning bar, almost. The room still danced behind him and around him, but less forcefully, and the ache in his head dulled. Jordan's hand was on his hand, her long, dark fingers pressing a charm into his palm—a closed eye in iron, with a narrow white feather wound through the metal.

"Does this help?"

"You," he said, finding that words came more easily now, "had no business chasing him away."

"Don't give me too much credit. You did more than enough." He'd heard doctors sound that way before, when operating on patients they judged terminal. "I just helped the process along. Follow me."

"No," he said, but she was already leaving. He hated this feeling: drowning in foreign waters. It reminded him of Cairo, of smoke-filled basements and impossible visions, of 1968 and the year he'd first met Jordan Rhemes. Back then he'd thought the only secret world was the one where he lived and worked. He slid out of the booth and pursued her, shakily, one hand always touching something solid: the side of a booth, a table, the wall, a bare water pipe. Jordan's skirt swayed ahead of him, but her shoulders were fixed and steady as a battleship prow. "It's only a headache."

"Even you do not believe that," she said. "I did not save your life back in Egypt to watch you decay now."

"I can handle this on my own," he said.

She laughed.

Tanya steered the girl toward a stack of wooden pallets. "Climb. Get up high." They climbed up to the low roofline of Bar Vodnář and settled on the edge of slate tiles; Tanya kicked away the pieces of lumber closest to them so no one—or rather, no thing—would find an easy path up. "All right. Can I trust you to stay put long enough for me to explain?"

The girl nodded. Her face was still soft around the edges, but her eyes sparkled with youthful determination. Tanya remembered that feeling from her own days as a student back at Moscow State. Back before she was assigned here, at the frontlines of the stalemate.

"My name is Tatiana Mikhailovna, but please, call me Tanya, if you like. I'm a cultural secretary at the Soviet embassy"—the lies flowed easily as water these days—"but that isn't why I'm here tonight. There are people hunting for you. I want to protect you from them, but I need your cooperation."

The student hunched her shoulders forward, drawing back from Tanya. "Hunting for me? People from your . . . embassy?" She said the word plainly enough—not dipped in the venom

Tanya would expect from one of the Dubček sorts, but the distrust was clear.

"No. No, nothing like that." Tanya shook her head. "Let me ask you . . . uh, Comrade . . ."

The girl hesitated, then shoved her hands into her pockets. "Andula."

Tanya gave her a sheepish smile—a well-worn tool in her kit for softening up a potential asset. "Andula. *Děkuji.* *Thank you.* "Have you experienced anything strange lately, perhaps when you cross through Staré Město?" She gestured toward the winding street beyond their alleyway. "It might be more intense during periods of low tide, or when there is a full moon, or—or perhaps when Venus is visible in the—"

Andula's stare was inching wider and wider, the sort of expression usually reserved for dealing with ranting lunatics.

Tanya cleared her throat. "What I mean to say is, have you noticed any strange sensations in this part of town? A headache, perhaps, or a tug of some sort, deep in your gut."

"I haven't a clue what you're talking about. I . . ." But then Andula's eyebrows drew downward. "Wait. No, now that you mention it, I did feel ill the other day, when I was collecting my stipend at the university offices not far from here. And then tonight, it was like this—I don't know, this . . . pressure, just in the back of my skull." Her eyes narrowed. "Your friends at the 'embassy' haven't done something to me, have they?"

"No, I assure you—it isn't that at all." Tanya laced her fingers together, the leather of her gloves squeaking. Where the hell was Nadia? She should have dismantled the construct by now and joined them. Somehow, for all her brusqueness, her partner was always better at explaining these things. The best Tanya could hope for was to spin an intriguing enough tale that the girl's curiosity or confusion would keep her from running. "There is no easy way to explain this, Andula. You are what is known as a Host. A vessel for one of the thirty-six elementals that power the world's sources of magic. Because of what you are, you are in danger from those who would use you to—"

Andula scrambled to her feet, tiles crashing to the alley floor beneath them. "All right. I think I've heard enough."

"Please. Just let me finish." Tanya pinched the bridge of her nose. "It's very important that you hear me out—"

"*Get back!*" Nadia roared in Russian as she tumbled into the alley's mouth. She wasn't alone—she was coiled around the main body of the construct, ungloved hands clawing desperately at the copper components that traced strange shapes all around its trunk. The construct lurched, menacing, toward the roofline, and leaped at them. For one moment, the phosphorescent eyes and gash of a mouth carved into its rocky face seemed to fix right on Tanya and the girl before Nadia was able to throw enough weight to send it crashing back to the alley floor.

"Wait right here," Tanya said to Andula—no more softness, no apologetic tone. No more time. She clenched her teeth and jumped down from the roof.

Tanya dug a charm out of her pocket and snapped the twigs on it in half to activate it. As she tossed it against the construct, the twigs turned into vines, flourishing over the construct's trunk, tangling around its limbs. Nadia bounced to her feet, nimble as ever. "Are we close enough?" she asked in Russian.

"It'll have to do." Tanya pulled out the components bag and dumped it open on the construct's twitching form. Flashing metal filings, herbs, flint, more twigs. She added a gob of saliva to the mix, then stepped over the construct to join hands with Nadia.

A bluish-gold glow seeped out of the spell components. It swirled into the air and wrapped itself around the two women, gilding the construct, the pile of discarded crates, the edge of the roof as they began to chant. Old Slavic words tangled into Latin; Aramaic put in an appearance. The longer they chanted, words droning as the intensity swelled, the more the glow illuminated, until it was pouring out of their mouths with each phrase and slicing through the cold night air.

The construct rattled beneath them, trying despite the vines to continue its grim march. *Just a few seconds more,* Tanya prayed as she let her chant punch through the night.

Then the vine snapped, and the construct lurched forward.

2.

Following Jordan through the bar's back rooms, Gabe clutched the charm and told himself that the metal's temperature made the difference. Gave him something to focus on. Or perhaps it was the pain of the amulet's edges digging into his palm that clarified his mind. The symbol did not matter, nor did the feather. He would be mad to think so.

Maybe he was.

She led him through a door, lit a candle, and continued down a sloped passage lined with shelves piled high with stock. Most of the Vodnář's customers would have been surprised to see what stock, precisely. The hall's first turning held the usual: beer bottles and cleaner, pallet boxes of chips, a vat of nuts, liquor. After the second turn bar supplies gave way to drying herbs and fruits, and what he hoped were roots—the light down here wasn't good, and some roots did look like mummified hands.

After its third turn, the hall might have been a museum storeroom. Wrought-metal charms filled one shelf; along another rested a line of ancient nails sorted painstakingly by size and type of head, each tip stained with what Gabe hoped was rust. Large stylized masks in the shape of birds' and lions' heads, or in shapes he did not recognize at all, rested on the top shelves, staring down like angels in judgment. Beneath them lay drums and flutes made of beechwood—that had to be beech, though the grain looked more like bone. One shelf sported only gleaming knives. He could almost hear the candlelight against their edges.

At the hall's end stood another door, which opened into an office: leather chair, fine old desk, packed with so many herbs and unguents the smells clashed and overlapped into a dank, rich jungle musk. Jordan fit the candle she carried into an iron holder.

"Close the door. Sit."

"What," he said, "no skull? I thought the candle's supposed to, you know, sit on the skull."

"Perhaps I will have yours out for the purpose. Sit."

He sat. The throbbing headache returned. He pressed the talisman to his forehead.

She grabbed a bronze bowl off one shelf, tossed it on the desk, lit a small gas flame under a black kettle, and circled around the room, gathering herbs and screwed-shut jars.

"What are you doing?"

"Trying to keep you in one piece. This is the worst the headaches have been, yes? The worst since Cairo?"

He crossed his arms. "That's none of your business."

She slathered a scoop of what looked like black tar into the bowl, added three handfuls of three different herbs, and mixed them into a paste with a flat blade. "It is all of my business, and very little of yours. By rights you should never have been drawn in to this world. You have tried to ignore it. You have tried to *cowboy* through, and perhaps now you may see that this is not helpful? Ignoring your difficulty hurts you, and your mission."

"I know this talk," he said. "You're buttering me up for a pitch."

"I am trying to help you."

"I won't betray my people."

The kettle whistled. Jordan poured water into the bowl, mixed the paste as if she were making cocoa, then added more water. "No fresh goat's milk, sadly, but this will have to do. Drink, quickly. It will help the pain."

He set down the charm and raised the bowl. The bronze warmed his hands. "This is steaming."

"It will not hurt you. I promise. Try not to breathe the fumes."

He met her eyes and drank. Oily liquid, gritty with powder, ash, and herbs, slithered down his throat. The pain receded. His vision cleared.

"I am not pitching you," she said. "And I do not wish you to betray anyone. There are people who have dealt with problems like yours since long before you were born—and long before your country was born, as well. They will help you, and then you will be able to do your job again. Will you listen to what I have to say, at least?"

Gabe finished the bowl, set it down, and slid it back to Jordan. The pain felt like a radio on in another room—easily ignored. "Fine," he said. "Tell me."

Jordan squeezed his shoulder and smiled. "You stumbled into a new world in Cairo, a world on whose edges I've lived all my life. There are two factions: Call them the Ice and the Flame. Their leaders have been fighting a secret war for a very long time, with people like me caught in the middle." Her smile turned sad. "Sound familiar?"

He nodded.

"Good. When you need to vomit, use the bucket beside you."

Tanya and Nadia chanted, bathing the alleyway in shades of blue and gold, even as the construct lurched out of its bindings. The glow wormed into its articulated stone joints; the "eyes" in the hollows on its head burned a hot white. It leaped once more for the roofline, where Andula, the terrified student, crouched. But they didn't relent, letting the ancient languages twist and flow.

Then everything happened at once: Andula's scream, the sparks showering from the construct's joints, the flash of light that hit Tanya in the chest like a fist. Her hand ripped out of Nadia's, and she tumbled backward into the heap of broken wooden pallets. Flecks of wiring and crystals sprayed across her lap—the creature's elemental components.

They'd done it. They'd overloaded the construct with energy direct from the ley lines, more than it could possibly contain. It had been reduced to its base parts, all of the power its creators had stored within it unleashed in a single burst.

As for the matter of just who'd created it . . . well, she and Nadia would have to deal with that soon enough.

"*Blyad*," Nadia swore, heaving a chunk of rock off her arm. She was sprawled across the alley floor, her dark hair pooled beneath her. Tanya had to blink a few times to clear the after-flash in her eyes to make sure it wasn't blood.

"What the devil was that thing?" Andula screeched.

Tanya and Nadia exchanged a look. "I need to gather components," Nadia said. "So we can track down the creators."

Tanya sighed and climbed back up to the roofline with Andula.

"As I was saying . . . You are a Host. You were born attuned to a particular elemental, and, through some means, have been activated. Your elemental has come home to roost, you could say." Tanya smiled darkly. "Witches like me are able to use these elements for good, but there are witches who would use them for more sinister purposes too. And they would very much like to harvest this elemental from you."

"Harvest? *Harvest?*" Andula crawled back on the roof, away from Tanya. "What is that supposed to mean?"

Tanya chose to ignore her question for the moment. "These witches—the Acolytes of Flame—someone from their organization created that device. An elemental construct. Its sole purpose was to track you down for them. Fortunately for you, members of the Flame aren't the only people capable of wielding elemental magic."

The girl's eyes were wild. "And what would it have done if it caught me?"

Nadia trilled with laughter. "Oh, *milaya devushka*. Trust me, you don't want the answer to that."

The crisp night air crackled in the heavy silence for a few moments. "It was tracking me," Andula finally said. She watched as Nadia wrenched apart two chunks of crystal that had been fused together. "Like—like a radar, or something."

"Yes, much like that. The Acolytes of Flame are attempting to collect all of the Hosts like you," Tanya said. "They want the elementals for themselves."

"So there's something inside of me? Right now?" Andula pointed to herself. "What is an elemental, and what does it want with me?"

"It wants *you*. You were born to be together; you were meant to be the Host for the kind of elemental power it represents—like

THE WITCH WHO CAME IN FROM THE COLD

water, or electricity, or earth, so you can use its power to its fullest potential. Think, Andula—have you always had an affinity for water, perhaps, or a particular type of flower? But it wasn't until you were activated by a strong burst of energy that your elemental could find you." Tanya's expression softened. "Don't worry—it can't harm you. This is what you were made for."

Andula laughed, a dry and bitter rasp. "I've never known you *KaGeBezniks* to be big on matters of fate."

Nadia and Tanya flinched as one. They exchanged a glance, a long, wordless debate; then Tanya closed her eyes with a faint nod. "We're not here as *KaGeBezniks*," Nadia said at last.

"No? Then who are you? What do you really want with me?" Andula folded her arms across her chest. "How can I trust you? How do I know that this 'Flame' is the group that means me harm, and not you?"

"We're with the Consortium of Ice," Tanya said, resting one hand on Andula's knee. She was careful to keep her palm curved down, concealing the tiny charm nestled in her hand there. "And we're here to help."

Gabe thought that by the third heave, surely there couldn't be anything left. He was wrong.

Jordan rocked back and forth in her chair and kept talking, as if his guts weren't lying in a bucket between them. "The Ice likes the world more or less the way it is. They are . . . prigs, for the most part, but less vicious than the Flame. I have contacts among them. If anyone knows how to deal with your pain, they will." She passed him a tissue.

"I don't need their help" would have sounded much more

authoritative if his stomach hadn't chosen that instant to double him over, dry-heaving.

"That should be the last." She passed him a glass of clean water once he finished. "Rinse your mouth well. You don't want any of the stuff you drank lingering between your teeth."

He rinsed, spit, and wiped his mouth, then tossed the tissue in the bucket. "Is there a place I can dump this?"

She nodded to a door he hadn't noticed before. "Washroom."

By the time he returned, she'd wiped the bowl clean and burned a handful of herbs within.

Gabe took his seat. "I can handle myself."

She laughed. "Like you handled Drahomir?" Jordan did not let the silence linger long enough to compel his answer. "How long can you keep this from your comrades at the embassy? Or from their bosses back at Langley? The Ice can teach you to deal with your problem."

"Can't you?"

She shook her head. "I can treat the symptoms. The problem beneath, I cannot touch. And if you let that problem go untended, the symptoms will grow beyond my ability to calm."

"That doesn't sound good."

"No," she said. "You must speak with Alestair Winthrop. He is a"—she searched the air above his head for the right word and settled on—"cultural attaché at the British embassy. One of your people."

Gabe crossed his legs and leaned back. She hadn't said "operative." She hadn't said "spy." "A cultural attaché?"

"MI6," she said. "So, really your kind of people. It's not like I'm sending you to the KGB."

"Was that an option?"

Jordan's smile was very white, but in other respects nothing like a shark's. "Your service and his are friendly. If your comrades, or Langley, discover the relationship, they might even be pleased: Interagency cooperation is so difficult to achieve, especially in the field."

"And he's a . . . whatever."

Her face screwed up. "'Sorcerer' is the term they prefer. But yes. From as old a family as they come. The Ice cares about things like that: bloodlines, titles, families. Prigs, like I said."

"And he's MI6. Of course."

"I don't care for the Ice at all, Gabriel. But Alestair is a good man. He will help you."

"Yes" was the word on the tip of his tongue. It tasted smooth, round, soothing, cough-drop fresh. But with the pain gone, training caught him like a trap. An officer massaged an asset through the stages of the recruitment cycle like a priest led parishioners through the Stations of the Cross: Find a potential source, trace the outlines of his needs or hers, build a relationship through trust or fear or common cause, and then recruit. Coax the player into the game.

I am not pitching you, Jordan had said. But that was the cycle's core, the double blind, the story told and sold: This isn't a process; these steps aren't mechanical. You're special. We care.

Magic was real. Cairo streets twisted through his nightmares. Jackals laughed, and metal feet clattered down cobblestones in memory. Knives gleamed in shadows, their edges blood wet. He saw those dark dream visions waking, sometimes, before the headaches came.

Jordan wanted to help. Or wanted him to feel that's what she wanted.

He swallowed the yes, said "No," and stood. The room did not tilt or sway as he approached the door.

"Gabriel—"

"No," he repeated, finding it easier the second time.

She rounded the desk, reached for his arm, but did not touch him. "You cannot ignore Cairo forever. Sooner or later you will have to face the wounds you took. Sooner or later you will have to trust me."

He couldn't bear to say no a third time, so he walked through the door and shut it behind himself.

Karel Hašek watched with one perfectly crinkled eyebrow as Vladimir spread the contents of his satchel on his desk, early morning light painting them with a softness that, having failed, they didn't deserve. Molten tangle of copper wiring. Crystal fragments. A bundle of herbs or flowers, singed beyond recognition. A chunk of quartz. Vladimir snapped the satchel closed, then crossed his hands before him, waiting for his boss to speak.

"What?" Karel asked. "That's it?"

"That's all we recovered from the alley where we located it, sir." Vladimir's thick fingers clenched around the satchel straps. "I suspect that whoever dismantled it most likely took the rest with them."

"Whoever. *Whoever.*" Karel raked a hand through his dark curls. "And who, pray tell, do you think is capable of dismantling such a construct?"

Vladimir's throat bobbed; he looked around the study, half-afraid the rest of their coven might pour out of the shadows at any moment. "The—the Ice, sir?"

"Yes. Yes, the Ice. But what are they doing in Prague?" Karel shoved away from the desk and began to prowl, pacing in long strides. "When was the last time they bothered to track down the Hosts on their own?"

"All they seem to care about is interrupting *our* work," Vladimir said.

"Always we must stay two steps ahead, Vladimir. Never be the one to pursue. What good is it doing the Soviets to chase after the Americans, after all? Kennedy said he wanted a man on the moon—the Soviets poured all their funds into trying to beat them there. No. Too late. They tried to squash our spirit here, in Prague, but by stamping out one fire, they ignited a dozen others. So it will be for the Ice."

Vladimir studied the map pinned up behind Karel's desk. Hand drawn, centuries old, the political boundaries embarrassingly outdated. But the stark diagonal lines formed an uneven grid that never budged. Whatever they accomplished with the ritual, with all of the Hosts bound together as one, that grid would remain, ready to serve them. An endless power source for their endless reign.

"But they have our Host," Karel continued.

Vladimir cleared his throat. "We cannot be certain of that. If we can identify the Host through what remains of the construct, we might be able to locate him or her through more . . . conventional means."

"Mm. Perhaps." Karel plucked up one of the crystals, turning it over in his fingers. A splinter of darkness lingered at the center. Vladimir couldn't remember if it had been there before their ritual or not. "Or at the very least, we might locate these Ice interlopers. That could be far more valuable, in the long run."

Vladimir blinked a few times, then forced himself to nod, even as he was trembling inside. "Naturally, sir. But—but in the meantime. What shall I . . . tell the others?"

"Tell them we'll need to conduct a new ritual sooner than we anticipated. I'll check the charts, the almanac, but I think there are several auspicious times ahead." Karel grimaced. "It would be better if we could gain access to the confluence beneath Bar Vodnář."

"The one the Rhemes woman owns?" Vladimir asked. His shoulders rolled back as he stood up straighter. "I think we might have a solution to that."

Karel seized his coat from the rack and swung it on. Heavy tweed, a fine English cut—something from before the tanks rolled in. "Then see to it." He pulled on his cap. "I have a lecture to give."

3.

CIA Prague Station was born from an architect's mistake.

The embassy building that housed the station was a sharp Georgian beauty curled around a tree-strewn courtyard, and its large third-floor chambers might, in a distant aristocratic past, have been drawing rooms or libraries or studies—not that Gabe knew the difference between the three.

Those rooms, the few times Gabe had been inside them, demonstrated that the architect knew how to produce a decent space. Light filled the chambers from their plush carpeted floors to their high ceilings, and pale blue plaster walls created a flawless illusion of openness. Which, of course, made them utterly unsuited for intelligence work.

But between and behind those chambers—now repurposed as filing rooms or meeting halls or public offices—tangled a warren of coffin-size rooms where two grown men would have to exhale to pass abreast, improbable cul-de-sacs, doors built for hunchbacks, S-curve crawl spaces with ceilings that belonged on a submarine, opening onto oddly cornered cubbyholes twice as tall as any room in the rest of the house. All windowless, of course, even the one room large enough to stash four officers' desks side by side. They'd been servants' quarters once, or storage, meant for heavy use by people the building's proper residents preferred to ignore.

Which, come to think, remained an apt description.

They'd carved a window for Frank's office during renovations, a smoked-glass slit broader on the inside, like an arrow loop. That had been their one concession to design or comfort, a status symbol and a generous allowance for the chief of station. When Gabe first arrived in Prague, he had imagined they made the window narrow for security reasons, but today he thought there might have been a different sort of foresight involved. Granted, Gabe had put on weight since his college days, but even in football trim he wouldn't have been able to throw himself out of that gap.

Franklin Drummond, chief of Prague Station, had killed seven men with a shovel in a foxhole in Korea. Gabe knew this, as did everyone in the station, even though Frank never told the story and no one else did either. Secrets of many kinds moved around and through Prague Station, and some you learned just by breathing in.

Today, that story Gabe had never heard was impossible to forget.

"Sit," Frank said when the door closed. Frank looked tired, but his clothes were military crisp. He dressed sharply, fit perfect, always ironed—as if at any moment he might be under inspection. As a black man in the CIA, he probably was. Frank held his officers to the same standard, and from the look of things, Gabe wasn't holding up. "And take me through it one more time."

"I'd rather stand, sir, if it's all the same to you."

"It is not all the same." Frank's voice tightened and tensed as he circled the desk. "It is not all the same because one of us has a leg missing, and that one of us just happens to be your command-ing officer, who is confused, and frustrated, and angry at what looks to be a first-degree failure of basic intel work last night. So sit down, Pritchard, and walk me through this mess again."

Gabe sat. Frank sat.

"Well?"

"I screwed up," Gabe said.

Frank lifted his clipboard with a typed report. "Officer Toms praises your work on the handoff. The potential asset enjoyed the game, won big, for which I'm sure Accounting will thank you, and then the pair of you skipped off to a nice smoky bar for the final pitch." He turned the page. "At which point, Toms continues, the, let's just say 'high-value' target, whom we have spent, and you have spent, six months and significant departmental resources developing, emerged from the bar 'spooked' and 'shaking,' which are not, in my professional opinion, words I would use to describe a successfully recruited asset. Would you agree?"

"Sir, I—"

"Would you agree, Pritchard?"

"Yes, sir, I would agree. Those are not words I would use to describe a successfully recruited asset. Nor would I describe what I did last night as successfully recruiting Drahomir Milovic."

"What would you describe it as?"

"I screwed up, sir. It's in the report."

"The report indicates that you suffered, and I quote, an 'intense headache' during the pitch. That you took suddenly ill, and asked the asset to leave rather than placing yourself in a situation where the two of you might appear on hospital records together."

"That's the shape of it, yes, sir."

"You're looking well today, Pritchard."

"It was a twenty-four hour bug, sir. I thought I could keep it together for the op."

"You went into a delicate recruitment op, which we've been planning and prepping for months, sick."

"I was feeling off yesterday morning. I didn't want to cancel at the last minute. It could have made us look bad."

Frank threw the clipboard on the desk, folded his hands, and leaned across toward Gabe. "Friends cancel on friends all the time because they're sick. We could have changed the schedule. This week, next week, makes no difference. But you got to the pitch, and you blew it. Best case scenario, Milovic's just worried about you. Worst case, which is likely, he knows you were trying to set him up for something, and he's worried about *us*."

"With respect, sir, I know this is bad. I'll make it right."

"Over a few months, during which we could have used you on other targets."

"I know," Gabe said. "I'm sorry. I've had a lot on my plate recently—"

"A lot on your plate." Frank's eyebrows rose, as if he'd never heard those words in that precise combination before. "A lot on your plate. Boy, you've been dropping more balls than a drunk juggler. My girls have a Labrador—you know, those big dogs with the floppy ears?"

"I'm familiar with the breed, sir."

"Now, I've known smart dogs in my time, and this is not one of those. When I throw a stick, she'll run in the opposite damn direction. But my girls love their dumb dog, and because I love them, I love her, too. I don't mind that the dog can't do what the damn thing's bred for, because I don't need it to. But I don't have room for two pets in my life. Whatever unscrewed your head at Cairo

Station, you'd best get it screwed back fast. I took you on because Killarney said you needed a change of venue, that you were a good officer, and I've seen some shades of that. But you better show me more than shades soon. There are boys dying for the chance to prove themselves here. We're on the front lines of the Cold War. We are in no-man's-land." His eyes met Gabe's. "And no-man's-land is no place for someone whose head is not in the game."

"I understand, sir." Gabe's heart beat fast, but his voice, at least, he kept level. "I'll get it under control. I'll do whatever it takes to land the asset."

"Damn right you will. One more screwup, and there's no way in hell I'm letting you touch ANCHISES next month."

"Leave it to me, Chief."

Frank pulled the report from the clipboard's jaws, opened a desk drawer, and dropped the papers in a file. "Show me what you can do, Pritchard. Get this done." Without looking, he slammed the drawer shut.

Tanya rushed through the Soviet embassy's hallways, sleep-crusted eyes squinted against the harsh morning sunlight. The worst sort of January day—inexcusably cold and unforgivably bright. Last night's encounter with the Host and the construct still rattled around her thoughts. It had been a perfect pitch. She'd laid out precisely why the Flame posed a danger, and why the girl needed the Ice to keep her safe. But it had been too much to swallow, Tanya feared. The girl needed time to regain her footing.

And then there'd been all the paperwork for the Ice afterward, prepping the report, picking through the construct's pieces for clues . . . And, of course, strategizing how they'd explain to their superiors that they hadn't persuaded the Host (*Andula, her name is Andula*) to turn herself over to Ice protection.

But the girl would come in from the cold, Tanya told herself. They always did, once they saw just how determined the Flame was. Just how cruel their methods.

None of it mattered, though, the moment she walked through these corridors. Here, she was the *KaGeBeznik* Andula had accused her of being; when she was here, there was no room in her mind for anything else to matter. Her grandfather had pulled countless puppet strings to land her this prestigious assignment in Prague, the sort of post every ambitious officer's-school graduate would happily claw her eyes out for, and she couldn't show one ounce of weakness.

We need you in Prague, he'd said. *It's vital to our success.*

She'd just laughed. *For the Ice? Or for the Party?*

He hadn't answered her for a long time; the tightness around his eyes had begun to frighten her. He'd always been that rarest of breeds—the unserious Soviet. The carefree true believer. *Both, if you can,* he'd said, finally. *But in this, you must put the Ice first.*

She hadn't believed him then. Still didn't want to now.

Tanya shoved open the door to the concrete *rezidentura* vault, buried like a tainted piece of evidence in the embassy's basement.

Heads snapped up at her entrance, eighteen minutes late—including, she noticed with a scowl, Nadia's. Hadn't Nadia said something about heading to the bar, even after they'd finished up well past one? Tanya ducked her head and made her way down the swaying, clanking metal staircase, feeling the heat of every single one of her colleagues' stares.

No encrypted cable messages from Moscow awaited her—no updates on her grandfather, no word from KGB headquarters, or from anyone else. She spun the dial to unlock her file safe and started to dig through the folders inside but already knew what they'd all contain. A couple of surveillance shots of suspected CIA and MI6 officers, none particularly damning. Some of the people she was developing for recruitment—mostly university students who might someday, eventually, inform on their capitalist-leaning peers; a few handsy businessmen; and the dossiers of a couple of maids who might, if their third cousins were to be believed, *might* clean the American ambassador's home . . .

They were Nadia's potential agents, really; as her supervising officer, Tanya had encouraged her to pursue contacts at the university for some easy recruitments to get her initial numbers up. Their encounter with the Host the night before played through Tanya's mind again. A university student herself. *Andula Zlata.* Tanya scribbled the name into a new information request form. She'd check KGB records first—then, if she couldn't find anything there, she'd run it by the Czech secret police service, the StB. Andula had agreed to meet with them in two days' time, after she'd had enough time to mull over Tanya's pitch, but if the Flame was already on her trail, it never hurt to be prepared—

"Morozova." Rezidentura Chief Aleksander Komyetski loomed in his private office's doorway. "A word, please."

Tanya dropped the form on her desk and shuffled toward his office. Nadia met her eyes as Tanya passed her; Tanya gave her the faintest shake of her head.

Chief Komyetski—Sasha, as he insisted even the most junior officers call him, in the spirit of socialist equality—was already seated at his desk when Tanya entered. A brutally sheared bonsai tree occupied one third of his desk, while a variety of chessboards covered shelf space, a few side tables, and two chairs. Sasha acknowledged her with a nod but didn't motion to the sole unoccupied seat as he rolled his own chair toward one of the chessboards farther afield. He clenched a scrap of cable traffic in his fist; Tanya's heart leaped at the sight of it. Word from Moscow? An update on her grandfather's condition, perhaps.

Sasha squinted at the paper, rubbing his free hand against his jowls. After a moment's consideration, he changed to squinting at the chessboard instead. "Ah!" His whole face glowed as he slid his knight into position and struck out the unseen opponent's bishop with a *click*.

Tanya's shoulders drooped. Of course. One of his countless games of correspondence chess with his chums back at Lubyanka and the rezidenturas across the globe. She shifted her weight and waited.

"Officer Morozova." Sasha turned his wire-thin smile on her. "I thought it was time that we discussed . . . your goals in Prague Station. Specifically, that you are not meeting them."

Tanya felt her throat harden like ice, holding back all the objections she wanted to make. "I—I recruited over a dozen agents in my two years in Madrid," she finally managed. "One of them was a British Royal Air Force attaché. He gave us—gave us vital information on NATO discussions."

"So you did." Sasha wheeled past her, making his way toward another board.

"It's not even been two years since the Soviet tanks rolled into Prague to crush the rebellion," Tanya said, panic raising her tone. "The people are deeply distrustful of us—we have few friends among the Czechs."

"All issues my other officers face," Sasha said with a wave of his hand.

Tanya clenched a fist at her side. "I graduated top of my class at the academy. Top marks at Moscow State's graduate program."

"Yes, yes. And we all know your family's credentials, as well." Sasha settled another chess piece into place. "But what are you doing for me here in Prague?"

Tanya's teeth clicked together. "It . . ." She swallowed hard, trying to vanquish the desert in her mouth. "It takes some time, sir, to familiarize myself with the new environment. We face far more hostility from the Western services here than we did in Madrid. But I'm building—building relationships. I have several developmentals in progress." She glanced down. "I understand that the CIA station chief is aggressively thwarting our pitches, and I don't want to get overeager without taking the necessary precautions . . . but you are correct, Comrade. I will do better."

The click of another piece falling. "Everyone knows what a Morozov is capable of accomplishing. I know you will live up to your name." The smile that shoved at Sasha's chubby cheeks sent a chill down Tanya's spine. He wheeled back behind his desk and gestured to a board on the far corner. All the pieces were lined up in starting position. "Come, Morozova. Sit. Would you like to play?"

Tanya hesitated, fingers curling around the top of the empty chair. She was fairly sure she had one too many games running at the same time as it was.

Two sharp knocks rang on Sasha's office door; then the door swung open. "*Izvinitye*, Comrade Komyetski, I was looking for—ah. For Comrade Morozova." Nadia cracked a wide grin. "I have the information you requested on the university student you're developing. You know. The one you think is ready to be persuaded . . . ?"

Tanya took her hand off the back of the chair she'd been about to sit in. The university students were Nadia's to recruit. But the tension in her partner's smile was growing by the second. "Oh! Oh, yes, of course. Thank you, Comrade." She hurried toward the door. "Come, I'll show you how to study a developmental's dossier, if you like. A good opportunity to prepare you to manage your own cases."

"That'd be most helpful. As long as Chief Komyetski is finished," Nadia added with a shy glance toward Sasha.

His lips rolled into a smirk. "Go on, my dear, we were only having a little chat."

As soon as they were out of Sasha's hearing range, Tanya rounded on Nadia. "Please, this is your developmental—I can't just take it from you."

"You need to boost your recruitment numbers to get Sasha off your back. Besides, you're the boss—you have priority. Around here, anyway." Nadia cracked her gum with a grin. "After we're done with the dossiers, I think we should both spend some more time at the university library. Check up on our new friend."

Tanya scooped up the information request she'd filled out earlier. *Andula Zlata.* "My thoughts precisely." She reached into her pocket and closed her hand around the bit of crystal she'd scavenged from the construct. "And then I'd like to do some research of our own."

Jordan picked up her phone on the seventh ring and didn't miss a beat when Gabe said, "Introduce me."

Nor did she look up from the bar when he entered the Vodnář that night, snow melting on his overcoat. Smoke burned his eyes. He peeled off his gloves and folded them in his coat pocket as he descended into the dark.

In the corner, behind a pillar—the table to which he'd guided Drahomir last night. Gabe draped his coat over his arm.

A man sat in the booth, reading: blond and long and pretty, a fencer or a gymnast gone soft with age. He wore a tweed jacket and a silk tie, either of which Gabe would have bet cost more than his own present wardrobe in its entirety. When the Brit saw Gabe, he closed the book—*Tiger, Tiger* (Gabe had never heard of it, maybe poetry or something)—and smiled with the farthest corners of his lips, not baring teeth. A spark in the man's blue eyes suggested merriment or larceny. "Good evening, dear chap. Please." He extended one hand palm up across the table.

Gabe sat. A drink appeared at his elbow. "Jordan says you're the man to see."

"Very right." The Brit didn't look much older than Gabe himself—a handful of years at most—but his voice suggested otherwise. A put-on, Gabe thought, but maybe not, considering. This was a world inside the one he imagined he knew, with secrets of its own. "I am certainly a man, and I've had scads of people eager to see me, from time to time."

"I'm Gabe Pritchard."

"Alestair Winthrop." The man's handshake felt firm, not strong, like he was made from math rather than muscle. "The fourth. Cultural attaché of Her Majesty's government. And I understand you're an analyst with the American Department of . . . Agriculture, was it?"

"Commerce," Gabe said.

"Oh, Commerce, indeed." Winthrop folded his hands on the table. "We do love our masks. Miss Rhemes did me the favor of arranging this meeting, but she left the details of your story imprecise, their relation up to your own discretion. I understand that your main interest tonight thrusts toward neither, shall we say, commerce nor culture, mine or anyone else's. Beyond that I'm afraid you must be forthright, if I'm to aid you in any way save offering the considerable pleasure of my after-dinner conversation."

Gabe felt the cold glass in his hands and pondered walking out. He remembered Frank. He remembered Cairo.

He stared into the light in Winthrop's eyes.

"Something went wrong in my head in Egypt," he said. "And Jordan thinks the Ice can help."

"Well, now." Winthrop unfolded his hands, laid them palm down on the table, and leaned in. "Perhaps we can, at that."

ГРАНДФАТХЭР

EPISODE 2

A VOICE ON THE RADIO

Cassandra Rose Clarke

Prague, Czechoslovak Socialist Republic
January 21, 1970

1.

Tanya peered out the window at the street below. The lamp at the corner burned yellow, but otherwise the street was dark. Empty, too. Good.

She checked that the window's latches were still locked and then drew the thick curtain across the glass. At the same time, she snapped the braid of dried herbs she carried in her left hand, releasing a scent like old tea. The magic wafted on the air around her: a simple spell, designed to make passersby on the sidewalk below ignore her apartment building.

The windows in her kitchen and her bedroom had already been secured. She cut across the apartment to her door, and for a moment she laid her ear against the cool, slick wood and listened to the sounds of the hallway outside. Music drifted from Mrs. Budny's apartment across the way, but that was expected: Every evening Mrs. Budny's radio was a constant hum in the background. Tanya ran her fingers over the lock, made sure it was clicked into place. Then she crumbled the herbs and sprinkled the dust on the floor.

Everything was where it needed to be. Everything was secure.

Tanya slipped into her kitchen and knelt to open the small cupboard next to the refrigerator. She couldn't remember the last time she had cooked with most of the tarnished pots crammed inside. She removed them one at a time, careful that they didn't clank as she lined them up on the linoleum.

When she had set the last of the pots on the floor, she reached deep into the cupboard and pressed the latch that collapsed the false wall at the rear; there was a sharp pause, like the apartment was holding its breath, and then the back of the cupboard slid into Tanya's hands. She set it aside and leaned into the hidden compartment. Her hands found the radio, cold metal and rough dials. She pulled it out and sat on her heels. The radio was a small thing, scuffed from use, the numbers fading away into ghosts. Tanya stood up and set it on her kitchen table, then slid into a chair and switched the radio on. She didn't bother plugging it into the wall; this radio didn't need electricity to run.

The radio flared with static. Tanya turned the dial, ears straining. She wasn't listening for music or messages from the Party. This was not that sort of radio.

The static roared. Tanya edged the dial forward. Maybe he wasn't going to speak with her today. Sometimes his voice didn't come through. Sometimes conditions weren't right.

But then she heard it, a familiar whisper in the radio's white noise. Tanya froze, finger hovering near the dial.

"—Ya, my little bird—"

She let out a long breath. Nudged the dial. Instantly the static vanished, and the voice rang out through her apartment like a bell.

"*Dyedushka*," she murmured. "Are you there?"

"I am here. I am always here," the voice said. Tanya slumped back in her chair and closed her eyes. That way it was easier to pretend her grandfather was in the room with her, and not lying comatose in a hospital bed in Moscow. That this voice was really him, and not a magical recording, trapped inside a plastic-and-metal box and enchanted to speak and respond as if it really were her flesh-and-blood grandfather. "What matters do we need to discuss tonight?"

Always straight to business. That was one way the disembodied voice captured her grandfather. That was the Ice, really.

"There's a Host in Prague," Tanya said.

"Have you secured this person?"

Tanya opened her eyes and looked down at the radio. The dial was set to 1320. The channel was different every time, as if her grandfather's enchantment was floating aimless through the radio waves.

"No," she said. "I gave her a pitch and two days to make her decision. I was certain she'd come with me. But she didn't."

A long pause. Tanya could hear the static through the speakers. "Why not?"

"She's frightened," Tanya said, defensive. "The Flame sent a construct after her. It was her first real experience with magic." Two nights ago she and Andula had met in the shadows of Letná Park. They had strolled through the frozen trees, and Andula had babbled her reasons for refusing: "I have obligations, to my family—my mother hasn't been the same since my sister vanished two years ago." And: "This is not my world." And: *"I'm not sure I believe you."*

"The Flame," her grandfather's voice scoffed. "Yes, that sounds like them. Always so showy. The old ways are better, yes? We don't frighten the Hosts."

"Of course not," said Tanya. "But she's still refusing to exfiltrate with me. We're watching her; we have her under protection. . . ." She sighed and glanced at the curtains covering her windows, keeping her shielded from the outside world. As a little girl she'd been close to her grandfather, who had been warm and loving despite the formalities of Ice propriety. Sometimes she hated that all she had left of him was this voice in a box, this clever simulacrum. She knew she was perhaps being greedy, that without magic she would have nothing. But, she thought, nothing might be easier.

"Well, she isn't from one of the families. Not if the Flame was able to get so close to her so quickly."

"I agree," Tanya said. "But that doesn't mean we should just let the Flame recruit her."

"No," her grandfather's voice said quickly. "Not a Host. She must come over to the Ice. You know that."

Tanya nodded. For the Flame to gain control of a Host—the results could be devastating. The Flame wanted magic to burn through the fabric of reality, to leave the earth scorched and blackened. They claimed it was the only way to start anew, that the burned-away reality would prove more fertile for change. The idea terrified Tanya. Yes, the Ice ways could be frustrating, so rigid and tied to the past, but at least they didn't mean annihilation.

"I am only suggesting," her grandfather's voice said, "that you must approach her differently, if she is not of the Ice. There are procedures, *Vnuchka*, proper ways of acting."

Tanya sighed. "I haven't forgotten."

"Well, I don't know what influences you're under, living so far away! You mustn't forget where you come from. Remembering that, remembering your heritage, that will help you recruit the Host."

Tanya rubbed at her forehead. "I was hoping for a bit more specific advice, *Dyedushka*." The voice in the radio always seemed to have a stronger obedience to the established order than the grandfather she remembered. She sometimes thought her grandfather's spark of magic had been designed to be the perfect bureaucrat, the type of man no human could ever actually be.

Her grandfather's voice laughed, although in the distortion of the radio it was not the warm laugh of the man who had sat with her by the fire telling her stories of magic and sorcery. It was broken and brittle. Cold. A winter laugh.

"You always want specific advice, my little bird, when the best advice comes from the past. You are too modern. Our ways have worked for thousands of years. We take the cautious approach. When the time is right, the Host will come to you. For now, you must concentrate on keeping her away from the Flame. These things cannot be forced. If they were forced, we'd be no better than our enemies—is that not so?"

Tanya rankled at the idea that her grandfather's construct thought she wanted to use Flame methods, wanted anything to do with their riotous, transformative magic.

"The Host is vulnerable," she said. "I don't think it's wise to take such a passive approach—"

A burst of angry static erupted out of the speakers. "It is not a passive approach, Tatiana Mikhailovna. It is *our* approach, born out of centuries of practice. Wait. Watch. Keep her away from the Flame. When the time is right, then we will act."

Tanya's face flushed hot. She knew there was no point in pushing the matter. Her grandfather had designed his construct to be the perfect sorcerer of the Ice; it won every argument just by digging in and staying there. The one unifying Ice practice, really. Staying put.

"Fine," Tanya said. "We'll continue what we're doing. But if the Flame recruits her—"

"You won't let that happen," her grandfather's voice said. It was starting to distort; it was pulling away, ending the conversation before she did. "You are a daughter of the Ice and of Russia both. You will not bend to the whims of your enemies."

The static flared on "enemies," swallowing her grandfather's voice whole. Tanya stared down at the box sitting on her table. It was just a broken, dead radio now.

Gabe followed Alestair through a knot of snow-covered trees, a string of curses running through his head. It was too quiet out here in the woods to mutter them aloud; any sound, from the crunch of snow under their feet to the huff of their breath, was amplified in the empty forest.

"Almost there," Alestair called out, glancing over his shoulder. He strode through the frozen wilderness outside Prague as if he were strolling through a London park on a sunny spring afternoon. "Tell me, old boy, what do you feel?"

"Cold." Gabe peered up at the tangle of black tree branches overhead. Alestair hadn't been forthcoming about why they were here—as he had driven Gabe to the outskirts of the city, he'd made small talk about his time in the field, discursive little stories that had the whiff of fishermen's tales about them. Any questions Gabe asked about where they were going, and why, Alestair had deflected, eyes twinkling.

Up ahead, Alestair chuckled. "Funny. But try to focus. We're getting closer, and I'm sure you'll be able to feel something. You just have to *try*. Give it the old college try, that's what they say in America, isn't it?"

Gabe grunted in response. It was colder out here than it was in the city, and the air knifed across his face. He could barely feel his nose.

"What am I supposed to be—"

"Shhh," Alestair said, still picking his way through the snow. "*Concentrate.*"

Gabe sighed. He didn't know what the hell he was supposed to be concentrating on. There was nothing out here but trees and snow and ice. Even the wind was still.

A few years back he'd watched some trashy horror movie as part of a double feature: a gaggle of wild-haired women sacrificing goats in the woods, calling down Satan. He wondered if Alestair had seen the same movie. Seemed unlikely. This whole trip felt like an interagency prank. Take the American out to the woods, scare him a bit, send him back.

But then he felt a prickle of electricity run over his skin, like he'd brushed against a live wire.

"What the hell?" He stopped and glanced around, his muscles tense. The prickle was still there, although it didn't hurt, not exactly.

"Ah." Alestair paused. "I see we've found it."

"Found what?" The prickle was deepening into a low magnetic hum. Gabe felt it in his bones, his skeleton a lit-up neon sign.

"The ley line." Alestair stood beside him and closed his eyes. With his blond hair, he looked angelic out here in the snow. "It's been a while since I've stood on one in the wilderness." He looked over at Gabe. "There are so many distractions in the city, you don't always feel the power of the lines. Too much noise, too much movement." Alestair flicked his hand around dismissively. "It's a bit like the stars, I always thought. You're aware of them in the city, but when you step out into the wild, they're magnificent." He gazed upward, even though it was the middle of the afternoon, and the sky was the steel gray of a gun barrel.

"What the hell are you talking about?" Gabe asked. The hum didn't seem so strong anymore—was it actually fading or had he just gotten used to it? His head was starting to hurt, that stinging pre-headache that always announced the imminent arrival of a migraine. Fantastic.

"Magic, my friend, magic." Alestair thumped Gabe on the shoulder. "If you take five steps to the left here, you'll be away from the ley line."

There it was again. *Ley line*. It was a phrase Gabe had heard before—although he couldn't quite place it. Jordan, maybe? That didn't seem right. He associated it more with San Francisco hippies. Crystals and incense. Ley lines.

Still, Gabe stepped off to the left. The humming faded away, although the pain in his head remained. Alestair was studying him, his expression unreadable.

"You brought me all the way out here to show me magic exists?" Gabe shook his head. Laughed. "I already know magic exists. Trust me. I've seen that shit."

Alestair smirked. "You're quite mistaken. I brought you out here to show you how magic works."

Gabe's stomach went leaden. He looked at his tracks in the snow, the blurred patch where he had stood, and felt his bones vibrating inside his skin. "I don't care how it works," he muttered. "I just want to know how to deal with it. I just want the headaches to stop."

"Of course you do, and as I promised Jordan, we'll find a solution. But until then, you'll need a means of controlling them. And that means understanding magic." Alestair looked over at him, his eyes crinkling. "I'm afraid you're a part of this world now."

Gabe scowled, feeling sick at the idea that Alestair was right.

"Fortunately, anyone can learn magic, just as anyone can learn to play the piano. And just as with the piano, learning's no guarantee you'll be *good* at it, but at the very least you'll understand what you've gotten yourself into." Alestair breathed out a puff of white air and walked over beside Gabe. He gazed out at the woods. "Magic is part of the earth itself," he said. "It formed out of the elements into a pattern of lines that have no sense of queen or country—they existed long before we did."

Gabe shifted his weight. His headache pulsed. Always the worst possible time.

"If one wishes to cast a spell," Alestair went on, "one only has to reach out and pluck those ley lines—metaphorically, of course— in the right pattern. Spellwork really is like music. Do you play anything?"

Gabe shook his head. He was trying to work his way around the pain in his head to sort this out. Lines of magic. Strumming a guitar.

"Ah, no matter." Alestair smiled. "Musicality isn't required of a sorcerer."

"I don't want to be a sorcerer," Gabe said. "I want to undo what happened to me in Cairo." He paused, remembering the heat of that back room. There was that tangle of bodies, that weird ceremony—

He frowned. Alestair was still smiling at him.

"Is Cairo on a ley line?" Gabe asked, voice low.

"I think he gets it!"

"Is it or not?"

"It is." Alestair dipped his head in a nod. "A rather powerful one, if I recall correctly. Are the pieces starting to fall into place?"

"Maybe." Gabe walked closer to the ley line, and he felt the humming at the back of his jaw. He took a step back; the humming disappeared. "It's just so damned *weird*."

Alestair chuckled. "You'll get used to it. You may even start to recognize the ley lines in Prague, as well. Several major ones run through the city."

"Have you ever"—Gabe felt stupid using the word—"plucked it?"

Alestair glanced over at him. "I have," he said with a slow smile. "I once coordinated a spell with a sorcerer in Taipei and another in Abidjan, in the Ivory Coast—not an easy affair, but certainly easier these days. Technology is a marvel, even if it isn't magical."

"Coordinated?" Gabe thought of Cairo again. Was that what he had stumbled upon? Some kind of coordinated spell?

"Well, of course. An individual sorcerer can't do the big spells himself." Alestair grinned. "It's yet another inconvenience of the Cold War. Access to lines can be difficult, for all that the miracle of long-distance phoning has given us. You need a point in East Berlin, another in Canada—it can be difficult. But we find a way. Rituals—the preferred term for those coordinated spells—have a long history on both sides of the sorcerous divide. All the major spells require a formal ritual, with a multitude of sorcerers plucking at the ley lines simultaneously. But an individual can still do a few tricks. Here, let me show you."

Alestair stepped onto the ley line and then broke off a twig from a tree growing nearby. He held the twig up. Gabe felt like a bored nephew watching an uncle's magic trick. But then Alestair closed his eyes and murmured in a language that Gabe didn't recognize. It was guttural and ancient, and Gabe felt a creeping sensation at the back of his neck, as if he were being watched. The pinprick of pain in his head flared. And at the same moment, so did Alestair's twig, a tiny yellow flame shooting up into the cold air.

"Nothing much more than a parlor trick, really, but—Gabriel!" His voice seemed far away. Gabe clutched at his head. The pounding drilled deep into his brain, and he landed on his knees in the snow with a shout.

"Gabriel!" A hand on his back. Alestair was kneeling beside him. "Oh dear, is it one of your headaches?"

"Yeah," Gabe muttered. The tide of pain was subsiding; but like the tide, it left a residue in its wake. Gabe dug the heel of his hand into his forehead.

"And it struck as I was pulling the fire, didn't it?" Alestair helped Gabe to his feet and guided him through the snow, away from the ley line. The pain quieted a bit more.

Gabe nodded. The *language*, that had done it. Those eerie words. "What were you speaking?" he asked, turning to look up at Alestair.

"A spell." Alestair led Gabe over to a nearby tree, and Gabe leaned against it. The pain was gone except for one stinging point. "In an ancient language, the name of which has been lost to time."

"I thought coming out here was supposed to help me." Gabe gazed at the snow-covered forest. Jordan had promised Alestair would be able to help him, but they were no closer to a cure here in the wilderness than he had been sitting in the back room of Jordan's bar.

"I'm trying to help you, yes." Alestair ambled through the snow, his hands tucked in his pockets. He didn't look at Gabe. "But your headaches are magical in origin, which means you have to understand magic if you're to truly defeat them. I can't simply wave a magic wand and make them go away." Alestair fluttered one hand lazily through the air.

"Too damn bad," Gabe muttered. In truth he had hoped that

was exactly what Alestair could do—say a few unsettling words on a ley line and banish the headaches completely. "They're interfering with my job."

"I imagine they are, here in Prague."

Gabe nodded. He pressed his back against the tree. Wet snow seeped through his trousers, chilling him.

"This is a good thing, though," Alestair went on. "The first step to finding a cure—a true cure, not just treatment for the symptoms—is to understand the disease."

"Do you understand the disease?" Gabe peered up at him.

Alestair paused. For the first time, a breeze gusted through the forest, rattling the branches of the trees.

"Not yet," he said. "But I will. That I promise you."

2.

Joshua Toms was feeling conflicted. Frank wanted to see him and Gabe in his office, which could mean one of two things: Gabe was about to get another dressing down for that massive recruitment failure three nights ago and Josh was inexplicably being called in to watch, or the university lecture they were attending in half an hour was a hell of a lot more exciting than Josh had been led to believe.

"Dammit," Gabe muttered from his desk. "This couldn't wait until after we got back?"

"We have plenty of time," Josh said, sliding away from his desk and grabbing his jacket from the back of his chair. Gabe stood up, pushed a hand through his hair. He didn't look like he felt well. His skin was grayish and pale, and he had a permanent band of sweat ringing his forehead. A week ago, Josh might've thought Gabe was hungover. But after what happened with Drahomir, he didn't know what to think.

"Yeah, wouldn't want to miss the lecture," Gabe said, sounding defeated.

Josh didn't answer, just headed toward Frank's office. He didn't like the university assignments either. No one did: They were boring work, tedious, and never amounted to much. But they were part of his job, and he was going to keep sitting in on those lectures as long as Langley required it. Even if he was pretty certain this particular assignment was a direct result of Gabe's screwup the other night.

Josh rapped on Frank's office door. Gabe slipped up beside him, hanging his head and rubbing his fingers over his brow.

"You feeling all right?"

"I'm fine," Gabe muttered.

"Come in," Frank called out, and Josh pushed the door open. Frank sat at his desk, half-hidden behind stacks of paper.

"Close the door," Frank said, gesturing at the two of them to step inside. "Have a seat. I know you're on lecture duty. This shouldn't take long."

Josh glanced over at Gabe, who had managed to straighten himself up in Frank's presence. Not that it helped much.

Josh sat down stiffly, not sure what to expect. Frank leaned back in his chair, steepled his fingers. He wasn't looking at Gabe. Maybe this wasn't about Drahomir after all.

"We need to talk about ANCHISES," Frank said.

Josh perked up, heart fluttering in his chest. There'd been whispers around the office for weeks about that name. All rumors—nothing substantial. Still, Josh had let himself get his hopes up. As a junior officer, taking part in such a potentially important op would be a tremendous boost to his career. "Are we on board, sir?"

Frank looked at him. "That's the plan, Toms. Assuming you two can show me you're capable." Frank glanced over at Gabe when he said, "You'll be capable, won't you?"

"Sure thing, sir," Gabe said.

"Good." Frank paused, taking the two of them in. Josh perched on the edge of his seat, hungry for details. "You ever heard of Maksim Sokolov?"

"The Soviet scientist?" Josh glanced over at Gabe, who leaned forward, his expression intense.

"The one and only. It appears he's had a change of heart regarding his political allegiances."

"A defector," Gabe murmured.

Frank scowled. "Glad to see you haven't totally lost your touch, Pritchard."

Gabe flinched at that, looked away. Josh felt a momentary twinge of pity.

"You're right, though," Frank went on. "Sokolov will be attending a physics symposium here in Prague in a little over a month, and our office has been put in charge of exfil. This is a big one, boys, and we don't have a lot of time to get ready."

Josh forced back a gleeful smile. Finally, a chance to work on something big, something that actually mattered. Sokolov was one of the USSR's top physicists, a man whose brilliance could be seen sparkling behind his hard eyes even in photographs. He'd helped design the *Luna 1* engine back in the fifties, and even though the US had won the Space Race, the Stars and Stripes now permanently flying on the surface of the moon, his defection would be a major coup.

"The op will take place during the symposium itself, which means we've got to clear the building. That's where you two come in." Frank waggled his finger back and forth between them. "I need a full report of the Troja campus, and the hotel where the symposium's being held. I want the layout, possible points of entry, exits, hideaways—the works. Nothing's too obvious. We need a hard plan if we're going to do this right."

Josh's mind was already whirring. Maybe he could slip into the lecture halls after their assignment today. It was in a different part of Charles University from the lecture, but he looked enough like a grad student that it shouldn't arouse suspicion.

"I need both of you to be in this a hundred percent." Frank looked at Gabe as he spoke. "You understand?"

"Of course, sir," Josh said brightly.

"Yes, sir," said Gabe.

"Good." Frank was still watching Gabe, appraising him. He didn't comment on the waxen skin or the sunken eyes, though Josh knew he saw them. Frank didn't miss much. "Now, you two have an assignment to get to, if I'm not mistaken." He flicked his hand toward the door. "Get on with it. Sokolov's not here yet."

Gabe and Josh stood up. "The students await," Josh said.

Gabe didn't respond, just shuffled over to the door. Josh moved to follow him, but then Frank said, "Wait," and they both stopped and looked his way.

"Not you," Frank said to Gabe. "Just Toms. He'll catch up."

Gabe glanced between Frank and Josh. "Right," he said, and slipped out into the hallway.

Josh's heart thudded. *Something else?*

"This'll only take a minute," Frank said. He settled back into his chair, the leather creaking. Something in his countenance had changed, and Frank looked older. Tired.

"Thanks for doing this," he said. "The university assignments are bullshit, but Gabe hasn't been himself lately. The last few weeks . . ." Frank let the sentence dangle, and he gazed over at the tiny square of gray light that was his office window. "I know the man he can be. That's why I wanted something simple to get him back to fighting form."

"I completely understand." Josh fiddled with his coat, trying to smooth out a wrinkle. Frank watched him with that weighty gaze, and Josh dropped his hand. "I don't mind the university assignments."

"You're one of my best officers," Frank said. "You know that, right?"

Josh smiled. "Why, thank you, sir."

Frank didn't return the smile, though. He just studied Josh, his hands folded on the desk in front of him. Josh glanced around the room, wondering if Frank expected him to say something else.

"I saw something the other day," Frank said.

"Sir?" Josh blinked, not certain where this conversation was going.

"You were talking with that little flop of a man from the mail room. Maybe standing a little too close."

Josh's cheeks burned. Bile rose up at the back of his throat. "That wasn't—what you think it is. Some of my correspondence got mixed up—"

"Good," Frank interrupted. "You know I like you, but Langley's not going to put up with that kind of—*relationship*."

"It was just a question about correspondence!"

Frank leaned forward over the table, hands folded. He had figured out Josh's secret during Josh's early days, Josh knew—he had been careful, the way he was always careful, but Frank had been through a war and countless bureaucracies—all of it as a black man. It was hard to get anything past him. It was difficult enough keeping it a secret back home, all that hush-hush spycraft against his own agency just to go on a date. And here, his sexual history was even more of a liability.

"I know it was." His voice was as gruff as ever, but something in his posture had loosened, suggesting a sort of fatherly affection. "But I thought you could do with a reminder. After all, ANCHISES could be a major career builder for you."

"Yes, sir," Josh said. Blood rushed in his ears. God, he hadn't even *thought* about relationships since he got here. The job was his first priority. But he'd learned to live with this kind of suspicion a long time ago.

"Which is why I want to make sure you're being careful out there." Frank tilted his head toward the window. "I'm sure you are. But don't forget that all the successful exfils in the world aren't going to protect you if a Soviet figures out your—proclivities."

"I know that, sir."

"Of course you do." Frank almost let a smile slip. "I'm just telling you to be careful. Pritchard's been screwing up, and I don't need you following after him."

"I won't, sir."

"Good." Frank nodded, as if the conversation had gone the way he wanted. "You better get out there before Gabe takes off without you."

"Of course, sir. Thank you."

Frank waved a hand to dismiss him, and Josh stepped out into the fluorescent glow of the hallway. Gabe was leaning up against his desk, arms crossed, waiting for him. Already had his coat.

"You ready?" Gabe called out.

They had an assignment. And yeah, he was ready.

Gabe settled down into the hard, molded plastic of his seat, and he stretched his and Josh's coats over the space beside him so no one would sit down next to them. The throbbing in his head had finally subsided. It usually wasn't too bad at the office—apparently that meant the embassy wasn't built on a ley line. He wondered how the boys in Langley would feel about that, that there was a secret out there they couldn't touch. Even so, all through that meeting with Frank a sharp pain had burrowed into his temple. At least the headache hadn't incapacitated him, the way it had the night with Drahomir. Maybe that meeting with Alestair had helped him more than he thought.

The lights in the auditorium dimmed. The place was only half-full, and the audience was made up mostly of bright-eyed students, no one of any interest. Of course not. This was punishment.

A woman walked onstage, her blond hair shimmering in the spotlight. The audience applauded politely; Gabe slapped his hands together a couple of times. Out of the corner of his eye, he saw Josh straighten up, suddenly interested. Zerena Pulnoc. Wife of the Soviet ambassador. Gabe had met her once or twice on the dip circuit; she always regarded him with a kind of bored languor, as if he were a TV show she couldn't bother switching off.

In front of her crowd of university students, though, she glowed like the moon. She smiled brightly and said, "Welcome, comrades! I am *so* delighted you could attend. This afternoon, the Chancellor's Lecture Series has quite a treat lined up for you." She paused for effect, her gaze spilling across the audience. "Our speaker today is a distinguished academic and a thoroughly charming gentleman—I've had the pleasure of dining with him several times." Another smile, this one dimmer, more understated. "Here to introduce Karel Hašek's accomplishment is one of the members of the Komsomol youth league. Please welcome Andula Zlata to the stage."

More applause. A girl stepped into the spotlight, one hand clutching a crumpled sheet of notebook paper. She looked small and wan compared to Zerena, as if Zerena were sucking all the light away from her. The girl stepped up to the microphone and in a shaky voice began to describe her experiences in Professor Hašek's medieval history class. Gabe wished he could just go to sleep.

The girl finished, the audience applauded, and Karel Hašek stepped onstage and made a joke that elicited a few strains of awkward laughter from the students. Gabe tuned him out; he knew what to expect at a lecture like this, the usual filtered-down Marxist nonsense about the glory of the proletariat, although in this case Gabe suspected it would be given some kind of medieval-ist glaze. Peasants instead of the proletariat, then. He wasn't here to learn, only to observe. And so, as Hašek spoke, Gabe scanned the students sitting in the dark room. A few of them tilted their heads together and whispered, occasionally shooting quick glances across the room at a compatriot. Nothing. Not a goddamned thing. Really, what did Frank expect?

Gabe leaned into Josh. "See anything interesting?" he murmured.

Josh shook his head. "Nothing. You?"

"Nope." Gabe straightened up in his chair. Hašek was still talking. Zerena and the student—Andula? Aneta? He'd already forgotten; Christ, he should probably ask Alestair about that—sat behind him onstage, watching intently. Gabe checked his watch. Another twenty minutes, then the reception.

A few rows in front of him, a figure slipped into the theater. A woman, going by her silhouette. Some latecomer. But then she stepped into a shaft of light spilling in through an open door, and Gabe recognized her with a sharp jolt of surprise.

Tatiana Morozova. She wasn't a student. She was in the files back at the office. She was KGB. Undeclared, of course, but her name and photo were printed in the booklet of suspected officers Gabe studied in his downtime. She'd attended university in Moscow, had a well-connected family. Officially she had some job at the Soviet embassy—a political secretary, if he remembered correctly.

Morozova stepped into the shadows again, and then draped herself in a chair near the aisle. Was the KGB interested in Hašek for some reason? Had this bullshit assignment turned out to mean something after all?

Gabe watched Morozova out of the corner of his eye, careful that she didn't see him staring. Hašek sounded like he was coming up on the end of his speech—he'd already built up to a crescendo of Marxist fervor a few minutes ago as he'd described the violent transition to capitalism, and now they were on the downward slope. Gabe flicked his glance over at Morozova again. She sat straight up in her seat, watching the stage.

"—and that is why students such as yourself are so important," said Hašek with a quiver in his voice. "Because only the youth can lead us away from the mistakes of our past. Thank you."

Applause rang out in the auditorium.

Gabe nudged Josh. "I might have something."

Before Josh could say anything, Zerena took to the podium again, and she beamed out at the audience and invited them to join Professor Hašek for a reception in the lobby. Hašek himself stood off to the side, his hands clasped behind his back, looking down thoughtfully at his feet. And the student, the girl who had announced him, she was still sitting in her seat, staring out at the audience, toward the part of the theater where Morozova was sitting. In the glare of the spotlight, the student's expression wasn't right. She looked frightened, maybe. Anxious.

Was the KGB here for her? Not Hašek? Or was it just stage fright?

More applause scattered around the auditorium. People shifted in their seats and began to stand and move toward the aisle. Morozova stayed put.

"What was that student's name?" Gabe's skin prickled. "The one up on stage."

Josh peered at him. "What are you seeing?"

"Did you catch her name or not?"

"Uh, yeah. It was Zlata. Andula Zlata."

Andula Zlata. The name meant nothing to Gabe. On the stage, Zerena gestured toward the girl and then said something, and the girl stood up and moved toward her. Professor Hašek gave her a warm smile. Together, the three of them walked offstage.

As soon as they vanished into the wings, Morozova stood up and walked toward the lobby doors.

"The reception." Gabe grabbed his coat. "Now."

"Come on, Gabe, just tell me what you've got." Josh was already sliding out of his chair.

"I don't know yet." They left their seats and made their way into the lobby. Cold gray light poured in through the windows, saturating the colors of everything: the students' clothes, the paintings on the wall. People milled around, their voices low and sparkling. He scanned the room. Froze.

There was Morozova, standing in a corner, sipping a glass of wine, pretending to admire one of the paintings: some lurid landscape, everything cast in dull golds and browns.

A peal of familiar, twinkling laughter cascaded across the

room. Zerena. Gabe turned toward her, as did half the faces at the reception. She was leading Hašek toward the temporary bar, and Andula trailed behind them, her skin pale and her eyes shadowed.

It was the student. Gabe was sure of it.

"So what's your theory here?" Josh's voice was low and close to Gabe's ear. "Something with Hašek?" He nodded at Zerena and Hašek sipping their wine.

"Not Hašek. The girl. Andula." Gabe stepped away before Josh could answer; he was determined not to lose sight of her. Another student, dark-haired and bespectacled, had walked up to her and was trying his hardest to have a conversation. Andula tilted her head toward him and nodded, but her eyes bounced around the room. She fidgeted with the hem of her sweater.

And then she went very still, and the color drained from her face. The dark-haired boy kept chattering as if he hadn't noticed. Gabe was close enough that he could catch fragments of the conversation—something about a mutual mathematics course.

"Excuse me," Andula said suddenly, too loudly. And then she strode away from the boy, leaving him looking vaguely stunned.

Gabe grabbed a glass of wine from the bar and whirled around, taking a long drink as he scanned over the rim of his glass. There. She was cutting a clear path to where Morozova stood beside the painting. Morozova straightened at Andula's approach, her expression calm and professional. Gabe maneuvered around the room, sticking to the perimeter, hoping he could blend in with the knots of students. He caught sight of Josh frowning at him. No matter. He'd explain in a minute.

Morozova was talking to the girl, her body angled away from the party, her head tilted down. The girl shook her head, glanced over her shoulder. Christ, she looked *terrified*, and for a moment

Gabe went cold all over, afraid that Morozova had spotted him. But no, the girl wasn't looking his way. Wasn't looking at Josh, either. She turned back to Morozova, ran her fingers over her hair. Morozova leaned in to her, looking for a moment almost concerned, almost maternal. She put one hand on Andula's arm. Andula shook it away.

"Gabriel Pritchard."

Gabe closed his eyes, took a deep breath. *God damn it, not now.*

"My, my, my. I'd no idea you were so fascinated by Prague's history."

Zerena slid up beside him, her chin lifted, the ends of her mouth teasing at a smile. Gabe forced himself to smile back.

"Zerena," he sighed. "You're looking as lovely as ever this after-noon."

She laughed, hard and glittering and fake, and reached out one hand, a slim silver bangle shining on her wrist. "Surely you'd like to meet our speaker, Professor Hašek? Karel, darling, come over here for a moment."

Gabe ground his teeth together. He didn't dare glance over at Morozova and Andula, not when Zerena was so close.

Hašek stepped up beside Zerena, who put her hand on his shoulder. Her nails were as sharp as her cheekbones.

"Karel, did you know you had an *American* in your audience?" She bared her teeth like an angry cat. Gabe imagined it was sup-posed to be a smile.

"An American!" Hašek spoke in English. "Tell me, did you enjoy the lecture, Mr.—"

"Pritchard," Gabe said, and then, in Czech: "Really, Czech is fine."

"An American who bothered to learn Czech! And you speak it so well. Isn't that a curiosity."

"I'm sure you'll find Gabriel to be an *exquisite* curiosity." Zerena's nails flashed. "And I'm sure he would be delighted to discuss some of the points from the lecture. Wouldn't you, Mr. Pritchard?" There was that angry-cat smile again. Gabe returned it with the most neutrally pleasant expression he could muster.

"Absolutely," he said, looking at Zerena. Then he turned to Hašek. "Unfortunately, I told my friend I'd meet with him, and I'd hate to leave him alone. . . ." He glanced around the room and found Josh ambling through the crowd, a drink in one hand. "And there he is now. Thank you, Professor Hašek. The lecture was fascinating. Zerena, it was a pleasure, as always."

Zerena stared at him, sharp and cold and full of harsh white light, like a diamond. "As always, Mr. Pritchard."

Gabe slipped away from them and headed toward Josh. His eyes, though, darted in the opposite direction, toward the corner where he'd last seen Morozova and Andula.

It was empty.

Tanya and Andula stepped out onto a narrow, enclosed courtyard tucked around the side of the building. Icy wind gusted over the walls, blowing Andula's hair into her face. Tanya walked quickly around the edge of the courtyard, her boots crunching on the old snow. No one was out here. They were alone. Good.

"What are you doing at the lecture?" Andula cried. "I told you I didn't want anything to do with this!"

Tanya whirled around to face her. Andula stood on the opposite side of the courtyard, her hands tucked under her arms, her coat flapping around her knees. She shivered. Maybe because of the cold. Maybe not. Tanya remembered what Andula had told her at their meeting in the park, about her sister's disappearance during the Prague Spring.

"I'm trying to keep you safe," Tanya said.

"How did you even know I would be here today?" Andula said. "Have you been following me?"

Tanya sighed. Andula watched her warily, and when Tanya took a step toward her, Andula took a step back. Tanya considered her options; right now, she decided, it would be better not to lie. Too much.

"I'm not here as KGB," she said slowly. "But I still have KGB methods at my disposal."

Andula's face went pale.

"I told you," Tanya said. "I'm here to *protect* you. Yes, the Ice has been watching you, but only because the Flame wants to grab you for themselves—"

"And you thought the Flame would be here? At the university? At Professor Hašek's lecture?" Andula glanced around the courtyard, fearful. "Is one of those things coming after me again?"

Tanya reached into her pocket and fingered the charm she had tucked away there. She and Nadia had created it from the scraps of the construct that came after Andula; it was designed to send out a pulse if the construct's creators were nearby. It had been still during the lecture, but Tanya did not want to take any chances.

"I don't know." Tanya walked over to Andula, and this time the girl didn't step away. "We seem to be safe right now."

"So there's still a chance they'll come after me."

"There's a very big chance." Tanya paused, took in Andula's frightened expression. "You mustn't underestimate the Flame. Their name is appropriate. They want to use you to burn this world down."

It was starting to snow, delicate flakes drifting down from the gray sky. Andula looked away from Tanya and stared across the courtyard. Tanya didn't push her. She thought of the advice from her grandfather's construct: *When the time is right, then we will act.* But when was the time ever right? This moment in this courtyard, everything quiet and muffled by the snow—why couldn't this be the right time? The Flame was watching Andula too. And they weren't going to wait.

And then there were those Americans at the lecture. Tanya had noticed the one—tall, broad shouldered, bland faced, so quintessentially how Americans pictured themselves—watching her at the reception, sliding through the crowd with his wine glass, like that could disguise him. He might be Flame, but she doubted it. He was far more interested in her than he had been in Andula.

"Why?" Andula whispered, still staring up at the sky. "Why did this happen to me?"

"We are born into the places in which we're born," Tanya said. "Some things cannot be changed."

Andula's shoulders hitched. For a moment, Tanya was afraid she was crying, but when Andula looked away from the snow, her eyes were dry. "I don't want this," she said. "You tell me the Flame wants to use me. Why should I believe you?" She stared at Tanya. "How do I know this—this Ice doesn't want to use me up too?"

Tanya kept her voice neutral. "A fair question."

Andula watched her. Waiting.

"The Ice wants the world to stay as it is. Even with all its imperfections, this is our world, our reality—why should we change that? We have no need to use you the way the Flame would. We only want to protect you. That's all."

Andula toyed with a button on her coat, twisting it on its

threads. The snow swirled around them. It was falling more thickly now. She seemed close to accepting, closer than she had been the night in the park. Maybe the time was right, after all. Maybe she just needed that one extra push.

"There was a man at the lecture," Tanya said. "An American. Did you see him?"

Andula dropped her hand away from her coat button. "What? An American? Are they Flame too?"

"Some of them." Tanya glanced out at the empty courtyard, filling up with snow. "This one, I don't think so. But he was CIA. He came to the lecture, he sat in the audience, and you didn't even see him there."

The wind whipped Andula's hair in front of her face. "What are you saying?"

"I'm saying you cannot protect yourself," Tanya said. "I'm saying that if you want to be safe, you need the protection of the Ice. This American didn't attract your notice, and he didn't even have magic on his side." Tanya hoped this was true.

Andula's eyes were wide with fear. She shook her head. "No," she whispered. "No, I don't believe you."

Damn it. Her grandfather was right, after all; Tanya had pushed too much, too soon.

"You saw that construct," Tanya said. "You saw what they are capable of. We can keep you safe—"

"I didn't ask for this!" Andula shrieked, her voice cracking through the frozen air. "My whole life, I've been good. I've been loyal to the Party; I've served my country. This isn't *fair*."

"This has nothing to do with politics," Tanya said quietly.

"Then why did you tell me a CIA man is following me?"

"He's not following you." *I think.* "I was only trying to show you that there are layers to this world, layers you haven't been trained to see."

"And let me guess: You'll train me," Andula said in a mocking singsong. "In some labor camp, yes? To keep me *safe*? Just like the StB wanted to keep my sister safe?"

"That is not what this is about. There are no Ice labor camps." Tanya knew she had lost control of the situation. Andula's face was red, her eyes bright. The falling snow confused things, like they were talking through static. "Listen to me. If you don't want to come with me now, there are ways to contact us if you change your mind. We won't approach you again until you contact us first."

Andula shook her head. Tanya grabbed her by the shoulder and looked her straight in the eye. Andula was terrified. Tanya could see it, could sense it. She should have listened to her grandfather. She should have waited.

"We're watching you, yes," she said, "but only to keep you safe from the Flame. If you change your mind, place a lit candle in your window."

"I thought you were with the Ice," Andula snapped. "Not the Flame."

Tanya sighed. "It's not an Ice trick. There's no magic in it." She let go of Andula's shoulders and took a step back. "I hope you change your mind, Andula Zlata."

Andula watched her through the snow, her eyes brimming with fear.

"A lit candle," Tanya said. "That's all you need to call us to your aid."

Andula didn't move, and for a moment Tanya felt a flicker of hope that she was relenting. But then she turned and stalked out of the courtyard, leaving Tanya alone in the cold and the snow.

◆ ◆ ◆

"Did you see her?" Gabe asked. Off to the side, a group of students erupted into laughter.

"Who?"

"The woman who was standing over by that painting." Gabe tilted his head in that direction. Josh stared at him. "Short, wearing a blue sweater. Light brown hair. Had it pulled back. You didn't see her?"

"That describes half the women in this room." Josh crossed his arms over his chest. "Just tell me what you think you've got."

Gabe scowled in frustration. "I don't know what I've got. She was speaking with Andula Zlata. Off in the corner." He lowered his voice. "Her name's Tatiana Morozova. She's KGB."

Josh's eyes widened. "And she was talking to Andula? The girl from the lecture?"

Gabe nodded.

"You think Morozova was grooming her?"

Gabe peered around, taking in the scene: groups of students, talking together with earnest expressions, laughing, waving across the room. They had the carefree look of youth about them; they probably didn't worry about anything more than an exam or a research essay.

Except that Andula Zlata hadn't been carefree. She'd been terrified. Confused.

"Maybe. I don't know. Something about it seemed—off."

Josh frowned. "Off?"

"The girl was *scared*. If it's a grooming, it's going badly." Gabe's chest tightened. "We need to find her. Andula."

Josh stepped toward him. "If the KGB finds out we're here—"

"You didn't see the girl's face, Josh." Gabe stomped away from his partner, heading toward the exit. He shoved the door open just as Josh slapped a hand on his arm.

"Where are you going?"

Gabe shook him off. "Where do you think? I'm not just leaving her to that Russian woman."

Josh had that blank expression of someone desperately trying not to roll his eyes. "Don't be stupid. We can take the information back to the office. Let Frank know. But chasing down KGB agents isn't why we're here right now."

A flurry of movement rippled through the reception. Gabe leaned away from Josh. His heartbeat quickened. It was her—Andula. She pushed through the crowd, her coat buttoned up to her throat and her hair and shoulders dusted with snow. Her head was tilted down so that her hair spilled over her face, and her hands were shoved into her pockets. She looked like she was trying to shrink herself down into invisibility.

Where the hell was Morozova?

"Gabe, don't even *think* about it."

Gabe ignored him. The girl was making a beeline for them—Gabe sidestepped out of the way, turning his head to the side. Not that she was looking at him.

She breezed past, so close that Gabe caught a whiff of a sweet, cloying perfume. She pushed open the doors, and cold air trickled in from the entryway.

"I'm going after her," Gabe muttered.

"Gabe, this isn't protocol. I know you feel awful about Drahomir, but there's no reason to go against orders like this. We've got their names, we've got a location—let's just take it to Frank."

Gabe bristled at Josh bringing Drahomir into this. That girl was *upset*. Shaken. If this *was* an attempt at grooming, Morozova was terrible at it.

He shrugged on his coat and slipped outside. The girl was several paces ahead of him, the heels of her boots clicking against the sidewalk. Snow fell in thick swirls, muffling the whole world. Good. It should keep her distracted. Keep her unaware.

He followed. As Andula moved farther away from the university, her steps slowed. She seemed to be heading in the direction of the river. An apartment, maybe? Or an arrangement to meet some other contact? Maybe one she felt safer with than Morozova?

Pain began to creep back into his temple. God *damn* it. Not now. Gabe rubbed at his forehead, trying to will the headache away. Christ, he didn't have time for this hocus-pocus bullshit.

The headache subsided. A little.

Andula stumbled over a crack in the sidewalk. She let out a shout and stomped her foot against the ground. Then she stopped and stood there. Gabe slowed. There was a shop up ahead; he could duck inside and watch her from the window if he had to.

Andula covered her hands with her face. Her shoulders shook. Gabe realized she was crying.

He was approaching the shop. *Move, move,* he thought at the girl, and then his chest twinged in an inner reprimand. The poor thing had been terrified back at the reception. Who the hell knew what they had on her? What they had threatened her with?

Gabe slid into the shop. The air was warm and dry and smelled of spices. His head throbbed with a sudden, single bolt of pain, and behind his eyes he saw a flash of Cairo, a narrow alley glazed with sand, yellow eyes watching from the shadows. As quickly as it came on it disappeared.

At least he could still see Andula from the window.

"Hello!" a voice creaked from the back of the shop. "Can I help you?"

"I'm only looking," Gabe called back. He picked up a bag of flour and pretended to examine it as he watched Andula across the street. She kept crying there in the snow.

Footsteps shuffled from the back of the store. "Are you looking for anything in particular?" the shopkeeper said. Gabe glanced back at him; an old man, bent over at the waist, wobbling on a cane. He looked back out the window. Andula was still there. Still crying.

"My wife wants to bake koláče tonight," Gabe said, watching Andula. "She sent me to the store."

The man sniffed in response. Outside, Andula was wiping her eyes. She lifted her head, peered around—did the KGB have a tail on her too? Gabe hadn't noticed anyone.

She wiped at her eyes, smoothed her hair back. Gabe set the flour on the shelf.

"Don't want those koláče after all?" said the shopkeeper.

"It's not that." Andula was moving again, her steps shaky and unsure. "Only that I just remembered we have flour at home."

And then he plunged back out into the cold street. Andula turned a corner up ahead; Gabe tensed, but when he rounded the wall a few moments later, he spotted her easily. His headache had become dull and distant; if he focused on Andula, he could tune it out. They were parallel to the river now; he could smell it, metallic and acrid, like old gasoline. This time of year the water turned to slurry, and the barges piled up, blocked by ice floes freezing the water outside the city.

Andula walked, and he followed. Snow tumbled down from

the sky. They walked past a barge bobbing in the river—old, rusted metal and dead engines. Waiting for its turn to move along. The wind gusted Andula's hair back, and she leaned into it, her hands shoved into her pockets. The wind was colder here, and damp from the river. Gabe's head throbbed.

Jesus Christ, not now.

He forced himself forward. The pain in his head grew, spreading like molten silver from his temple to his brow, down into the space behind his right eye. He curled his hands. The sounds of Cairo came back to him, that piercing sharp laughter, the howl of a storm that wasn't really a storm. He forced himself back into the present. He wasn't in Cairo; he was in Prague. The air was cold and damp, not hot and dry and baking.

He kept his gaze on the girl. The wind howled off the river, low and keening, like it contained the trapped voices of the dead.

Andula turned sharply into a narrow street. Gabe waited a few moments before following her. She was walking more quickly now, almost a jog, her shoes tapping against the cobblestones. Was she trying to lose him in the tangle of buildings? It seemed strange for a university student to know even that basic bit of tradecraft.

But then she stepped onto a path leading up to a shabby concrete apartment building. She reached into her purse and extracted a key. Gabe stepped into a doorway of a building across the street, pretended to check his watch, like he was waiting for someone. His headache had faded. *The river,* he thought. *It was the river that was doing it.* Maybe a ley line ran underneath the Vltava.

Andula unlocked the door, but she didn't go in. Instead she stood in place, glancing around. Left. Right. Not behind. She didn't look *at* him. Another tail, after all? He still hadn't noticed anything, but then, he had been distracted. The pain.

Andula slipped the key out of the lock and disappeared inside. The door clicked shut behind her.

Gabe considered his options. He could try to get inside the apartment building, see if this was her place or if she was meeting the KGB here.

Or he could suck it up and take Josh's advice. Let Andula go, for now, and find out what the office had on her. There had to be something, if the KGB was interested. *Had* to be. If nothing else, he could confirm this was indeed her address. Then come back later, with backup, the way he was supposed to do things.

He ducked out of the doorway and headed back the way he'd come. He hoped Josh would have something on Morozova's movements at the reception.

Gabe trudged down the street. His footprints, Andula's footprints, had been covered over by the falling snow. His head pulsed as he neared the river. *Christ. Magic migraines.*

But Morozova and Andula, that felt real. The battles between East and West, between communism and democracy, those, at least, he still understood. They were something he could grasp at, to keep him from drowning.

3.

"We don't have anything on her."

Gabe was back in Frank's office, two days after he'd tailed Andula Zlata to her apartment. The report Gabe had typed up after getting back from the lecture was fanned across Frank's desk.

"What do you mean?" Gabe leaned forward. "There's got to be some reason the KGB would be interested."

Frank shrugged. "She's not the sort they usually go after. Doesn't have the kind of connections that would be useful to them. It looks like her sister was involved in the protests back in sixty-eight—"

Gabe's heart surged with excitement. "Well, there's your connection." He leaned back in his chair. "Something with her sister."

"The sister's gone," Frank said. "And Andula herself avoided all that mess. She's boring. I'm not *doubting* there's a connection there, but we sure as hell can't see it." He fixed Gabe with a hard scowl. "And while I appreciate you showing some initiative, there wasn't any reason for you to break protocol like you did."

"She was being tailed. I thought she might be in danger."

"You didn't see the tail," Frank said. "Said so right in your report. You didn't see much of anything, in fact, save for a moment of contact at the reception."

Gabe huffed in frustration. "That's all it takes."

"I don't disagree." Frank wove his fingers together on top of the scattered file. Gabe remembered the frantic urgency of typing it up, hitting the keys on the typewriter so hard that the ink in the letters smudged. "But there was nothing about the contact that required you to break off with your partner and tail the girl like that. You should've brought it back to me. Let us follow up on it."

"I told you—"

"Dammit, Pritchard, I know what you told me." Frank shoved away from his desk and stood up. Gabe felt his mood darkening. When Frank stood up, you knew he was irritated. God help you if he started to pace. "But that assignment was a chance for you to show me you could keep up with a textbook job." He walked over to the window, a slight limp from his prosthetic. "You might have found something, and I appreciate that, I do. But after what happened with Drahomir—"

"This has nothing to do with Drahomir," Gabe said, annoyance flaring at the back of his head.

Frank moved across the office, his hands clasped behind him. When he paced, Gabe could see the soldier in him, and he knew not to talk back. Gabe slouched down in his chair. Frank stopped beside his desk and stared at Gabe, eyes hard and piercing. "You really going to tell me that?"

"I really am."

Frank picked up his pacing again. "And I think you're full of shit. You screwed up Drahomir. You're trying to show me you won't screw up again." He glanced over at Gabe. "But breaking protocol's not the way to do it. You didn't have reinforcements. You didn't even take Josh with you, for God's sake. Say you were right . . ." Frank's steps thumped softly against the carpeted floor, one lighter than the other. "Say this Andula Zlata's more interesting than she looks. Say she hadn't been going home to her apartment—"

Gabe's interest piqued at that; so the building definitely was her apartment. Good to know.

"—but to some KGB safe house. Say there were guards, they spotted you, shot you clean through before you knew what the hell had happened." Frank turned his angry scowl over to Gabe again. "Then where would we be?"

"Come on," Gabe said. "You know I'm better than that."

"Do I?" Frank gave a sharp little laugh that burned at the back of Gabe's head. "I thought you knew what you were doing with Drahomir, too."

"I did!" Gabe snapped. "I got a head—I wasn't feeling well. I should've called it off. I know that now. But this was different."

"You're on shaky ground, Pritchard."

Gabe glowered at Frank, and Frank glowered right back. Nothing would faze an old army man like Frank.

"Headquarters determines when someone like Andula Zlata is of interest to our organization. All we needed was a report from you. But breaking protocol like that—it was a stupid move, Pritchard. A dangerous one."

Gabe crossed his arms over his chest. Frank had a point. He'd gone to the lecture unprepared for anything beyond a mild altercation, and he could have been walking into a trap without backup. At the same time, though, Andula Zlata felt too important to let slip away. He couldn't say why. Call it spy's instinct.

There was something about her, deeper than the surface.

Frank stopped pacing. He braced his hands against the desk and leaned forward, sliding into Gabe's line of vision. "We need you following protocol once ANCHISES starts up."

Gabe sighed. "Yes, sir. I realize that."

"There are going to be a lot of moving pieces. You run off and do your own thing, you leave a bunch of guys standing around with their thumbs up their butts. You want that, Pritchard?"

Gabe shook his head.

"Good. I didn't think so. If this Andula Zlata thing turns out to be something bigger, that's fucking fantastic. But if it turns into nothing—and right now, that's what it's looking like, a whole pile of nothing—you running off against orders isn't going to impress Langley. You need to keep that in mind."

Gabe sat still for a moment, his arms crossed, frustration burning a hole inside him. Frank slid into his seat, although he didn't stop glowering at Gabe.

"I understand, sir," Gabe finally said, voice so low it was almost a whisper. Frank didn't take the bait.

"Good. Now get the hell out of my office."

Gabe stood up. Frank was still scowling at him. He went out to the hallway, feeling stunted and angry. Josh was waiting for him, leaning up against the wall, looking concerned.

"Everything go okay in there?" he said as Gabe brushed past him.

"Went exactly how I thought it would."

Josh had pushed himself away from the wall and was following Gabe over to the desks. The office hummed with activity. Gabe rubbed at his head. Still had traces of a headache.

"Are you sure you're okay?" Josh asked, frowning.

Gabe dropped his hand to his side. "I'm fine. Just want to get some work done." He glanced over at Josh. "ANCHISES is coming. We've got a university building to report on."

Tanya took a bite of the potato pancake she'd bought from a street vendor a few hours ago and then glanced out the car window. "She hasn't left," Nadia had said when Tanya slid into the passenger seat beside her to trade shifts. "No one's gone in. Haven't sensed any magic, either."

"Has the Flame made an appearance?" Tanya asked. "Or the CIA?"

"No. No one's interested in our little *devushka*. At least not tonight."

Nearly four hours had passed since then. The pancakes had gone cold and greasy. The window of the Host's apartment was lit up, a golden square in the snowy darkness. Sometimes Tanya saw a shadow pass by. Andula pacing out her worries, she imagined.

Tanya pulled out another pancake and ate it distractedly. She ran over her memories of the reception two days ago, the CIA man eyeing her furtively through the crowd. He'd followed Andula after she'd left, stalking her through the snow all the way to her apartment. She still wasn't convinced he wasn't here now, but she hadn't seen any sign of him. No movement in the darkness.

Odd. Very odd.

Something flickered in Andula's window. Tanya tossed the pancakes aside and grabbed her binoculars. Her heartbeat quickened. The curtain drew back, and there was Andula, her hair pulled back in a messy bun. She peered down to the street.

"What are you looking for?" Tanya murmured.

Andula stepped away from the glass. Tanya cursed, set the

binoculars on the passenger seat. Someone was out here. Andula must have sensed something, or heard something—

But then Andula returned.

This time, she had a candle.

"Bozhe moi," Tanya muttered. "Finally." She yanked the keys out of the ignition and checked to make sure that her gun was still strapped to her leg.

Andula lit a match and touched it to the candle's wick. For a moment she stared out at the street, as if she expected danger to be lurking in the shadows. Then she vanished from the window.

Tanya stepped out of the car. The street was empty, yesterday's snow crusted over. Tanya slipped her hand into her pocket and touched the construct charm. Tonight, it was still.

She skittered across the street to the building's entrance. Then she pressed the button to call Andula and waited.

Morozova was moving. Gabe shifted, his legs numb from cold and disuse. He'd been up on this rooftop for the last few hours. A personal project, on his personal time. Frank didn't need to know about it.

Morozova waited at the door to the apartment building. Gabe quickly scanned the darkness, trying to decide what had prompted the movement. The street was completely empty. Only a handful of the apartment windows even had lights on.

Lights—

There. That candle. Third row from the top, smack in the middle of the building. Had it been there a few minutes ago? Shit. He'd been so focused on Morozova's car that he hadn't registered activity in the apartment windows.

He swept his gaze back down to the front door, where Morozova stood with her arms crossed. He hadn't been able to learn much more about Andula Zlata other than what the office's files had already revealed: that this was her address, that her sister had vanished back in '68, that she was otherwise an incredibly dull target.

The door swung open. Gabe leaned closer, peering through his binoculars. Andula. She gave Tanya a flat, defeated look, and then she stepped away from the doorway so Tanya could step inside.

"I knew it," Gabe whispered as the door slid shut.

Andula did not look at Tanya as she led her up the stairs to her apartment. She clutched the banister tightly, her knuckles turning white. On the second-floor landing, she said, "You were watching me, weren't you?"

"We were protecting you."

Andula paused. For a moment they stood unmoving in the stairwell. Then she turned toward Tanya. Her face was bare, her eyes sunk low in her skull. She did not look like she had slept.

"Thank you," she finally said.

A few minutes later, they were inside Andula's apartment. It was small, smaller than Tanya's, the furniture faded and threadbare. The candle flickered in the window. Tanya strolled across the room and extinguished the flame between her thumb and forefinger. Then she set the candle sideways on the frame, pulled the curtains closed behind it: *All is well.*

"Lock the door," she said.

She listened as the door clicked shut, as the lock slid into place. When she turned around, Andula stood with her arms crossed, looking very small.

"The other day," she said. "After the reception." She lifted her head, looked Tanya in the eye. "Were you 'protecting' me then? When I left?"

"I was, yes."

"Did you use—um—" Andula shook her head. "It feels so strange to ask this—did you use magic?"

"Magic?" Tanya frowned. She hadn't even *felt* any magic that afternoon. "No, I didn't."

Andula nodded and looked away. Tanya realized her eyes were brimming with tears. "Someone was using it," she said. "I—I felt it, this surge of power."

"When?" Tanya stepped toward her.

Andula wiped her eyes. "Here."

"What? You mean in your apartment?"

Andula shook her head. "No. It was outside. As I moved to come in." She took a deep breath. "And as I was walking along the river—"

The river. "That's not surprising," Tanya said. "The river is important, magically speaking."

"I walk by the river every day," Andula said. "I've never felt anything like this before. *Ever.*" She pulled at the hem of her sweater, her hands working nervously. "I could feel it building up as I walked home. This—pressure, like a storm cloud in the back of my head. And then when I was at the front door, I felt a bolt of electricity, like I'd been shocked—it just slammed into me." She shook her head. "It didn't hurt, not really, but it *frightened* me, and I was afraid one of those—those things from the other night—"

"A construct," Tanya said. "That's what we call the thing from the other night." She was trying to make sense of this. A wave of magic as Andula walked home? Why hadn't Tanya felt it, with all her charms and knowledge?

"Yes, a construct. I was afraid it was something like that, that I would be attacked—but then nothing happened." Andula sank down into her couch. She looked wilted. Deflated. "I haven't left my house since then. But you probably know that."

A hint of sharpness in her voice. Tanya didn't answer.

"Is this going to keep happening?" Andula looked up at Tanya, her eyes pleading. "Am I ever going to have a normal life again?"

Tanya sighed. She'd almost had Andula at the reception. She would not lose her now. So she had to answer this carefully.

"I want to tell you yes," she finally said. "And I think it's certainly possible. But you will not be able to have a normal life on your own."

Andula's eyes glimmered. She lowered her head, trying to hide her tears. Tanya sat down on the couch beside her—slowly, carefully, the way she would approach a frightened animal. "What you felt the other day, that wasn't a construct. I would have felt it too, had that been the case. But there are other things—other forces—that you will be sensitive to, as a Host." Tanya paused, studying Andula's reactions. "Your elemental will tune you in to them. Perhaps that's what you experienced."

"I don't want this." Andula's voice was small.

"I know it's an enormous change. And I can't tell you I know what it's like. But I can promise that the Ice can help you find that normal life." Tanya paused, watching Andula closely. "I swear to you."

Andula didn't respond.

"Look at me," Tanya said. "My life—well, I wouldn't say it's normal, but it's not divorced from the normal world."

"You're hardly a good example, *KaGeBeznik*."

"That's why I said my life isn't normal." Tanya smiled, although it was not returned. "But the sorcerous world need not swallow you whole. You can make a space for it, live alongside it. That's the Ice way. The Flame way, it's different." She shrugged. *Let the Host come to this decision herself.* "If you come with me, I'll help you find your normal life again."

Andula nodded. She looked at Tanya with red-rimmed eyes. "That's all I want," she whispered. "I didn't ask for this—to be a Host."

"No Host does," Tanya said. "But please, let me help you. Let *us* help you."

Andula turned toward the window. The light from her floor lamp illuminated the streaks of gold in her wild hair. And just for a moment, Tanya thought she could see it, the power of the elemental that coursed through Andula's system, that ignited her, that fueled her. Just for a moment and then it was gone.

"All I've done for the last two days is think," Andula said. "I couldn't sleep, couldn't concentrate on my classwork. All I could do was think about what you told me. The pros and the cons. I even made two lists, side by side. I couldn't make up my mind."

Tanya's heart pumped. Her breath caught in her throat. *So close.* She didn't dare ruin it by opening her mouth. She'd learned her lesson the other day. Andula needed to find her own final nudge. Tanya couldn't do it for her.

"The Flame terrifies me," Andula said. "You, you only scare me." She peered up at Tanya. She looked haunted.

"I don't meant to scare you," Tanya said. "But the truth of the world can be frightening."

Andula nodded. "Yes. Yes, it can." She closed her eyes. Took a deep breath. Tanya's fingers curled.

"When I lit that candle, I didn't know what I would say to you." Andula's eyes flashed open. "But I realize now I'd already made up my mind."

Tanya nodded. Excitement prickled over her skin. It was going to happen. She was certain of it.

"I'll come with you," Andula said. "If you promise to keep me safe."

Tanya was engulfed by a wave of relief. She turned to Andula and looked her right in the eye, to show she was telling the truth.

"I promise," she said.

ПУРСУИТ

EPISODE 3

DOUBLE BLIND

Max Gladstone

Prague, Czechoslovak Socialist Republic
January 26, 1970

1.

W e shouldn't be here," Josh said. Gabe shouldered deeper into his overcoat, and did not agree out loud.

Prague Januaries ran bitter and deep. Chill wind whistled off the frozen Vltava down narrow medieval streets and over tile roofs. Earlier in Gabe's career—in Indochina, in Cairo—crouching sunburned and sweating in some perforated awning's excuse for shade, he'd dreamed of a post where they'd heard of winter. The world had turned since then.

Gabe glared at the dormitory across the road through the Moskvich's tinted windshield, wishing they could run the engine, or at least the heater, or, hell, drink coffee. Why not wish for an American car while he was at it? About all you could say for their midrange Russian clunker was that it wouldn't raise eyebrows—which was about all that counted for a stakeout. You never could tell who was watching: StB, KGB. He supposed he should add *Acolytes of the Flame* to that list now too. In the parked Moskvich, Gabe and Josh were as unobtrusive as two CIA officers could be in Prague's university district after dark.

"You tailed the mark from her apartment," Gabe said. "I saw her go inside. She's there."

"She is, all right," Josh said. "Third floor, corner, by the window."

Gabe checked through his monocular. Their target, Andula Zlata, stood backlit in the window, pale and scared. Behind her, a tall blond student knocked back a glass of vodka and wound a scarf around his neck. Another girl wrestled with a thick winter coat. "Looks like they're leaving. You're sure they'll go out the front door?"

"All the dorm exits lead to the street. But, Gabe, you know what I mean." Tension edged Josh's voice. "We shouldn't be here watching her at all. Stakeouts on college girls, God. Frank still has a chip on his shoulder about our screwing up Drahomir's recruitment. If you want to prove you're not crazy, you're doing a bad job."

"I'm the one who screwed up the Drahomir op," Gabe said. "You did fine."

"That's not what he implied."

Gabe risked a glance away from the window. Josh, in monochrome blue like an architect's pencil drawing, sagged against the car door, his chin balanced on his tented fingers. His right hand smoothed out an imaginary wrinkle in his slacks.

"He lit into you?"

"Not in so many words. But it was clear I had disappointed him. I don't like to disappoint people, Gabe. Especially not Frank. This girl better be important."

"The KGB thinks she is. We've got nothing on her, no signs of interest, no significant political activity—but Morozova went from approach to pitch in twenty-four hours."

"Must be nice to move that openly."

"That's a crazy pace even for them. This has to be big."

"What's she studying?"

"History."

"History?" Josh turned from the window, astonished. "Why would they be extracting a history student? Grooming one, sure, cultivating, but extraction?"

"Makes you curious, doesn't it?"

The party emptied. Gabe timed the students' progress against his resting pulse. *Know the target, feel the target: sliding on her jacket, one hand steadying herself against the doorjamb, figure twenty people in that room all walking together. The stair, most likely, is halfway down the central hall, and the building's about a football field long. Three flights of stairs. Another forty feet to the front door. The average human pace length's about a yard, walking speed of around three miles an hour unburdened in flats, knock that back a third because they're in a group and some are wearing heels . . .*

"You ask me," Josh said, "this whole thing's a put-on. The handler doesn't want this girl. She just wants to make us jump, waste our time, and boy did she."

Gabe rolled his shoulders. Too tight—too long in this car. Too long sitting down, recently. "Worst-case scenario, fine, they make us jump; we waste a night's sleep. We'll get plenty of rest when we're dead."

"Hey, you want to stay up all night just to follow the Prague State University pep squad bar crawl, be my guest."

And the front doors should open . . . , Gabe thought, *now.*

Right on schedule. The students shuffled into wet drifting snow, huddled in jackets, flushed with booze and cold. Gabe found the girl: Andula Zlata. At the rear of the pack, eyes wide and liquid despite the cold. Pale, afraid, hungry. And there, by her side, tall, angular, unafraid—Morozova.

"The handler is in play," he said.

✦ ✦ ✦

Tanya Morozova pulled her jacket close and took Andula's—the objective's—arm. She checked the street. A row of parked cars stood across the road, some windows tinted, others not. A man huddled inside a thick jacket at the corner past the bus stop, holding a folded newspaper. Waiting, but for whom? Rooftops clear, and windows. Might be a problem. Might not. Safer to assume the former.

The man was not so immediate a nuisance, though, as the big dumb blond comrade to her left. Marcel was walking a step too close for comfort and stank of the vodka he'd downed before they left the party. "The city," he slurred, "she impressed me, too, when I first arrived. How long will you stay?"

Andula's distant relative had been her hasty cover. Fortunately, students, draped in the invincibility of youth, tended to be trusting. Certainly Marcel had not questioned her story—he was too busy trying to talk her into bed. "Not long," she said. "I am sorry. I must speak to my cousin."

"We have such a night planned!" Marcel did not seem to have heard. "The joys our city offers—they will stun you."

"Perhaps." She turned her back on him and pulled Andula ahead, into the warm huddle of students shambling toward the bus stop. Andula felt stiff, scared, under her hand. Tanya had hoped a drink would bolster the girl's courage, but her courage needed more bolstering than her bloodstream could support. "When the bus arrives," Tanya said, "we must move quickly. Do what I say, when I say it. We have taken precautions to deter pursuit, but the elemental inside you will draw certain eyes."

Andula tensed. "They're watching us now."

"Yes. Relax. Walk."

"They'll find us," she said, her voice uncertain. "I could feel the one who followed me. How can we lose them?"

They clustered at the bus stop, a clutch of sheep gathered against the winter. "Act naturally," Tanya admonished.

"None of this is natural."

Fair. Headlights flashed up the street. The bus approached. So did the man in the thick jacket. Another fellow in an overcoat, this one wearing earmuffs and a fur hat, emerged from an alley across the way. Sloppy, if they were professionals—but not all the Flame's acolytes had intelligence training. The one across the street might have a weapon; the newspaper man's hands were in plain sight.

"Oh God," Andula whispered. "He's there."

"The man across the street?"

"No. Third car down, the Moskvich." She pressed closer to Tanya. Her breath steamed. "I can feel him."

Newspaper ambled closer, head down, doing his best uninterested, uninteresting saunter. No one innocent would spend so much effort seeming so. Earmuffs glanced left and right as if preparing to cross the street—his gaze drifted smoothly past Tanya and Andula, but hitched on the newspaper man. An exchange of glances.

The Moskvich had tinted windows. Perhaps there was a suggestion of movement inside. Tanya felt nothing when she looked at it, but then, she was not a Host. She did not breathe the secret powers of the world. She merely used them, when it suited her.

She giggled as if Andula had said something funny, and leaned close to her, covering her mouth with her hand. "Do not look. The man with the newspaper. The man across the street. They are hunting us."

Andula tensed and almost looked; Tanya felt a stab of sympathy as the girl caught her breath. *Poor girl. So few harbors remain in our storm-tossed world for sailors like you.* When she drew her hand from Andula's mouth, the girl said, "We should run."

"Wait for the bus," Tanya said. "When it comes, we board. Now, please, laugh, as if I have told you an embarrassing fact about Marcel."

The girl's laugh, when it came, was strained and hollow.

Josh put down his monocular. "Okay, that's Morozova. What now? Do we approach? Try to scare her off?"

"Looks like someone beat us to the punch," Gabe said. "Newspaper. Earmuffs."

Josh shook his head. "What is this, amateur night? Spy camp? If that's the KGB's second-string team, they're definitely pulling your leg with this job."

"That's not KGB backup," Gabe said. "Look at the girl—she just made them, and she's terrified. No Russian team would be that obvious. That's another squad—and they're moving in."

When the bus arrived, Tanya pulled Andula to the front of the gaggle of students so they could board the bus first, ignoring the others' groans and Andula's own yelp of protest. Descending passengers shot them dirty looks; a short woman in a black overcoat shoved Andula against the wall of the bus, and the girl gasped in pain. A thin line of blood ran down her pale cheek.

Nadia worked fast. In less time than Tanya would have needed to draw the blood, Nadia had cleaned it from her thin knife onto a piece of wadded cotton, placed the cotton into a silver locket, and shucked her black overcoat from her shoulders.

"You cut me!"

"Hush," Tanya said. "Give her your jacket." She did not greet or acknowledge Nadia. The last passengers left the bus, and students herded on. Andula, trembling, wordless, handed her jacket to Nadia, who passed Andula the overcoat. While Andula struggled with the bulky black garment, the knife flashed again, and Nadia withdrew her hand, clutching a few strands of the girl's bright hair.

"What—"

Before Andula could finish her question, Nadia darted out into the night, no time wasted in farewell. Tanya guided Andula to a seat, pressed her down, and stood above her like a mother bird over her child. Nadia could take care of herself. "She will buy us time."

"Holy— The girl's on the run!"

Gabe shook his head. "No she's not. It's a look-alike. Zlata's on the bus, with Morozova."

"No way. She slipped out the doors; she's running past the dorm now."

"Are you crazy? That's not the target. The height and hair and build are all wrong."

Josh banged on the dashboard. "I followed her from the apartment over here. That's Zlata, dammit!"

The bus closed its doors and pulled away from the curb.

"We're going after the bus," Gabe said.

Josh threw up his hands. "You're the one who wanted to follow her. Newspaper and Earmuffs are running after her now. I'm telling you, that's our mark! You're the one who talked me into this damn scheme. If we're doing this, we might as well do it right."

"Zlata's on the bus." Gabe turned the key and shifted into drive. "Trust me."

"Not this time." And before Gabe could stop him, Josh slipped out the Moskvich's door into the dark.

Gabe cursed. On the one hand he had Josh, on his own, chasing a dead end, possibly into a trap. Why was he so sure? Everything about that decoy was wrong. On the other hand, the student, target, lure—whatever Zlata was, she was disappearing into the KGB's mouth.

No time for clarity. Josh could handle himself. Gabe pulled the door shut, pressed the gas, and followed the bus into the cold and dark.

2.

Josh, running, cursed Gabe, himself, Frank, Prague, the Holy Roman Emperor Charles II, and the Soviet Union. Most of those were merely implicated in the present mess; the real fault lay with Gabe, obsessed with a meaningless Czech student and stubbornly blind to the fact she'd been switched for a body double. Gabe, whose madness must be catching. Why else was Josh now pounding down the sidewalk, chasing this joke of a mission?

But he couldn't blame anyone but himself for the grinding pressure on his lungs, for the fact that after a few minutes' run his legs felt like lead and his blood like lava. Should have kept up the PT after basic. Should have found hobbies other than reading, chess, and overwork. Should jog in the mornings, maybe. He'd meant to, before he learned what winter mornings in Prague felt like. If he got through this, he'd buy sneakers. Long underwear. A better coat.

The girl cornered hard and sprinted down an alley. Newspaper and Earmuffs followed; Josh settled into a pace he hoped he could sustain.

What he'd do when he caught the girl—or when Newspaper and Earmuffs did—was a question he hadn't yet answered. He had a sidearm. He could shoot—targets. People wouldn't be so different, he told himself.

God. He didn't want to kill anyone. Not tonight.

Newspaper and Earmuffs were halfway down the alley. Josh ran harder to catch up, hoping they were too focused to hear his footsteps. Streetlamps lit the girl's black hair—no, she was blond, must be a trick of the light.

His legs didn't like him. The feeling was mutual. Josh ran faster.

"There's no need to complain," Tanya said. "The cut was shallow. Look, the bleeding has already stopped."

"But why?" Andula kept the handkerchief pressed to her face.

"Sympathy."

"I don't understand."

"With a bit of blood, a bit of hair, and the right tools, Nadia can pass for you. The trick will not work in direct light, nor will it last for long, but it can distract pursuit."

Andula huddled into the black overcoat. Not good. She was drawing away, into herself, away from the chase. Tanya should have warned her about the blood. Now she needed to reforge trust, create common cause.

It was not hard to make herself look worried. She thought about Nadia, fierce, in flight; pictured the men following her, imagined what Acolytes of Flame might do to a captured agent of the Ice. Nadia could fight them, and she was strong, but only in foolish fairy tales did the stronger fighter always win.

"I'm sorry," Andula said. "Your friend will be fine."

Tanya drew a ragged breath. The truth, as always, was the best lie. "Yes," she said. "I hope so."

Andula removed her glove and laid her bare hand on Tanya's wrist. Her touch was warm and sharp, with a soft tingle like mint or electricity. Was that the elemental beneath the girl's skin? Or was it Tanya's own spark of loneliness, an ache so desperate she could not admit it even to herself?

A tint-windowed Moskvich passed the bus on the left.

"Can you stay with me," Tanya asked, "for what comes next?" She forced that brief thrill of contact back into the locked and chained pits where she kept everything she did not have time to feel.

Andula's wide brown eyes were soft. "I'm ready."

Of course you are. I have made you ready. "That car." She pointed. "Is it the one you saw before?"

Andula's breath caught; her lips opened but the word "yes" did not quite make it out.

Tanya set her jaw. "Thank you. Now, please listen. This next part will be tricky."

Karel Hašek should not have been chasing a fugitive Host down back alleys after dark—by all rights he should have been home now, poring over tomes and texts or marking papers in comfort, glad of the several thick walls and roaring fire between himself and the cold. He and Vladimir had hoped to observe, to follow the Host and her Ice handler, but they could not pass up so golden an opportunity. For the Host to have slipped her handler's custody! "Do not run," he shouted—or tried, it being difficult to shout at full sprint. "We are here to help!"

The Host crossed the street, diving out of the way of a passing truck. The truck swerved but righted itself. Vladimir followed the Host into the alley, and Karel followed Vladimir, feeling triumphant. He knew the university grounds, their cobblestones and corners, better than any student. This particular alley branched west out to the street again, and, a little later, branched east; the Host, running, might assume they'd think she had taken the quick escape of the western branch and try the east instead—only to catch herself in a dead end.

The Host's jacket flared around the eastern turn. Karel ran faster, ignoring the pounding in his chest. The revolver in his inside jacket pocket pounded against his ribs. He would not need it. The Host would join them. They would free her from the lies of Ice and feed her the truth of Flame.

He rounded the corner.

The girl lay crumpled near the wall.

Vladimir approached, his knife out. Thug. "Girl," Karel said. "We will not harm you."

She did not move. Collapsed, no doubt, when she found she could not escape. She despaired. He had to make her believe she was safe, for now.

"I do not know what lies that woman told you," Karel said, gasping for breath, "but we are your friends."

"I think she's out," Vladimir said, tilting his big ox head.

"Pick her up, then!" Karel clutched the stitch in his side and winced. "We have to get her into hiding before the Ice finds us all."

Vladimir lurched toward the fallen girl. His knife glinted in the shadows. "Miss?"

"Put away the knife, you fool!"

Vladimir reversed the blade so it lay against his forearm, but did not sheathe it. "Miss?"

Karel limped closer. Vladimir knelt by the girl, prodded her shoulder with one meaty finger—

"Karel, she's not here."

Karel blinked snow out of his eyes. "What are you talking about? I can see her."

"I don't understand either," Vladimir said. "There's a coat, and a locket, but no girl." Vladimir lifted something glistening and silver from what Karel could now clearly see was a pile of rags. The locket shimmered and glowed like torn foil cast into the air at sunrise. It pulsed. It growled.

"Vladimir, put that down!"

But too late, too late—and then the world was light.

Gabe followed Morozova and the mark, hoping they would stay inside the bus. He knew no good way to tail pedestrians from a car: There were too many places cars couldn't go, and a car could not match a walking pace. He kept a few lengths ahead of the bus; when it stopped, he saw the *KaGeBeznik* lead Andula out, and he parked and almost left the Moskvich, only for the women to circle back onto the bus again at the last moment.

He threw the Moskvich into drive and followed as casually as he could. Morozova must have seen him; he would have seen her if their situations were reversed.

He turned onto a side street and sped through intersections to beat the bus to its next stop, a few blocks south of the Staré Město. He only almost killed himself once, fishtailing on slick cobblestones. He parked and left the Moskvich, ditched his hat, but kept his overcoat. No sense freezing on the trail. Hunched shoulders and bent knees would change his height a few inches. He paused in front of a shop upwind of the bus, produced a cigarette, and smoked in the snow.

If Morozova had made him, or the car, at the bus stop, he might have thrown her off by veering away. If they didn't dismount here, he'd board the bus himself, a tipsy Czech apparatchik stumbling home from a late night at the office, or a bar, or both.

Gabe did not think of this game as *cat and mouse*. It was dangerous to cling to the fantasy that pursuer and pursued were different animals, living out their fate. In the real world, a cat could not become a mouse, or a mouse a cat. In Gabe's world, that shift might come at any time. Chases turned when you least expected; your careful preparations pitched you straight into a trap.

He avoided thinking about Josh.

The bus stopped. He smoked, and watched reflections.

He found the women more easily than he'd expected. Andula drew the eye in a way Gabe couldn't explain. Morozova manipulated her charge well, moving them within a clump of bystanders; she'd hidden her own hair beneath a knit cap, and seemed shorter— swapping heels, perhaps, or walking with a stoop.

As they neared, he looked past them, raised his hand as if greeting a friend just now exiting the bus, and brushed toward the rear of the crowd. Morozova's eyes tracked over him, locked briefly. She quickened her step.

As the women passed him, Gabe realized he felt distinctly aware of their presence and location, especially Andula's. Not merely conscious, as he would have been of any mark—*aware*. If he'd thrown a rock over his shoulder, he could have struck Andula Zlata in the arm. Like someone had switched on a radar screen in his skull.

He spun on his heel and tailed them north into the snow and swirl of the Staré Město.

Josh saw a blinding flash around a bend in the alley and heard a wet thud. He pressed himself against the alley wall and stilled his breath. There was no cover here. Then again, that hadn't been a gunshot.

Footsteps on iron echoed through the silence and the snow. He looked up to see a woman descending a fire escape set into the alley wall. Josh recognized her, and didn't, at once. He'd seen her before, some part of his brain asserted: short, muscular, dark haired, this was the woman he'd chased down the alley. That was the hair off which the streetlamp light had reflected.

But she was not Andula Zlata.

Gabe had been right. But Josh could have sworn, *had* sworn, he was chasing Zlata, as sure as he would have been swearing he had skin. Surer, in fact, than he ever should have felt about his ID of a target running in the dark. He was no field agent like Gabe. What had made him so positive that he'd left his partner and chased this woman into certain danger?

The woman leaped from the fire escape and landed in a fighter's crouch in the snow. The steam of her breath wreathed her face and spread out behind her in the wind. She looked fierce, and cold.

She rubbed her arms and walked toward the western alley.

Josh almost followed her. Then he heard the click of a gun being cocked.

"Do not move," a man said in Russian. Earmuffs emerged from the bend in the alley ahead, a revolver leveled at the woman. Josh, to his surprise, recognized the man, now that he wasn't chasing behind him at night. What was Professor Karel Hašek doing with a gun in a back alley in Prague? Some sort of StB/KGB feud? "I will kill you."

She turned. Josh did not need to see her eyes. Even from this distance, the scorn she directed against Hašek set the air wavering.

"What did you do to him?"

She raised her hands and walked toward Hašek, as if he were an unwelcome suitor and the revolver a rose. "Your friend will be well." Josh recognized the accent on her Russian—Moscow, and the countryside before that. Interesting. "Put down the gun."

Hašek's revolver shook. He did not seem entirely certain where the woman stood. "Put your hands behind your head. Kneel." Josh slipped his own sidearm from his pocket.

The woman did not move. "Throw the gun away, and we both leave this alley. Your friend will recover. You should go to him. No one should lie out in the cold on a night like this." She was a body's distance from Hašek now—either his body, or hers.

"Down!" Hašek barked, and raised the gun.

At which point Josh shouted, "Hey!" and ducked.

Hašek glanced up the alley, but no shot came. Kneeling, head covered with one arm, Josh heard a man's cry and a muffled thud; when he glanced out from behind the trash bins, he saw the Russian woman standing over Hašek, who lay bleeding on the ground. She blew on her knuckles, drew a handkerchief, and wiped the blood from them.

She picked up the revolver, slid it into her purse, and raised one hand in greeting. Josh, confused, raised his back.

Snow fell between them. Hašek, fallen, groaned.

"Wait," Josh said, and his words broke the spell.

She ran. He followed.

She was long gone by the time he reached the road.

"Can you explain," Andula asked Tanya after they slipped out a café side door, having switched coats, "why we're moving like this?"

"To check for accomplices," Tanya replied without turning her head. Rooftops clear, no watchers outside the café. The square was broad and sparsely populated. On the one hand, they couldn't melt into the crowd; on the other, it would make any surveillance team easier to spot. "I think he has none. That presents certain options."

"What options? Can you—will you—" She slowed; Tanya grabbed her hand and tried to pull her back to pace. "Are you going to kill him?"

"No," she said. "Violence attracts attention. We want you to disappear." A juggler fountained balls in the shelter of a balcony. Tanya guided Andula through the audience, checking over her shoulder as they passed. If Tanya were tailing someone, if she'd just found herself doubled back upon without spotters to assist, she'd slow and sweep the square right to left, in the hope of catching a familiar pattern. So, if someone was following—there. She recognized the tail—a grim, brown-haired man in his thirties—from the university party; she'd pegged him then for American intelligence, but now she was less sure. He did not even slow. He turned toward them and followed. Tanya avoided meeting his gaze by the narrowest margin. No sense letting him know she was aware of his presence—if she let on, he'd be watching for her to try an escape.

"He has your scent," she said. "Like the construct did that first night."

Not American intelligence, then. Flame, perhaps. Deal with

the current scenario before advancing to the next. "Follow me." They slipped across the square. Andula burrowed into her coat. Tanya relaxed her shoulders. She could not waste energy on tension; when they moved, they would have to move with speed.

They walked east, toward the towers of the Charles Bridge. "Is he still following us?" she murmured. "Don't look. Can you feel him?"

"He's following us," Andula said.

"He is following your elemental. That gives us an advantage. He is trained in pursuit, but he's not using that training now. Your elemental calls to him." The Old Town Bridge Tower rose ahead, peaked and enormous, painted dark by age. Men and women and children drifted beneath it across the frozen Vltava, even in this weather, even at this time of night. Buses plowed furrows through the snow. "The world is wrapped in lines of force," Tanya said. "Like electricity, but flowing without wires. This power is the air the elementals breathe, the ocean through which they swim. People sense these things without recognizing them. We build great roads and structures where they lie. A bridge has crossed the Vltava here for eight hundred years at least, because there is power in this place."

"Can that power . . . help us?"

Tanya felt, in spite of herself, a stab of guilt. "I do not have the tools, or the time, or the comrades, I would need to use that power. Humans cannot call upon such might unaided."

They passed beneath the arch. He followed them. Tires ground snow to slush. She walked faster, following the burned-metal-and-cardamom smell of magic to the center of the bridge. A bus cleared the western bank, approaching. Barges lay frozen in the river far below.

"But you," she said, "are more than human." She removed her glove, turned, and stared into Andula's eyes. "Take my hand."

Crossing the bridge was Morozova's first mistake. She'd led Gabe on a good chase even with an untrained girl in tow. If the student was a plant, she'd been chosen for her total lack of field competence. Not even an expert could fail so adroitly. Gabe could have followed her with ease, even if he had not been able to *feel her in his mind*. Zlata was easy to spot, that was all. She moved wrong, turned wrong, looked at things the wrong way. Carried herself as if the sky were about to collapse, or the earth erupt beneath her feet. Morozova barely kept her in line.

That's what he told himself.

His head ached as he approached the river, but he pressed on. While the two women crossed the Charles, Gabe could close the distance. If they boarded a bus, he'd see it. They couldn't even make the desperate jump off the bridge in this weather. The ice would break them, and if by some chance they broke the ice instead, they'd drown.

He felt them stop before he saw they had.

They stood by the railing, facing downriver. He slowed, approached. *Don't spook them; don't draw attention to yourself.* Damn Josh, dashing off like a greyhound after a metal rabbit. Gabe could have used a partner here.

He felt another tug in his brain, a gentler twin to his pull toward Zlata, from the ice-locked barges on the river. He ignored it and sidled closer.

Morozova and Zlata joined hands.

When they touched, the world shook.

He'd been caught in an earthquake before, in Burma. The same queasy terror corkscrewed through his gut now as then, this shaking not some random ragged pulse like a drum set thrown down a flight of stairs, but a rhythm. He felt himself move in harmony with it, saw the river too pulse, not with light but with something *like* light, sound made visible, tangible by this new sense, this *presence* inside his brain—welding him together only to pry him apart again.

The world was an instrument, and God's hand plucked the strings.

Gabe fell to his knees on the Charles Bridge like Saul on the Damascus road and clapped his hands over his mouth to contain his howl.

How long does the end of the world last?

Forever, and no time at all.

When Gabe recovered, his legs were wet with melting snow. A crenellated wall of black fabric surrounded him. Concepts righted themselves slowly, filtering his senses' bloody report. The battlements were coats, the crenellations concerned faces, locals peering down as he knelt on the Charles Bridge. His watch told him ten minutes had passed.

He roared to his feet, furious, unsteady, scattering Samaritans—but Zlata and the Russian were gone. Not on the sidewalk; buses and passing cars had long since cleared the bridge in both directions. He couldn't feel them anymore.

Gabe ran to the railing; foot traffic had mushed away the women's trail. He set his hand on the stone rail where he remembered seeing Zlata's rest, and found it warm, though the stone to either side lay cold.

He swore into the dark, into the river.

THE WITCH WHO CAME IN FROM THE COLD

Tanya could have skipped to the safe house, laughing like the girl she'd never been. She did not. She kept her head. She forced herself to work, to be a spy, an officer, an acolyte, when every cell in her body wanted to sing. An ecstatic silent symphony vibrated within her as she led Andula Zlata to the safe house.

While Tanya kept herself together, Andula was glowing and giddy as a first-time drunk in love, or a first-time lover, drunk. She gaped at spires of buildings that were once churches and at castle battlements; she ogled the cold-scarred faces of passing ancient women in the street; she hummed, poorly, tunes Tanya did not recognize but which sounded like nursery rhymes. "I have never," she said for the third time as they rounded the last block to the safe house, and she decided she loved the word and repeated, "never never never never nev—" flying up the tonal scale and down again, now elated, now furious, now laughing too hard to finish. "Never! Felt anything!" She left *like that before* implied.

Not that Tanya was in any condition to argue. She could barely frame words without shouting. Barely imagine the possibility of pursuit and ambush, barely watch the streets ahead. They must seem drunk. They *were* drunk, just not on liquor. She'd taken part in rituals before. You spoke the words when others did; you moved the knives in sync as well; you performed the strange broken math and arrayed the ritual apparatus. But she had never led the work. She had never held a Host's hand while she twitched the reins of the world.

They reached the green door and she raised her fist to knock, but before she could, Andula caught her by the wrist, and she stumbled against the wall, remembering the power of Andula's touch. And this girl with the power of a god, she *giggled*. "Is that how it always feels?"

"I hope so." Those weren't the words she'd thought to say—they were too naked. "I've never been this close to the center. And we didn't *do* anything—we didn't play a chord, just plucked a string. In real work, you'd move in concert with other Hosts, and with acolytes better than me."

"You"—Andula grinned—"are fantastic."

"There will be others around the world, working the same magic, together. You'll save us all, piece by piece. And you," Tanya said, and for once, just once, she did not spin this, did not control, "are fantastic too."

She tried once more to knock, but Andula—the Host—Andula hugged her, fierce and hard and warm and young and good.

"Thank you for this," the girl said.

At last they pulled apart. Tanya knocked on the green door four times, then twice, then three times, and the acolytes received them, and led Andula, smiling, to safety.

"Fuck," Gabe said when he finally caught up with Josh in the Vodnář later that night. Josh was finishing his first drink; Gabe went to the bar, bought two pints, and settled in the booth across from him.

"Fuck," Josh replied. They tapped glasses. The beer tasted crisp and fine. Josh didn't point—he was too well-bred—but he indicated Gabe's torn trousers and dirty jacket, the bruise on the side of his face where he'd struck cobblestones, with a jut of the chin and a raised eyebrow.

THE WITCH WHO CAME IN FROM THE COLD

Gabe leaned back and let the whole evening, the chase and his plans and his hopes, out in a single long breath. "Fuck."

"You were right," Josh said.

"Of course I was."

"That woman running from the bus wasn't her—it was some other Russian. She took out the two chasing her." The way Josh clipped that story made Gabe think maybe there was more to it, but he didn't press. "One of those was that professor, by the way. Hašek. So that's interesting. But the Russian sure as hell wasn't Zlata. So we have at least one more description to add to the *Audubon Book o' Spies*, if nothing else."

"I tailed Morozova and the girl into the Old Town, but they lost me."

"Looks like they jumped you."

"I fell."

Josh leaned back and quirked an eyebrow. "You *fell*? What happened?"

"I've been getting these headaches lately. Bad ones. Got another while I was chasing the student, real nasty, like a seizure, almost." No sense telling him about the Ice, about the magic—not when Gabe wasn't sure what to believe himself—but Josh had done him a favor, despite his misgivings, and deserved to know as much as Gabe could tell. And after so much silence, it felt good to tell someone something.

"A *seizure*? Have you seen a doctor?"

"I . . ." Gabe lifted his glass to his lips and tried to gather his thoughts. "More or less. We're getting it under control. Isn't yet, though."

"If I'd known, I wouldn't have left you." Josh pressed himself back against the booth, as if trying to topple it with his weight. "I was so sure, though. What the fuck are we going to do, Gabe? We split up. You lost the target. And I don't imagine you've told Frank about these headaches."

Gabe set down the glass before the tremor in his hands could betray him. The jukebox started up a Joplin record—Scott, not Janis.

Josh drummed his fingers on the table. "We checked out equipment for this job, so we have to write it up—and all this stuff is too weird to sweep under the rug. Good thing for us both that Zlata doesn't look important, or we'd catch hell for losing her, even if you did start watching her on your own initiative. But this local group working against the KGB, Hašek and his buddy, what are they about? Infighting among the happy family? Are they allies? Crooks? Crooks we could use? That gives us *something*. I'm still worried about you. Frank isn't happy."

"I know." He remembered Frank glowering in that tiny office. "I owe him a win."

"And soon. Losing Drahomir was a big hit. This—you found a Russian op, sure, but we lost the girl. We don't think she was important, but we don't know why they thought she was. It's not clean enough to save you."

No tea leaves clustered in the bottom of his pint glass to be read, but if Gabe squinted, he could see the concave wet bottom as a crystal ball; *Mirror, mirror, on the wall*; or maybe *The Wizard of Oz: There's no place like home*—

No. He did not need magic to win this thing. This was not Cairo. All he needed was simple tradecraft.

"We don't spin it at all," he said with a smile he knew would read as wicked.

3.

Nadezhda Fyodorovna Ostrokhina greeted every morning as a war. In war, you relied on plans and procedures, discipline and determination. You could not control the enemy. Often, in her line of work, you could not even control initial conditions—whether or not you slept the night before, the prevailing political wind, ambient weather, and so on. So you offered the enemy, which for Nadia meant *the world*, as few openings as possible. Eliminate weakness with training.

It had been well past midnight when she finally returned to her small apartment, having shaken any potential magical or physical tail, yet Nadia nevertheless woke as usual at 5:29, one minute before her alarm, sat up smoothly, and flipped the switch before the alarm could speak. The kettle whispered on the burner while she performed one hundred push-ups. While the tea steeped, she held her plank.

She read as she sipped another cup of tea and ate her egg. She'd spent the last three weeks on *East of Eden*, her second time through. English frustrated her, but Steinbeck was worth it. This morning she reread the chapter about qualities of light. She balanced a knife by its tip on the middle finger of her right hand. When she finished the chapter, she closed the book and drank the last of her tea.

Reading was like any other form of exercise: Too much, without rest, would destroy the very muscles one wanted to develop.

And that was her morning, even after a night spent wandering through cold streets until she'd ground out every trace of mystic residue Flame agents might have left upon her. She had crossed and recrossed bridges until her legs ached and she was clean.

Still, war or no, Nadia wanted nothing more from this day than to sit behind a desk, shuffle developmental papers, and drink strong tea until the end of her shift.

So naturally, when she reached the rezidentura vault, she found Chief Komyetski waiting behind her desk in the otherwise empty office. "Comrade Ostrokhina! Early as ever, I see. I value your dedication."

"Good morning, Comrade Komyetski." She sifted through the pile of mail in her inbox. Nothing urgent—information requests she'd issued yesterday come home to roost—but the sorting let her survey her papers, which seemed undisturbed. Not that she'd leave anything incriminating at her desk, no one would be so stupid, but if Komyetski had searched her desk and left a sign, that might indicate, for example, that his interest in her was personal—that he did not want to call an embassy team to give her papers a thorough search. Her brief glance revealed no obvious tampering. "I like to start work on the day before the day starts working on me."

His laugh echoed off the bunker walls. "I appreciate your attitude. Come. Let us speak in my office."

She followed him into his small room. Every flat surface

THE WITCH WHO CAME IN FROM THE COLD

supported at least one chessboard. He closed the door after her. She expected a quick debrief, down to business, but when he closed the door behind her, she found herself waiting in front of his empty desk, listening to the wall clock tick. She wondered if he was watching her from behind—Sasha lacked the lascivious reputation of some of her previous commanders, but Nadia had lived long enough to recognize reputation as an imperfect indicator of human quality.

She turned. Sasha stood in front of a chessboard balanced atop a stack of folders. His hand hovered over the black queen's knight. His thick fingers twitched closed and open. His forefinger almost touched the carved horse's head, but he pulled his hand back as quickly as if he'd brushed a hot iron.

"I do not understand, Comrade," Nadia said. "You play over the post. You could touch the pieces if you wished, or move them. It's not a formal move until you send it to your partner."

He looked over in apparent shock, as if he'd forgotten she was there. Nadia could have done without that particular bit of low-class subterfuge. He had not called her into his office to forget about her. Nor had he made her wait to impress upon her his power to do so: No officer of his skill needed resort to such pettiness. He wanted to convey, by his distraction and his easy old uncle's smile, a sense of harmless vulnerability. Good, kind Sasha, regrettably forced into a position that sometimes makes him cruel.

"I suppose I could," he said, "but I respect the principle. The smallest touch is a commitment." With a triumphant laugh, he took up the queen's knight and captured a white pawn. "Thank you for waiting, my dear. I commend you; your work this last year has been exemplary. You are a model citizen and officer."

"Thank you, Comrade Komyetski."

"Sasha, please. It can be Sasha between us."

"I am only performing my duty," she said, and because it was unwise to disobey a commander in his own office: "Sasha."

"Of course." He rounded his desk, working the white pawn between his thumb and finger. "Your developmentals have progressed admirably. You are accumulating field experience at a respectable rate, and your occasional personal entanglements have posed at most the smallest hindrance to embassy security."

Nadia did not let herself tense, nor did she relax. That was not a threat. She took lovers; so did other officers. The material world demanded she satisfy material needs. That her lovers insisted, too often, on misinterpreting the nature of her needs, or theirs, was not her fault—but she did not relish KGB security's involvement in her affairs. "My personal life does not interfere with my work. I have not always been fortunate enough to find partners who understood that I would not set them before the Party."

"You are not the first to experience such a problem."

Offering common cause? Backhandedly rejecting her excuse? Both? Neither? "I am glad to know I am not alone."

"You are not. I plan to commend you to my superiors."

Plan. So that was the nature of this conversation. Stick presented, and carrot. *What direction do you want me to run, Comrade Komyetski? How high do you want me to step?* "Thank you, sir."

Komyetski placed the pawn atop the blotter on his desk and tilted it on its edge. "You have a talent for identifying loyalty among developmentals. I wonder if you might have a similar facility with identifying disloyalty among officers?"

"I do not know what you mean, sir."

He rolled the pawn back and forth, wearing a small groove in the blotter. "You work closely with Comrade Morozova."

"I do." *Do not hesitate. Trust procedures, and plans, and discipline.*

"Have you noticed anything . . . erratic in her behavior?"

"Erratic, sir?"

"It is a word in the Russian language," he said with an utter lack of expression. His eyes remained on the pawn. "Surely you have encountered it before."

"I do not think Morozova's conduct is . . . erratic."

He released the pawn and looked up. "She is your superior. I appreciate your loyalty. But, Comrade, there are many levels of superior. I do not mean to suggest that I am suspicious of Comrade Morozova."

Of course not.

"But her recruitment numbers are not improving at the expected pace. She seems distracted. She trusts you, as anyone would trust a model subordinate. I merely ask: If you learn of any way I could help her—if you learn the source of her discomfort, and share it with me, well . . ." He took the pawn in his palm, closed his fist, and opened it again, finger by finger, to reveal his hand was empty. "I could ease her pain."

"Thank you, Sasha," she said. "I will tell you what I find."

"I'm so glad we understand one another," Komyetski said. "That's all, Comrade. Back to work for us both, alas. I look forward to your report, some other early morning."

"Thank you." Nadia stood and left. The knight, she saw on the way out the door, had forked a bishop and a rook.

Drahomir Milovic, assistant undersecretary for the Ministry of Economics, often took his tea in a small cafeteria down the street and around the block from the ministry offices. This, Gabe knew.

He knew Drahomir drank tea without milk or sugar. He knew that while Drahomir drank tea, he read a two-week-old copy of the *London Times* he brought to work in his valise. Gabe knew a great many things about Drahomir Milovic.

He knew all these things because he had studied the man like any hunter would his prey—scouted and plied him, and prepared him for the shift, so subtle he might not even realize he'd shifted, from developmental to asset. Gabe cultivated Drahomir's interest in American culture, and sold him the song of freedom. Drahomir did not need much convincing. He'd seen Soviet tanks roll through his city. He was not a fighter, or a fool. But he was a patriot.

And Gabe had brought him to the pitch and flubbed it. He'd suffered an attack at the wrong moment and scared Drahomir off. He'd meant to wait, give the man time to cool, find a gentler way to approach him. But there was no more time to wait.

Nor was there time to hide.

He sat across from the man in the cafeteria, in full view of the street. "Hi, Drahomir."

The assistant undersecretary looked up, and his brown eyes widened. "Gabriel! I am glad to see you well."

"It's good to see you, too." Gabe did not return his smile. A smile did not serve the mask he had to wear today. "We need to talk about that card game."

"My friend." Drahomir leaned in. "Are you certain this is the right time?" The cafeteria was almost empty, but almost wasn't enough: A cashier stood behind the register; an old woman slumped over her soup three booths down.

"Let's talk outside," Gabe said. "Leave the tea. You'll be back."

The streets were noisy, public. Traffic trundled past. Gabe took Drahomir by the arm and guided him down the sidewalk. "You know, or suspect, what I was going to ask you the last time we spoke. Who I work for. How you can help us."

"Gabriel." Drahomir stopped. Gabe swung to face him. "I do not understand."

Gabe kept his voice level and low. "You do. But I want you to look like you don't, like we're arguing—about cards, say."

Drahomir reared back and raised his hands and cried, in Czech: "I do not believe you!"

"Good." Gabe stabbed his finger into Drahomir's breastbone. Their faces were inches apart. "We need your help. We need you to work with us."

"You play a game with me, and you lose. And now you cry, and curse me!"

"The Russians are abducting people, Drahomir. I followed a KGB operative last night; she stole a history student right out of her dorm. The student's name was Andula Zlata." He grabbed Drahomir's lapels and pulled the man toward him. "Check your records. Zlata's gone."

"Why?" Drahomir roared. *Overdoing it,* Gabe thought. Spittle flicked against his cheek.

"I don't know what they wanted with her, but she's gone now. Your daughter's in university, isn't she?"

"What can I do to be rid of you? The game was played and won—that should be the end of it."

"We need you, Drahomir. Your people need you."

Drahomir's teeth flashed white, and blood flushed his pale skin. He was breathing hard. But he nodded, too, once, clearly: *Yes.*

"Look into it, Drahomir. See if I'm right. There's only one catch: I can't work with you anymore, not after contact in public like this. So I want you to do two things." Gabe wrapped Drahomir in a wrestler's hug, prelude to a throw. "If you want to work with us, wear a white flower to the Soviet ambassador's birthday bash. Someone will contact you—not me. We can't see one another again, after this."

"And second?"

"Hit me. Now."

The man might have been stone for all he moved. His jacket smelled of mothballs and tea. Then he shoved Gabe back, and Gabe didn't even have to fake surprise when Drahomir's fist slammed into his face.

He sat down hard on the concrete, blinking up into stars and sunlight and sky the color of cold steel.

"That," Drahomir said, "is what you get for accusing Drahomir Milovic of cheating at cards. Go, my friend. We are done."

No one helped Gabe to his feet, which was just as well.

4.

Drahomir packed a mean right hook. By the night of the ambassador's birthday, the swelling around Gabe's black eye had receded, but even with concealer he looked like he'd gone three rounds with Muhammad Ali.

The ambassador's birthday party, at least, was swank. Everyone who was anyone was there, and some who weren't. Unseasonable flowers erupted from vases against the wall. The chandelier glittered. A quartet played something Gabe did not recognize. Apparatchiks and ambassadors' wives glitzed across the parquet floor, leaving invisible trails of secrets and perfume. Zerena Pulnoc shone at the apex of a clique to which Gabe would never be admitted, which suited him just fine. Her husband, man of the hour, was nowhere to be seen.

Embassy staffers clustered by a cold buffet, funneling caviar into their mouths; Gabe found a flute of a beverage that looked like champagne and tasted like battery acid, and settled back beside the entrance to watch.

"Prokofiev," Josh said at his shoulder.

"New guy?"

"The music. You look horrible."

"After all the time I spent dressing up pretty for you? I'm hurt. You seen Milovic yet?"

"I just arrived." He tugged at a sleeve. Gabe would have felt naked wearing Josh's slim-cut suit. No give in those soft gray checks. "Wait. There. Far wall, in the corner, by the roses."

Gabe let his eyes drift that way, under the pretense of following a girl's long legs. There Drahomir stood, smoking, laughing too loud at some friend's joke—Gabe recognized the friend, a ministry coworker. A chrysanthemum bloomed in Drahomir's lapel, a little white sunburst against the black. Gabe clinked glasses with Josh. "That's our boy. Yours, now."

"Little Drahomir, all grown up. You'll miss him?"

"Something awful." Six months of work handed off to a friend with a punch and a flower. "Try not to lose too much money to him, okay?"

"I meant to lose, that one time."

"Sure," Gabe said, knowing it was true. "If you say so. Go on. Socialize."

"Cheers." Josh grimaced down the last of his champagne and marched onto the dance floor.

Now, time to find Alestair.

One could not, more's the pity, disregard an invitation to the ambassador's birthday gala, not if one's embassy cover indicated that one served as a cultural secretary, and especially not if one were already on fragile terms with one's superior. So, while Tanya had hoped to spend the weekend locked in a closet with a stack of paperwork to catch up on the more infuriating and time-consuming demands of her position, her Saturday was instead spent preparing for an ambassadorial birthday party that the ambassador himself, to believe gossip, would not be attending. He was indisposed. But Zerena Pulnoc, gleaming doyenne of Prague's diplomatic circle, would let nothing curtail her husband's birthday bash, not even the man himself, sick and moaning in his suite. So Tanya armored like a knight with makeup and shoes and her finest dress, and when she could delay no more, proceeded to the ballroom for battle.

She didn't intend to stay long. Appear, be seen, and retreat to fight another day. She swanned into the chandelier-lit duck pond of the party and danced a turn with a young embassy security sergeant who looked less gawky in dress uniform. Smiling, she thanked him for the dance and turned away, hoping to find Nadia and an exit.

A tower of diamonds and blue silk blocked her path: Zerena, divested for once of hangers-on and junior acolytes, tall and sharp and thin, with a smile bright as knives and about as gentle. "Tanya Morozova! Dear." She held out her hand. "Such a pleasure to see you." They embraced, and Zerena kissed her on the cheeks. "I feel ashamed for having taken so little time to talk with you these last few weeks. You poor girl, you look exhausted."

Tanya tried to sound . . . buoyant. "Zerena," she said, because the ambassador's wife had insisted on this point, refused to let herself be addressed with any honorific, even *Comrade*, which might have been an affectation had it not seemed so precisely calculated. "Thank you for your concern. I'm fine, really—but what about you? The strain must be terrible, your husband falling ill so suddenly." The concern sounded forced, even to her.

If Zerena noticed, she seemed not to care: "Oh, dear Andrei will be well. He's so noble, you know, if I may use that word—he wouldn't dream of disappointing his friends by canceling the gala. I admire that—let's call it courage—in the Russian spirit. You have more than a little of it yourself, Tanya. Working late hours, eager and determined. I hardly expected to see you last week at my little youth league soiree, though I suppose Sasha must prod his grubby fingers into every pie." She chuckled, and Tanya looked for an escape. "Not," Zerena said with sudden horror, "to suggest you were grubbing. Your presence was an unanticipated delight. Did you attend for pure business, or dare I hope you enjoyed the affair? Might we see you again?"

"I always find Communist youth leagues charming." Had Zerena seen her with Andula at the lecture? Did she know Andula had disappeared? Was she threatening something?

"Your use of 'charming' suggests that we entranced you somehow. Please, tell me: Have you met someone?" Zerena laid a hand on Tanya's arm. "I wouldn't blame you. Some of the young men are so dashing, full of zeal." She shivered, her face mock-rapt. "Did anyone catch your eye in particular? I could arrange an introduction."

The door was only ten feet away. If she threw Zerena back, she could make it in thirty seconds, having added *mortally offending the ambassador's wife* to her recent list of tradecraft victories.

She heard a familiar scream and a fountain of curses. Turning, she saw Nadia dripping wet with champagne and ringed in broken glass, berating an apologetic waiter with air-burning Russian that the young man, fortunately, could not quite follow. "Excuse me," she murmured to Zerena, and whisked to Nadia's side. "Are you all right?"

Nadia glared at the waiter with an expression that promised swift and certain harm, and waved him away. Tanya grabbed a fistful of napkins from the buffet table and mopped her friend's shoulders clean. "What are you staring at?" Nadia growled to the dancers who'd stopped to look. They quickly discovered interests elsewhere.

"Thank you," Tanya whispered as she tried unsuccessfully to sop wine off the front of Nadia's red dress. "Come on," she said loud enough to be overheard. "Don't worry about it. You can change."

"My pleasure," Nadia said into her ear. "Sasha asked me to inform on you—can you believe that?"

"What did you tell him?"

"Why, yes, of course." She clapped Tanya across the shoulder; her hand was sticky with champagne. "You'll be a model Soviet citizen by the time I'm done with you. Hope you have room left on your jacket for the Order of Lenin."

Josh did not watch Drahomir Milovic work his way around the party's edge. If you watched someone, people could see you watching. He just waited and stayed aware.

He wasn't nervous. Nerves happened to other people. They tightened when you'd rather they didn't, like when you were ready to take responsibility for a high-profile source, to run an agent more important than any you'd ever run before, after spending most of your career as a desk-jockey analyst. Situations like that.

For example.

He was certainly not sweating. He gulped fake champagne that wasn't even trying too hard. And, when Drahomir was about to pass in front of him, he stepped forward and struck the man in his shoulder. Drahomir reeled back, and Josh caught him before he stumbled onto the dance floor. "I'm so sorry," he said. "Here."

"Pardon me." Drahomir's eyes narrowed. He recognized Josh, but didn't know how to play it. "I believe I know you from somewhere."

"Oh, I don't think so," Josh said. "Your boutonniere's crooked." He adjusted the flower. "It's a nice flower, if a bit crushed. Here, let me make it up to you—a drink, perhaps?"

"Tonight?" Milovic laughed a little too loudly. "I don't think you need to buy me a drink."

"Sometime it would count, then."

"I see," he said. "A pleasure to meet you."

And that was that. So much stress, for such a little thing.

Milovic moved on and left Josh strung out, unattached as any civilian. But the wine was bad, the dancing didn't interest him, and the Soviet army uniforms were a bit of a turnoff, all things considered. He could appreciate the caviar, at least.

He leaned back against the buffet table, munching caviar and crackers, when a cry made him glance left—to a young woman with dark hair and broad shoulders, standing beside an earnest, fumbling blonde. And he knew them both.

He turned his head so he could see them out of the corner of his eye. Morozova and the decoy, working together. Distinguishing features? Hair could change color and length. Focus on jawline, carriage, musculature, height. Everything he needed to add the new girl to the *Audubon Book o' Spies*.

"Fascinating night, isn't it, though?"

Josh realized that as he'd tried to watch the Russians without watching them, he'd ended up staring at someone else. And what a someone: a beautiful edge of a man, blond and lean and very British, his pedigree obvious even without that accent. He carried a martini glass, one hand in his pocket; his body described a gentle arc from feet through spine. "I didn't mean to stare," he said.

"Oh, that's quite all right if you were. I was referring to the evening overall." The man smiled as easily as he seemed to do everything else. "Alestair Winthrop."

"Josh," he said, and then "Toms," remembering that last names existed, and shook hands. "You're English?" seemed the dumbest thing possible to say under the present circumstances, so of course he said that.

"A humble subject of Her Majesty," Winthrop said. "Cast upon these distant shores like Viola on the seacoast."

"We're a bit north for Illyria."

Winthrop smiled. "You're not a sailor?"

"No."

"You'd be surprised how far a good storm can carry one." The Englishman's grip loosed, and Josh realized he'd held the handshake too long. "I've been posted to Her Majesty's embassy for three years, a pleasant length of time—long enough to grow accustomed to the weather, not so long that the post has lost its charm. You're new to the area, I take it—you'll forgive me, but I have an excellent memory for faces."

"A year last December," Josh said. His chest felt tight.

"That long?"

"I don't get out much."

"I hope you'll remedy that in the future. Zerena throws a fantastic party, but at the very least you owe it to yourself to attend a function that serves better swill than the Russian stuff."

Josh's mouth felt dry. He stuffed his hands in his pockets

because he wasn't sure what to do with them. He knew what meaning he'd have read into the man's advance in certain bars, in certain parts of New York, but what could it mean here? *Be careful,* Frank had said, as if Josh ever forgot. Some days—most—he wished he only had his country's secrets to keep.

"Thanks," he said. Kept his voice level, and his eyes. Kept his hands from fidgeting with his jacket, or his belt. "I'd like that very much. But I have to go. I'm sorry."

"Duty calls?"

"It called a long time back."

Winthrop smiled sadly. "A familiar experience, alas. Until next time, Mr. Toms."

"Mr. Winthrop."

Josh's heart didn't slow until he hit the street.

Gabe checked his watch. As soon as he'd seen Drahomir's flower, he'd cleared his checklist for this shindig, and Josh made the approach just fine, but you couldn't sway into the Soviet embassy and sway back out five minutes later. People noticed things like that.

So he spoke with a Frenchman about agricultural imports, promised he'd discuss the matter with his people at the embassy, drank too much whatever-this-was (it certainly wasn't champagne), ate too many passed hors d'oeuvres, and was about to leave when he noticed Alestair Winthrop by the buffet—guy must have come late, or else just now let himself be noticed.

He wound through the crowd toward Winthrop. "We need to talk."

"A pleasure to see you again, my man."

"Your nothing," he said, companionable as he could manage

himself. "This thing in my head cost me another job. I can't let it push me around anymore."

"Progress takes time." Winthrop steered Gabe by his elbow through the crowd. "And requires effort on your part. But we'll do what we can. In the meantime, I thought I might seize upon a rare opportunity to introduce you to one of our allies in the field."

Gabe thought, and did not say, that that field was Alestair's, not his. He thought, and did not say, that his interest in the Ice and their secret war extended only so far as they helped him to get a handle on his little problem. "More Brits?"

"Someday, perhaps," Alestair said. "But for the moment, please meet my friend—" and he touched a tall young woman in a brown dress on the shoulder. "Tanya Morozova, this is Gabriel Pritchard."

Then the rest of Gabe caught up.

"Pleased," he said, because he was a professional, "to meet you face-to-face."

"Likewise," Morozova said, and with equal venom.

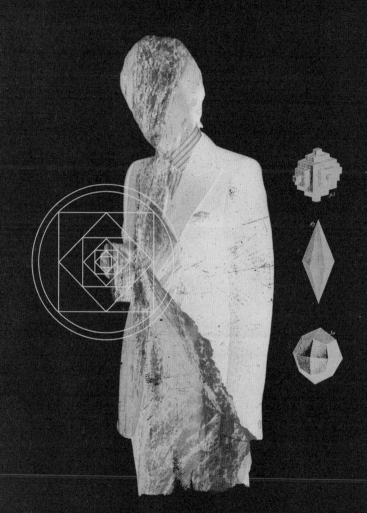

ДСЗПОЙД

EPISODE 4

STASIS

Lindsay Smith

Prague, Czechoslovak Socialist Republic
January 31, 1970

1.

The knock on Gabe's door ripped him from sleep with the force of a gunshot. He clutched at his chest, sucking down air, cold sweat wreathing his forehead as he tried to get his bearings.

Dark. Night. His apartment. He glanced at the wall beside his twin bed—he was alone. (No surprise there.) His sidearm was where he'd left it; he pressed the cold metal to his forehead and tried to think.

The knocking continued. Gabe racked his mind, trying to think who or what it could be now. Everything was going well with Drahomir; he'd handed him off neatly to Josh, so any issues that might arise—which they shouldn't—would be Josh's problem, not Gabe's. Surely neither Josh nor Drahomir had already done something stupid. And he hadn't been in Prague long enough to develop any other agents. Hell, he'd barely been in Prague long enough to make nemeses of the rival services. Except for that god-damned Ice woman, he'd barely roused their notice at all.

Ice. Magic. Right. The "Ice," who had an honest-to-God *KaGeBeznik* in their midst.

Gabe swung his feet over the side of the bed and slid into his slippers. The thing inside him was awake, as far as he could tell; maybe it never really slept. Sometimes he thought it ran in circles, senseless, like squirrels scampering through an attic at night. Well, if it had any warnings as to who waited on the other side of the door, it kept its silence.

Gabe slid the cover for the peephole up and was greeted with an outsize Wimbledon-blue eye on the other side.

"Jesus, Alestair." Gabe fumbled with the chain locks and dead bolts that scaled the side of his door—his fine motor skills still hadn't fully woken up. "Do you have any idea what time it is?"

"Oh, I reckon it's never too late for a few fingers of single malt." Alestair jabbed his hand into Gabe's for a forceful shake as soon as the door cracked open. "How've you been doing? Glad the office isn't keeping you out late, wining and dining some mustachioed Slavic goon or another."

Gabe suspected Alestair had consumed a few *hands'* worth of scotch already. "Just trying to get some goddamned sleep. *Shit,*" he added, weariness filing off the edges of his temper. "Next few weeks are going to be hell. Station inspection, and then . . ." Were the Brits in on ANCHISES? *Shit.* Maybe this whole midnight visit was an elaborate ploy of Alestair's to pry information out of him. He'd have to remember this trick for the future.

"All the more reason I think you'll be glad I dropped by." Alestair dug around in Gabe's cabinets, in what Gabe knew was a fruitless search for glassware free of water stains and detergent rings. "Has our fellow been letting you sleep?"

Gabe stopped in the doorway to his cramped kitchen. "He, uh . . . it . . ."

Gabe was still bothered by the strange pull he'd felt tailing

Morozova and her Czech student. The strange pull he'd felt by the Vltava. Almost like the thing inside him, the . . . *hitchhiker* had been—unsettled. Scared, even. Something to do with the Flame? Or something Morozova had done? It felt like the river itself, the water running beneath its frozen surface, *something* elemental had been ringing through him, plucking him like a string in a natural symphony. Not that it had sensed something malicious, so much as it had been overwhelmed. But ever since then, his new passenger had rested more easily within him. As if it had aligned with something, clicked cleanly into place at last.

"It's been . . . behaving," Gabe finally said.

Gabe wondered, now, whether Morozova's pursuit of the university student was part of her spy work or witchcraft. The puzzle he'd gotten so good at, the East-West game, had suddenly popped into a confounding third dimension. It hurt his head. Not that his head needed the help these days.

Alestair nodded to himself, apparently satisfied, and set two glasses on the wobbly kitchen table. "A start, then." He uncorked Gabe's bottle of Grant's and poured them both generous shares.

Gabe pinched the bridge of his nose. It figured that the first night he wasn't suffering the unsettling mental hangovers of the . . . thing roiling inside him, or else out late on "official" business, he'd come down with a stuffy Brit infestation. "What do you want, then?"

Alestair took a gulp of scotch, then recoiled as if he'd been punched. "Dear God. Certainly not whatever this abomination is." He shuddered, pounded one fist to his sternum, then took another drink, daintier this time. "I was at the Vodnář, chatting with Miss Rhemes—you know how it goes—and she voiced her concerns over your struggles in handling whatever it is that's jerking your chain, so to speak."

So this was all Jordan's fault. Gabe winced.

"Seeing as how you're so reluctant to take Miss Morozova's assistance . . ." Alestair drew a circle in the air with the glass. "I thought perhaps I'd volunteer my own services to educate you on the finer points of handling elemental magic."

Gabe glanced at the kitchen clock. In other words, Jordan kicked the Brit out to close for the night, and he was looking for an excuse to keep drinking. "Your *services*?"

Alestair pulled a smile. "In navigating your newfound magical aptitude, of course. You do want to actually make use of it, yes? It'd be a shame for it to go to waste."

Gabe snatched up his glass as well and chugged half the pour, just to make a point. "Oh. So I'm invited to your secret magic club?"

"Anyone *can* do magic, with the proper time and training. But can you imagine the chaos it would cause if the whole world were to attempt it? The misused energy it might send out into the world?"

Gabe scowled at him. "And you're choosing to let me in on the secret because of this—the thing in my head."

"Yes, well, your situation is something of an anomaly. An anomaly I mean to sort out." Alestair sipped at the scotch timidly, as if he were afraid it might bite him. "Fortunately for you, I've been doing some research, and I daresay that I think we can train you to use your fellow to your advantage."

Advantage. The dangle. Gabe saw the fishhook in Alestair's words but swam toward it all the same. What if he *could* use the hitchhiker to his advantage—in his work, even? A little dash of secret sauce, a rabbit's foot in his pocket to give him just enough of an edge to get back in Frank's good graces. Bend some ears his way, add a little charisma and persuasion to his patter, give him just a little speed over the *KaGeBezniks*, even Morozova—no, especially Morozova.

A new arms race. If the KGB was using witches to aid their spy work, he'd be foolish not to claim the same advantage for himself.

Oh God, but it was a wonderful prospect. An end to the spiral of stagnation and pratfalls he'd found himself in ever since that goddamned night in Cairo. Progress. No more worried looks from Frank and Josh; no more knowing glances and whispers behind cupped hands around the embassy. "Okay." He finished the glass. "Show me what you got."

Alestair grinned in return. "Come with me."

Alestair started with the simplest elements of all: a pinch of common dirt, nicked from some collectivist farm or another nearby; a vial of purified water; a twig he'd found from a tree that he was pretty sure was oak, though Gabe doubted tree identification had been part of his classical Eton education. Gabe sat with his back to Alestair while the Brit set the elements on the table between them, and Gabe focused. Alestair suggested he start by trying to sense any sort of change in how he felt—trying to see if each element tugged at the hitchhiker a little differently.

At first, Gabe felt impossibly ignorant, like he was too drunk to tell the difference between a good tequila and jet fuel. But slowly he started to notice little changes: The water had a taste, a quenching sensation to it that piqued the hitchhiker's interest a certain way. The twig smelled a little loamy and felt firm and fine-grained in his mind. Okay. He could get the hang of this.

"Good work," Alestair said after he'd successfully identified water, dirt, wood, blood, cotton, and fire all in a row. "Now let's move on to powering charms."

Powering things—now that's where the hitchhiker really gave Gabe hell.

The first charm, which Alestair claimed would erase the need for an hour of sleep completely by invigorating his bloodstream, bit back the moment Gabe tried to activate it. Or maybe it was the hitchhiker that lashed out—Gabe had no patience for the distinction.

"I think it worked in reverse," he muttered through what felt exactly like a sudden but raging caffeine headache.

"Go on. It's quite simple once you get the hang of it." Alestair had returned to drinking while he watched, as if charm activation were his new favorite country club sport.

After five more tries and an exhaustive repertoire of curses, Gabe snapped the charm to life. Some of the tension washed out of him; the tightness in his brain unspooled. He did feel better—not a full night's sleep better, but maybe a not-too-strong mug of joe better.

"Wait." Gabe stared down at the charm in his hand. "Most of Jordan's customers—I thought they bought their charms already powered." She'd given him a few charms as well, telling him he didn't need to do anything special to activate them.

Alestair's smile poked up from the other side of his glass as he took a drink. "Yes, ah, well . . . I had some theories about the way your 'condition' might work. Turns out I was right—you function as a very minor power source now."

"So I'm your new pet science project. Great."

Alestair ducked as Gabe lobbed the charm at his head. "Tell you what. You're doing so well—let's grab a round at the Vodnář to celebrate!"

Gabe sagged forward. "It's seven in the morning."

"Then we're just in time for that wonderful breakfast she makes."

Prague looked very different to Gabe through the lens of his new attunement. It *felt* different. As if a fine sheen of Soviet dust had been wiped away to reveal the ancient city beneath. Prague was alive and loud and clamoring for his notice. The more he practiced with Alestair, the more he found the subtle distinctions in different metals and stones and even soil from different regions; the more the riot of color and noise inside his head resolved into distinct shapes. He wandered the elemental garden that was Prague and marveled at each petal.

I could learn to live with this, Gabe dared to let himself think. Even if none of the witches he'd encountered thus far seemed to be able to tell him exactly what "this" was. He sensed a granite-and-quartz monument not far from the American embassy and drank up the fine speckling and the rock's subtle resonance with a trickle of power from the nearest ley line. *I'm going to survive. Thrive, even.*

"Whoa." Josh stared at him when he arrived for work the next Monday. "Your face."

Gabe's fingers darted toward his cheeks. He *had* remembered to shave. "What . . . ?"

"You're not frowning." Josh smirked at him. "It's—it's weird."

Gabe could get used to weird.

Drahomir: happy and producing some decent intelligence. Nothing too juicy out of him yet, but the best agents were steadily leaking faucets, nothing so egregious that it warranted calling the plumber, drip-dripping away for years.

Andula: missing, ever since that night he had chased her and Morozova through the streets. That worried Gabe. He poked around the university, spotted the group of friends he'd seen her with at the lecture, but with an unfilled hole in their cluster. Like they, too, expected her to be there and were still used to fitting their lives around her. What the hell had Morozova wanted with her? It had to have been KGB business—Alestair would have mentioned it if it was Ice related, wouldn't he? Surely Morozova hadn't put in the work to recruit Andula Zlata only to disappear her just as quickly.

But maybe the recruitment hadn't gone according to Morozova's plans. Maybe Andula got spooked—hadn't expected to draw any interest from the rezidentura—and ran. Ran where? He pulled out the file he'd started on her (and never finished) and started looking for leads. Maybe she'd gone back to her mother's farmhouse in western Czechoslovakia. . . .

Josh raised an eyebrow at him from across the desk. "Is that the coed girl's file?"

Gabe shot him a look. "I was just thinking—"

"I'm starting to think you have a little crush." Josh laughed, eyes sparkling. "We followed them halfway across the city, and nothing. I'm sorry, Gabe, but it's a dead end."

"She's missing. Hasn't been to class in a week. You don't find that just a little suspicious?"

"Could be. But it could be any number of things. Maybe she got some sense into her head, and she's having second thoughts about selling out her countrymen to the Russkies."

"They could have done something to her," Gabe said.

"And there's nothing you or I can do about it. It's beyond our jurisdiction. You know where else she hasn't shown up?" Josh thumped the stack of papers he'd been working through. "The guest list for the French National Day party. Isn't that what you told me to focus on?"

Gabe's gaze slipped toward the open door to Chief Drummond's office, where Frank sat peering at the latest cables from head-quarters. The chief was content for now, but Gabe couldn't rid himself of the sweaty film of their earlier conversation, right after he'd botched his first attempt at pitching Drahomir—what was it Frank had called him? A big dumb Labrador?

He was right; Josh was right—he couldn't keep fetching the same stick into eternity. The community had far too short a memory for him to coast on the Drahomir recruitment for long. If he was going to pursue the Andula issue, it would have to be on his own time—time he couldn't spare while he rebuilt his credibility in Prague Station. "And?" Gabe asked. "Any of the names on the guest list strike your fancy?"

As long as the hitchhiker was playing nice, he fully intended to rack up so many wins even Langley couldn't forget.

The hitchhiker was on full alert inside Gabe, attuning itself to the world around him as if it had raised its head and sniffed at the evening air.

Gabe stopped at the foot of the Charles Bridge. Sodium lights, sparkling up and down the banks; the cobblestone path; clay tiles; and a smear of dirt in the snowdrifts across the street. But no, there was something else mingled in there, something that didn't belong. The same dull, throbbing sense of *so much* he'd sensed when he'd tailed Andula and Morozova—only now he was better equipped to filter out the background chaos.

He tasted a tang like metal in the back of his throat and heavy heat in the back of his mind.

Blood.

Gabe paced south down the river path, and the blood faded. He approached the Charles Bridge again, and the sensation grew. Started to cross the bridge, but the *otherness* tugged him northward, just a little farther north, and he stepped up to the railing, garnering a few odd looks from wool-wrapped pedestrians.

Blood. That had to be the element he was sensing. Gabe hoped he wasn't standing over a crime scene. But there was something stronger beneath its pull—something *powerful*. Something that implied the blood had been used for magical purpose. It pulsated, charged by the ley lines and the willful intent of whatever witches had employed it.

Blood magic, though—that in itself felt sinister. What if whatever he was sensing on the bridge was somehow related to the Flame?

Gabe's gaze followed the path of the Vltava northward, or rather, the thin crust of glistening ice that the Vltava had become. It looked the same as it had the last time he'd seen it—snow wreathed, laced with animal tracks, punctuated by a few stubborn barges that were waiting out the cold snap. Gabe felt the distinct sensation of something shifting and shuffling in his mind as he focused on the barge nearest to him, just north of the bridge.

He turned away from the barge, and the hitchhiker shifted again—like letting out a sigh.

No coincidences—not in spycraft, and not in magic, Gabe told himself.

He exited the bridge and wandered north up the riverside path until he stood even with the barge. The thrum of blood was overwhelming now, loud as his own pulse in his ears. It wasn't just blood, he was a little relieved to note, not that he could be completely certain about all the other elements mixed in with it. There must have been dozens of them—iron and stone and copper and plenty more that he hadn't begun to identify. Salt, maybe. Something that felt smooth and shiny in his mind, like freshly dripped candle wax. And a scent that itched his memory more than it itched the hitchhiker, a fragrance like spices and smothering air and—

Gabe staggered and clutched for the stone railing along the river path. He heard chanting, a tangle of foreign tongues hidden in the shadows of his memories. He felt the sharp bite of a blade against thin flesh. Screaming—his throat shredded and raw.

Was he screaming still? Gabe squeezed his eyes shut and sucked in his breath until the memories slithered away. Slowly he eased open his eyes. No. He hadn't screamed aloud. Not here, in Prague—no one stared at him now, or paid him any mind at all. The scream belonged to the memories.

To whatever happened to him in Cairo.

Whatever was on that barge reminded him a little too much of those memories to ignore.

2.

Ahh, just the man I was hoping to see. Come, Gabe, sit. This—this, my friend, is Scotch whisky." Alestair waved the gold-filled glass in Gabe's general direction. "See if you can't train your fellow to recognize the real stuff. No more Shetland-pony piss."

Gabe seized Alestair's cane from where it was propped against the empty chair and fought off the urge to beat him with it. "We have a major problem."

Alestair sat up, though far too slowly; his gaze slid toward Jordan behind the bar before he turned back to Gabe with chilly regard. "What seems to be the matter?"

"There's a barge on the Vltava. I was walking past it, and I think I sensed something—"

Gabe swallowed. What was wrong with him? He hadn't even scanned the bar properly before he'd launched into his story. If Drahomir had overheard him, or that third secretary from the Ministry of the Interior, or whatever goddamned cultural attaché—

No. Just Alestair, Jordan, and a few shady types that had the wild-haired, charm-hung look of hippies or witches or both. Gabe dropped into the chair and clutched Alestair's cane in his lap.

"It's Flame. Has to be." Gabe spoke beneath his breath, despite the soupy psychedelic chords dribbling out of the jukebox in the far corner. "I'm telling you—whatever's on that boat, it has something to do with—with how I got this *thing* to begin with."

"Barge on the Vltava," Alestair repeated. "Flat bottomed? German registration, yes?"

Gabe reared back, blinking. "I—I think so, yes. What?" He leaned in, conspiratorial. "Does Ice already know about it?"

"Well, I should hope so!" Alestair laughed to himself. "It's our own. Nothing you need to worry about. Ah, but it's sweet of you to be concerned. I take it you're getting better at differentiating, then? Your little bloodhound is becoming quite the boon."

That was the trouble he had with reading old-school bureaucrats like Alestair, Gabe thought, searching the man's face. They lied so much it had eroded all hint of their tells. Even their truths smelled like they were dipped in bullshit.

"Sure," Gabe heard himself answer. "It's fine."

Jordan gave him a warning look from where she stood at the bar. Amazing how loud she could be without making a sound. Gabe almost felt duly chastened. But Gabe was almost a lot of things.

Almost a great spy. Almost a worthwhile investment for Frank. Almost a witch.

Almost willing to trust the Ice.

"Oh," Alestair remarked breezily, abruptly shifting topics far less adroitly than usual. "Before I forget. I've brought you something."

"Bribery? Really, Al?" Gabe managed a wry smile in spite of himself. "C'mon, what do you take me for?"

"Please, it's—it's Alestair." His eyelashes fluttered in mock distress. "And it's not a bribe. I think you might find it quite useful."

Alestair set something on the table between them, and Gabe turned his head this way and that, seeking meaning in this inkblot. It looked a little bit like the charms Jordan had pressed upon him—bits of cloth sewn together with some sort of element stitched into the pouches, like dirt or hair or iron shavings. But this one was fringed with a variety of strings and wires, each one wrapped around a different chunk of rock or twig or herbs; carved stone lined each face of the main pouch, each stone dented with a shallow groove as if there were something intended to fit into it.

"Just what I've always wanted. Al, you shouldn't have." Gabe tried and failed to find a suitable handle on the mess. He had no idea how to pick it up. "Did you make this at craft night?"

"Oh, don't be such a snob. It's an amplification charm—one of my own specialities." *Specialities,* Gabe echoed to himself. "You have access to twenty different elements in this charm. It required no less than six witches working in concert to charge that thing, but I think you'll find it contains sufficient power to utilize these elements for . . . well, for just about any spell you currently know how to wield."

The twenty most common elements. Gabe could sense the hitchhiker shifting around, leaning into the pull of each of the elements in their own way—the maple and the jade, the loamy soil inside the pouch, the crystal and quartz. Everything he needed to conduct a ritual of his own.

Assuming he was ever trusted with the knowledge of just how to do that.

Perhaps reading his expression, Alestair leaned forward and placed one hand gently over Gabe's wrist. "It is your choice, of course. But should you decide that you are comfortable with continuing along this journey with the Ice, then we can begin teaching you in earnest. Imagine it." Alestair's lips softened in a smile. "True mastery. No longer having to ask your friend there to work spells for you, or anyone else. You'd be in command of your own power."

Gabe barked a laugh. "Well, that's not entirely true, now, is it?" He frowned. "I'd be at the Ice's mercy."

Alestair leaned away. "The Ice can keep you safe," he said carefully. "Perhaps that's not such a terrible thing to be. Under someone's protection."

But Gabe thought that was something he was better off deciding for himself.

It was a Tuesday morning, and Gabe had hoped to spend his free morning sniffing around at the university and seeing if he could find anything about what had happened to the student, Andula. Then he needed to review guest lists and dossiers for that night's party for the French embassy's festivities. As if the assignment required any preparation beyond liver-strengthening exercises. But no, Gabe decided, this was far more interesting.

He let the clean February air gust over him as he studied the barge. Though the lower currents of the Vltava had thawed, the barge was still stymied by a thin crust of ice across the surface that refused to yield. The crayon-blue sky spoke sweet lies of warmth and sunshine, but Prague knew better; those twisting, snarled-up alleys whittled the wind down to a fine point, jabbing through every weak spot in his clothing's defenses.

The kind of weather where everyone burrowed their chins deep down in their scarves and kept their eyes on their own feet.

The perfect weather, Gabe thought, for getting up to nothing good.

Gabe moved down along the quay to get a closer look at the barge. The tinted glass of the cabin offered up only shadows, but Gabe was pretty sure he saw movement; he kept a safe distance, still trying to look like no one in particular, just a fellow out for an ill-advised morning stroll. He reached a bench at just the right angle along the quays to offer a windbreak and, taking a seat, pulled a notebook from his breast pocket and studied his scribbles with calculated earnestness.

Then he let his elemental senses out to play.

Blood—again he sensed it, overwhelming and dense and crackling with something that Gabe could only imagine must be power. The blood was definitely related to some spellwork—had been used as a conduit for a ritual, perhaps. But there were other elements in large doses too. Water, something far purer than what lurked under the river's ice, but it tasted frosty in Gabe's mouth, like accidentally swallowing an ice cube. When he tried to focus on it too much, it began to sting. Something else prickled his senses, hidden in whatever magic was emanating from the barge. But it was a duller sting—it reminded Gabe of novocaine, spreading in a slow creep of tingle and numb. Whatever element or mixture of elements caused that sensation, he knew it was a combination Alestair hadn't taught him.

Gabe waited a few minutes, watching the cabin for further signs of life, but whoever was inside had either stopped moving or had vanished into a lower deck, if there was one. No sign of any other guards, though Gabe supposed he'd have to rely on the hitch-hiker's senses to help him detect any sort of magical . . . wards? Sentinels? Did witches use such things? He tucked his notebook away and approached the boat, keeping one of the many shipping containers between him and the cabin to block the line of sight.

Gabe felt the spark, the awareness inside him lean into the motion. Something about those new elements excited it—or maybe the combination of them; Gabe couldn't be quite sure which.

He had to know what was on that boat—and why Alestair had seemed so cagey about it. If he was going to ever be able to trust the Ice, then he needed to see their dark corners as well as their glossy exteriors. Put this unease in him to rest so he could get back to his real work without magical conundrums following him around. The sooner he could do that, the better.

He studied the hull; the low ladder that swung up and over the railing and plunged into the icy Vltava. Chunks of fractured ice spiraled away from it, sloshing back and forth as the boat swayed, a dull echo of the roaring water beneath the surface.

The Vltava wasn't particularly deep, but he didn't relish the idea of plunging through the ice, which seemed just likely enough a scenario to give him pause. (A quick glance back up at the cabin—still no movement.) He circled past the barge, approaching the quay's pathway underneath the foot of the Charles Bridge, but could spot no other likely entrance point.

No, wait. There *was* one likely entrance point. It would just require some magical assistance. Fortunately, he had a leather satchel brimming with all the spare charms Jordan kept pushing on him—the ones he had thus far patently refused to activate.

Time to make use of them.

Gabe returned to the bridge to better position himself above the barge and, leaning against the railing, dug through his satchel. Which one did Jordan say would give him five seconds of invisibility? (Apparently any longer than five seconds and the spell needed multiple witches to charge, and as Gabe so loved to point out to her, she was somewhat short on friends.) Each charm he sorted through provoked a different reaction from the hitchhiker, pulling it this way and that, the different combinations of elements banging out ferocious piano chords on Gabe's nerves. There it was, the shimmering chunks of mirror bound with silvery wiring around a mixture Gabe couldn't identify. Then he scrounged through the bag for the charm to dampen sound for one second. "The silencer," Jordan had called it, "when you don't have a silencer on hand."

Gabe had imagined a very different use for that charm, one he hoped never to require. He liked this application much better.

All right, hitchhiker. Time to make yourself useful.

Gabe poured his energy into the invisibility charm, and as he glanced down at his hand clutching the charm, his skin shimmered and faded away.

Five.

It was time. He swung up and onto the railing of the Charles Bridge, then shifted the empowerment to the silencing charm—

Four, three, two—

His boots struck the top of one of the barge's shipping crates with only the faintest thump instead of the resonant bong he'd feared.

One.

Gabe was crouched on top of the container as he wafted back into view. He was visible now, but at least no one had seen the demented American flinging himself off the bridge, or heard him crash into the barge below. It was about the best he dared to hope for.

And given the nature of the rest of the charms in his bags—concealing a piece of text, twisting someone's opinion favorably toward you with the dimmest of pulls—he'd probably exhausted all his magical options for this mission.

Gabe shimmied toward the back of the container, the end farthest from the cabin, then dropped down onto the barge's deck. A sheet of ice coated the deck, shiny as a plastic slipcover. No handrails, only a slight lip to the barge—if he didn't keep his balance and his grip, he was sure to go sliding straight into the river. Gabe reached out to steady himself on the heavy padlock that sealed the cargo hold beneath the deck. Then paused.

The lock had been recently used, the ice around it chipped clean away. Maybe the Consortium of Ice was using the barge for storage, then. A base of operations.

But for what? Ritual components? Taking advantage of the ley lines in Prague to charge up some charms before shipping them around the globe? Alestair had made it sound like the Ice's top priority in Prague was to prevent the Flame from gaining access to either Hosts or the unique power sources available in the city. But he also had sounded none too interested in letting Gabe in on the barge's contents. Which either meant it wasn't at all related to those goals, or was related in new and terrifying ways that he didn't want Gabe to know about.

Gabe looked forward to finding everything Alestair didn't want him to know.

Gabe dug into the front pouch of his satchel, where he kept his more mundane tools of the trade. If this had been a Prague Station operation, Frank would've burst a vein on his forehead at the idea of one of his officers out picking locks in broad daylight. The nature of the station's spycraft in a city, rather than a war zone, meant Gabe primarily served as a wordsmith, wooing men like Drahomir, and almost never anything as risky as B&E. Gabe rarely got to work the type of ops that involved putting his foot through things: doors, walls, skulls.

Gabe pulled a slender file from the pouch and got to work. The pins in the lock stuck easily enough in the cold, even the springs reluctant to uncoil. But when he tugged at the padlock to open it, it clicked but didn't budge.

Gabe tugged harder, then harder still. He got the distinct impression the hitchhiker might have been laughing at him.

Spellwork—it had to be. Some sort of warding. When he gripped the lock tightly, he could feel the faint shift on his tongue and his skin, pulling him like a weak magnet. As he adjusted to its frequency, it soon became clear that the ward was stronger than he'd first thought. Dammit. He didn't know enough about magic to understand how the wards even worked in the first place, much less to puzzle out a way to get around them. Time to look for another means inside. Maybe if he had the luxury of coming back at night with some bolt cutters, or something that could dismantle the hinges on the hatch door, where they might not have thought to ward it—but he was already spending too much time on this bizarre quest as it was.

The loud crack of the cabin door banging in the wind stopped that line of thought.

"Who's there?" someone called out in Czech.

Gabe quickly sorted through his options. He could try magic—maybe if he didn't mind setting his hair on fire, or something similarly clumsy. He could try to hide, he could face down a wary and possibly dangerous witch, or he could dive into the frigid Vltava. The last one was no option at all, not in this cold. The first option—hiding—would be his usual choice, but he suspected that whoever was operating on this barge wouldn't be as easy to evade as the vodka-addled StB agents he was accustomed to giving the slip.

Well, if he couldn't use magic, Gabe decided on the next best thing: bald-faced lies. Which always kind of looked like magic anyway.

"Arnissen," he said, pulling a name like a rabbit from the depths of his working memory, and realizing only too late that it was the name of one of his targets at tonight's party. "Piers Arnissen. Morozova sent me?"

The man rounded the containers. Gabe noticed, with what he hoped was a straight face, that his interlocutor had a pistol tucked in his waistband partially concealed by a heavy parka. He supposed there were some threats even magic couldn't guard against.

"I have not heard this name." The man's words hung in the air before him, little white tufts of suspicion.

"Well, you should have. She asked me to come in, special, to do inventory." Gabe took a deep breath—now for a big leap. "She wanted me to make sure no one was walking off with the . . ." Gabe searched his brain for an appropriately vague word. "Merchandise."

There. Give the KGB woman something to chew on if she got wind of him snooping around.

"Merchandise." The man laughed, but there was no humor to it, no glimmer of joy to his eyes. "No, no one informed me of this. How did you get on this boat?"

Gabe cursed himself for not pocketing one of those charismatic charms. "The same way you did." He gave him a blank look and hoped the man's conclusions could stand in for whatever means, magical or non.

The man eyed Gabe again, rubbing his mouth and chin, disrupting the weft of his thick, dark mustache. "I was not informed of this," he said again. That lovely Slavic devotion to hierarchy, tinged with the bitterness of being left out of the loop. Gabe had used it to his advantage more than once.

"So check it with Alestair. Please—be my guest." Gabe smiled with only a hint of teeth. "Bring him down here, make *him* explain the need for inventory. I'm certain he'd be just *thrilled* to step away from his sensitive operation to have to repeat himself when you missed his message. . . ."

The man's other hand, the one not rubbing at his chin, was dipping toward his waistband.

"Of course," Gabe said in a rush, "I have my credentials."

The man rocked back on his heels. Just a fraction.

"From Alestair. Yes? Is that what you're looking for?"

"Let me see it." That accent made everything sound like a death threat.

Gabe reached into his satchel. "It's right in here. I'm going to take it out very slowly. See?" He'd been on the other end of this sort of exchange enough to do the work for both of them. Didn't stop the fresh bead of sweat from running down his temple as the man hovered over him. "Showing you my bag . . . taking it out very slowly . . ."

Gabe's fingers curled around the main body of the charm Alestair had given him, an involuntary reaction. A thousand different sensations played across his mouth, his nose, his skin, his inner ears. Alestair had said it required a fairly sophisticated ritual to craft a charm like this one. Gabe just hoped that it was sophisticated enough to mark it as Alestair's own work.

The man's hand moved away from his waist and he reached for the charm.

"Oh," the man said as his fingers brushed against the charm. "Oh. I see."

Gabe resisted the urge to gloat, though it took some effort. "Is that enough of a credential for you?"

Something whispered between the two of them; Gabe might

have thought it was only a breeze if he hadn't been training with Alestair. Now, though, he knew better. The man was channeling something. Testing the charm, maybe, to verify its provenance. Perhaps there was some sort of ritual he could conduct to prove that Gabe hadn't killed Alestair and ripped the charm from his cold, dead (but still well-moisturized) hands. Who knew what magic was capable of? Not Gabe—he was humble enough to admit that to himself.

Depending on what he discovered inside the boat's hold, though, maybe it was finally time he learned.

"Yes," the man said at last. "That will be acceptable."

The boat guard wrapped his fist around the lock; if he noticed it had been picked, he gave no hint of it. Another whisper, strumming across Gabe's senses in a subtler, sweeter-tasting way, and the lock popped off.

"You go ahead," the man said. "I'll wait for you out here."

Only because he was looking for it did Gabe notice the tension in the man's throat, in his upraised chin. Whatever was inside, the guard wanted no part of it.

Gabe raised the hatch's lid and lowered himself into the hold.

3.

Somewhere in the depths of the Soviet embassy, a clock chimed. Zerena Pulnoc looked up from the letter she'd been writing and pressed her lips together. Her guest was late. Not that she expected any better from him, but it disappointed her all the same. This was Prague, after all. The jewel of Eastern Europe, the glittering gold gate of the Iron Curtain. She shouldn't have to resort to such primitive, unreliable sources to get things done.

And yet. Here she was.

She turned back to the letter before her—the tangle of Roman letters and Arabic numbers spaced out into a long and rambling message, its secrets illegible to anyone but the intended recipient. A one-time pad was a precious thing, unbreakable, as long as it was used properly. Which was to say, exactly once.

Zerena found that the same applied to most things and people in her life.

A short knock at the door, hesitant and light. A sneer curled her upper lip as she lifted her head, mentally marking her place in the message she was encoding. "What is it?"

One of the maids—Erzebet, something of the sort—stuck her head through the office door. "They've brought your dress choices for tonight's party. Did you want to select one now?"

Zerena let the pen tip rest against her lips for a moment, then glanced back at her correspondence. "No. Leave them in my dressing room. I'll deal with them later."

"Of course, ma'am." The maid dropped into a curtsy without coming fully through the doorway, then left with a soft click of the latch.

Zerena smiled to herself. How bourgeois. She was a student of the revolution, an architect of the cold snap that put an end to the Prague Spring, and here she was, ensconced in her castle, with the servants bending to her will like flowers to the sun.

But she'd earned her place here. She'd done what anyone had the capacity to do, if not the fortitude. And there was plenty more work to be done.

Zerena finished transcribing her notes, waved the paper dry, then folded it up. She had just unlocked the drawer where she kept her seals when another knock came on the door.

"Please, come in." Zerena slipped the letter into the drawer and settled into the wingback chair.

Marcel. One of the Komsomol youth league students at the university she'd taken under her wing. Only—she checked the slender watch on her wrist with no particular effort to conceal that she was doing so—twenty-three minutes late. "I trust you're late because you were being thorough."

She could toss the rope to him, but he had to swim to it himself, and Marcel did not. "I—I'm sorry, ma'am. I had to speak to Professor Hašek after class, and then drop some books at the library on my way over here, and . . . Well, it's not important to you."

Zerena leveled her gaze at him.

"Anyway, you did get my—my message, yes?" He shifted his bag from one shoulder to the other. "For our 'friends' in Moscow?"

Zerena considered a withering response, informing him he wasn't half so subtle as he believed himself to be, but decided against it. The information he thought was invaluable was useless; it was everything else she needed from him. But to get that everything else, she had to keep him happy and his ego sufficiently stroked. For now.

"Oh, yes." She gave him a cold smile. "I've already cabled it back to them. I know they will be very pleased with your work."

The tension in his shoulders dissipated at that, and he hazarded a grin.

"You're providing a very valuable service to the cause, Marcel. Turning the tide in the university, leading them away from all those foolish Dubček sycophants."

Zerena picked up her pen again and let it dance through her fingers for a few seconds, as if hesitant. "I do worry, though. About your attention to detail."

He swallowed, Adam's apple twitching at his unbuttoned collar. "What do you mean?"

"I've heard some troubling things about your friend. The girl who presented Professor Hašek at the lecture, yes? With the . . ." Zerena pantomimed over her own razor-straight hair.

"Andula?" Marcel ventured.

"Yes. That was it." Zerena snapped her fingers. "I have not seen her around in several days. And none of your other friends have either."

Marcel puffed up his chest. "Andula's clever, but she'll never be loyal to the cause, if you don't mind my saying. I think it's a waste of your efforts if you're looking to recruit her."

Zerena peered down her aquiline nose at him. Didn't say anything, just held the stare for several seconds until the boy took a step back.

"I—" He swallowed again and clutched his satchel higher against his chest. "I'm sorry, ma'am. It was only my opinion. . . ."

"It was a very limited one," Zerena said. She tossed her head back, pale hair cascading. "Her willingness to aid us is only a very small part of what use she can serve."

Marcel raised one eyebrow. "How do you mean?"

"You did not notice the American men who took an interest in her, after the presentation?" Zerena laid the pen back down before her. "The blond man, and his curly-haired friend. Trying to speak to her. Perhaps too eagerly."

Marcel shook his head. "No, I—"

"And who do you suppose those men might be? No, no, it doesn't even matter—any permutation is unwelcome. What matters is that they showed her too much interest. The reason, too, is unimportant. They believe Andula has some use to them. And so, we must make her useful first."

"You think the Americans have detained her?" Marcel asked. "I just don't think they—they would have taken her, or—I mean, she has family in the countryside, and maybe she went to see them for a sudden illness, or—or who knows? It could be anything."

Now it was Zerena's turn to lift a brow. "You never mentioned her family in the country before." She made a note in an open leather-bound journal before her. "What else have you forgotten to bring up?"

"No, I've told you everything else I know." He frowned. "I'm sure she's fine. I'll do my best to find out where she's gone. Maybe Professor Hašek knows—we attend his class together. Or our friend—"

"You understand why I must worry for her," Zerena continued. "You would wish me to worry the same way for you, yes?"

He lowered his gaze, speaking to his shoes. "Yes, ma'am."

"There are so many unfortunate things that can happen to people like us. To people who dare to take risks."

He worked his jaw. "I'll do whatever it takes, ma'am, for the good of the cause. I promise you."

"I know you will." Her smile bared just a sliver of teeth. "But you must remain vigilant of these dangers. From the Americans. From other forces besides. I would hate for something similar to befall you—all because you could not pay attention."

"I—I understand." He held one palm up, wincing away from her.

"You understand. And you will find out what happened to Andula, as well?"

He nodded again, backing up into the door.

"I'm so very glad to hear it." Zerena reached for the drawer once more. "Best of luck on your exams, Marcel."

Tanya couldn't shake the restlessness that she'd felt since she delivered Andula safely into the Ice's care. Usually, when a mission was complete, she slipped into an easy state of bliss—everything was a little sunnier, a little softer, gold tinted in her eyes. This assignment, though, carried the pinch of a chore left undone.

But she'd done everything. She found a Host, rescued that Host from the Flame (even if it had been closer than she'd liked), and gotten her safely into Ice custody. What was left? True, there had been . . . complications. (A good Russian euphemism, like a scrap of gauze over a gaping wound.) That rogue witch, or whatever Alestair was considering him, stalking her over half of Prague. Gabriel. The American. The other *shpion*.

Tanya watched him now, from the far side of the French embassy's great hall. He was laughing with his other spy friend, the young one, without the slightest whiff of concern. Winthrop swore he was "on the up and up," and that even if he wouldn't join the Ice in their efforts, he'd at least try not to actively sabotage them. But they'd said the same of that Rhemes woman, and she'd caused more than a few "complications" herself.

Tanya didn't like to leave things unfinished. Loose ends had a way of unraveling further, and tangling up into a noose. Maybe Andula was safe for now, but she couldn't risk Gabe interfering with the next Host they encountered, or deciding he himself was better off casting his lot in with the Flame.

American or not. CIA or not. The world of magic was too dangerous to leave open—the damage he could cause, too great. She needed to make him understand.

"Thank God," Gabe said, draining what Josh estimated to be his third or fourth glass of champagne. "I thought I'd never get the taste of *Sovyetskoye shampanskoye* out of my mouth."

"You know, they make mouthwash for that," Josh said.

But Josh already knew what Gabe was going to say. In Communist Czechoslovakia, vodka tastes like mouthwash and mouthwash tastes like vodka. Josh knew this less from an eerie sense of déjà vu and more from a certainty that they *had* had this exact conversation before. That was the problem, he was finding, with these embassy parties. There was an impossibly narrow band of safe topics along the spectrum that comprised Joshua Toms. He had to keep threading the same needle, over and over.

Sometimes, though, it couldn't be helped. No matter who might be listening, Josh had to shed his character for the sake of the team. Like when he caught Tatiana Morozova glancing their way a second time. The second time he'd noticed, anyway.

"Soooo," Josh said, drawing the vowel out while he shuffled to place himself between Tanya and Gabe. "What's the word with that Russki broad? From the lecture?"

Gabe's knuckles went white around the stem of his empty champagne flute. He brought it to his lips and tried to take a swig, but there was nothing left to chug.

Was Gabe afraid? Embarrassed? Whatever emotion was now etching itself into Gabe's too-blank face, it wasn't the reaction Josh had been hoping for. He tried to shrug away the doubt Frank had draped around him like a shroud. If there was anything between Gabe and a KGB agent—Josh's mind spun, whirling around and around on that thought with unstoppable force. It didn't matter what it was—sex, espionage, even a shared love of Spartak hockey. It would only end badly for Gabe.

Josh had to be wrong. *Please, God, let me be wrong.*

"Which one?" Gabe asked, lowering the glass. "The frosty-looking blonde, or the brunette who looks like she could punch your lights out?"

Josh forced himself to smile. Gabe was indulging him—that had to be a good sign, right? If he really, *really* didn't want to throw a spotlight on his relationship with the *KaGeBeznik*, he would have evaded the conversation. Unless he was all too aware of how conspicuous such avoidance would be and was compensating. "The blonde. I could swear she's making eyes at you." Josh made his

THE WITCH WHO CAME IN FROM THE COLD

grin wider; it came a little easier. "Maybe you could play her, let her think she's honeypotting you. She's not so bad-looking, right?"

"Right." Gabe wheezed out a laugh. "Thanks, Toms, but I'm not quite desperate enough to start taking your advice on the ladies."

Josh laughed too, because he wanted to be able to laugh with Gabe again. He hoped it didn't sound too hysterical.

Gabe slung his arm around Josh's shoulder. Josh noticed a smell clinging to him—not alcohol, which he would have expected; it was sharp, a little metallic, like rust or—or blood. Josh didn't want to consider that possibility.

"Lemme give you a freebie, Toms. See that fellow over there?" Gabe gestured through the curtained doorway that led to the gentlemen's lounge, thick with cigar smoke and the scent of cognac. "The German in the cheap suit."

"Cheap to you, maybe." Josh grinned and fingered the nap of his corduroy blazer, which was looking a bit worn despite his best efforts.

Gabe nudged him and clung tighter. "He works a lot of business ventures in Berlin, east of the wall. Manages to play nice with both the DDR and the Stasi enough that they look the other way."

"Sounds like a fun guy."

"And," Gabe added, leaning forward with more emphasis than he would if he were sober, "I hear he loves nothing more than to blather away about musty old German tomes."

"Now who's trying to play matchmaker?" Josh nudged Gabe in the ribs. "Really, though, I've got my hands full with the new friend you introduced me to. You sure you don't want this one? Might give you a slam dunk." *Might put you back in Frank's good graces,* Josh added silently, and hoped Gabe wasn't so drunk that he didn't pick up on the implication too.

"*Psssh.* I'll be fine. I've got some long-term plans I'm developing. This one has you written all over it."

Josh stepped forward, just enough to make Gabe's arm fall away from him. Then he spun on Gabe. Looked him over—his . . . coworker? His friend? Could he still lay claim to that, with that uneasy tension sliding between them so much these days, their third wheel?

Gabe smiled at him. Sloppy, but genuine, crinkling the corners of his eyes. Surely they could mend whatever this rift was. Gabe's dry spell, his off year, his slump. Josh hadn't been in the business long enough to hit his yet, but he'd heard they were always looming. No way to avoid it entirely. He hoped that when his came, he could plow through it, same as Gabe.

"Thanks. You're a real pal." He clapped Gabe on the shoulder, then began to ease his way toward the boys' club. A dozen possible opening lines shuffled through his mind. The game was on.

4.

Gabe staggered forward the moment Josh left his side.

Shit. He needed to—dammit. No. He did *not* need another drink. He was already feeling wobbly after skipping lunch. The hitchhiker, which had been strumming at elemental chords for most of the day, was now returning to its old state of maniacal hammering. Pounding at his head. Josh had said Tanya was watching him, which was about the last thing he needed, and there were no signs of Alestair, the first thing he needed. Alcohol-sharpened anger flashed through Gabe. Alestair and his dumb face, just begging for Gabe's fist. His fingers curled reflexively; he dug his knuckles into his thigh. He'd rather claw his own skin off than spend another fucking minute in the French embassy with all these stupid fucking people.

Like worrying about the KGB wasn't enough to keep him stressed out and paranoid; like that blond witch bitch wasn't twelve different kinds of bad news. Now he had a whole new set of magic-related problems to worry about, distracting him from his real job. The drafty embassy was barely warmer than the winter night beyond the glass windows, but sweat made a waterfall down Gabe's back as he wove through the crowd. He was done. He was just done with everything.

His headache turned sharp, like the hitchhiker already knew what he was thinking. Hell, maybe it did. But it didn't matter. To hell with magic, to hell with how "useful" it might prove—Gabe was going to find a way to tear it out.

He barely remembered to smile widely at the French agricultural secretary, toss out his customary "How're you?" as he ambled past in search of a remote bathroom. Flicked at the lock, fumbled with his trousers, aimed for the toilet. *Deep breaths, Pritchard. Get through tonight, then figure out what needs to be done.* He washed his hands in the scalloped basin, then ducked his head down and washed his face, too. Tried to get the splotchy red to even out.

He straightened and reached for the towel. But someone was already handing it to him.

"Jesus fucking Christ!" Gabe leaped up so hard he smacked his head on the angled ceiling of the half bath. Tanya Morozova stared back at him in the mirror, trying to conceal a faint smile. Gabe whirled around toward her, his first instinct to reach for her throat, before he thought better of it. He was sober enough to realize he didn't want to start an international incident, at least. "How long have you been standing there?"

Tanya thrust her shoulders back, trying to look taller than her modest height. Her dark blond hair was pulled back in the kind of sleek bun even Bolshoi ballerinas would envy. It added a certain severity to her expression, not that she needed the help. "We need to talk about the Ice, Gabriel."

"Here?" Gabe snatched the towel out of her hand; felt a little better when she flinched. "Right now?"

THE WITCH WHO CAME IN FROM THE COLD

"No one followed either of us. So, yes, I do think this is the safest place for it."

"Sorry, honey. You and the Ice had your chance."

He reached for the door handle, but she caught his wrist first. Gabe ripped his hand back. It came out of her grip easily, but already she'd swung her other hand up toward her face, palm flat, as if to block from a follow-up blow. Gabe laughed in spite of himself. She had asked for a talk, but clearly she expected a fight. *Okay, KaGeBeznik.* Gabe leaned back against the sink and crossed his arms. *Let's see what your game is.*

The hitchhiker was no longer hammering in his head; if anything, it seemed soothed by Tanya's presence, as if it were in harmony with whatever elements were closest to them right now. Figured that it'd be a filthy traitor that way.

"I understand why it is . . . difficult for you to speak to me," Tanya said.

"Oh, I'm not sure you do."

"I do not know what was done to you, but Winthrop has explained some of your situation to me. I know you didn't ask to be a part of this world, this . . . this other war." She canted her head to one side, an oddly delicate move. But it had to be calculated—Gabe didn't think the KGB ever did anything that wasn't scripted from the start.

"No," Gabe said, trying to keep his voice low, though he suspected he wasn't doing a good job of it. "I didn't."

Tanya winced and kept her eyes closed for a few seconds, perhaps searching not just for the right words but the right English ones. "But Alestair seems to think that you—"

"How often are you talking to Alestair, anyway?" Gabe asked. "It's incredibly stupid. For both of you."

"When it comes to magic, it does not matter!" Tanya's voice was tense, quiet, but forceful, like pressing her thumb over a hose. "I do not care. East, West, none of that will matter if the Flame is allowed to succeed."

The alcohol was clarifying in Gabriel's veins, distilling into pure anger. "Sorry, doll." He bowed forward until his eyes were level with hers. "You're barking up the wrong tree. You say it doesn't matter—" He grinned. "But I've heard that pitch before."

Something elemental crackled in the air, pulling the hitch-hiker out of its brief lull. Gabe hadn't seen Morozova reach for a charm or any other magical item to activate—was it coming from her? Or somewhere else?

"You don't understand what the Flame is capable of. What they intend to do."

"Don't care," Gabe snapped.

Tanya's ivory cheeks flushed pink. "Their plans—they make fools of us. All our silly little games, passing codes and numbers and secrets around . . . the danger the Flame poses makes them look like nothing. Crumbles it all to ash."

"Doesn't look like nothing to me. To the Czech people your tanks rolled over. Or the millions of Russians your own leaders put into the ground—"

"Millions?" Tanya cried. "The Flame will kill *billions*, Gabriel. The fascists could only dream of the power the Flame is trying to grasp. They want to elevate all those they deem worthy of magic and its nuances, and all the rest—"

Gabriel had had enough.

His anger ballooned out of him, honing the edges of every element he could sense into a fine blade. The bathroom, tucked beneath a staircase, seemed to shrink, or maybe he was growing;

he planted his forearms against either wall as he lunged toward Tanya. She stumbled backward and landed on the closed toilet seat.

Was she afraid of him? Was that fear, finally, in that softness of her Party-stoic face? Good. He relished it. Maybe fear was elemental too, sweeter even than French champagne and bubbling just as steadily under his skin. Gabe's grin was a creature all its own.

"You deliver these grand speeches about what monsters the Flame are, as if you're not their goddamned twin." He bent down, casting a shadow over her wide eyes. "But I've seen the Consortium of Ice for what it really is. Ice, Flame—it's all the fucking same."

"What are you talking about?" Tanya whispered. Her voice trembled so much she might have even meant it.

"Your little secret barge on the Vltava. Don't think I haven't seen it."

Tanya's eyebrows wrenched upward. "What about it?" She was good, he'd grant her that. Gabe should try to recruit a KGB instructor someday. Teach Prague Station a few tricks. "It's for rituals—all the spell components we require to perform massive rituals along the ley lines. You did not ask Alestair about it? Part of our fight against the Flame."

Gabe bashed one fist against the wall, no longer caring who heard. "What the hell kind of spell requires so many frozen bodies!"

Tanya's lips popped open; she made one tiny sound before her voice dried out. The rosy tint to her face was fading fast. Her lower lip quivered as she worked her jaw.

She didn't know. She really hadn't known.

"There must be a dozen of them. Frozen—I couldn't tell if they were dead or alive, but the ice holding them—it wasn't natural."

"You're lying," Tanya managed.

"Why the hell would I lie about this? They're all locked up in a chunk of ice like some kind of witchsicle. Trapped in some kind of . . . stasis, or something. I don't even know."

"But that's—" Tanya's knees came up to her chin as she curled into a ball. "That doesn't make sense. Why would they—"

"What? You're going to pretend you didn't know? God, you people are so sick." Gabe dragged one hand to his face and wiped away the sheen of sweat that clung to it. "Is that why you're giving me the hard pitch? Do you want to lock me up too? Shove me in a freezer, figure out what kind of botched spellwork made me into what I am before you take me out for good?"

"What you are?" Tanya echoed back, her tone watery as if she couldn't parse out the English phrase. Then she shook her head, freeing wisps of hair. "No. You are lying. There is no reason—we have no need—"

Gabe laughed, loose and ragged, as if something was tearing out of him. Not the hitchhiker, unfortunately. His grip on reality, maybe. The last shred of hope that maybe he could learn to live with this curse.

"You didn't even know. Of course you didn't. Ice couldn't trust you with this knowledge. Ahh, and I bet you thought you were something special to them."

Tanya's eyes flashed with pure hatred now. "You do not know what you are talking about." She lurched up from the toilet. "You are a fool. And it will get you killed, Gabriel."

Gabe shook his head. "Ice, Flame, it's all the same. You can keep your goddamned magic. Just like your dear leaders and their show of making a world for all the workers, isn't it? Give anyone a sliver of power, and they'll find a way to abuse it."

Tanya thrust the heels of both her hands square into Gabe's

gut, just beneath his sternum. The air whooshed out of him all at once, briefly, mercifully, catching him off guard long enough that it rattled even the hitchhiker. Then she stormed out of the bathroom and was swallowed up by the droning chatter of the embassy.

5.

Jordan Rhemes tipped the boiling pot forward. Her shoulders eased at the familiar hiss of hot liquid hitting the tempered glass; she watched the caramel-colored broth swirl around the assorted herbs and filings in the glass flask, waiting until they reached just the right consistency before pulling the pot back. Counted backward, from ten. Then opened herself to the currents of the ley lines.

One-woman rituals were a hell of a lot more powerful when you had the convergence of two major ley lines at your disposal.

Once her chant was finished—a graceful twist of Aramaic and Coptic with a few Egyptian flourishes—she shoved a cork stopper into the flask and returned to the main bar.

"Freshly empowered," she told the man waiting at the counter. "You'll use it in the next five hours?"

"I—um—" He retreated into the upturned collar of his coat.

Jordan held out a palm. "Y'know what? Don't answer. Just use it in the next five hours." She winked. "And thanks for watching the bar."

"Of course, of course." The man picked up his glass, although it was empty; Jordan noted the weathered envelope tucked beneath the coaster and slipped both smoothly behind the bar. "Thank you again, Miss Rhemes."

"Anytime, Pavel."

As Pavel tucked the flask into his coat pocket, Jordan scanned the bar. Late afternoon was always a comfortable slowness, just enough customers to keep her busy but not so many she felt rushed. Some Slovak witches who liked to order shots while they bitched about the Russians cutting them off from their suppliers; a trio of men who whispered together in German, talking equally as often about shady business deals as fishing trips; and the usual parade of spies who didn't think she'd pegged them as spies.

Then Jordan spotted the two men sitting at a four-top, drinking nothing, saying nothing. The foremost of them wore a tweed coat with leather patches at the elbows and had his hands laced together on the table as he stared into the middle distance. Everything about him was angled, precise—his combed hair, his fine nose, his faint smile so unwavering it might have been his stock expression. The man beside him, shorter, rounder, arms wrapped around a leather satchel, looked considerably more vexed, though he, too, said nothing, and never once glanced toward his companion. She tried to catch their eyes, but neither looked her way.

That should have been her first warning.

"Are you gentlemen ready to order?" she asked, loudly enough to cut in on the other conversations around her. Jordan wanted eyes on her, and on these men. Witnesses. Just in case.

"Ah. Hello, Miss Rhemes." The taller, particular one looked up at her without moving his head. "Please, allow me to introduce myself. I'm Karel Hašek, professor of medieval European history and sociology. And this is my associate, Vladimir."

Jordan cut her eyes to Vladimir for a brief, forced nod before turning back to Karel. "I see."

"Yes, I am confident that you do. This is quite a fascinating piece of land that you have, Miss Rhemes. But I am certain you know this already."

Jordan straightened, hoping the movement distracted them from the hand she slipped into her pocket. "It's been in my family for some time."

"That isn't the only thing that has been in your family for some time," Karel said.

The words glinted like a knife between them. Jordan fought against her instinct to take a step back, to put space between her and this man who was undoubtedly some sort of witch or another. If he knew about her family's history in Ice, then he probably knew that she wasn't exactly well-liked in the Consortium. But then, he might not be Ice at all, but something else entirely.

She liked that possibility even less.

"There was a book in the library at our university." Karel pulled a handkerchief from his breast pocket and began wiping his glasses. "In the special collections. Only serious scholars were permitted to view it—doctoral candidates whose theses directly related to the subject matter. A wonderful book. I've written a few papers on it myself—and written other things using it, besides."

Jordan knew what kind of books they kept in Prague libraries, away from anyone who might use them for harm. Emperor Rudolf in particular had liked collecting grimoires, and the witches who used them. Ice didn't much care for leaving that kind of knowledge where anyone could find it.

"But this is not in keeping with the spirit of global communism, now, is it? Knowledge for all. Power for all. Doesn't matter whether the

Party really means their bullshit—and let's be honest with each other, we all know they don't. Yet Marx and Engels had one bright idea."

Karel replaced his glasses, then turned toward Jordan with his whole body. His eyes were light gray—the leached-away fog of February mornings and thick ice.

"Resources," he said mildly, "are meant to be shared."

Jordan glanced back to the empty tables. She'd have felt a lot better if Pavel were still around. The tavern was too wide suddenly, too hollow. Not nearly enough patrons. She clenched the chunk of stone tight in her pocket.

"Sharing," Jordan repeated. "I was never very good at that."

Karel's smile was even colder than his stare. "Yes, so I understand. But you must know, these little charms, these brews, these solitary rituals . . . Isn't it just a waste? I'm sure it keeps you in business . . . barely . . ." He peered over the edge of his glasses at the dim bar, the tufts of dust she knew gathered in the corners. "But imagine what could be done with it in others' hands."

"The Vodnář isn't for sale." Jordan tried to keep her tone as sturdy as the rock she was clutching.

"Oh, no, I don't imagine it is. But surely there are other . . . arrangements we could come to."

Jordan swallowed. "I doubt that."

"Think about it." Karel stood up; a moment later, Vladimir joined him, still clutching the satchel to his chest. "There must be something you want, Miss Rhemes. You'll know how to find me when you decide what."

Jordan watched them leave with her heart in her throat. She'd assumed they were Flame, but Flame didn't give up so easily, she thought.

It was hours later that she realized she hadn't even considered what might have been in the bag.

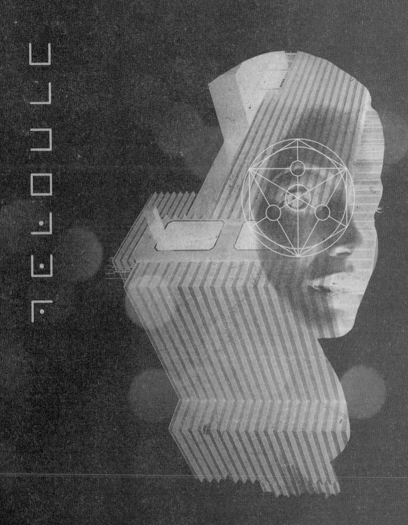

EPISODE 5

THE GOLEM

Or

WHAT HAPPENS IN CAIRO . . .

Ian Tregillis

1.

"Have you any idea," Jordan panted, running a kerchief across her brow, "what they do to grave robbers?"

Gabe whispered, "No. But I'm sure you'll tell me."

"I won't, in fact. You know why?"

As it happened, he knew very little beyond the crushing pressure in his head—the hitchhiker was in fine form tonight. Or maybe he'd concussed himself when he took a header on the cobbles of the Staré Město that morning. It was all he could do not to bite through his tongue, so he let the crunch of his shovel be his answer.

"Because," she continued, warming to her subject, "*nobody* knows the penalty for grave robbing these days because nobody has been stupid enough to *try* it."

"Less hissing, more digging," he managed.

His shovel hit another root. They froze like fawns caught in the headlights of a speeding truck until the echoes faded.

They worked amid ten thousand graves. A clammy winter fog had rolled off the Vltava, a mile or two to their west. Tendrils of that same mist, silvered by the moonlight, drifted like revenants through the underbrush of Prague's overgrown New Jewish Cemetery. The fog turned their discrete flashlight beams into shimmering and very indiscreet haloes. It was cool against Gabe's skin, but exertion and a hyperactive hitchhiker had him sweating like he'd just stepped out of a sauna.

Jordan picked up her shovel and rammed the blade into the earth. *Crunch.* "When you showed up at the bar tonight, asking for help *again*, I thought, sure, why not, he's making a good-faith effort to work with Alestair."

Gabe grunted. Alestair's "lessons" had been helpful, but they came with a hefty dose of Ice propaganda. And like some uncouth developmental, Gabe had nearly swallowed it, hook and all. But then he followed the hitchhiker to the barge and found . . . well, whatever it was, he wanted nothing to do with it. He'd solve his problems on his own, thank you very much.

"I thought it would be something simple." *Crunch* went her shovel, *sluff*, another load of earth tossed aside. "But here I am robbing a grave, awaiting a Kafkaesque nightmare when the police inevitably catch us."

The displaced earth took on a metallic ozone tingle beneath the scent of moldering leaves. Something in the leaves drove the hitchhiker nuts. Gabe groaned, using his shovel as a crutch.

"I swear I can feel it," he gasped. "We just . . . have to . . . dig a little farther. I can't stop now."

They'd excavated a hole nearly two yards deep. Despite the static sizzling in his brain, he noted faint scents of salt and sandalwood rising from Jordan's clammy skin. She smelled like a shipwrecked schooner carrying spices from the Near East. The hitchhiker had all Gabe's senses revved up to redline.

Her eyes were unreadable in the moonlight. "The Golem of Prague is a myth, Pritchard."

The hitchhiker hit him with another seizure. "I'm not so sure," he gasped.

She leaned on her shovel. "You've wandered through this graveyard like a tipsy sailor for nearly an hour. You haven't found it because it doesn't exist."

"Wasn't wandering," he managed. "Homing."

He'd been about as aimless as a compass. What Jordan took for wandering had been triangulation, of a sort. He didn't know how he knew where to go, only that he did. Same way he'd zeroed in on that wretched barge.

A car rumbled slowly down the macadam just beyond the graveyard wall. In unison, they snapped off their flashlights and hunched in the shadows, listening for the slam of a door or the shouts of discovery. Gabe counted thirty heartbeats before exhaling.

Jordan shook her head. The gesture sent eddies of silvery mist gamboling through the gravestones. "We're running out of luck. So listen to me, okay? The golem is a legend. It's a comforting fairy tale and nothing more."

Gabe wanted to say, *Well, I'm pretty certain that something is sure as hell down there.*

Instead, it came out as "Gunnnghhh . . ." He doubled over again.

"Gabe, you're drooling." Jordan handed him her handkerchief and grabbed his coat lapels. "We're leaving."

"No. We're too close now."

He managed to lever himself upright. Swaying like a prizefighter, he hefted the shovel and kept digging. Jordan made to take it from him just as his blade thunked against something hard. "Shine your light down there."

"Gabe—"

"Please, just do it."

Jordan sighed and cupped her hand around the beam to lessen the inevitable fog halo before clicking the switch. His shovel had splintered the planks of a crude casket.

"Huh," she said.

The screech of tires pierced the night. Gabe dropped to his knees and started brushing away the dirt with his hands. The touch of the casket jolted him like a live wire. There was an inscription on the wood. Hebrew, of course.

"Can you read this?" he mumbled. The taste of blood filled his mouth.

The soft glow of approaching flashlight beams pierced the gloom. One set to the north and another to the east, moving quickly.

"Damn," said Jordan. "We're blown. Time to go."

She grabbed Gabe by the shoulders and tried to haul him to his feet. He shrugged her off. Jordan tumbled backward. Her flashlight went sailing in a high arc, spinning like a lighthouse beacon, visible clear across the graveyard.

Shouts and whistles echoed through the cemetery.

"We have to go, NOW! They'll have us surrounded."

The urgency in her voice penetrated his fugue. "Yeah, okay—"

A muddy fist like the river incarnate punched up through the moldering planks and clamped around his wrist.

Eighteen hours earlier, Gabe had been crouched under the open hood of the Moskvich, which was parked slightly askew over a curb at the edge of the Old Town Square. He cranked the socket wrench. Then he shook feeling back into his numb fingers, stretching until his back popped. And watched the passersby.

"Overalls, flat cap, seven o'clock," he said.

Josh fished out a toothpick and grimaced at the side mirror. He dug at an incisor for a few moments before saying, "You mean Boris Badenov over there?"

"Must catch pesky moose and squirrel," Gabe said in his best caricature of a Russian accent. Josh snickered.

"Okay," said Gabe, serious again. "Try it now."

Josh hit the starter. The engine coughed for a few seconds as if considering the suggestion before deciding, on balance, not to bother.

"Nope," said Josh. "Still dead."

"Thanks, Mr. Peabody. I hadn't noticed."

The temperature had dropped overnight. The Gothic towers of the Church of Our Lady before Týn were a pair of burned Christmas cookies dusted with powdered sugar. The cold provided a superb cover. For a car designed and built by the damn *Russians* of all people, the Moskvich exhibited a profound and illogical aversion to cold weather.

Josh muttered under his breath. "Piece of crap."

Gabe spit the taste of copper from his mouth and sighed. "Oh, come on, you hunk of junk." He peeled off the useless gloves and puffed on his fingers a few times before pulling them back on. He crouched under the hood again, splitting his attention between the heap of fine Soviet engineering and the midmorning police presence.

Frank had them assessing potential routes through the Staré Město, in preparation for ANCHISES. It was scrub work, and they knew it. If the officers working ANCHISES found themselves herded into the wide open spaces of the Old Town Square, it would mean so many *other* things had already gone so enthusiastically to hell that the op was a catastrophe. Gabe's screwup with Drahomir had cast a pall over Frank's faith in him; he'd salvaged that, but the clouds hadn't dissipated. So Gabe would eat this slice of humble pie, plaster a shit-eating grin on his face, and ask for seconds like Oliver goddamned Twist if that's what it took to get a place at the table again. He shivered in the shadow of the Old Town Hall while the ticking of a medieval astronomical clock flicked ice water at him.

At least Josh was in a good mood. He didn't mind being on the periphery of the preparations. It meant he was involved, and the boy was hungry for any piece of ANCHISES.

Still slouched behind the wheel, Josh said, "Look sharp. Got two VB homing in." VB: *Veřejná bezpečnost.* The Czech regular police. "And based on their expressions, I question your mastery of local parking regulations."

"Quiet, you. Crank it again."

Gabe dropped the tradecraft and focused on the car. The butterfly valve was sticky. It shouldn't have been cold enough for fuel to gum up the valves, but God only knew what passed for gasoline here. Half the cars in Prague ran on a hair-curling witch's brew of kerosene and vodka.

"Sir! Sir, please, a moment."

Gabe pretended not to notice the cops. To Josh, he called, "Okay, I think I got it this time. Try it now."

A metallic tingle scraped Gabe's tongue like a wire brush. The insulation on the spark plug wires looked dodgy; he must have brushed one with the wrench. He pretended to adjust the valve. At which point he "noticed" the police.

"Yikes. You startled me," he said in English.

"Ah." The cop made a gesture that encompassed both Gabe and Josh. "Americans?"

"Yes," said Gabe. He peeled off his gloves and started blowing on his fingers again. "Cold Americans."

The cop frowned at the gloves. He clucked his tongue. "No lining." He folded back the cuff of his own glove just far enough to display a thick layer of fur. "Rabbit," he said. "Much better."

Gabe nodded appreciatively. "*Děkuji.*" He gestured at Josh to start the car again, but the cop intervened.

"Sir, please. You can't leave your auto here." He pointed up and down the cobbled lane. "Narrow street, yes?"

"Oh, we're not leaving it. We'll leave as soon as my friend learns how to start a car without flooding the damn engine." On cue, Josh jabbed the starter again, giving the gas pedal a good stomp to ensure the engine flooded.

Gabe tossed his hands into the air. "Now you've done it, you dimwit."

The younger policeman shook his head. "Sir, please. This lane is not a—" He and his colleague exchanged a few quick words in Czech and English. "It's not an 'auto shop,' yes?"

"Oh, we don't need a shop. I can fix this myself."

Gabe started to lean under the hood again, but the VB guys intervened. "*Ne, ne.* You must go now. Already it is too long." The other cop pantomimed pushing the car. "You push your auto away from the square."

Gabe sighed. Their chances of successfully surveilling the square had fallen between slim and none. Best to move on gracefully. "Very well."

"We'll help you," said the older policeman.

"Thank you," said Gabe. He leaned under the hood to clear away the wrench. The copper taste came surging back with a vengeance. Gabe banged his head on the hood when a jolt shot up his spine. It felt like a thousand volts. He tossed the wrench aside and slammed the hood, glaring through the windshield at Josh.

"Hey, lead foot! Are you trying to kill me?"

Josh's eyes widened. He gave a minute shake of his head. *I didn't . . .* , he mouthed.

Oh crap. Gabe hadn't brushed against the spark plugs. It was the hitchhiker again.

The VB guys had both retreated a step. Gabe ransacked his mental filing cabinet for a way to cover his gaffe. Every drawer came up empty. But it wouldn't have mattered anyway: The jolt ricocheted back down his spine as if completing an ethereal electric circuit. He jackknifed at the waist, slammed his forehead against the cobbles. The younger cop tried to catch him. And that's when Gabe tossed his cookies all over the nice policeman's fancy gloves.

Tanya's breath wriggled through the woolen balaclava like steam from a leaky radiator. It frosted her eyelashes. When she squinted, the world became a dark kaleidoscope. She'd been crouched behind a riverbank piling since the wolf hours, that loneliest stretch of night. She shivered again. It had to be at least ten degrees colder now than when she'd begun her hypothermic vigil.

The barge was a long, low thing, of a type used to transport bulk freight like sand and gravel. The corrugated iron hatches comprising the deck rose only midway between the water and the top of the tugboat's pilothouse.

It certainly didn't *feel* special. It elicited no tingle in her magician's intuition. Was Gabe having her on? Perhaps this was a—what did the Americans call it? Oh yes: a *snipe hunt*. But on the other hand, placing the "safe house" on running water and keeping it in constant motion would cloak it from divination. It was a tale of sophisticated magical tradecraft, yet Gabe knew too little of such things to spin a plausible lie. So either he really had found something, and badly misunderstood it, or somebody was coaching him. Either way, she had to know.

The bow rested against a piling in the center of the Hlávka Bridge. The tug pilots had chosen this expedient rather than mooring along the riverbank while waiting for congestion downriver to clear. Was the subsequent tactical advantage just a coincidence? Mooring along the bank would have made the entire length of the barge vulnerable to boarders. Instead, this arrangement forced would-be visitors to either drop down from the bridge or sneak across from shore in a rowboat—both options in plain view of the tug's elevated pilothouse. It was an excellent defense against incursions.

Well. Mundane incursions, anyway.

From a coat pocket Tanya produced a length of copper wire and a lipstick tube filled with the ashes of a particular species of Vltava river grass. Gathering enough in the middle of winter had been a chore, and she wasn't certain that the withered brown foliage would suffice in lieu of healthy greenery. She had to hope it did. If she got this wrong, or lost her concentration halfway across, she'd probably freeze to death.

She smeared ash along the length of the wire and then wrapped the copper around her index finger, working from the tip to the base, then around her hand. The configuration resembled the coils of an electric space heater.

Shadows inched across the river, night's rear guard ceding the field to sunrise. In moments, she gauged, the rising sun would peek over the bridge to shine directly into the frosty forward windows of the pilothouse. And, she hoped, momentarily blind any observers. She crept around the riverbank piling.

Every military and intelligence service in the world had its own version of the lieutenant's prayer: *Please don't let me screw this up.* Every sorcerer had her own version. Tanya whispered this to herself now. She prepared a chant; it rested on her tongue like a mouthful of broken glass.

Then she waited. And waited. Until—

There! Sunlight glinted off the windows.

Tanya retreated a few steps, clenched her wire-bound fist, and spit the pent-up chant at the river. Before her mind had time for traitorous second thoughts, she sprinted straight toward the icy water.

The copper coil pulsed with searing heat in the instant before her foot broke the surface. She gritted her teeth against the pain. The magicked coil sucked all the heat from a tiny section of the river; the water directly under her boot flash-froze into a thick plate of ice. She skipped forward like a stone across a pond. The coil instantly went cold, then flared hot again just in time to prevent her next footfall from plunging into the river. The wire pulsed like that—frigid one instant, blistering the next—in time with the rapid rhythm of her footsteps. Tanya left a trail of floes in her wake as she sprinted across the river. She lunged, caught the barge prow, and scrambled aboard.

Crouched in the recess between the forward cargo hatch and the bridge piling, she listened for the thudding of steel-toed boots and the metallic *clack-chack* of chambered rounds. But nothing broke the tranquility of early morning on the river. If she hadn't been wary of her breath giving her away, she would have sighed.

Nothing tingled her nape; nothing fizzed at the tip of her tongue. She was lying on the damn thing and the barge telegraphed less occult significance than a dead trout.

If I wasted those ashes on a barge full of gravel, it will not matter how much Alestair vouches for you, Gabe Pritchard.

She couldn't open the hoppers without standing in plain view of anybody on the bridge. She squinted. Actually, she couldn't open them at all. Nobody could: the forward cargo hatch was welded shut.

Tanya was still pondering this when the putter of a two-stroke motor broke the soft lapping of water against the hull. The pilothouse's portside door creaked open, and a voice called across the misty waters in phlegmy Czech.

"You're late."

"You're drunk," came the reply from the motorboat.

Ah. The shift change.

While the tug pilot bantered with his relief, Tanya scooted to starboard. She found an inspection hatch built halfway down the length of the vessel. This lacked the grimy weathering of the rest of the vessel, a recent retrofit. It was fastened with a padlock. Tanya unwrapped an inch of copper from around her finger and worked it into the lock. The keyhole sported fresh scratches; somebody else had picked it recently. None of the Ice's usual wards were active either. Someone hadn't been following Ice protocol to check and recheck the wards, not that Tanya should be surprised. She spun the wheel; the hatch swung open soundlessly.

The cargo hold's magical aura hit her between the eyes like a hammer. It carried a hint of numbness, like the lingering traces from a shot of anesthetic. The hatch closed behind her, plunging her into darkness. She turned on her light.

"*Bozhe moi!*"

The flashlight dropped from her slack fingers to roll along the keel. The barge wasn't filled with wheat or gravel or anything so simple. The cots were piled two and three high in places.

Tanya gathered her wits and her flashlight. Only then did she realize how steamy her breath had become. It was *cold* down here. Even colder than the river.

Roughly half a dozen cots were occupied, but not by people. By blocks of *ice*. She played her light across the nearest slab. It contained a sallow, middle-aged man with a widow's peak of shocking white hair.

Are they dead? Or just deeply unconscious?

What *was* this place? No wonder Gabe had been horrified.

Tanya worked down the line, searching for any sense of who these poor souls might be or why it was necessary to place them in stasis. But they'd been stripped of any identification. What was the pattern here? What could—

Tanya froze, clapping a hand over her mouth.

On the sternmost cot, all by herself as though it were a place of honor, Andula Zlata lay encased in ice. Like the victim of a fairy-tale curse.

Who do I work for?

Had she been duped by Flame all these years, an unwitting acolyte tricked into thinking she served a noble cause? Or—even worse—was Ice run by twisted madmen?

Grandfather. I must speak with Grandfather.

Another horrifying thought: *What if . . . what if Dyedushka already knows about this? What if he knows and condones it? What if—*

From outside came a muffled shout. Heavy footsteps rattled the decking. The inspection hatch opened.

The door to Frank's office still hadn't opened. Had Josh been in there the entire time? How much could they have to discuss?

Gabe paced through the embassy corridors. He passed Alestair, whose cover identity from MI6 occasionally brought him to the United States embassy, by virtue of the US/UK special relationship. Today his contribution to the defense of the West against the creeping scourge of communism consisted of leaning rakishly against a filing cabinet and regaling a member of the secretarial pool with an improbable tale.

". . . Now, this was a bit of a sticky wicket, you see, for at that moment I was—"

"Have you seen Josh?" Gabe burst in.

"I think he's in the chief's office," said the secretary. Her name was Junie something, as Gabe recalled.

Alestair nodded at him. "Ah, Gabriel, my lad."

Yeah, we're all just good pals, aren't we? Nothing sketchy about you or your magical allies and their floating coma ward. Gabe resisted the urge to punch him.

"You seem a bit ruffled. You are well, I trust?"

Gabe jerked a thumb over his shoulder. "How long has Josh been in there with Frank?"

Alestair deadpanned, "Until a moment ago, I gather."

Josh looked like Gabe felt. But the sight of Alestair seemed to brighten him. Gabe sighed.

"Ah, Mr. Toms. A pleasure," said Alestair.

Josh nodded. "Gabe. Frank wants to see you."

Gabe took the younger officer by the arm and led him a few strides away from the others. He bent close, lowering his voice. "What'd you tell him? You were in there a long time."

"I told him the truth, okay? That you're acting weird, that I'm worried about you."

"Worried about me, or about what I might be doing to your career?"

Josh scowled and shook Gabe's hand from his arm. "I didn't tell Frank anything he wouldn't have heard sooner or later anyway. Better for you if it's sooner. You want to get ahead of this."

"I can't get ahead of anything when you go running straight to Daddy the moment we get home."

"I was trying to clear the runway for a soft landing."

Gabe ran a hand through his hair. "Thanks. "

As Gabe turned to leave, Josh said, "Just to warn you? He's pretty angry."

"I'm sure I'll survive." *My career, however* . . .

Josh blinked. "You remember the shovel story?" He whistled softly as they rejoined Alestair and Junie. "Seven guys."

"Seven?" chimed Junie, looking slightly pale. "Oh my."

"Ah," said Alestair. "Now *that* reminds me of Calcutta . . ."

Gabe knocked on Frank's open office door. "Sir?"

The station chief stood with his back to the door, gazing out the window. "Close the door. Sit down."

Gabe did. "Sir—"

"I said sit. I didn't say speak." Frank turned his attention from the window and pointed to a photo on the desk. "Remember my girls' dog?" He shook his head. "Damn thing's still pissing on the dining room rug."

"Sir—"

Fiddling with a buckle on his suspenders, Frank said, "You don't piss on your own floor, do you? When you're at home, I mean."

Gabe blinked. "Uh. No, sir."

"Of course you don't. You're housebroken. A proud day for your parents, no doubt. So I can't help but wonder why you insist on pissing all over everything we do here."

Gabe kept his mouth shut. After a fraught silence, the station chief said, "That was your invitation to explain yourself. Succinctly and persuasively."

"I haven't been feeling well."

"Pritchard, if this were a head cold, I'd tell you to walk it off. But there's not feeling well and then there's acting like you've got a brain tumor fixing to bust your melon wide open."

"I don't have a brain tumor, sir."

Frank stopped and looked up. "You sure about that, son?"

What if it *was* all in his head? What if the hitchhiker was a figment of a diseased mind? The hallucinations, the phantom sensory impressions, the seizures . . . but then Gabe remembered that awful barge, the way he'd felt its proximity, the way it drew him like a magnet. That was no brain tumor.

"Yes, sir."

"Well, that's a shame," said Frank, "because then we could write off your behavior as a medical issue." He opened a drawer. "Instead, it's a question of how many loose screws you have rattling around up there."

"Sometimes I wonder, sir."

Frank produced a half-empty bottle of scotch and two tumblers. His prosthetic leg made a hollow *clunk* when he kicked the drawer shut.

"We all do. That's our legacy." He splashed a finger of booze into each glass. Pushing one across the desk to Gabe, he said, "Those of us who have been in the shit."

Early as it was, Gabe knew better than to refuse. They raised their glasses in unison.

"*De oppresso liber,*" said Frank.

"*Semper fidelis,*" said Gabe.

Clink.

It burned all the way down. The smoke that filled Gabe's sinuses tasted like a burning oak barrel.

"How long were you in the marines before they pulled you for intelligence work?"

"Not too long, sir. Middle of my first tour."

"That's plenty long. I've heard about those jungles. I know what you're going through." Frank fell quiet for a moment. "I saw some shit in Korea."

Gabe coughed. "I hadn't heard, sir."

Frank rolled his eyes. "Jesus. Please tell me you're a better liar in the field than you are in my office."

"I like to hope so."

"Prior to this posting, your reputation was solid."

"And after this posting?"

"That's up to you. We've fought hot wars, you and I, and now we're fighting a chilly one. We're not that different. Lord knows there were times when I didn't have my head screwed on right."

"I appreciate it, sir."

"Don't mistake me. I'm not turning a blind eye, and I'm not forgetting anything. But you pulled the Drahomir debacle out of its nosedive, and even showed some grace in handing it over to Josh. That earned you this courtesy chat. But when you walk out of this office, you're officially out of second chances."

"I understand, sir." Gabe set the shot glass on the desk. Lightly.

"Maybe you are smarter than that damn dog, after all."

That evening, Gabe spent more time and money than he could afford staking out a booth at Vodnář. He waited until most of the clientele had stumbled home. Jordan set down the glass she'd been drying and tossed the dishrag over a brass fitting along the bar.

Without preamble, Gabe said, "I need a favor."

The glare she shot him could have stripped paint. "You do understand that favors aren't like liquor, right? It's not the sort of thing where one runs a tab."

"It's about Cairo."

Jordan held his gaze for a long moment, before finally relenting with a heavy sigh. "Low blow, Pritchard. Low blow." She squinted, pinched the bridge of her nose. "I'm listening."

"Two shovels."

She blinked. Brightened a bit. "Not what I expected to hear. But okay. I can do that."

"I need something else, too." She cocked an eyebrow. "I need help robbing a grave."

2.

Haret el-Yahud, Cairo
March 19, 1968

Gabe Pritchard's posting to Cairo in '68 was his first turn through the Levant. But in the aftermath of the Six-Day War, the atmosphere in the country was less Cecil B. DeMille and more Carol Reed. Less than a year after those brief hostilities, the streets of Cairo still bristled at the humiliation.

Getting your ass kicked will do that.

Three months in Cairo and Gabe had yet to glimpse one serving girl clad in defiance of the Hays Code. This particular morning, for instance, he'd spent crouched in an oven-hot storage space over a cobbler's shop in the Haret el-Yahud, the Jewish quarter. Twice in the past week, his target, a Mossad agent, had visited an antiquities shop across the street.

The previous June, Israel had tripled the amount of territory it controlled in less than a week. When the concerted attack by its neighbors ended in fiasco, Israel took the Sinai Peninsula and Gaza Strip from Egypt (officially the United Arab Republic), the West

Bank and East Jerusalem from Jordan, and the Golan Heights from Syria. Yet a mere ten days later, the Israeli government voted to cede the territorial gains back to Syria and Egypt—all except the tiny Gaza Strip. But SIGINT suggested Mossad had moved several assets into Gaza immediately after the takeover, even before the ceasefire took effect. Almost as if they'd been poised at the border just waiting for somebody to wave them in.

There were obvious public diplomatic reasons for the concessions, of course. But the flurry of covert activity cast a peculiar light on the situation. From the sidelines, Sinai and Golan looked just a bit like misdirection. A magician's trick.

Nine months later, CIA Cairo Station identified one of the same Mossad assets in the medieval quarter, posing as a scholar of antiquities. Gabe's bosses wanted to know why. Surveillance had turned up nothing unusual on the man, so Gabe had headed a high-risk/high-reward operation with the local lamplighters. Penetration of a hotel room safe revealed the Mossad man carried artifacts taken from the Qasr al-Basha, a Mamluk-era palace situated in the Old City of Gaza.

It was starting to look more like plain old graft rather than intelligence. It certainly wouldn't be the first instance of a case officer using information gleaned from work to pad the retirement account.

Gabe's job was to confirm that explanation. If the Mossad officer strolled into the store of a gray-market antiquities dealer carrying the Mamluk artifacts, then exited empty handed, that would be fairly convincing. Especially if, on the way out, he obligingly carried a burlap sack bulging with cash. Gabe wasn't counting on it, though; much to his disappointment, conditions in the field rarely embraced the tidy internal logic of a Bullwinkle cartoon.

Foot traffic picked up as the morning wore on. A woman unlocked the shuttered shop: late forties, early fifties, long dark hair with a hint of gray, slight build, five-six to five-eight. The Mossad man's contact?

Business was slow on midweek mornings. Jordan Rhemes took her time reconciling the cash register. There hadn't been many trans-actions the previous day; the pushy "scholar" who didn't know a Berber from a barber, had once again driven her few other custom-ers away with his dogged refusal to accept no for an answer.

Just the thought of him wearied her. If he showed up a third time, she might be forced to use the scimitar under the counter to behead herself. But then her cousin Hakim would inherit the shop, and the poor witless boy would have to sand all of Jordan's blood out of the floorboards. That didn't seem fair.

She set her cup of tea on a display case containing Berber relics—bracelets, earrings, a fragment of undecipherable writing, a Moroccan wooden comb—and opened a pulpy biography of T. E. Lawrence, settling in for a long, quiet morning. She found her place in the book and reached for the cup, but paused at the wisps of steam dancing above the brim. They swirled as though caught in a breeze. But the chimes over the door weren't moving. If there was a draft in the shop, it wasn't coming from outside. Brow furrowed, she closed her eyes and felt a faint tickle against her skin. She closed and locked the shop again. There was nothing out of place. Nothing broken. But something ruffled the fringe of an Algerian Kabyle rug hanging behind the counter.

The rug concealed a door. A special door. A heavily locked and warded door. A door she opened infrequently, and only for very special customers. A door she'd chosen *not* to open for the self-proclaimed scholar. A door she checked every evening before closing up shop.

Oh no.

With one hand she eased her blade from the scabbard beneath the counter. With the other, she clutched the charm at the hollow of her throat. The ancient words she whispered chilled her lips as they escaped in visible puffs of breath that should have been impossible even on Cairo's very coldest winter days. These, too, shimmied in the draft. She closed her eyes, concentrating on the chant. When she'd drained the charm, she opened her eyes again. Had customers been present to witness this, they might have remarked on how Jordan's eyes had changed, as though now limned with phantom silver. Her magic-enhanced senses heard no concealed heartbeat, tasted no sweat of hidden assailants.

She hefted the blade and swept aside the wall hanging. The door was closed. Mostly. But the paint on the doorjamb was badly gouged. It looked like somebody had forced the door with a crowbar; the damage to the frame prevented it from sealing properly. So now it admitted a soft but incessant zephyr from the cavern beneath the shop.

The wards—powerful disincentives against tampering, laid in place by her grandfather—should have prevented such a crude assault. Jordan studied the door with magicked eyes . . . and gasped. Tendrils of dread braided her spine. The wards weren't ruptured. They were *gone*.

Careless, careless. How could I be such an imbecile?

She knew instantly who had done this: the so-called scholar. He'd been obsessed with Mamluk artifacts; he sought to reunite a set of relics, or so he'd claimed, and had practically demanded to see anything she might have had in her collection. She'd demurred, telling him simply that she had none, which was the truth. When she'd laughed at his money, he'd grown angry and stormed out, scowling like somebody determined to do something unwise. She'd laughed that off too. After all, her shop was warded.

She should have realized that he wanted to see her special wares not because he thought he could cheat her out of something valuable and easily fenced, but because he understood their true significance.

And that meant one thing: a Flame acolyte. Had he come from Ice, the artifice would have been unnecessary. Though Jordan tried to keep them at arm's length these days, the legacy of her family's long association with the Ice made for decent, if somewhat muted, relations. They would have had the courtesy to be up front with her.

How could I be so stupid?

She pushed the door open and stepped behind the rug into a dark tunnel. Jordan flicked a switch. Then, still wielding the blade and her magicked senses, she descended, dreading what she'd find. If they'd cleaned her out, the chaos those maniacs could wreak . . . A single one of these items in the wrong hands could be disastrous. How many might suffer because of Jordan's carelessness?

The tunnel had been chiseled into the bedrock under the city by unknown persons for unknown reasons centuries or even millennia ago. She'd been coming down here since she was a little girl. She knew its every twist and echo. But this morning it had an odd scent, so out of place it took her a moment to identify it. Petrichor: the clean, heavy smell of a cleansing rain on hot stone. But the tunnel was kilometers from the Nile. It was never damp down here. Apparently this was also the scent of broken protective wards. She wished she didn't know that now.

She'd expected to find the shelves toppled, every item missing or destroyed. But at first glance it almost appeared that everything was undisturbed. Almost.

To magicked eyes, the lacuna blazed like a bonfire on a moonless night. The items on the shelves were undisturbed: vials containing the ashes of rare plants; unremarkable crystals containing trace amounts of exotic metals; bracelets woven from the stems of flowers that had grown in only one bog on earth, a bog which had long since been drained; fulgurites unearthed in high desert valleys accessible only by mule; a dinner-plate-size piece of bubbled green trinitite from a military base in New Mexico; sundries from every corner of the globe. Jordan saw this instantly from the shape of their accumulated magical aura. But the rarest and most powerful items were stored within hidden clefts chiseled into the cavern walls. One such cleft emitted no magical aura. It was empty.

She didn't need to consult her inventory to know what had been stolen. The fake scholar's obsession allowed only one possibility. He, or his Flame allies, had stolen a clay figurine discovered by Napoleon's staff in the Ottoman fortress where the campaigner stayed for three nights while preparing for the Siege of Acre. The place had many names, for it had changed hands many times over seven hundred years, most recently during the Six-Day War: Napoleon's Fort. Radwan Castle. Qasr al-Basha.

Her family had never unraveled a purpose for the figurine, though it had been imbued with staggering elemental power. Whatever its true purpose, the homunculus had been wrought by a master sorcerer in a bygone era. It crackled with a power that nobody should wield. Not even Ice. Certainly not those anarchic bastards in the Flame.

Jordan doffed her scarf and uncapped a vial of ashes. She tapped a thimbleful of fine gray powder into the center of the silk, then she bit her thumb and spit a drop of blood into the ash. Next, she set a pale blue crystal into the grit and folded the scarf closed. After tying the bundle together with a leather cord, she placed it in the secret hollow where the figurine had rested for generations. The artifact's unique magical aura had seeped into the surrounding stone; Jordan's makeshift magic dowser-cum-compass absorbed the residuals and began to vibrate, almost imperceptibly, in sympathetic reaction.

She jammed the bundle in her pocket before taking a moment to peruse her special inventory. She donned a bracelet of flowering grasses still green as the day they'd been picked a century ago, and placed a patinaed copper coin under her tongue. It tasted not of metal but of salt. Back upstairs, Jordan retrieved the scimitar scabbard and hid this beneath her robes. She took extra care to lock the hidden door and re-create the wards before departing.

Gabe, sweating to death in his airless garret across the street, perked up when he saw her depart.

"Well now, hello," he said, watching her set off at a fast walk. "Where are *you* going in such a rush this morning?"

In one hand, Gabe had an officer of a foreign intelligence service carrying priceless archaeological relics. In the other, he had a woman who ran a shop clearly specializing in rare items. The math was adding up to graft, not a geopolitical conspiracy of musical chairs. But he wasn't paid to judge books by their covers.

Grateful for any break from the stakeout, he set off to follow the woman.

A single tail through the crowded rabbit warrens that passed for streets and alleys in Cairo was less than ideal; he should've had a team for this. But he'd never find her again if he peeled off to run back to Cairo Station. She acted indecisively: lingering at intersections to study every path before continuing, stopping suddenly and changing direction, looping back and traversing the same alley over again. At first he thought these were artless attempts at tradecraft, intended to reveal any followers. But she acted as if searching for something, following a trail he couldn't see or hear or smell.

His tradecraft was solid, though, and he managed to keep her in sight, even when she strode through a crowded pedestrian market. She never saw him.

Of course, she didn't *need* to see him to sense him. Jordan had given all of her senses a sorcerous jolt. The follower she detected almost certainly worked for, or with, the man she tracked. And probably intended to kill her.

She hadn't expected that this day would be her last. Suddenly, she missed her father and mother more than she had in years.

It was an irritated loneliness, however. She'd broken with Ice years ago. It figured she'd die doing their dirty work for them, and those idiots would never even realize the service she'd rendered.

Then the tugging in her pocket turned into a vibration as she neared the ley line beneath Masr el Qadīma: Old Cairo. Her makeshift dowser trembled so rapidly it started to hum: The clay figurine was nearby. But, given the man trailing her and his probable intentions, it seemed unlikely she'd ever get it back to her shop intact. The best she could hope for was to destroy or corrupt the statuette before the Flame absconded with it.

She had to work quickly before her follower intervened. She ducked around the corner and into the shadow of a minaret. Momentarily out of his sight, she snapped the bracelet. This released the magic that had sustained the dead grasses; the sundered bracelet browned and withered even before it hit the ground. The grass puffed out a little cloud of silvery seeds as it crumbled to dust. They drifted to Jordan's feet, tickling her toes just as her follower turned the corner.

Surprise creased his face. "What the hell?"

For a moment, Jordan feared the spell had failed and that he was alarmed to find her standing ready to confront him. Her hand went to the scimitar. But then he frowned and sprinted to the end of the alley, the breeze of his passage fluttering the hem of her shawl. She counted sixty seconds after he disappeared around the corner. Then she doubled back. The concealment glamour cloaked her even in bright sunlight, rendering her shadow a gossamer silhouette. She was almost atop the Cairo ley line.

The dowser brought her halfway down the street to a sun-bleached wooden door that had once been painted a mesmerizing azure like the doorways of Mykonos. She knocked. No footsteps echoed through the house; nobody called out. Jordan knocked again, more loudly. Still no answer.

She bit her cheek until the iron tang of blood mingled with the saltiness of the charm beneath her tongue. Then she worked up a good bit of saliva and spit on the lock. Her spittle, foamy pink with blood, sizzled on the escutcheon. The brass filigree corroded. A moment later, there came from inside a metallic *clunk* suggestive of a brass doorknob hitting the floor. The door swung open at the touch of her fingertip.

✦ ✦ ✦

Gabe turned the corner into an alley. He'd unfolded the Cairo street map from the breast pocket of his shirt. The accoutrements of a tourist were a flimsy disguise, but better than nothing.

The shopkeeper had vanished as if swallowed by the sun. But halfway down the alley he now saw two men lugging crates from the back of a truck through what appeared to be a service door. Gabe passed them without stopping, too engaged in berating his map to pay them any notice.

One of the men was the Mossad officer from Gaza.

Okay. This is good enough, Gabe told himself. *You found them. You can pin this place on a map. And you've pushed your luck to within a hairsbreadth of reckless. Time to go back to Cairo Station and share what you've learned. Let the people who really know this city do their thing.*

He stopped where the alley merged with a crooked lane. And sighed. *Why do I never listen to good advice?*

He doubled back. The men were gone, but the truck hadn't moved. The keys were still in the ignition.

Also on that same ring? A key to the service door.

Jordan was grateful for the lingering effects of her enhanced vision. The building had no windows, no skylights—even at midday it was dark as sin. No mere house, this place—it fairly thrummed with the power of the ley line running directly through its foundation. If this were an Ice property, she'd have known about it before now. That pointed to Flame. And the site was well-suited to major works of magic. Her magicked ears twitched at the faint murmur of voices emanating from beneath the floorboards. Of course. Whatever they were doing, they'd want the figurine as close to the power source as possible.

Like her shop, this place had been built over a cavern hewn into the ancient bedrock of an ancient city. The stairs didn't creak; these, too, had been hewn from the bones of the earth. And worn smooth by countless feet, it seemed, much like the marble outcrops of the Acropolis. Still wrapped in gossamer shadow, she reached the bottom lightly as a cat, then crouched behind a pillar that had probably been supporting the roof of this chamber since Tutankhamen's grandfather was a newborn.

Half a dozen men and women milled about a long, low wooden table in the mustard-yellow lamplight of the chamber, clearly waiting for something. Each corner of the table sported a shackle on about a foot of chain. On an adjoining plinth sat the clay figurine stolen from Jordan's shop. A pick poised to strum the ley line.

The ages of the assembled Flame sorcerers ranged from mid-thirties to just shy of crumbling dotage. Jordan didn't recognize any of them, but she could speculate about the oldest person in the room. His age and accent clued her in: Terzian, an Armenian who'd been a noteworthy Flame acolyte decades ago. She'd heard of him over the years—every Ice sorcerer in this part of the world had heard the terrible stories—though few claimed to have ever seen him. Ice considered him a unicorn.

He spoke now to a woman perhaps twenty years Jordan's junior, in a voice like the creak of a sepulchre door. But the ley line had Jordan's enhanced senses crackling.

"I envy you, girl."

The woman closed her eyes and dipped her head low, a gesture of humble thanks. "I'm honored, sir. But this should be your moment. You've worked toward this for so long . . ." She trailed off, the unspoken conclusion hanging in the air between them.

"Too long. The decades weigh too heavily. I wouldn't survive the procedure."

Procedure?

That was the end of their conversation, for then two men descended the stairs, each carrying a chest. Jordan held her breath, but the newcomers walked past her hiding spot without twigging to her presence. When they joined the circle around the table, she recognized the pushy "scholar" who'd been visiting her shop.

"Just got off the telephone with Rome and Peking," he announced. "They're in position."

This catalyzed the group into action. Terzian went around with a knife and a cup, collecting blood from all the acolytes. The new arrivals opened the chests and distributed charms to the assembly. The accumulated power of the objects, exponentiated by the ley line, imbued the chamber with an almost unbearable physical pressure. The woman to whom Terzian had spoken lay upon the table. Two others snapped the shackles around her wrists and ankles, while another gently placed a leather bit in her mouth. She gnawed on it, then gave him a sharp nod.

Jordan had never heard of any ritual like this. Something the upper echelons of Flame had been pursuing for decades. That wasn't promising. The figurine was apparently the lynchpin of the operation. She gauged the distance from her hiding spot to the plinth. Could she sprint across the room and smash the clay before they tackled her? Proximity to the ley line had turned her simple concealment spell into a cloak of shadow darker than the finest sable—

The chanting began the moment the subject was settled on the table. The syllables of a nameless language reverberated through the stone chamber, strumming the ley line and assaulting Jordan's enhanced senses like knitting needles jammed into her eardrums. Now was her chance, while they wove the basis of their spell, before the intended effect took place. But eavesdropping on the chant was like peering through a thick fog—it afforded glimpses of something hidden, a sense of the sorcerers' intent.

No, that can't be right. That's not possible. Surely even Flame isn't this reckless?

She prepared to hurl herself across the room. She crouched, pulling into herself as though her entire body were a spring. She visualized the choreography, the last actions she'd ever take. *Leap out of hiding, shove him aside, vault that table, grab the figurine and hurl it to the ground. . . .* She could do it, though she would have felt more confident had she been fifteen years younger. She made her peace, drew a calming breath, and counted. *One. Two—*

From behind her came new footsteps and a sharp inhalation. The man who'd followed her from the Haret el-Yahud—he might have been an American—sidled down the stairs. Jordan tensed. But the look on his face made it clear he wasn't a part of this. And the scent of his sweat told her he didn't understand what he saw. It frightened him.

It scared Jordan, too, because she *did* understand what was happening. Even if she couldn't quite believe it.

The chanting reached a crescendo. The magical call and response lured something unfathomably ancient from the bones of the earth. The lamps flickered in a nonexistent breeze. The universe convulsed. *Something* entered the chamber.

Terzian lifted the clay figurine in his left hand. A *hollow* figurine, Jordan remembered. She'd never put any significance upon that, until now. His other hand held the knife. He raised his arms,

THE WITCH WHO CAME IN FROM THE COLD

brandishing both over the woman on the table. Jordan had the gist of it—the ceremony was akin to a magical blood transfusion. But the clueless American didn't understand.

"Holy shit," he blurted.

Part of Gabe wondered how his report would go over with the station chief when he got to the part about cultists and human sacrifice. At the very least he was looking at a six-month psych eval. The rest of him knew the worry was moot because his chances of getting out of this room had just taken a torpedo below the waterline. They'd heard him. And, as one, they turned to stare at him. Even the poor woman on the table, the whites visible in her terror-widened eyes.

"Kill him," said a man who looked old enough to be dirt's older brother.

Jordan knew a second chance when she saw one. She leaped from her hiding spot, elbowing a Flame sorcerer in the neck as she strove to cross the chamber. It was like trying to dive into molasses. The summoned entity carried massive metaphysical heft, which pushed against Jordan's concealment spell like a magical headwind. She vaulted the table—"Oof," said the woman chained there—swung her legs up, and kicked.

Just as Gabe turned to run, a shadow streaked across the room. But this shadow was a physical thing, and it lashed out at the earthen doll in the old man's hand.

The heel of Jordan's boot connected with Terzian's outstretched hand. The clay shattered.

The old man opened his mouth to rage, but the destruction of the spell's focus released the accumulated magical potential in an instant. To Jordan, it was as though she'd bitten a live wire. Her concealment spell shattered. But to the Flame acolytes blood-bound into the magical weavings, it was a metaphysical hand grenade. They collapsed, a roomful of marionettes with broken strings. The chamber reverberated like an overstretched drumhead, crackling with a vast store of dangerously unconfined magical potential.

I'm going insane. One moment there was a roomful of cultists getting ready to murder him, the next moment they were sprawled on the ground moaning, while the woman from the shop appeared out of nowhere. The intended victim was out cold.

Three things happened at once. Jordan turned to grab the interloper and flee. But the idiot American stumbled the rest of the way down the stairs, apparently intent on freeing the shackled woman. And the inhuman entity became an intangible maelstrom as it ricocheted through the chamber, seeking a host it could no longer perceive. So it tried to wedge itself into the nearest healthy body.

The American arched his back and screamed.

✦ ✦ ✦

Jordan caught him before he cracked his head on the floor. She was tempted to leave him there. She couldn't afford deadweight—by tomorrow morning, every Flame acolyte within two hundred miles would be searching for her. But she knew they'd torture the foolish American, running enchanted flensing knives through his soul until there was nothing left of him but a drooling, quivering heap, all because of her careless mistake.

Jordan lugged him up the stairs. He improved, slightly, with distance from the ley line. She dragged a yammering madman into the sunny alleyways of Cairo.

3.

Gabe convulsed. The golem's touch turned the crackle in his head into a full-blown electrical storm. The taste of metal filled his mouth; the smell of ozone filled his nose. The seizures made it impossible to speak. It was as though the golem and the hitchhiker were opposite magnetic poles desperate for fusion, and their only obstacle was Gabe. Something invisible wormed deeper into his mind, en route to the golem.

His scream filled the graveyard. The police shouted to each other, blew whistles. Flashlights approached.

Jordan took his free arm and pulled. But she might as well have been a newborn kitten trying to nudge a boulder.

Words filled Gabe's head. Words from a language he didn't understand, but which he somehow knew was older than his species. Alien language spilled from his mouth. Meaning, comprehension, discretion—none of it mattered. Only giving voice to ancient truths. He became their vessel. His lips, tongue, teeth, throat, and lungs worked of their own accord. The words couldn't be whispered; they had to be yelled. They left an ashen taste in their wake.

Jordan wound back and slapped him across the face hard enough to snap his head aside. It should have hurt, but all he could feel were razor-edged syllables shredding his vocal cords. He spoke a curse and tasted blood.

"Shut *up*," she hissed, "and help me free you."

He tried to say *I'm trying*, but all that came out was "G-g-glarghgghghunngg."

The crunch of footsteps on gravel approached from the fog. Jordan released him and scrambled from the hole. She crouched behind a grave marker and hefted the shovel like a baseball bat. She wound up like Babe Ruth.

Alestair emerged from the swirling fog. The steel ferrule of his umbrella clicked lightly on the gravel as he paused to survey the situation. He tipped his hat to Jordan.

"Miss Rhemes. A pleasure, as always."

He crouched at the grave's edge. The shouts and whistles drew nearer, as did the flashlight beams lighting up the fog. Alestair looked at Gabe, then to the inhuman hand holding him fast. He clucked his tongue.

"Oh, my dear boy. I must say, you are *terribly* predictable."

Gabe replied, "BWLEGH PLYXCH JTCLPHVISK!"

Alestair cocked an eyebrow. "Indeed." From the breast pocket of his suit he produced a flask.

As he uncapped it, Jordan said, "Oh, come *on*. This really isn't the time—"

But instead of taking a swig, Alestair splashed the contents over the clay hand clamped around Gabe's wrist. The fingers snapped open; Gabe tumbled backward. The thing in his head still vibrated like a bone saw poised to split his skull, but at least his thoughts were his own again.

"What the hell was that? Holy water?"

"There's no need for blasphemy, Gabriel. Merely a dash of water from the Vltava." He recapped the flask and tucked it back in his pocket. "I fear it's unlikely to slow our friend here for more than a few moments."

Already the clay fingers were wiggling. There came a scraping and crunching, too, as if the hand's owner was clawing free of its grave. Together, Jordan and Alestair hauled Gabe from the hole.

"Well, then. Ms. Rhemes, Mr. Pritchard." Alestair gestured with his umbrella, away from the flashlights and shouts that were moments from converging upon them. "This way, if you please. I advise haste."

Tanya sighed when her apartment building hove into view. Or she would have, if not for the shivers racking her body. It had been a long, miserable walk from the river. Her boots squelched; she left a trail of muddy footsteps and silvery exhalations in her wake.

It was cold in the river. Very, very cold.

She lingered at a corner to let a boisterous trio of students stumble past. Better to let them go ahead; she probably looked like a river witch, complete with mud in her hair. Two women and a man crossed the street, his arms over their shoulders. One of the women happened to glance in Tanya's direction as they passed. She was so young.

Oh, Andula. What have I done to you? Tanya started hyperventilating. *What did Ice do to you? What have they done to me? What lies have I served?*

She waited for the students to sway around a corner and out of sight before she walked the last few yards to her building. First, she would peel off her sodden clothing and bundle herself in every blanket she owned. And then she'd pour herself a drink. And maybe a second. And then she and Grandfather would have a very direct conversation. If necessary, she'd stay up all night interrogating the construct.

She trudged up the stairs. Staving off death from hypothermia had drained every charm on her person. And that had been a narrow thing. Back home in Volgograd, she'd seen men and women who spent every day in various levels of stupor, forever trying to forget the Battle of Stalingrad. And she'd seen what happened when somebody so deep in the bottle was deprived of alcohol. Tanya's hands shook like that now as she fought to get her key into the lock.

She managed eventually, but only after a conspicuous amount of jangling, and not before spiderwebbing the escutcheon with new scratches. Once inside, she threw the locks and slumped against the padded door. Her frostbitten heart beat so hard, the pulse of blood in her ears boomed like a kettledrum. She stood there for a long moment, catching her breath, before engaging in the battle to remove her boots. Those she let fall where they might. Exhausted, horrified, and chilled to the marrow, she shuffled to her bedroom, trailing articles of sodden clothing.

It wasn't until she had dragged the covers from the bed and wrapped herself like a Bedouin that she realized she hadn't needed to turn on any lights. Not in the hallway, not in her bedroom. She hadn't left them on when she left, had she? That was the kind of wasteful excess one expected from children and Westerners. Tanya tiptoed out of her tiny bedroom and peeked around the corner to the other branch of the hallway.

Lights blazed in every room of her apartment. In the water closet. In the sitting room. And, at the end of the hallway, the kitchen . . . whence came a faint, high-pitched warble and hiss, as of somebody tuning a radio.

Oh no.

The warbly static from the kitchen crystallized into her grandfather's voice, as if the person turning the construct's dials had thrown a net into the aether and pulled his soul down to earth like a wounded bird.

"What matters should we discuss?" said the construct.

The intruder's chuckle was terribly familiar.

No, no, no no no.

Delaying only long enough to don a proper robe, she padded barefoot to the kitchen, hoping like mad that she'd misheard. She'd misheard; she'd misunderstood; there was an innocent explanation. There wasn't. Sitting at her kitchen table, fiddling with the knobs on her grandfather's radio, was Aleksander Vadimovich Komyetski, chief of KGB Prague Station. Her pots and pans were piled on the floor beside the cabinet.

"I'm disappointed and frightened, Tatiana Mikhailovna. A strange man enters your flat, and you do nothing to confront him? How fortunate for you that it was only me, your true friend with nothing but fatherly affection and your best interests at heart."

A long, fraught moment passed before the gears in Tanya's rattled mind engaged sufficiently for conversation.

"Sir? What are you doing here?"

"I was worried about you, Tanya. No sign of you in the office all day, and even dear Nadia had no idea of your whereabouts. We feared something terrible had happened."

She'd thought her errand to the barge would take at most an

hour around sunrise; it was probably now after midnight. Evading the guards on the barge and shaking the pursuit had taken many hours and one desperate plunge into the river. She hadn't reported to KGB Prague Station all day.

"And—my, my—I see my fears have been realized," he continued. The scent of his breath told her that along with Grandfather's construct he'd also found the last of her alcohol. So much for that drink she'd been hoping for. "Why are you all wet, dear Tanya, with mud in your hair?"

"I jumped into the river," she said. At least that much was true. The most foolish, most immature part of her hoped they'd just concentrate on the river and he wouldn't mention the construct in his hands.

In response to the furrowing of his brow, she added, "It was a desperate situation. I was being followed. They may have been with a Western service." All technically true; she knew nothing about the Ice staff stationed on the barge.

Sasha shook his head. "My, my, my. It hurts my aging heart to think you nearly came to trouble. Of course, if you had followed procedures and hadn't been acting alone, perhaps you wouldn't have found yourself in such dire straits. At *my* station, we take care of each other. Yes?"

"Yes, sir. Always."

"We're a family." He nodded solemnly. But then he tapped the radio with a fingernail and chuckled. "But speaking of family!" A punch of dread threatened to double her over. "This strange device. When I found it, at first I thought, *Oh no! Our dear Tanya has an unreported radio.* I cannot tell you how it pained me to think you might be listening to Western numbers stations."

This was bad. This was Siberian-gulag bad. She started to shake again, but not from cold. "Sir, I can explain—"

He carried on as if she hadn't spoken. "But, oh, my relief. It barely receives anything, and nothing on a shortwave band. Just a lone disembodied voice claiming to be somebody's grandfather."

Oh, Grandfather, what secrets did Sasha trick you into revealing?

Her half-frozen, three-quarters-terrified, fully unprepared mind scrambled for purchase on the slippery conversation. "It must be malfunctioning. . . ."

No, no, you fool! Don't admit your guilt! With one telephone call, Sasha could have her family's stipends slashed. Or have them rounded up as dissidents.

He nodded. "Of course it is. Why, it's not even plugged in! Besides, I understand your only surviving grandfather is very ill. He's in a coma in Volgograd, yes?"

"Yes, sir."

He reached forward and patted her hand. "You needn't worry. Soviet doctors are the best in the world, you know. And a veteran of the Great Patriotic War? Remarkable men like that receive the very best care. I'm sure there's little danger of anything happening to him."

The veiled threat was a fist clenching her innards. She pressed a hand to her stomach, gasping for air. "Sir—"

"You're also quite remarkable, Tatiana Mikhailovna. More lives than a cat! First, you survive a plunge into an icy river in January. Then, when you're found to be in possession of an illegal radio, who should be the one to find it but me? Again, such luck! Because I know your loyalty and dedication are absolute. A lesser apparatchik would seek to misconstrue this for his own benefit."

She blinked. What was happening? Her mind was too cold and slow to keep up.

He stood. "Which is why, in order to protect you, I will take this strange device. It is the best option, yes?"

Bozhe moi. Dyedushka.

She gaped at him like a goldfish. "I . . . I mean, I think . . ."

Again, he waved her quiet. "Now, now, don't worry about thanking me right now. Perhaps an opportunity will show itself in the future."

"Opportunity?"

"A favor. I'm doing you this favor now, and maybe there will come a time when I need a favor from you. As I said, we take care of each other."

There was another word for it, of course. Blackmail.

He shrugged. "You're a highly resourceful woman, Tatiana Mikhailovna. Should it ever come to that, I'm sure you'll be equal to the task."

He donned his coat, and with it a mantle of avuncular concern. "Take tomorrow off. Stay in bed, lest you catch a cold. Sasha's orders! I'll ask Comrade Ostrokhina to check on you. She'll bring pierogi."

He said this last with a smile and a wink, as if he hadn't just threatened to have her grandfather murdered and hadn't just made it nauseatingly clear that, for all intents and purposes, he owned her now.

Sasha paused in the doorway. "You should think about moving. The superintendent of this building is not an honest man. Rumor has it that for a shockingly small bribe he'll let a strange old man enter the apartment of a perfectly respectable young lady such as yourself. I fear for you, living in the midst of such despicable moral turpitude. Good night to you."

And with that, he was gone, her grandfather's construct tucked under his arm.

✦ ✦ ✦

Gabe stumbled between the graves, arms over Jordan and Alestair. Sandwiched between her sandalwood and his cologne, he felt like a shipwreck in the men's department of Harrods. Alestair led them through the darkness with the surety of a bat, steering them toward the east entrance.

New noises had joined the sound of pursuit. First, a tremendous crashing and shattering, as though something were punching free of an old wooden casket. Then a slow but steady crunching, as of lumbering footsteps on gravel.

A few dozen yards ahead, a trio of flashlight halos loomed amid the graves. Alestair paused for a moment, as if consulting an internal map. Abruptly he said, "This way," and pulled them north into an older section of the cemetery. They passed rows of grave markers. "Here," he said, just as abruptly. And pulled them into a crouch.

They'd stopped behind a gravestone so blackened and weathered by age as to be unreadable. Gabe would have thought the occupant long-forgotten, yet somebody had recently left a posy. It was more grass than flowers, but still a nice gesture.

Jordan frowned when she saw it. "Hey, wait a second—"

Alestair wrung the posy like a dishtowel until it tore apart and the bundle coughed out a little cloud of seeds and flower petals. It elicited a strange but not unpleasant tingle in what Gabe had begun to think of as his other-sense, a legacy of the hitchhiker. It felt like soft magic.

The MI6 sorcerer whispered, "That should buy us a few undetected moments."

Moments later, a policeman stalked past their hiding spot. Gabe could see the man's silhouette in the fog and hear the rustle of his clothing. But the cop didn't even slow when his flashlight beam swept over them. His footsteps receded into the graveyard.

Gabe frowned. "What the hell just happened?"

For the first time all night, the hint of a smile played across Jordan's face. She whispered, "Alestair salted the entire graveyard with charms."

Alestair shook his head. "Merely a few strategic locations. But one does strive to be prepared."

"I wondered why you bought up so much of my inventory."

Prepared. What had Alestair said? Something about being predictable . . . "Wait a second. You knew I was going to try this?"

Alestair shot his cuffs. "I suspected that sooner or later you'd go looking for the golem." From somewhere in the fog came a shout, followed by a heavy crash, as of a shattered gravestone. "I didn't suspect you'd meet with such spectacular success."

"But how? I never told a soul before tonight."

"Prague is rife with tales of the golem. But to those of us embroiled in this occult conflict, the descriptions have all the hallmarks of an extremely powerful construct. Many on both sides have sought it. It's difficult to resist the allure of such a seductive legend."

"But in all this time, nobody has ever found it," said Jordan. "Because it's only a legend."

"So thought we all." Alestair shrugged. "Any traces of the animating spellwork must have dissipated centuries ago. Rendering it utterly undetectable. That is, until the remarkable Mr. Pritchard came along."

Gabe massaged his aching wrist. His skin exhibited a distinctly hand-shaped wheal. Had the golem squeezed any harder, it might have ground his bones into powder.

"Speaking of which. I know our mutual friend here has been prone to indelicate actions of late," Alestair continued, "but I am somewhat taken aback to find you involved in this ill-advised venture, Miss Rhemes."

"I owe him." She shivered, hugged herself. "What happened to Gabe . . . it was my fault."

"You refer to Mr. Pritchard's infamous misadventure in Cairo, yes? A ripping yarn, no doubt. Although when a fellow makes discreet inquiries—all through the proper channels, mind you—one finds details devilishly thin on the ground. I rather suspect that you, Miss Rhemes, are the only person who knows the full story."

She bit her lip and flicked a nervous glance at Gabe.

Though his head spun like a tornado, he understood the gesture. "Oh my God. You've always said you *found* me in that stinking alley. Have you any idea how frightening it is to wake up with a gaping hole in your memory and nothing but disjointed fever-dream nightmares where an entire day should be? For years I've worried that I'm losing my mind. But you've known all along what happened and what's wrong with me, haven't you?"

Jordan shook her head. "No, no. Gabe, I swear, I don't know what happened to you. I can't offer you any certainty. Just a crackpot theory. Or, at least, I thought it was crackpottery until tonight."

"If you don't spill the beans right now," Gabe whispered, "I will stand and belt out 'The Star-Spangled Banner' at the top of my lungs until every policeman in the city finds us."

Jordan looked away. "I only know what I think I witnessed that afternoon."

"All *I* know is that I woke up in an alleyway with a daylong gap in my memory. So let's hear it."

To Alestair, Jordan said, "It was the Flame. We barged in on a sorcerous work-in-progress. Big one. A geographically distributed operation. Cairo, Rome, Peking."

"An operation intended to achieve what, exactly?" The Brit was all business now. For a moment, the languid Etonian old-boy charm evaporated, revealing the hardened MI6 lamplighter at the core.

"I think they were trying to hollow somebody out. To create their own Host."

For a moment, nobody said anything. The only sounds were the occasional shouts of the Veřejná bezpečnost officers searching for them.

"Believe me, I know how it sounds," she said. "As time went on, I convinced myself that I'd misunderstood what I'd witnessed. I chalked it up to adrenaline and fear. But the way Gabe's proximity energized the golem construct . . . I'm not so skeptical any longer."

"You believe the elemental intended for the Flame volunteer ended up in our Gabriel."

"He's not a Host, though. So it *can't* join with him." Again Jordan shook her head. "Instead, I believe it's lodged halfway, like a couch stuck in a doorway."

"Now that," said Alestair, "is an elegant and intriguing hypothesis."

"Well, great. That solves it then. I just need to find some college students," Gabe hissed. He paused to spit the taste of copper from his mouth. "I'll pay them with beer."

Jordan gave him the side-eye. To Alestair, she said, "Are we certain we can't leave him?"

"Would that we could, my dear."

A new round of shouts echoed through the fog. At first just a couple, as policemen called to one another. Then more voices joined in, a chorus of alarm. They were converging on something.

Alestair stood. "Perhaps we should depart."

Jordan helped Gabe to his feet. "Thank you, Alestair. I wasn't prepared for this. I'm glad you were."

The tumult turned from shouts to screams. A heavy impact shook the cemetery, and then something large and limp came flying out of the darkness. It landed nearby with a meaty thud. As one, they stared at the dead policeman.

"I confess, I wasn't quite prepared for *that*."

EPISODE 6

A WEEK WITHOUT MAGIC

Michael Swanwick

Prague, Czechoslovak Socialist Republic
February 14, 1970

1.

Bar Vodnář was knee-deep in shadows and bad memories when Tanya walked in the door. But already there was a thin blue haze of cigarette smoke in the air, mingling with residual traces of beer, frankincense, angelica, and sage. The more exotic scents lingered from Jordan's weekly purification ceremony, a ritual performed only when the bar was closed.

There were only four patrons so far: three Czech apparatchiks and Arnold Lytton, a former CIA officer who—on being put out to pasture—found himself compelled to stay, yearning to be let inside again, hoping against hope that he would be called back to duty. His was a common type in Tanya's world, the human residue of long-forgotten struggles, addicted to a way of life that no longer had any use for him. She despised him for it. Not bothering to return his nod, she went to the bar and waited impatiently.

Jordan returned at last from setting votive candles on the tables and slipped behind the bar. "Look at you—all dressed up and ready to party. Did the KGB finally issue you a sense of fun?" Tanya had noticed that Jordan always touched one particular brass bracelet with two fingers when she said things like that, and somehow nobody ever overheard them. So she had given up on trying to shush the woman, even though her words were criminally indiscreet.

Scowling, Tanya placed a box that had originally held *Krasny Oktyabr* chocolates on the bar before her.

"Are you trying to seduce me? Because, frankly, you're not that—" Jordan's hand lightly touched the box, then flew up like a startled bird. All trace of humor fled from her face. "Why are you bringing *these* here?"

"I need to hide them someplace safe for a week." *Or possibly forever,* Tanya thought, though she refrained from saying that aloud. When Jordan remained silent, she added, "An inspection team is coming in from Moscow tomorrow. If these were found . . ."

"It's no skin off my nose."

But it was, of course, and Tanya knew that Jordan understood that very well. The bartender's neutrality was only tenuously maintained, through a combination of her usefulness to both Fire and Ice and the amount of effort it would take to bring her down. If the existence of a secret war of magic being fought right under the noses of the intelligence community were to come out, Jordan would suffer as much as anyone. "You're a perceptive woman," Tanya said. "You must know how little I trust you. . . . Just how serious does it have to be for me to ask this of you?"

For a long, still moment, Jordan said nothing. Tanya held her breath. In truth, she was not much afraid of Moscow Center's inspectors. But *Sasha* terrified her. Her superior might very well invade her apartment again, and she could ill afford the consequences should her gear be discovered. Either he would know what it was and what it was for, or he would want her to explain everything to him. She did not relish the confrontation either way.

Scowling, the bartender lifted the box. She kicked a step stool into position so she could reach the shelves above the cash register and placed the box holding Tanya's tools and weapons as high as possible, alongside a clutch of dusty but expensive-looking bottles.

Tanya felt her heart stutter at the sight of them so exposed. "Will they be safe there?"

"Have you never read Poe's 'The Purloined Letter'? Hide things in plain sight. If you're staying, you'll need to buy a drink."

"I'm not staying. Thank you, Jordan. I owe you one."

Jordan made a sour face and shrugged. "Why not? Everybody else does."

At that moment, a tall man in a panama hat breezed through the door. He doffed his greatcoat, revealing a linen suit as white as his hair and far more appropriate to the tropics than to a Prague winter. Obviously, he was new in town. A scar slashed across one cheek rendered his startling good looks all the more intriguing. "Martini," he said in an American accent. "Dry, straight up, with an olive. Don't stint on the gin."

Choosing a booth by the wall, he removed his hat, tapped out a cigarette from a pack of Marlboros, and lit it with a Zippo lighter.

Tanya turned to leave. He couldn't possibly be a spy—too damned gaudy. Then the newcomer cried, "Arnie!" and waved to the only retired CIA officer in the room. Lytton smiled and raised his glass in salute.

Damn.

She had to find out who this guy was.

But not now. Tanya couldn't linger. She had to show her face at the National Gallery for the opening of a show of old masters on loan from the Hermitage. It was simultaneously the dullest and most glamorous part of her job to attend such gatherings. Nothing interesting ever happened at them.

Deep in the National Gallery, deeper into the administrative recesses than any visitor had a right to be, Gabe was puking his guts out. Minutes earlier, he had been holding but, ironically enough, quite deliberately not drinking a flute of Georgian "champagne," when the monster inside his head had reached down to roil his stomach. Like a wounded animal, he had fled the reception and found refuge in an unlit corridor. Stumbling as he went, he'd grabbed at door handles until he'd found one that opened and found sanctuary here.

It had, thank whatever nonexistent gods overlooked the welfare of wayward spies, turned out to be a bathroom.

The vomit gushing into the delicate porcelain sink—hand-painted with Tyrian purple gentians—was green and foul-smelling. Fat drops of sweat poured from his throbbing head like rain. Meanwhile, the thing within him reached down to caress and then squeeze his bowels. An instant ago, Gabe had imagined his situation couldn't possibly get any worse. Now, however . . .

Somebody rattled the bathroom's doorknob.

"C'est occupée!" Gabe growled in his very best Metropolitan French. *"Va te faire foutre, trouduc."* Just to throw off the scent, should the intruder later wonder exactly who he might have been.

Whoever it was went away, possibly to alert the guards.

Gabe knew all the ways an agent might get in and out of a secure building. His previous cover identity, after all, had been as the chief of diplomatic security for the Cairo embassy. But he had no idea how he was going to get out of the fix he was in. If he was discovered—no, make that *when* he was discovered—his career was as good as over. He would be a laughingstock. Worse, he would have rendered himself visible in a way no intelligence officer should ever be, constantly pointed out, invariably noticed wherever he went, the guy who was found spewing filth from both ends in an art museum. He was well and royally screwed.

And then, abruptly, he was fine.

What the hell had *that* been all about? One minute, he was looking at a painting, and the next . . .

The noise that issued from Gabe's mouth then was half relief, half despair, and half disgust. Swiftly he made himself presentable and cleaned away all evidence of the embarrassing incident. The bundle of towels he'd used to mop things up, he hid in the back of a linen closet for some horrified janitorial staffer to discover a week from now. Time for him to slip away quietly.

As he was making for the exit, however, Gabe saw Morozova standing by herself at the edge of the mixer, talking to no one and looking extremely bored. On a desperate impulse, he seized her wrist and pulled her into a shadowy side gallery.

And realized that he had a demon by the arm. Morozova's eyes were murderous. Her free hand was raised and cocked in a way that Gabe knew meant she was ready to drive its heel into his nose and, with any luck, splinters of his skull into his brain. But then, seeing who he was, and evidently judging him unlikely to try anything physical in so public a space, Morozova lowered her arm and wrinkled her nose. "You smell terrible."

Quietly, urgently, Gabe said, "I need your help. I need help from . . . your organization."

"Let go of me." Morozova pulled her arm free of his grip.

Fiercely she said, "That door is closed. Forever. You can just pretend it never existed."

Whoops. Mentally Gabe took two steps back and one to the side. *That* had been badly played on his part. Apparently the bad blood between them was stronger than the desire she'd shown earlier to recruit him into her organization. No, wait. Her tone suggested she was unhappy with more than just him. Her KGB masters, perhaps? Or was it the Ice? If, at his instigation, she had looked into the barge filled with the frozen victims of her organization, she might well have suffered a massive loss of faith in her own people.

Whatever was going on, it was the kind of situation Gabe knew how to exploit.

His personal problems were nothing compared to an opportunity like this. Gabe felt like an actor who'd just heard his cue. Time to stride onstage and play the fool. Let her think that he thought she could be manipulated. Then see what she did.

"Listen to me," Gabe said in his most unctuous tones, channeling his inner bad boyfriend. "We had a thing going here, a professional connection. Don't cut me off like this. Keep the relationship open: Surely we can work together on matters that don't threaten either of our sponsors. We complement each other. Seriously, there must be something you want. Some small favor. Ask."

For a long moment, Morozova considered his offer. Gabe could almost see the gears turning. "As it happens," she said at last, "there *is* something you could do for me."

2.

There was a wall across the street from Tanya's apartment, too tall for a passerby to see over, but not too high for somebody to place something atop it. The morning after her encounter with Pritchard in the gallery, Tanya discovered that Nadia had placed three small stones in a row there, easily visible from above. So she was not surprised to find a rolled-up newspaper outside the neighboring apartment door—the one that nobody lived in. She took it in and shook it open over the kitchen table. A folded sheet of paper fell out. It read simply: *Family crisis. Cover for me. N.*

Tanya understood this to mean that Nadia was off on Ice business. Which would have been inconvenient at the best of times, but at this particular juncture was maddening. She had questions, *pressing* questions, for Nadia about the Ice's handling of the Hosts. Nor was she thrilled at the prospect of having to cover at the embassy for a subordinate when the inspectors descended upon them like hyenas upon carrion.

Still, what could not be mended had to be endured. Tanya turned off the lights and put the electric kettle on for tea.

As could have been predicted, Tanya was not at her desk for fifteen minutes that morning before she was summoned to Sasha's office. A stranger waited there, a man who seemed a caricature of himself: morbidly obese, with a doughy face, jowls, brown age spots, and, on his eyelids, skin tags like little flesh tentacles that jiggled as he talked. Tanya found it hard not to stare as they exchanged meaningless preliminaries. No reason was given for his presence, so he was obviously the head inspector.

Sasha introduced him as General Boris Petrovich Bykovsky, adding in an almost whimsical tone, "You can speak as openly before him as you would before me." Obviously, a guarded warning. Then he told the general that Tanya was his most trusted subordinate, which made her wonder.

"Not half so trusted, I am sure, as Sasha is to me," General Bykovsky said with finality. "We are like brothers."

A complex look passed between the two men. They both turned to Tanya. "You have an eager air about you, Comrade," Sasha said. "Perhaps you have something you wish to ask me?"

Tanya marshaled her courage. "Sir, I request access to the files and authorization to use the photocopier room. I've chanced upon an opportunity to slip the Odessa file to the Americans."

Sasha's eyebrows flew up. "Did you really?"

The Odessa file, a carefully constructed lure labeled *Electro-magnetic Bio-information Transfer*, contained A. L. Ivanov's paper from the *International Journal of Parapsychology* on eyeless seeing, the mimeographed transcript of a symposium on the use of Tesla coils as anti–remote viewing devices, a secret and totally fictitious speech by Kosygin on the importance of psychic research, and a background paper on an experiment in telepathic communication between Sevastopol and two nuclear submarines using ELF transmitters as boosters. It was by no means a comprehensive file or even a particularly coherent one. Rather, it was quite cannily the sort of thing a curious *rezident* might assemble out of bits and pieces that came his way, in the hope that it might eventually add up into some useful clue as to what his superiors were up to.

But when Tanya gave a severely edited version of her discussion with Gabe in the gallery, she was astounded to hear Bykovsky abruptly shut down Sasha's growing elation. "I absolutely forbid any file leaving the building. Discipline has obviously gotten slack here. Why would we give such valuable information to our enemies?"

Tanya bent her head deferentially. "With all due respect, sir, the file is nonsense. Bait. Half forgery and half the work of crackpots. But if we can get it into the hands of the American intelligence community, the Odessa file has the potential to make them waste millions of dollars creating their own psychic research program."

Sasha added, "Moscow Center concocted the scheme. They are most eager for it to go forward."

"As far as you are concerned, *I* am Moscow Center. So, no, Moscow does not desire any such thing."

"Then . . . I am to drop the American contact?" Tanya asked.

Bykovsky assumed what he obviously thought was a clever manner. "You could always seduce him."

Tanya felt her lips turn cold. "I am not a—"

"We have made a good beginning here," Sasha said, clapping his hands together, "and I trust that we will all build upon it. The first thing I will need from you, Comrade Morozova, is a typed report of your contact with the opposition officer. I'll expect it on my desk by noon. With three carbon copies, please."

So there went most of Tanya's morning. When she delivered the handwritten copy to the typing pool, she discovered that the general had spent the interim spreading terror and confusion among the clerical staff. Bykovsky was the sort who liked to change procedures without bothering to understand them first. First, he had told the typists they were not to make carbon copies anymore. Then the file clerks were instructed to merge individual files into group dossiers arranged by "affinity clusters," whatever those might be. After which, anything on paper was immediately classified secret, including blank forms. All typed materials were henceforth to be handled only by those graded as intelligence officers or higher. Which meant that, in essence, nobody in the clerical staff had the clearance to read or handle anything they typed or filed. In the aftermath of this cascade of new and contradictory regulations, one typist, Ekaterina, came to Tanya, biting back tears. "Please, Comrade. Tell me this is some sort of test."

"Keep calm, and do what you can. Everything will be normal again soon," Tanya lied. She assumed her most stalwart and capable face. "Meanwhile, in the absence of carbon paper, I'm afraid you'll have to type this out four times. I'll need all the copies by noon, so please make it your top priority."

"But . . . four copies!"

"You're not the only one with problems, Comrade."

To Tanya's complete and utter surprise, the report and its three hand-typed copies were finished in time, despite all the chaos. Apparently she was not as unpopular with the typists as their behavior had always led her to suspect.

Bykovsky had requisitioned Sasha's office for his own use, but when Tanya arrived there, the general was out for lunch. Sasha accepted the papers, placing them print-side down on an empty space of the desk where his bonsai used to be—facedown positioning of all documents being another of the general's innovations. Then, sitting on a chair not behind but to one side of the desk, he said, "So. How are you enjoying the new regime?"

"I am confident we will quickly adapt to the changes."

Sasha looked longingly at the tables where he normally kept his chessboards. They had, it seemed, been deemed a distraction from his work. "Have you ever seen the British James Bond films?"

"I saw *From Russia with Love*. It was nonsense."

"My old friend Borya has seen every James Bond film three times." For a long time, Sasha said no more. Tanya, who knew better than to let him goad her into speaking simply to fill the void, matched him silence for silence. At last he continued, "Boris Petrovich has risen as far as he possibly can in the KGB. Now he is angling for a position on the Politburo. For that to happen, however, he must first draw the attention of those on the top. He needs a spectacular accomplishment. For his purposes, closing down a corrupt and dysfunctional station would be every bit as useful as reforming it. So, trust me, he's nobody you would want to make unhappy."

As Tanya wondered at this unexpected show of friendliness—callousness? a display of power? business as usual?—Sasha's face turned uncharacteristically grim. "Nor, my dear, am I. Whatever else happens in the course of this very long week, I do hope you'll remember that."

That same morning after the meeting in the gallery, Gabe had a long and depressing breakfast in a rundown café in the New Town. When he arrived at his desk, he found the embassy buzzing with bland, pink-faced accountants. "Oh Lord," he muttered. He had forgotten that it was inspection season, that time of year when, the winter holidays over, busybodies on both sides of the Cold War descended upon embassies everywhere to make life a living hell for poor, long-suffering spies.

He also found three identical messages demanding that he report to Frank's office immediately. There Gabe saw, lined up on a table, an array of half-empty liquor bottles, prescription bottles with their labels carefully turned to the wall, a switchblade, and a short stack of magazines.

"It's a funny thing," Frank said. "No matter how secret you try to keep these things, word always goes out about an inspection the day before. Somebody always tips somebody else off." He did not mention that he himself had issued the warning. "A cleaning team went through the offices last night looking for anything an employer might not want to find in the desks of his employees and, predictably enough, they came up empty-handed. However, as it turns out, our auditors expected this to happen. Which is why, without notifying me, they previously had three days' trash diverted to a warehouse. When it was sifted through, all kinds of crap was discovered."

"I know whose switchblade that is, and—"

"So do I. He'll have his little souvenir back just as soon as our esteemed colleagues from Accounting are gone." Frank opened a drawer, fished within, spilled a handful of trinkets onto the desk: bits of carved bone, a white feather painted with red stripes, glass beads and twigs lashed together with silver wire, and the like. "What do you make of these?"

"Um . . . hippie jewelry?"

Frank stared at Gabe, unblinking, for long enough that Gabe

began to sweat. He knew better than to break the silence, though. Silence was the easiest way to get someone who was feeling guilty to blurt out something incriminating. Instead, he matched that gaze with his most stalwart mask of an expression and just the hint of a smile. Frank would know what he was doing, but it was exactly what an honest spook *would* do.

"Yeah, I've got no idea either." Frank swept the things back into the drawer and handed Gabe one of the magazines. "How about this? What do you think?"

The magazine was titled *Dynamic Nudist*. Gabe flipped through it, paused midway through, and grinned. "I think that I wouldn't mind playing volleyball with the blonde."

"Right answer."

"Sir? I'm afraid I don't understand what a wrong answer would be."

"Faggots like magazines like this because they allow 'em to look at naked men—if they're caught they can claim they were ogling the broads. I wish someone would tell whoever-it-is to keep this crap at home. Or, better yet, to just use his imagination." Frank tossed the magazines into a wastebasket.

"Oh," Gabe said.

Then he realized that Frank was looking at him expectantly, waiting for him to say something. Not about Josh—that matter was closed. But Frank's unblinking stare said, clearer than words, *Do you have something to tell me?* The best means of concealment was always the simple, if carefully pruned, truth.

Gabe cleared his throat. "Sir, I must report a contact with a KGB officer last night." Frank did not look surprised. Which meant that someone had seen Gabe talking with Tanya and fingered him. Josh? No, more likely somebody from outside the

Company, looking to curry favor with Frank. Or just some idiot yanking Gabe's chain. "She wanted information on a new player in town. I said I'd see what I could do."

"So what did you do?" Frank asked.

"I had breakfast with Arnie Lytton."

It had been heartbreaking how the old man's eyes had lit up when Gabe walked into the café, and pathetic how eager he was to tell everything he knew. Not that he knew all that much. But at least now Gabe had a name, Magnus Haakensen, and a nickname as well—the Norwegian. Haakensen had been on the circuit for years. He told good stories, and he bought his share of the drinks. Nobody knew who he worked for—nobody, the implication was, particularly cared. He was just one of those characters who popped up wherever spooks gathered.

As Gabe was leaving, Arnie had grabbed the sleeve of his jacket and begged for work. "Surveillance, sabotage, message running, *anything*, Gabe. I've got a good record—I can do the work. You have no idea what it feels like being on the outside." Which was not entirely true; Gabe understood the old duffer well enough. He just didn't have any use for a relic from a different era, with reflexes gone slow and a brain clogged up with old tricks. But he had lied and promised to do his best to find something. Just to get free of the poor son of a bitch.

"And the KGB officer?"

"Tanya Morozova. We've talked about her before. Ostensibly third cultural secretary at the Soviet embassy, but of course we know better. Very serious, very professional. A true believer. We've met a few times before this, just casual talk. This time she suggested we might do each other a small favor from time to time."

"Huh. Sounds like she's trying to get you a little bit pregnant."

"Funny thing, that's my assessment of the situation as well."

"Let's turn the tables on her, see how much time she can be conned into wasting on you. Let her think you might want to play volleyball with her. Without your spending an equal amount of time on her, understand? Some of us have got work to do. Anything else? No? Scram."

Gabe started to leave.

"Oh, and Langley's sending in a new boy to oversee you on the extraction. Name's Dominic Alvarez. We'll be having a conference on that the day after tomorrow."

On the way back to his desk, Gabe did a few mental calculations and was appalled to discover exactly how much grunt work he had just volunteered to do. Then he saw Josh, feet up, reading that day's *Lidové noviny*. Gabe clapped a hand on his shoulder. "Josh, old buddy, old chum, old pal! How's about giving me a hand today? I've got a bitch of a workload, and it's all dull as ditchwater."

Laughing, Josh swung his feet to the floor, putting down the newspaper. "You make it sound so delightful. How can I resist?"

Paperwork was the bane of every spy's existence, but sharing it created a camaraderie second only to that involving live ammunition.

Gabe and Josh spent the next several hours working the phones and the fax machine in order to assemble a file on Haakensen to present to Tanya. Gabe also wrote up his encounter with her and a summary report of his breakfast with Lytton. He'd have to fill out an expense voucher as well, to be reimbursed for the morning's watery eggs, soggy toast, and weak coffee. It would have been easier just to pay out of pocket, but contacts with the other side always looked suspicious, and he wanted a paper trail a mile wide for this little game he was playing with Comrade Tatiana Morozova.

"Excuse me." One of the crew of interchangeable accountants who had been sifting through the embassy's financial records, this one bespectacled and pale-scalped under a severe crew cut, stood blinking before Gabe. "Is this a good time for you?"

"As a matter of fact, buddy, this is a perfectly terrible time for me. But never mind that. What can I do you for?"

"Well, you can . . ." The accountant stopped and, all in a rush, said, "You guys are doing a great job, I just wanted to say that."

Most people didn't know what Gabe did for a living, so he didn't get this reaction very often. But he understood it. To someone on the far fringes of the intelligence community, a desk man, an encounter with an officer who presumably went out into the real world and did things to shape the destiny of nations would be like meeting Mick Jagger. "Well. Thank you for telling me that. It means a great deal to me."

"You've been chosen at random to fill this out," the accountant continued. He held up a binder whose contents were a good inch thick. "I'm afraid you won't like it."

Gabe's stomach sank. But he turned on the easy grin, the pleasant manner. He had learned long ago that this was the best way to handle people he found difficult to like. Act like the guy they'd most want to have a beer with, the new neighbor they'd immediately invite over for a barbecue. "Before we make that kind of judgment, let me glance over this thing. Maybe it's not as bad as you think."

Swiftly Gabe riffled through the binder. The introductory section spelled out a fourteen-step protocol for an hour-by-hour expenditure/benefit accounting of all his activities performed in the past six months. The rest went downhill from there. He doubted he could fill out this bastard in less than a day.

Okay, then. The gloves were off. Gabe let out a long, low, and perfectly insincere whistle. "Wow. Filling this in would be an honest-to-God violation of national security."

"It would?"

"Trust me. If I created this documentation and it fell into the wrong hands, it would be a road map detailing my duties, methods, and operational preferences. A map leading straight to my dead body in a dark alley. You don't want that on your conscience, do you?"

"No! But I'm still on probation. If I can't do my job, I'll lose it." The man was close to tears. Who would have guessed that accountants were so emotional? "I had an offer from J. P. Morgan, you know. I passed up good money so I could serve my country." Or that they were so patriotic?

Gabe snapped his fingers, as if he'd just had an idea. "I'll tell you what. You and I both agree that this form is total bullshit, right? I literally cannot fill it in without committing an act of treason against the United States of America. But you can."

"I can?" The accountant looked confused.

"Of course." Gabe guided the man to his chair and sat him down behind his desk. "You can't give away any secrets—you don't know them. It's just a lot of boilerplate, really. All you need to know to make it look good is that my job is forty percent agency paperwork and planning, twenty percent embassy paperwork, and forty percent ops. Add to that another twenty percent soft surveillance—going to lectures and such—but be sure to mark it 'off the books.' Otherwise I'm entitled to overtime, and getting paid for work I don't do is a fast way into the federal prison system."

"I really shouldn't . . ."

"I've done some things in this job I wasn't proud of. But by God, I did them for my country." Gabe lifted his head nobly. This was no time for subtlety. Locking eyes with his victim, he said, "I'd sleep a lot better knowing that you've got my back."

"Well, I suppose . . ."

It was so easy that Gabe found himself wishing the guy worked for the Soviets. He'd have had him trapped, turned, and depositing spools of microfilm in bus station lockers within the week. "That's the spirit," he said. "When you're done, let me know, and I'll give it to Amanda in the typing pool."

The afternoon passed slowly, but not a fraction as slowly as it would have without Gabe's little act of deceit. When the Time/ Efficiency Accounting Systematics Documentation—as the heading on every single page solemnly proclaimed it to be—was finished, he stood the accountant up and gave him the firmest handshake of his life. Then he sent him on his way.

As he was leaving the embassy at the end of the day, Gabe realized that he'd never learned the accountant's name. He almost felt bad about that. Turning to Josh, he said, "You know, your typical KGB officer might be working in a treacherous den of thugs and assassins in the service of a filthy cause, but at least they don't have to put up with all these goddamned bean counters."

Josh made a wry face. "I said something like that to Frank once, and he told me I should be grateful I had to deal with so few of them. He said that we had no idea how much crap he was protecting us from. So I dunno. You have to take the good with the bad, I guess."

"Oh yeah, speaking of that. Frank wanted me to have a word with you about your choice of reading material . . ."

♦ ♦ ♦

Tanya had never seen an organization fall apart so fast: Prague Station, which yesterday had been solid as solid could be, was crumbling before her eyes. Having thoroughly demoralized the clerical staff, Bykovsky was now working his way through the intelligence officers. One by one, they were called to his temporary office, and one by one they returned to their desks, looking shaken and alarmed.

Meanwhile, Bykovsky's underlings, grim creatures who might or might not have been accountants but certainly looked like they would be at home in a brawl, were ransacking the very files nobody was supposed to touch anymore, shredding some, adding to others, and assigning each a randomly chosen file number by which they were now to be organized. The original titles were written down on yellow legal pads that would be kept under lock and key in Sasha's office. However, since the numbers were random and the titles listed in no particular order, it was a system which guaranteed that, once implemented, no information would ever be accessible again.

Even Sasha was beginning to look panicked.

Finally, late in the afternoon, the general summoned Tanya. "You have doubtless heard that I am instituting more stringent internal security policies. From now on one of your duties will be to turn in weekly reports detailing the activities of"—he consulted a paper—"Nadezhda Fyodorovna Ostrokhina."

"Sir, Nadia answers directly to me. So her activities are already a part of . . ." Then, in midsentence, she got it. "You want me to spy on her."

I can do this, Tanya thought. *Nadia spies on me; I spy on her; we each attest to the ideological purity of the other.*

"Nobody can be above suspicion. Listening devices will be provided. Incidentally, why isn't she here today?"

"She—"

"Also, what have you done about the American since we spoke yesterday?"

"Nothing, sir. I've been busy with paperwork."

"No excuses. I want action. Either bed him or kill him."

Tanya's mouth fell open. Prior to this very moment, she had thought it something that only happened to people in pulp novels. While she was grappling for a less than suicidal way to phrase her complete and utter unwillingness to attempt to engage in either disastrous suggestion, she was dismissed and the next victim was sent in.

Her hands itched for the tools she had left with Jordan.

Later in the day, Tanya noticed Sasha retrieving something from his office desk. With a sinking sensation, she saw that it was a travel guide to Hawaii.

3.

After a second day of solid paperwork, Gabe found it a pleasure to be out on the street again. He and Tanya met, as if by accident, at a Peter Max exhibit sponsored by USAID. Indeed, it was by some standards coincidental, as neither of them had made prior arrangements to do so. But there were only so many places that people like them would be on any given evening.

They had stalked each other through the show and wound up in a dogleg at the far end of the gallery, well beyond the magic table with the crystal bowl of spiked punch and stacks of paper napkins and plastic glasses where the coursing guests put an end to their relentless advance on art and culture in favor of as much free booze as they could swill down and still walk home afterward. Nobody was paying the least attention to Gabe and Tanya whatsoever.

Gabe gestured expansively toward a multicolored painting of the Statue of Liberty. "Forget all those musty old oils at the National Gallery that your country stole from Europe. This is America in all its polychromatic glory."

"I agree. It's bright and splashy and utterly without a soul."

With an easy grin, Gabe said, "You're saying that the country that gave the world James Brown and Elvis Presley has no soul? C'mon."

"Whatever soul it might have, there's no romance in it. Do you know the difference between Soviet men and Americans? They both want the same thing from women. But Americans just . . . go for it. Like they are grabbing a beer in one of your commercials. Russian men understand romance. Do you know what you'll see on the Moscow Metro when work is letting out? Men with soulful eyes and bouquets of flowers in their hands— for their wives, for their girlfriends, for young women they hope to make smile."

"When was the last time you saw a Russian smile?"

"When was the last time you brought a woman flowers?"

"Ouch." Smiling, Gabe handed Tanya a bright yellow plastic bag. "This is for you." A coffee table book of pop art that he'd have to file an expense report on in the morning. Lowering his voice, he said, "The file's in there too. It's a duplicate—keep it if you like. Your man's name is Magnus Haakensen. Born to a Norwegian blue-collar family in Minneapolis. Saw action in 'Nam and by some rumors served in Army Intelligence. Hooked up with the Irish Republican Army. Had to leave Ireland quickly, which led to some less than savory rumors that he was turned by the Brits. Popped up in Israel, where he fought in the Six-Day War. So he may be working for Mossad."

"Stop. You are making my head hurt."

"He's been seen in all the hot spots in Africa, all the usual bars in Europe, and of course in Hawaii—so it's also possible that he's one of yours."

"How would that make him one of ours?"

"Everybody knows how you guys feel about Hawaii. That's where all the KGB generals go when they retire."

"That's a cliché."

"Only because it's true. Most likely Haakensen is a freelance spook, picking up work where he can get it. I wouldn't worry about him if I were you. In any case, he's not one of ours, so do with him as you wish."

Tanya nodded. "And what are you hoping to get in exchange for this information?"

"It's not worth much. You can do me a favor somewhere down the road."

"Just how stupid do you think I am? No favors. Payment up front." Tanya took a folded piece of paper out of her clutch. When Gabe reached for it, she drew it back. "It's true that Russians don't smile unless we have a reason to. But we are famous for our sense of humor. Let me tell you a joke: A man walks into a diner and sits down at the counter. He has just lost his job, his wife, and his life savings. He is feeling very close to suicidal. The cook asks him what he'll have, and he says, 'Two fried eggs and a kind word.'

"A few minutes later the cook puts a plate of eggs down in front of the man. He looks up and says, 'How about that kind word?'

"The cook leans forward and whispers in his ear, 'Don't eat the eggs.'"

Tanya handed Gabe the paper. "I was hoping to have something better for you than this, but . . . well. I'm going to give you two things. The first is the address of someone who may be able to help you. She's not aligned with either the Ice or the Flame, and she's got a drinking problem, so she's always in need of money." She tapped the paper. "And the second is a piece of advice. As a fellow human being, I urge you to take it."

"What's that?"

"Don't eat the eggs."

Tanya's apartment in a crumbling *khrushchyovka* in the New Town was like every other apartment she had ever lived in—a Soviet apartment, identical from Saint Petersburg to Kamchatka. The door opened into a hallway with a coatrack on one wall with a rubber tray where one could trade one's shoes for a pair of slippers beneath it. Bedroom to one side, water closet, bath, and kitchen to the other.

The electrical wiring was a disaster. Of necessity, Tanya habitually turned off the lights before plugging in the electric kettle to make tea. Otherwise, she was likely to blow a fuse. Tonight, when the water finally boiled, she yanked the cord, turned the lights back on, and slapped some brown bread and cold fried fish on a plate for a late dinner. Sitting down at the kitchen table, she opened Pritchard's file and began to read.

Haakensen had had an adventurous life, there was no denying that. Much too adventurous for her to take him very seriously. Probably that was all that had kept him alive—being a daring but small fish in a very dangerous ocean. Too small to be of any serious interest to the sharks and orcas that swam there.

When she'd read the précis, Tanya slid out a grainy wire photo of Haakensen in the Atelier Bar in Helsinki. There were more such of him in spy bars in Cairo, London, Johannesburg . . . Looking at them, Tanya had an idea. She felt the corners of her mouth tugging upward.

Tanya got out her typewriter, an elegant little Groma Kolibri with green casing, and set to work.

There were three rocks on the wall again the next morning. Tanya fetched in the newspaper. Today's note read: *Bring me up to date? Let's have bagels for breakfast. Eight o'clock. N.*

It was not exactly a subtle code. Tanya and Nadia met in the Old Jewish Cemetery. It was a cluttered, cold, and morbid place, gravestone upon gravestone upon gravestone clustered ridiculously densely. Here the dead were buried three deep. Tanya could feel the heavy thumb of the past bearing down hard on her whenever she visited this particular spot. But it was a place where they could talk without being overheard. Here she could shout if she wanted to—and today she might well decide to scream.

Nadia was waiting for her at the very center of the graveyard.

Without so much as a hello, Tanya leaned her portfolio against a stone and said, "Tell me exactly what the Ice is doing with the Hosts."

Nadia looked surprised and then bored. "You know all about our relocation program. We—"

"Don't you dare lie to me. I know what you do to them! Andula Zlata trusted me, and I betrayed her. Just as I trusted you. Just as you betrayed me."

"I have no idea what you're going on about." Nadia folded her arms. "I don't think you do either."

"Don't play stupid. I broke into the barge." Tanya saw Nadia's face go stern and blank. Holding back her emotions as best she could, she said, "I saw everything—the bodies frozen in stasis, the hexes holding them there, the blankets so old they were beginning to disintegrate . . . The dust was an inch thick on some of them! I saw a girl there—" She choked with anger, managed to go on. "A girl I'd talked into coming over to our side."

Nadia relaxed. "So that was only you?" she said, amused. "I lost three days moving that facility and trying to track down who had breached our security. You covered your tracks well, incidentally."

Tanya was furious. "I swore to that child on Lenin's grave that we were going to help her. Because I thought it was true."

Glancing away, Nadia said, "You're growing tedious, girl. Live in the moment. Embrace the all. Stop annoying the snot out of me."

"Just who do you think you're talking to? I'm your direct superior!"

"And just who do you think you're yelling at? In the Ice I'm—" Nadia caught herself and stumblingly said, "I'm your fellow soldier. We're on the same side, after all. We shouldn't be arguing like this."

Tanya got it now. The chain of command within the Consortium of Ice was murky at best. One received directions in the form of whispers and hints. Orders arrived unsigned. Duties were simply understood. She was not meant to know who her immediate superior was. And what better way for a superior to hide in plain sight than by working as her subordinate?

"So you lied to that girl," Nadia said. "So she spends the rest of her life asleep. So what? Do you imagine that's not better than what the Acolytes of Flame had in mind for her? Tell me the truth, now. If it were *you*—which option would you choose?"

"I . . . I . . ." Tanya found herself gasping for breath.

Unexpectedly, Nadia laughed. "Oh, you! You should see your face." She punched Tanya lightly on the arm. "Cheer up. The past doesn't matter, and the future isn't here yet. Yes, things may look dark from time to time. But we are alive, and this is good."

Tanya was being thrown a lifeline, and they both knew it. She could grab on to Nadia's words and let herself be pulled back to land, back to her status as a good soldier for Ice. Or she could go rogue and . . . do what? Find common cause with the Flame? Not likely. Try to go independent like Jordan Rhemes? Even if she'd had Jordan's resources—and she didn't—she had family back home who could be made to pay for her disloyalty. Give up magic entirely? There were some things that, once seen, could not be unseen.

All she could do was to stay in place and pretend she liked it.

"I have a present for you," Tanya said at last. She picked up her portfolio and unzipped it. Then she handed Nadia the book Gabe had given her. She had brought it in case she and Nadia made up. Which they hadn't, of course. But she didn't want the thing, in any case. The stench of CIA perfidy clung to it.

A look of spontaneous joy blossomed on Nadia's face. "Cool! I love these guys. Peter Max, Andy Warhol, all of them. So open! So carefree!"

That was one of Nadia's great strengths, that she could compartmentalize her feelings. Her pleasure in the book was doubtless real. But no one who knew her as well as Tanya did could possibly believe they were on a good footing again.

She found the Norwegian sitting at what clearly was well on its way to being his usual booth in Jordan's bar. When he saw Tanya approaching him, he shifted the ashtray to his far side so the smoke from his cigarette would blow away from her. Her opinion of the man inched upward.

"You are Magnus Haakensen," Tanya said.

"Guilty as charged. And you are clearly somebody interesting. Miss—?"

"Tatiana Morozova."

"Miss Morozova, it is a pleasure to meet you. I believe you are precisely the person I am looking for."

At that instant, Frank Sinatra's "Strangers in the Night" began playing on the jukebox. "Dance?" Haakensen asked. Without waiting for a response, he stood and gently tugged her out into an empty space between tables. They slow-danced. Despite the ridiculous disparity in their heights, Tanya had to admit that the man knew how to lead.

"We are drawing attention," she said.

"Look at me. I couldn't be inconspicuous if my life depended on it. Even without the white suit, everybody's going to be watching me. I make a little cash out of that fact from time to time. Somebody needs to do business in a place like this, so they enter two minutes after I do. I walk in with a big smile. I talk people up; I share confidences; I tell stories. I suck up all the attention in the room. Meanwhile, my nondescript partner does whatever it is we came to do and leaves."

"Is that what you're doing here? Drawing attention away from someone?"

"Do you see anybody here I might be distracting attention from? I'm here on my own dime tonight. I'm looking for the other side of the curtain."

"I beg your pardon?"

"Remember how it felt when you first got into the business? How exciting it was to be in on what was *really* going on? You passed through a curtain, and suddenly the things you read in the newspaper made a new kind of sense. Well, over the past few years,

I began picking up on hints that there's a whole other level beyond that one. People chanting at night inside government buildings. Embassy officials crucifying cats in graveyards. A few odd words with no context to make sense of them: 'Ley lines.' 'Ice.' 'Flame.'" Haakensen stared down into Tanya's eyes. "I see that you know what I'm talking about."

"I can't help you."

"Can't or won't?"

"In this instance, they are both the same thing. However, I might have work for you." She named a price and, as expected, his mouth twisted with distaste. The KGB paid its agents notoriously badly.

"Tell me what I want to know, and I'll do your job for free." Sinatra crooned on until, recognizing that he'd been shot down, Haakensen said, "Or I could do it for a kiss."

Tanya raised an eyebrow questioningly.

"I'm a romantic."

"Congratulations. You've put the humorless Soviet bureaucrat off her stride, and she is now so flummoxed you can trick her into saying things she shouldn't. That was your intention, wasn't it?"

Haakensen smiled ruefully. "It was worth a try."

"Do you want the money or not?" Tanya watched Haakensen intently, and when she saw that he was about to shake his head, added, "The organization you're looking for is called the Ice. I'll tell you the name of a city where they're recruiting. After that, you're on your own."

Haakensen sighed. "Give me the details."

4.

It wasn't strictly necessary to have the conference room swept for bugs—the monthly sweep of the embassy had been completed only four days before—but when it came to ANCHISES, Gabe wasn't taking any chances. When the tech crew finally declared the area clear, packed away their arcane electronic gear, and left, he turned to Frank. "It's all yours, sir."

"Thanks." Frank went to the door. "You can come in now."

The man who entered reminded Gabe of nothing so much as a bantam rooster. Compact but tough. He didn't so much walk as strut. His dark brown eyes glittered with energy. Could that possibly be an American flag pin in his lapel? By God, it was. Inwardly, Gabe groaned.

"Boys, this is Dominic Alvarez. He's going to be overseeing ANCHISES."

"You must be Gabriel. Obviously, that makes you Joshua." Alvarez's handshake was strong, fast, efficient: pump down, pull up, release. "Sit down, both of you. I've got something to say before we start." He did not sit down himself. He seemed to be too full of nervous energy for that.

"Everybody has a hobby. Some men collect stamps; others collect blondes. There are people who write poetry, climb mountains, fire guns at paper targets. My hobby is history. Now, I could spend my time refighting the Battle of Waterloo or trying to figure out a way the South could have won the Civil War. Worthy studies, both of them. But my passion is the Bay of Pigs invasion, the most perfect military failure in American history. How did it happen? What lessons can we learn from it? How can we keep from ever doing that again?"

Oh great. Dominic was not only a by-jingo bourbon-and-branch-water flag-thumper, but an armchair general to boot. This was going to be one long afternoon.

Alvarez charged on, warming to his subject. "Now, there were a lot of reasons for the fiasco. The training camps in Guatemala were an open secret. Boats sank on coral reefs that weren't on their maps. The B-26s arrived late, which is why a couple of them were downed by friendly fire—you didn't hear that from me, incidentally. A hundred little snafus went into making the Bay of Pigs invasion the sublime fuckup that it was.

"But they all boil down to one thing: We got cute. What we should have done was go in with everything we had: the army, the navy, the marines, the air force. We would have been in Havana by nightfall, and Castro would be folding laundry in Leavenworth now."

Alvarez paced briskly back and forth as he talked, stopping in his tracks whenever he paused for emphasis. "Now. To ANCHISES. A Soviet scientist wants to defect. We want to help him do so. There are two ways the extraction can be handled. We can go in like the *Mission: Impossible* team with a glittery plan requiring a thousand moving pieces coming together with split-second precision . . . and create another Bay of Pigs. Or we can play it sweet and simple. Which will it be?"

Frank had been slouching in a chair off to one side, staring at the ceiling. "Don't look at me," he said. "I'm hands off, this operation. The only reason I'm sitting here is so I won't look too stupid in front of my superiors if you three jokers screw up."

Gabe cleared his throat. "We were thinking the best way would be two men, a reliable Czech driver, and a Volvo in good repair. Two spare tires and a can of gas in the trunk, a semiautomatic pistol in a clip beneath the dash in case things go haywire. Our man walks in one door, guides the package out another; they get in the car; next thing Sokolov knows he's in Radio City Music Hall, watching the Rockettes."

Turning to Josh, Alvarez said, "That the way you see it too?"

"Sir, it is."

Alvarez slammed his hands together. "Then we are all on the same page. Now, let's get down to brass tacks."

Gabe and Josh had put together a plan that they thought was tight. By the time Dominic was done with it, a drill sergeant could have bounced a dime off its surface and nodded in grim approval. Jingoist or not, Dominic knew his stuff.

They were just wrapping things up when there came a knock at the door, and Frank's secretary entered with a tray carrying four cups of coffee, a sugar bowl, and a pitcher of milk. When the door closed after her, Dominic whistled softly. "Now that's what a secretary ought to look like. Red lipstick and a tight skirt. None of this libber nonsense."

"Look but don't touch," Frank growled. "No intra-office

fraternization while I'm in charge. Understand? It degrades morale."

"Message received, sir," Alvarez said. "Loud and clear. Still, a man can dream. America is the land of dreams, after all."

When the coffee was done, Frank dismissed everybody with: "Good work, all of you." Which, coming from him, was unexpectedly high praise. "Gabe," he added, "you stay behind."

When the others had left, Frank leaned back against the table, a gesture far too casual to be anything but premeditated. "What's your feel for ANCHISES?"

Cautiously Gabe replied, "I am beginning to feel decidedly upbeat about this operation."

Frank took his cigarette out of his mouth, glowered at it as if it were something distasteful, and laid it aside in an ashtray. "I like you, Pritchard. You remind me of a guy in my platoon in Korea, name of Stinky. Good kid. Probably deserved better than the nickname we gave him, but what the hell. We were in the ass-end of nowhere in the ruins of what used to be a village, and the Chinks had us pinned down. Nowhere to run, nowhere to hide. Couldn't even see the enemy; we were firing blind. Then they stopped shooting at us. Sometimes they'd do that, hoping to trick you into standing up. Ten minutes went by, maybe twenty. You have no idea how slowly time can pass under such conditions. Thirty minutes in, by my guess, Stinky raised himself up on his elbows, gave me that big, goofy, shit-eating grin of his, and said, 'I'm pretty sure they're gone, sir.'

"Which is when a bullet ripped through his skull." Frank sighed, stood, picked up his cigarette. "Don't get cocky. I don't want to wind up with your brains spattered across my face."

◆ ◆ ◆

Magnus was in his usual booth in Bar Vodnář when General Bykovsky strode in looking stern and excited, as men tend to be when they get their first taste of spycraft. Assuming all had gone according to plan, just minutes ago the general had received a telephone call from Tatiana Morozova promising to share information of the greatest importance. Without actually having said so, she would have presented herself as an ambitious underling with something juicy on her boss. Bykovsky would have tried to talk her into coming to his hotel, of course. She would have insisted that would not be safe. Finally, they would have settled upon this ostensibly neutral setting. By the way he held himself, the general was carrying heat.

It was astonishing how the least whiff of tradecraft turned grown men, even war veterans, into little boys again, avid to shoot dead every Apache in the playground.

"General!" Magnus said. "Come sit with me."

Bykovsky looked carefully around the bar. Then, face stony, he slid into the booth opposite Magnus. "You know me, then?"

"Beyond the obvious, that you're Soviet military of command rank, served in World War Two, and are currently in Prague as a member of the intelligence community, I have not the slightest idea. My name is Magnus Haakensen, by the way."

A hint of a smirk materialized on the general's face. "'You know my methods, Watson.' I have the posture of a military man and, I flatter myself, the air of authority that befits my rank. My nationality is written on my face, ergo I am Soviet. Given my age, I naturally served in the Great Patriotic War—what Russian did not? But what's this about the intelligence community?"

"I'm in it myself. I know the type." Magnus did not mention the gold-and-steel Rolex peeking out from the general's sleeve:

expensive, obvious, and just a trifle vulgar. The man wearing such a thing would consider himself very important indeed—and other than the IC, what was there in Prague to draw such a personage? Anyway, Tanya had told him all he needed to know about the general. "Also, you *are* in a spy bar."

"I am?" Bykovsky looked about the place with new interest.

"You are. Your Cold War is being fought in a gentlemanly manner. You share a watering spot with your enemy; perhaps you even nod to him as you enter the room. When I was in the Irish Republican Army, we played a rougher game. There were Catholic bars and Protestant bars. You knew which ones you belonged in and which were worth your life to enter. Once, I was sent to Derry—"

"Londonderry, you mean?"

"You see? If we were in Derry—the name you use for the city depends on which side of the struggle you're on—you would have just signed your death warrant. A couple of the boys would leave their stools at the bar, take you by the arms, and frog-march you outside. There'd be a gunshot. A phone call later, somebody would drive up with a car to take away the body. The boys would return to their drinks and when the British Army came by the next day, asking questions, it would turn out that nobody had seen a thing. That's how you fight a guerrilla war. Like Mao said, the people are the ocean in which the revolutionary swims. But I started to tell you about the time I was sent to Derry. There was an informer there who had been responsible for the arrests of three good men, and nobody knew who it was. So I . . ."

Though the general listened with an air of open skepticism, Magnus knew that inwardly he was mesmerized. Soviet spooks all speculated about what they might have been and done in the days of the Russian Revolution, had they only been born earlier. Give them a glimpse of the real thing, of desperate deeds performed under the loosest of supervision, and their fantasies rose up within them to glaze their eyes and drown out all coherent thought.

When the story was done and had drawn a roar of laughter from the general—it was a genuinely funny tale, if a little gruesome around the edges—Magnus lifted an arm to catch the eye of the bartender. "Jordan! Vodka and a plate of bread for my friend." (His two rules for getting along in the world were *Learn the bartender's name* and *Tip well*.) Time now for the changeup. "When the Six-Day War began, I was attached as an observer to the Jerusalem Brigade, which meant that I wasn't supposed to so much as touch a weapon. But guess what? If you grab a rifle in the heat of battle and start firing, nobody complains."

The appeal of a story from behind the Israeli lines was that it gave the general the illusion of insight into the thinking of the other side. Not that Magnus had any such insight to peddle. But he needed to keep Bykovsky's attention, which this particular anecdote did easily.

"You were an observer. For whom?"

Magnus tapped a new Marlboro from its box and lit it with the coal of the old one. "That would be telling. Ah! Thank you, Jordan." He took command of the bottle and poured a shot for his guest.

"*Za zdorovie!*" Bykovsky downed the shot and pinched up a bit of bread to follow it with.

"*Khorosho poshla?*" Magnus asked politely, and Bykovsky nodded.

It was then that Tanya entered the bar. She froze. Magnus had to admire her skill. She feigned shock as well as anyone he'd ever seen—and he had known a great many inherently deceitful people in his time. Gesturing with his cigarette, Magnus said, "Looks like your girlfriend isn't happy about something."

"My—?" Twisting around in his chair, General Bykovsky was just in time to see Tanya's face shift from shock to anger.

She spun around and fled to the street.

Bykovsky went lumbering after her with Magnus at his elbow, unobtrusively hurrying him along, prepared to shove him forward if he hesitated at the door or to grab his arm if he tried to draw his gun. They stepped out of the bar together. And into a barrage of flashbulbs. By the time Bykovsky was done blinking, the car containing the photographer had roared into the night. Tanya was nowhere to be seen.

"You'd better go home and get some sleep, General," Magnus said. "I have a feeling that tomorrow is going to be a long day for you."

Prague after midnight was an unlit necropolis of empty streets. But from the heatless, unlit apartment that was maintained by the KGB precisely because it had a good view of the only hotel in Prague suitable for foreigners who might require surveillance, Tanya could see that the light was on in General Bykovsky's room. Evidently, he was finding sleep elusive. Doubtless, the enigmatic encounter at the bar had set his brain awhirl with speculation and worry.

It was time to make his day worse.

There was a live telephone line in the room, but no phone. No matter, Tanya had brought her own. With pliers and gaffer tape, she swiftly spliced it in. Then she dialed the same number she had called earlier, when she had presented herself as an ambitious and treacherous underling with evidence of misbehavior on Sasha's part. For just the briefest instant, she felt the icy touch of fear. Did she really dare threaten a KGB general?

She did.

In the coldest, most furious voice she could muster, Tanya demanded, "What in the name of hell were you doing consorting with the Norwegian?"

"Norwegian? What are you—?"

"You couldn't possibly be so stupid as to not know who Magnus Haakensen is. You should have shot him on sight. You're in a Warsaw Pact nation, you could have gotten away with it."

Bykovsky made shushing noises. "Now you are talking nonsense, Comrade. Why should I shoot anyone?"

"Don't you dare call me *Comrade*. It's too late for you. I'm going to save myself."

Tanya slammed down the phone. Then she went to the window.

Across the way, the general stood motionless, phone in hand. After some time he put the phone down and slumped into an easy chair.

Standing in the cold and darkness, Tanya projected herself into that despairing silhouette. By now, it would be obvious to him that he had been played for a fool. The question was, by whom? By Tanya? But she had very carefully asked for nothing. His old friend Sasha? The bastard was certainly devious enough to have arranged this. But for what reason? Blackmail? So he would go away and leave Sasha in peace? There were no answers to be had and every question would raise a dozen more in Bykovsky's brain. Paranoia would feed upon suspicion, and both would be fed by ignorance.

Slowly Bykovsky raised his hands to his head. His entire body shook. The man was weeping.

Tanya unspliced the telephone with a smile.

THE WITCH WHO CAME IN FROM THE COLD

5.

Tanya slept late the next morning. She had a leisurely breakfast and then picked up a copy of F. V. Gladkov's *Cement*, which she had been slogging through for some time, and read the last chapters. Then she considered her options. She could go shopping. Or she could do some cleaning. Certainly the apartment needed it. But in the end, she decided to go to the Hermitage show at the National Gallery. She had been in too sour a mood at the opening to enjoy it, and there were paintings on display that were unlikely to ever again leave the Hermitage.

It was midafternoon before Tanya put in an appearance in the rezidentura vault. Time enough, she judged, for things to have shaken down in her absence. The minute she entered, she could sense that things had returned to normal. The cacophonous mix of clacking typewriters and chattering voices had returned to its familiar rhythm. The undertone of hysteria was gone. Not one of the general's men was visible anywhere.

Ekaterina dashed up to clasp Tanya's hands. "I don't know how you did it, Comrade, but thank you." Her eyes shone. Had she been any happier, she would have smiled. Another typist, mousy little Anya, appeared with a cup of tea in her hands and placed it on Tanya's desk.

Tanya gaped at the cup in astonishment. Only Sasha himself possessed sufficient clout to demand that the clerical staff make tea for him, and they despised him for it. But there the cup was, with milk in it too. Then Tanya saw that throughout the vault, the clerical staff had turned their eyes to her. To a woman, they were all silently miming applause.

She felt a flush of unfamiliar solidarity and reddened. "I have no idea what you're talking about. I did nothing."

"Our oppressor suddenly gathers up his hooligans and leaves. The new rules disappear. Work returns to normal. Yet when you walk in, you show not a flicker of surprise. That tells us all we need to know," Ekaterina said. "Oh, and I should mention that you're wanted." She made a little upward jerk of her head. "Up there."

Sasha had restored his chessboards and their men to their usual places. They looked contented to be there. His wretched little bonsai was back too. "Sit down," he said when Tanya entered. Then, gesturing to the board before him: "Give the game a try. Just this once. You can have white."

Tanya stared at the board long and hard. Despite the offer (or maybe command), she did not sit. Then, finally, she pushed a pawn to f3.

Sasha advanced his pawn to e5.

Without hesitation, she moved another pawn to g4.

Sasha slid his queen through the opening he'd created, across the board to h4, putting Tanya's king in check. Quizzically he said, "Fool's mate."

"Congratulations. You win. I see you have your office back."

"It was the oddest thing," Sasha said. "When I came in this morning, General Bykovsky was waiting for me. He looked like the very devil. He demanded to see a file on a tall, white-haired master spy known as the Norwegian. Imagine my surprise to discover that such a file existed. Imagine my astonishment to learn that one Magnus Haakensen, a man I never heard of before today, is considered to be the most dangerous terrorist in all Europe; is allied with MI6, the CIA, and Mossad; and is the mastermind behind half the wars of oppression in Africa."

Tanya said nothing. The specimen sheet for her typewriter was on file, but she had long ago swapped it for that of a machine in the Polish trade mission. Whatever he suspected, Sasha could not be sure of her hand in it.

"Bykovsky had me stand before him like a schoolboy while he read the file. Then he asked for the 'other' photos. I knew my answer would displease him, but having no idea whatsoever what he was talking about, I told him there were none. What else might I have done? What would you have done in my place?" Sasha shook his head heavily, like a weary buffalo. "When I said that, he gave me a look that froze my blood. I fear that Boris Petrovich and I are no longer friends. Then, without saying another word, he swept up all his people and fled. Back to Moscow, I presume."

When Tanya still said nothing, Sasha asked, "Do I want to know the details?"

"No."

"Ahh, little Tanya, more and more I am convinced that you would make an excellent chess player, if only you'd apply yourself to it."

Tanya locked eyes with her superior. Let the bastard experience a touch of fear himself, for a change. Let him think twice before breaking into her apartment again and stealing what was hers. With cold menace, she said, "I don't play games."

The only time Tanya ever wished she could paint was when she stood on the Charles Bridge, savoring the silence of dawn. Every visit was different, and each was beautiful in its own way. Today, silvery mists rose from the frozen river as the sky above the horizon slowly turned palest yellow. The feet of the buildings in the Old Town were as darkly shadowed as the bridge itself, but their upper stories rose into the sunlight to turn eggshell white, and the apricot glow of their tiled rooftops made her soul soar. She came here when she could, though it grew increasingly hard to find the time, to clasp hands with something vital to which she could not put a name.

Midway across the bridge, Tanya became aware of a splash of red on the parapet ahead of her. Blood?

No.

It was a rose.

As she drew closer, Tanya saw that a dark rectangle of duct tape held the rose to the stone so a breeze would not blow it away. Closer still, she saw that someone had leaned a hand on the parapet to melt away the thin skim of ice covering it to give the tape purchase. Pritchard had been here, and not all that long ago. For a moment, she felt an unreasoning outrage at this breach of her privacy. Peeling off her gloves, she ripped away the tape and dropped it into the Vltava. Almost, she threw the rose after it. Was this supposed to be a gesture of thanks? Or was the American boasting that he was not the incompetent he seemed, but capable of ferreting out her most private and cherished habits? Or could it be a threat, a reminder that he could reach into her life anytime he so desired? Did she need to take precautions against him?

Finally, Tanya decided that this was nothing more than classic tradecraft. The American was messing with her mind, trying to make her paranoid, doing his best to throw her off her game.

She scowled down at the red blossom. Again, she felt the urge to fling it as far from herself as she could.

In the end, however, Tanya decided not to throw the rose into the cold waters. Instead, she lifted it to her nose and inhaled. Even in the cold winter air, its perfume was lush and rich.

Briefly—though she knew that it was pointless, for tomorrow would necessarily bring new disasters to which she might or might not be equal—Tanya smiled.

EPISODE 7

RADIO FREE TRISMEGISTUS

Ian Tregillis

Czechoslovak Socialist Republic
February 17, 1970

1.

I t was a ramshackle little place, part stone and part timber, with moss growing between the shingles and bird-bone wind chimes swaying from the eaves. Fifty meters from the nearest road, the cottage hid within a stand of pines in an isolated valley forty kilometers outside town. The roof had a pronounced sag, like a swaybacked horse. A lonely goat chewed cud inside a pen that looked unlikely to withstand the next strong breeze. The wind smelled of pine resin and goat shit.

Finding this place had taken all morning, half a tank of gas, and three stops for directions. Gabriel Pritchard couldn't afford the time, and he couldn't afford to leave a trail of people who might remember a man with a strong American accent. But nor could he keep living with a disembodied spirit lodged in his soul like a couch stuck in a doorway.

So here he was. Hoping like hell he hadn't been played for a fool.

He'd come on the advice of a KGB officer whom, quite frankly, he had no compelling reason to trust. Jesus, they didn't even *like* each other. If he died out here, it might be days or weeks before the CIA found his body—if they ever did. Perhaps he'd die in an ambush today, or be captured. Or perhaps the end would come when the hitchhiker finally burst his skull like an overripe melon.

Fools rush in, he reminded himself. But he knocked anyway.

From within he heard quiet voices and the squeak of a chair. Slow footsteps on creaking floorboards.

A woman old enough to be Gabe's grandmother opened the door. Behind her, bundles of dried flowers and herbs, dozens of them, hung from the rafters. A very large man, bald and meaty, ate black bread at the kitchen table. Too young for a husband or brother. Her son? Grandson?

Tanya had given Gabe an address, referring to a woman who might be able to help. He knew immediately what this place was and whom he'd come to meet.

He didn't know the Czech term. But in Latin America they'd call her a *curandera*.

The old woman was a hedgewitch. A cut-wife.

This was the ragged fringe of the USSR, where local superstitions hadn't been bulldozed by socialist realism. Here the cut-wife solved human problems beyond the purview of Marxism-Leninism. She lived on the outskirts of town because people feared her, maybe even reviled her at times, but they always stopped short of driving her away. Where else would they buy good-luck charms and love potions, have their fortunes divined or their most delicate problems solved with discretion?

For her part, she'd likely been expecting to find a girl on the doorstep. Somebody from one of the surrounding farms. Gabe could picture it now in his mind's eye: a freckled milkmaid—he gave her Pippi Longstocking braids, because why not?—who'd naively spent some unchaperoned time in a hayloft with a charming boy and now found herself in just a little bit of trouble. Such was a cut-wife's clientele.

Certainly she had not expected to find a man in his midthirties on the doorstep. And an American, at that.

They stared at each other for a long, awkward beat. To her credit, she didn't slam the door. She looked him up and down, as if assessing a horse or cow for purchase. He wondered if she'd want to check his teeth, too. Then she narrowed her eyes, and, just for a split second, the hitchhiker stirred.

Damn. She was good.

That's when she made to slam the door. Gabe was faster. He caught the door with his toe. She yelped in protest. The large fellow set down his bread, tugged at the napkin in his collar, and dabbed the buttery crumbs from his lips. Then he pushed his chair away from the kitchen table and stood. He tilted his head far to the left, set his hands on his jaw and scalp, and gave a little tug, cracking the joints in his neck. Then he tilted his head the other way and did it again. It was quite a show. All very deliberate, probably to give unwise visitors time to rethink just how badly they needed to overstay their welcome. Performance completed, he approached the door. His hands curled into fists, undoubtedly anticipating a short, intense conversation with Gabe's face. Gin blossoms pinked the man's nose and cheeks.

She's not aligned with either the Ice or the Flame, and she's got a drinking problem, Tanya had said, *so she's always in need of money.*

Gabe carried a rucksack slung over one shoulder, and he hefted this now. Glass clinked. The old woman cocked an eyebrow.

"*Slivovice,*" Gabe said. She licked her lips. He pulled open the rucksack, just enough to show her the bottles.

Cocking her head ever so slightly, she said over her shoulder, "All is well."

Baby Huey shrugged, turned, and lumbered back to the kitchen table. With the same deliberation with which he had prepared to show Gabe the error of his ways, he sat down, tucked the napkin back in his collar, and spread another spoonful of butter across his bread.

The woman reached for the sack. Gabe handed it over. The witch retreated a few steps, opening the door more widely. He entered. The hitchhiker stirred again; it tweaked his senses. The cottage smelled of freshly baked bread, garlic, thyme, incense, sweat, lavender, and half a dozen additional wildflowers and herbs he couldn't parse. The air within tasted of ash and tickled his tongue with the metallic tang of blood—she'd butchered a chicken sometime in the past few days. His host pointed to a chair beside the hearth. Gabe took a seat while she stowed the booze in a cabinet.

He could imagine the expense report now. *Ninety korunas: plum brandy (six bottles, top-shelf), for bribing the local hedgewitch.*

Baby Huey finished his meal and went outside. Soon the noises of wood chopping filtered into the cottage. The old woman stoked the fire, washed her hands in an aluminum basin, then dragged the only other chair before Gabe. She sat facing him.

"You have a ghost in you," she said. *Přízrak*: Ghost. Phantom. Wraith. Specter.

"Yes."

She took his hands, spit in his palms, slapped them together, and stared unblinking into his eyes. "How long?"

"Two years."

"That long? But you're not dead."

She pulled his hands apart and studied the pattern of spittle. Again, the hitchhiker stirred. She shook her head and dropped his hands as though they were hot coals. He wiped them on his trousers.

"It is in you too deep. I cannot help."

He sagged in his chair. *Damn.* Coming out here had been a move of desperation. Thanks to Alestair and Jordan, he now understood the magical nature of his affliction. He'd even learned to mitigate it, to a limited extent. But détente wasn't enough. He wanted a cure. He wanted his old life back. His old *self.*

Time for plan B, if his Czech was up to the task. Jordan had speculated that the hitchhiker was an errant elemental spirit. If that was true, then it had to have an affinity for a particular alchemical element. If Gabe could at least identify that, he'd have a strong lever for prying the damn thing out of himself once and for all.

"If you can't remove it," he said, "can you at least tell me its name?" *Název*: Name. Title. Her blank expression sent him rummaging his mental filing cabinet for any useful scrap of vocabulary. "Its . . ." Nature. Temperament. ". . . *povaha.*"

"You seek the *druh*?"

He didn't know that word. She answered his shrug in English: "Species."

Gabe nodded. She narrowed her eyes. He got the sense he'd lifted her opinion of him just the tiniest bit. Enough to help?

"That is very difficult," she said.

He pointed to the cabinet. "Too difficult for six bottles?"

This time he couldn't read her expression. But she did open a different cabinet, from which she retrieved a yellowed sheaf of papers. An herbal pharmacopoeia, he realized. Such lore was the lens through which she saw the magical undercurrents of the world. Undercurrents that were fundamentally elemental in nature, according to Alestair, for values of "element" more Mendeleevian than Aristotelian. When she flipped through the pages, he glimpsed astrological and alchemical symbols mingled with artful sketches of what he assumed to be local flora. He knew from his own research that certain plants bioaccumulated particular metals or minerals from the environment. It made a certain kind of sense, then, that a hedgewitch or MI6 sorcerer might make use of their ashes.

She used a mortar and pestle to hold the sheaf open to a long table of symbols: a list of elements and elementals written in several different hands in a hodgepodge of languages. Mostly Czech, of course, but he recognized bits and pieces of Latin, and even some English, as in the phrase "star regulus of antimony," whatever that meant.

They could dispense with three of the classic elements—earth, air, water—right away. He walked on the earth and breathed air literally all day and night, and his body was mostly water. If the hitchhiker were ravenous for any of these things, it would have torn him inside out long ago.

Of the big four, that left fire. The witch nicked his thumb with a knife, smeared the blood on the long stem of a dried nettle, and wrapped this around a candle. She lit the wick and pointed.

Gabe stuck his hand in the flame. And yelped. But the hitchhiker didn't stir. Gabe licked a fresh blister while she crossed off *oheň*.

The processes became more involved as the elements became more obscure. Though Alestair's exercises had proven useless at evicting the hitchhiker, Gabe had to give the old spy credit. Without the benefit of the Brit's tutelage, Gabe would have been utterly incapable of following what she was doing.

Sometimes she'd roll back his shirt cuff, then jab his arm with a long needle. A songbird beak clamped around a fossilized worm dangled from the eye on an almost invisible thread. Then, before the bleeding stopped, she'd press something to the tiny pinprick. It occurred to Gabe that he was undergoing something akin to magical allergy testing. And so it went all afternoon.

Until they got to mercury. For this, she opened the window and slipped a thermometer from its bracket.

Did he feel a little twitch just then? As though the hitchhiker had just rolled over in its sleep? If so, it was subtle, something he wouldn't have noticed prior to working with Alestair. Encouraging, though.

She took a chipped saucer from the cupboard. After working the thermometer free of its frame, she used the blooded knife to etch the glass. Then she snapped the thermometer in two and poured the contents into the dish. The bead of hydrargyrum, water silver, was smaller than the nail on his pinky finger.

He waved his hand over the dish. Nothing happened. The hedgewitch darted forward with the knife. He sighed, but, knowing the drill by now, he let her take more blood. Chanting, she flicked a crimson drop into the dish and then swirled it around until the liquids mingled. Then she gestured at him. He waved his hand over the dish again.

The contaminated mercury sprouted tentacles like a tiny sea anemone and reached for his fingers.

Olly olly oxen free.

Click.

The voltmeter needle swung hard to the right. It quivered like a hunting dog catching the scent of hare on the wind. Sasha dialed down the gain before the overtorqued coil shorted out. The Bakelite knob clunked twice. The needle relaxed, swaying until—like a tipsy sailor—it found an equilibrium that wasn't quite vertical.

He sniffed. A mélange of hot metal and burned lamination wafted from the meter. Or was that coming from the radio? He sniffed again. No, definitely the meter. It was warm to the touch.

The voltmeter would have sacrificed itself if so ordered. Its needle was slim as the line between sedition and loyalty, truth and falsehood, East and West. If only he had such a tool for probing the minds and hearts of those around him. A little red needle to tell him who was good, who was bad, who was loyal, who was not, who could be controlled, who could not. Alas.

He set the tool aside, taking care not to nudge the chessboards arrayed on his desk. One game was barely out of the opening, with Sasha playing a lovely King's Gambit favored by the great Spassky, while the other showed that Sasha's black pieces held a slight but winning positional advantage unless his opponent was crafty enough to force a bishops-of-opposite-colors endgame.

He turned his attention back to the radio he'd confiscated from Tatiana Morozova's flat. Right now it was plugged in to the outlet under his desk, its back cover laid carefully on the desk, a screwdriver and four screws sitting queenward of a forlorn king's bishop. It had taken some concentration to glean a sense of its operation: Sasha's time as a radio operator in the Red Army pre-dated transistors. He missed the triodes' cozy golden glow. The old tubes were superior in so many ways. One could often see a malfunction with the naked eye—a blackened grid, a broken filament. And he'd coaxed more than one broken radio back into operation just by giving it a solid whack. Transistors were too tiny. How could you whack something you couldn't see?

But the voltmeter confirmed that the circuitry worked as he expected. He'd found nothing unusual about the device.

No hidden antenna, no hidden modifications for receiving shortwave broadcasts. He'd managed to summon a voice from it earlier but could not seem able to replicate it. That was both a relief and a disappointment. How much stronger his hold over dear Tanya would be if he had found something truly incriminating. Such as the ability to receive Western number stations. Had there been the slightest possibility that she received coded messages from a handler in the West . . . well, that would have paid dividends for a long, long time.

No matter. He'd keep working on her. What was the next move? He envisioned several lines. The tactical approach: He could confront her directly, dropping the avuncular tone he'd adopted in her flat. But that lacked finesse. Better still, a *zwischenzug*: He could arrange the partially disassembled radio on display behind his desk and then conveniently "forget" about it before calling her into his office. Her roving eyes would get a good glimpse, and Sasha could watch her reaction. Or the strategic development: He could hold back, keep his power pieces in reserve, and slowly draw Tanya out. On balance, he preferred the strategic approach. But he'd keep the equilibrium-threatening in-between move, the zwischenzug, tucked in his back pocket.

For now, then, he'd leave the radio intact and locked in his desk. His army training came to the fore again, prompting him to unplug the radio before reattaching the case. It seemed well-grounded, but one could never be too careful. He waited for the faint hum of energized circuitry to fade. And waited. And waited. It took much longer than he'd expected. Transistors were supposed to be faster than vacuum tubes, weren't they? Perhaps he *was* a little rusty.

He sighed, shook his head, then lifted the cover. But as he flipped it over to ease it into place, something glinted under the fluorescent lighting.

He set the cover down again and rummaged in his desk for a magnifying glass. (A most useful tool. One could never examine photographs too carefully. Even when they came straight from the Kremlin. More than one Politburo member had fallen to an airbrush rather than a bullet.) It took a few minutes of tilting the metal plate back and forth, long enough to start wondering if he'd imagined it, before he saw it again. The faint shimmer of mica flakes. A smear of dirt? The radio had given off the unmistakable odor of singed dust when he'd turned it on—again, like the old tube radios. But no, this wasn't random.

The mineral had been laid down deliberately, painted in lines barely the thickness of a piece of cardstock. Now that he knew what to look for, he saw the ghostly shimmer ranged all over the radio's innards. Somebody had painstakingly inscribed the radio with a nigh-invisible circuit diagram of inert minerals. They couldn't have used a full brush—it must have taken just a single bristle to create such fine lines. This was extremely careful work.

Sasha set the radio down again, smiling. A classic move, and a personal favorite: the discovered check.

CIA Prague Station blew a collective sigh of relief.

It was a restrained relaxation, though, not *Apollo 11* crazy. *That* had been like a Christmas party in July, with an open bar and very good booze, with more than a few valiant souls blitzed out of their minds and perhaps just a bit of clumsy screwing in the broom closets. Nevertheless, the lightened mood hit Gabe the moment he entered the office. He didn't need the hitchhiker redlining his senses to detect an emotional sea change. Even Frank cracked a smile. Gabe marked the day on his calendar.

Over by the coffeemaker, Dominic flirted with Junie from the secretarial pool, who laughed girlishly at something he said. The entire office had warmed to Dom. Even a bullish jingoist could be a breath of fresh air in the tail end of a long winter behind the Iron Curtain.

They'd survived the inspection. The auditors had been most worried about big-picture stuff. Newspaper-headline, Congressional-investigatory-committee stuff. By that standard Prague Station was clean as a nun's knickers. It wasn't as though they'd doped somebody to the gills until he leaped from a hotel balcony, or dosed an entire French village with ergotism. It wasn't the 1950s any longer, for Chrissakes. All Gabe had to hide was accidentally resurrecting a centuries-old golem, plus the fact that it had murdered a policeman. Small potatoes.

Even Josh had weathered the storm. The inspectors had blown through without churning up details of his personal life. That was largely due to Frank. It would be good to raise this delicate point with the kid. This wasn't the time, though—at the moment, the kid sat at his desk looking pensive. He leaned with one elbow on the blotter, head resting against his fist, the other hand desultorily piling paper clips.

"It got to you, didn't it? You've glimpsed the glamorous life of the bean counter and now you're ruined for anything else," Gabe said. "Don't deny you were just daydreaming about paper clip audits."

"I've never seen you this chipper." Josh squinted. "Are you on uppers?"

Gabe imagined this was indeed how a stomachful of bennies

might feel. His visit to the hedgewitch had lifted a burden he'd carried for so long that he'd forgotten what it was like to stand straight without a crushing yoke bending his back. Knowledge was power, and this knowledge would give him the power to evict the hitchhiker once and for all. It made him giddy.

But he couldn't explain this to Josh. "Can't a guy just be in a good mood for a change?"

Josh shrugged. "Well, technically we're on US soil, and it *is* a free country. But give me some time to get used to the new Gabriel Pritchard. I'm accustomed to the moody bastard who likes to throw up on the local constabulary."

Gabe would never live that one down.

"Hey, Rocky, watch me pull a rabbit out of my hat." He leaned over Josh and mimed sticking a finger down his throat. Their laughter drew a few curious glances in their direction.

"Okay, okay. Truce," said Josh.

Gabe grabbed an extra chair. "So what's up?"

"Drahomir. Is he just naturally stiff?"

Ah. "I know you're eager to move things along, but you've got to have patience, okay? You've only been at this a few weeks. Remember, you're playing a long game here. A looong game. Don't think in terms of months. Think in terms of years. Careers."

"I get that. Honestly, I do. But our interaction is a bit chilly. He trusts you; he tolerates me." Josh shrugged. "How do I build on such a brittle foundation?"

Gabe leaned against the desk. "Open up to him a little bit. Make him feel like he's getting something personal from you. You want him to feel like it's a two-way street."

"Such as?"

"Drahomir loves the symphony. Just mention in passing some

concert you attended back in the States. Doesn't matter if it was Beethoven or Three Dog Night. The point isn't to have a conversation about music. Even if he doesn't take the opening, you've given him a point of connection. He'll remember you attend live music. And that's grist for the mill."

Josh mulled this over. Nodded. "Simple. I like it."

Later, Gabe found himself departing the embassy just as Alestair entered, shaking his umbrella. The Brit favored him with a genial nod.

"Good morning, Gabriel."

"Hi, Al."

He was two steps out the door before his thoughts boomeranged back to their shared misadventure in the New Jewish Cemetery. He turned and jogged back inside. "Hey, Al, tell me something. Is that flask of yours a family heirloom or did you pick it up locally?" He lowered his voice. "And did you simply dip it in the river, or did you have to do something special?"

Tonight, as with the past several nights, the clientele at Bar Vodnář leaned to the West. Ever since the Soviet general, Bykovsky, had gotten himself photographed on the doorstep practically holding hands with the Norwegian, traffic from the vodka crowd had been light. That didn't mean it was uneventful, though. Gabe staggered in around eleven.

He scanned the room with bloodshot eyes, looking like the very last thing in the world he needed was a drink. He clutched a handkerchief mottled with rusty stains, Jordan noticed, and kept dabbing it under his nose. But he put on a game face and ventured across the room, sending swirls of cigarette smoke eddying around his head. His legs were wobbly as a newborn foal's, and he stumbled against a table, spilling the drinks of the couple sitting there. After tossing a handful of coins and cash on the table by way of apology, he lurched onward and finally slumped against the bar.

Jordan did a double take. His eyes weren't merely bloodshot—the whites were genuinely red. He'd burst a vessel in each eye. Somebody had worked him over but good. No bruises or swelling, though. That was strange. She studied him more closely. His nose wasn't broken, though it had bled, as had both ears. A thin scarlet crust traced the contour of each earlobe to the hinge of his jaw, and tiny scabs dotted the corners of his eyes like sleep crumbs.

Jordan hastily moved to conclude her current transaction before he scared away one of her special customers. And because her extended clientele was none of his business. Fingers lightly brushing her bracelet, she said to the woman across the bar, "All right. I'll let you have it for twenty. But only because you're a regular and I like you."

Money changed hands, and so did a sun-bleached piece of the Atacama Desert. The woman on the neighboring stool took one look at Gabe, picked up her drink and her new charm, and moved to a booth.

Jordan gave his bloody rag a nasty frown. He stuffed it in his pocket.

Forgoing anything even remotely resembling a preamble, he said, "You were right."

"Of course I was." She stuffed the folded korunas into her pocket, then wrenched the cap from a beer bottle and slid it to another patron. "About what?"

Gabe tapped his temple with a quivering finger.

"Okay. I'll bite. What makes you say that?"

Though he looked ready to keel over at any moment, his eyes widened and his entire manner brightened. His hoarse voice crackled with excitement. He leaned closer.

"I've identified it. I know its affinity."

She blinked. "You don't say?"

He nodded. "I'm feeling very *mercurial* right now."

That sank in. "You're certain?"

"Oh yeah." The high-pitched thread of a madman's desperation wove through his laughter. "Yeah, I'm sure."

"I'm impressed. That must have taken some smart detective work." She looked him over again. Frowned. "So I assume this means you immediately followed it up by doing something dumb."

He tried to look innocent. But having clearly spent the earlier part of the evening bleeding from every orifice, he wasn't selling the schoolboy act particularly well.

"You did, didn't you?"

"Of course not." His hands shook. She could tell he was trying his best to hide it. "But, on an unrelated note," he said, "I will mention in passing that if you're in the market for a new thermometer or barometer, you're probably out of luck for a while. I happen to know that every place in town is out of stock. You can't get one for love or money."

"Pritchard, sometimes, I swear . . ." She clenched her eyes shut and pinched the bridge of her nose, as though fending off the first tendrils of a nasty sinus headache. Which, in fact, she was. She wondered what the symptoms of acute mercury poisoning might be, and whether she'd have to cleanse the bar after he left. Was it her imagination, or was there a greenish tinge to his pallor tonight? "Do I need to call an ambulance for you?"

"I'm fine. Honestly."

"That's a relief. Because you look like five miles of bad road." She reached under the bar and set a shot glass on top. Then she turned, plucked a bottle from the top shelf, and filled the glass with some of the most expensive booze she had on hand. "Anyway, this calls for a celebration. On the house," she announced.

He cocked an eyebrow at her. "Really?"

"Look, if you don't want it—"

"Very generous of you. Much obliged." He laid his hand beside the glass but didn't lift it to his lips.

"Drink up, cowboy, before I regret my good cheer."

He tried. He'd raised the glass about two inches before his fluttering hand slopped fine Kentucky bourbon all over the bar. Jordan snatched the glass from his hand and tossed back what little remained.

"That's what I thought. You did something stupid tonight, and it left you so jacked up you can barely lift a shot glass."

He frowned. "Dirty pool, Rhemes."

"Out with it. What did you do?"

"I tried to evict it."

All that blood . . . "Did you try to *cut* it out?"

"Of course not. I thought drawing it out would be easy. Seemed like it should be, uh, straightforward."

She pinched the bridge of her nose again. This headache wasn't going anywhere.

"I know you don't remember how it got there in the first place, Pritchard, but you can take my word for it. And maybe you'll notice I don't use words like 'easy' and 'straightforward.'" She sighed. "So what happened?"

"Before or after two ounces of liquid metal tried to climb up my nose?"

Jordan leaned left and right, squinting at the sides of his head. "Your nose?"

"And my ears, my eyes . . ." He trailed off, shifting uncomfortably on the stool. "Other places," he murmured.

Forget cleansing the Vodnář. She'd have to burn it down.

"Oh my God, Pritchard. I swear, if you start shitting blood in my bar, I truly will murder you."

He swayed. For a moment she thought he was going down, but he grabbed the brass rail at the last second and righted himself. "How would you get rid of it, then?"

"I don't know," she admitted. "Let me make a call."

Alestair arrived just before closing. He hung his umbrella on the bar, doffed his hat to Jordan ("Miss Rhemes, enchanting as ever, my dear"), and glanced at Gabe ("Good heavens, lad"). Jordan poured him a brandy while Gabe filled him in. She kept a hand on her bracelet in case the late-night patrons tried to listen.

Gabe concluded, "So. Knowing the hitchhiker's identity, can you help me get rid of it?"

"I have an inkling." Alestair shared a look with Jordan. The Brit frowned just a bit, calculating. What was he up to? "But I'm uncertain that it would be best for us to help you."

"Oh come on, Al. I obviously can't do it myself."

"You've demonstrated that with admirable clarity. I mean, have you considered appealing to Miss Morozova for assistance?"

Gabe groaned. He slumped over the brass rail and pressed his forehead to the polished wood. Jordan snatched a dishrag and tried to remember where she'd put the bleach.

"I know what you're doing," he said, his voice muffled. "Have you forgotten she's KGB? She might as well be radioactive." Then he sighed. "Do you think she can help?"

"I do. But are you certain you've given this due consideration? Yours is a unique situation. Don't be hasty." Alestair finished his brandy. "Haste makes waste."

Gabe hopped from the barstool on wobbly fawn legs. "Go jump in a frozen river. Both of you."

2.

The next day, while finishing his early breakfast of weak coffee and cold toast, Gabe glanced over the newspaper. And almost did a spit take. A body had turned up near the Legion Bridge. The man had been strangled and beaten with tremendous force—like the policeman the golem had killed in the cemetery. But the newest victim was a member of the Státní bezpečnost. State security: the Czech secret police.

Now even the reputable papers were speculating openly about the sightings of a strange figure and whether they were connected to the two recent deaths. But the average man and woman on the street would naturally assume the StB officer had been killed by sinister Western provocateurs. And that logic kept most people from using the word "golem." For now.

CIA Prague Station had picked up the bad news over the wire. The light atmosphere of the previous few days was nowhere in evidence. Nobody lingered around the coffeepot this morning. It was all hands on deck while their captain stood just outside his office, barking orders.

"We need to know the story here," Frank said. "Because in about"—he glanced at his watch—"three hours the early risers in Washington are going to see this on the wire, and we'd better have some goddamned answers by then."

By now the news was already old in Moscow. The Soviets took pride in their orderly cities. Rampant murders were a symptom of the sickness of capitalism; they did not happen in a workers' paradise. Which meant the CIA's local KGB counterparts were under twice as much pressure to find an answer. An answer that would almost certainly involve heaping blame upon the Western services.

Frank continued, "And we need to know who our friends think might be doing this. Everybody from loudmouthed students to escaped circus bears."

One didn't have to squint very hard to see the murders as a statement about the ouster of the Dubček government. The Soviets would see that angle: retaliation for the brutal crackdown on the Prague Spring. And they'd assume the West was stoking those coals. Which they'd use as an excuse for retaliation. Meanwhile, the Western services, suspecting the deaths to be false flag work, would cast equally wary gazes back across the Curtain. The rival services would be circling each other like feral tomcats.

Gabe rubbed his temples. Despite the risk to his career—and, given what the Ice did to people like him, perhaps his very life—he'd arranged to meet Tanya this afternoon. She'd be in a swell mood, no doubt.

"I only care about three things." Frank's prosthetic pushed little divots into the linoleum floor while he paced. It reminded Gabe, not for the first time, of Captain Ahab's whalebone leg. "I care about clean hands." *Stomp, stomp.* "I care about heading off every possible avenue our *KaGeBeznik* friends might use to connect this to us." Frank turned the corner, completing his circuit of the room. "And I care about keeping my people safe. As long as we don't know who's doing this, we don't know who they might target next. Doesn't matter if it's a lone lunatic or a crew of political radicals. As much as I hate calls from Washington, I hate calling next of kin even more." Standing again in the door to his office, Frank said, "We can be sure the local authorities have already drawn up a list of suspects."

They'd be combing those lists even now, Gabe knew. But the killer wasn't a political radical. It wasn't human.

Casually Gabe said, "The papers are drawing a connection to sightings along the river."

Josh's eyebrows tried to climb onto his scalp. "The 'golem' sightings?" He wiggled his fingers, putting scare quotes around the word. "You don't believe that."

"Of course not. But the return of the legendary golem, a protector of the oppressed, would make an excellent symbol for a dissident group chafing under friendly Soviet rule, wouldn't it?"

Frank chewed on this. "Long shot. But yeah, okay, I can see it." Gabe relaxed. Frank never wasted more than one officer on a wild-goose chase. He could still make his meeting with Tanya. "Sniff around, that's it. You smell anything fishy, you come straight back here."

"I understand."

Frank said, "Everybody else, put feelers out. Call on your developmentals and local contacts. Find out what they know. What they've heard. What they've heard other people have heard. Get everything."

Gabe headed for the coatrack by the door. Dominic raised a hand as if he were in a classroom. "I don't have any local connections, sir. What should I do?"

"You can go keep Pritchard out of trouble. Normally that's Toms's job."

Damn it.

Josh opened his mouth to object, but Dom cut him off with a slap on the back that echoed through the office. "I'll try to live up to your example," he laughed. Then he joined Gabe at the coatrack. "I can drive. It'll help me learn my way around."

Did Dominic notice the split second hesitation while Gabe again recalculated his day? He covered with a smile, making certain it crinkled the corners of his eyes. So genuine.

"Sure. That'd be great. Along the way I'll show you where the good cafés are."

"Now we're talking."

Gabe followed him out the door, pausing momentarily to throw an apologetic shrug at his partner.

The Moskvich bumped over a set of tram tracks. Gabe pointed to the left.

"That place makes excellent koláče. Probably the best in town. But"—he shook his head—"the baker's husband is an StB informant. So tread lightly."

"I'll stay out of there."

"Well, don't be rash. Seriously. Try their koláče."

"You're a hell of a tour guide, Pritchard." Dominic downshifted as they turned a corner. "So what's the angle here?" He brought the car to a smooth stop at a light.

"Angle?"

"Yeah. What's really going on? I've been around. I've seen some weird shit, okay? But then I get to Prague, and the moment there's a chance to take a breather people start chasing mythical creatures."

"Hey, I'm not the one who brought up the golem."

Dominic chuckled, shook his head. "Potato-eatin' peasants. Crazy."

He released the clutch so smoothly the finicky Moskvich barely hiccupped. Gabe was glad they had somebody so capable on board for ANCHISES. Short of political assassination, pulling a defector from the Iron Curtain was just about the trickiest operation a team could mount.

"Look, I don't want to step on any toes," Dom said, "and I'm not looking to put you on the spot. But I need to know if this will complicate the extraction. You seem plugged in. Will this splash back on us?"

"This isn't an op gone wrong, if that's what you're wondering. Not one of ours, anyway."

Dom turned past the National Theatre, heading for the Legion Bridge. He cleared his throat. "I gotta ask you something else. And it's not personal, okay?"

Gabe did not like where this was going. But he clung to the mask of cheerfulness. "Fire away."

Dom took his eyes off the road for a split second to nod at Gabe's hip. "I notice you touch that flask in your pocket every time somebody mentions the golem."

Gabe reeled as if slapped. He'd developed a tell. Dom hadn't been here a week, but already he was reading people like he'd known them for years.

I have to ditch this guy. I have to ditch him now. He'll sniff out Tanya in a heartbeat.

Dom continued, "Listen. I'm not passing any judgment, okay?

I'm no saint, believe me, and I'm not pointing fingers. You ever get posted to Buenos Aires, ask about me and you'll hear stories. But I need to know right now if you have a problem that'll become my problem."

"You can relax. It's not booze." Gabe squirmed in the seat to pull out the flask. "It's a good-luck charm."

Dom gave him the side-eye. "Lotta drunks say that."

"No, honestly." Gabe unscrewed the cap and held the open flask under Dom's nose. "Give it a whiff."

He did. And scowled. "What the hell?"

"River water."

"Remind me never to take a swim around here." Dom shifted again as they approached another turn. "I've seen some superstitions in my day, but that's a new one. I'll bet there's a hell of a story behind that flask."

Brother, you have no idea. "My priest gave it to me," said Gabe. "I'm supposed to keep holy water in it."

Dom laughed again. A genuine, full-belly laugh. He slapped the steering wheel. "I *knew* I would like Prague."

You're too good, Dom. Too good to be anywhere near me.

Gabe closed his eyes, leaned back in the seat.

"You okay?"

"Yeah. Little headache is all."

Gabe called up the exercises Alestair had taught him. He centered, focused, reached inward. Reached for the hitchhiker. Nudged it like a drowsy girlfriend's shoulder. *Wake up, sleepyhead. You want mercury? I know where you can find a nice juicy gob of it.* The Moskvich's trunk light operated by a simple mercury switch, turning on when the tilt of the open trunk sent a little bead of liquid metal rolling downhill to connect a pair of terminals. Gabe

THE WITCH WHO CAME IN FROM THE COLD

pictured this now. The hitchhiker stirred. *That's it. Wouldn't you love that delicious metal . . .* For a split second, he could have sworn he felt the mercury splaying against its glass cage, trying to slither toward him, desperate to merge—

Dom slammed on the brakes. The car skidded over uneven cobbles. "Gabe! Talk to me."

Gabe opened his eyes. They hurt. His face was warm and wet, he realized. He was bleeding from the nose and eyes again. He hoped those were the only places. Blood dripped from his chin and stained his shirt.

"Don't worry," he said. "It's not contagious."

Dom fished out a handkerchief. "Yeah, great, but what the hell is it?"

Gabe coughed. Blood had trickled down the back of his sinuses to tickle his throat, too. "Little souvenir from my time in"—for a split second he almost said *Egypt*—"the jungle. It comes and goes."

Dom narrowed his eyes. Calculating: He'd heard things about Gabe. Gabe remembered how Dom schmoozed the secretarial pool.

"You've kept this from the company medics." A statement, not a question. He'd heard things *and followed up on them.* Thorough. Dangerous.

"Yes," said Gabe.

He glanced at the handkerchief. Extemporaneous lies were anathema to good tradecraft. His mind raced. Lies worked best when they were mostly true. So he worked up his best preconfessional sigh, the sigh of a man gearing up to admit his darkest secret.

"Dom. Here's the thing. Nobody knows about this, okay? Josh suspects something's up, but I've managed to do some damage control in his direction. Frank will look the other way but only to a point. If this gets into my file, Langley will yank me stateside. It'll be the end of my career."

Dominic pulled a cigar from the inner pocket of his jacket. To Gabe's relief, he only chewed on it, rather than lighting it in the close confines of the Moskvich. Finally, he said, "My lips are sealed. For the moment. But if I suspect for one second this will compromise ANCHISES . . ."

"It won't. But I understand. Thanks, Dom."

They shook on it.

"Okay. Now what?"

Gabe suppressed a sigh. "Drop me at my flat." He gestured to the handkerchief. "It's rarely this bad. I'll be fine if I can lie down for a while."

Dom dropped the cigar in his pocket and slid the shuddering Moskvich back in gear. "Can do, chief."

"And here you thought keeping me out of trouble would be a cakewalk."

Gabe really did need to return to his flat. He had to change clothes before meeting Tanya. Showing up covered in blood would draw all kinds of attention their rendezvous didn't need. He stayed in his apartment long enough to make it look like he had taken a nap, just in case Dom was suspicious and chose to linger nearby. Then he slipped out the back.

He felt particularly self-conscious as he left his apartment building. It had taken a bit of effort to mollify Josh and get things back on an even keel. Now he had to start all over with the new guy. Dom seemed pretty okay, and that wasn't something Gabe said about every backslapping jingoist he met. But he'd have to

THE WITCH WHO CAME IN FROM THE COLD

step lightly around the man from now on. At least until he got rid of the hitchhiker once and for all.

You're already lying to your colleagues and collaborating with a KGB officer. At what point will the cost of this exorcism be too dear?

The ancient fort of Vyšehrad commanded a magnificent view of the Vltava. The twin neo-Gothic spires of the Basilica of Saint Peter and Saint Paul towered nearly two hundred feet over the river. Academic lore dated parts of the fortress all the way back to the Dark Ages; local lore said the hilltop was also the spot where the witch prophetess Libuše had envisioned the city of Prague.

Gabe had shed his coat by the time he passed, puffing and sweating, beneath the arch of Tábor Gate. It was a long, tall hill. And it didn't stop rising after he entered the Vyšehrad grounds. He'd changed out of his bloodstained shirt, but its replacement was damp with sweat by the time he turned right at the more ornate Leopold Gate. From there he stalked past a Romanesque rotunda, through manicured lawns and tidy white buildings with red slate roofs. Lovely place, even in winter. He'd have to come back in the summer, when the grass was green and the trees weren't bare. He checked his watch, then picked up the pace as much as he dared, trying to hurry without looking like somebody in a hurry. He passed a tripod of stone columns known locally as the Devil's Column and, finally, entered the cemetery adjoining the basilica.

Wandering through the graves, he took time to run his eyes over each inscription like a curious tourist. He seemed to be spending a lot of time in famous graveyards lately. Was that a reflection of Prague, or of him? Finally he spotted the KGB officer in a corner of the arcade that bounded the cemetery. She stood with hands in her pockets, gazing down at a tomb marker.

She wasn't alone. Her pal, the tall brunette, lingered nearby, carefully contemplating a gravestone, with a clear view of Tanya and anybody approaching her. Prague Station had a file on her: Nadezhda Fyodorovna Ostrokhina. AKA Nadia.

Gabe hesitated. He'd already told Frank about an earlier contact with Tanya; he had to step lightly in his next report, now that their interaction was a matter of record. Repeated contacts with the same *KaGeBeznik* would raise eyebrows. But meeting with *two* known officers . . . And that was just the spycraft angle. The Ice had a special boat for people like him. Were the Russians here as spies intent on squeezing a CIA agent, as sorceresses intending to capture a magical pawn, or both?

He backed off, did another sweep of the grounds. If the *KaGeBezniks* had other allies on-site, he didn't sniff them. Still, he considered waving off entirely. Would have, too, if not for the voice in the back of his head.

I could be myself again. Have my old life back.

His footsteps echoed beneath the groined vaults of the arcade. He came to a casual stop before a marble bust. Tanya dropped a flower on the grave of Antonín Dvořák. He recognized the blossom he'd left for her on the Charles Bridge, much worse for wear. She studied him from the corner of her eye. He tipped his head, ever so slightly, toward her companion.

"Well aren't you just two peas in a pod," he murmured. The KGB officer furrowed her brow. But she was too stubborn to admit she didn't understand the idiom. "We have a saying. 'Two's company; three's a crowd.'"

"Too bad," she said. But the glance she shot in Nadia's direction wasn't entirely friendly.

Oh ho. You didn't want her here either. Just how are things at the KGB these days?

And then, covering her tracks, she elaborated. "I'd be a fool to meet alone with you."

"I'm not crazy about this either, sweets."

"I didn't ask for this meeting."

Slowly he worked his way closer. Whispers carried under the arcade. He didn't know where to begin. "I need your help."

Tanya frowned. Another voice said, "We don't handle defections."

The other woman had joined them, he realized. She was dangerous. He remembered how easily she'd tricked Josh. It wasn't a simple disguise the night they'd followed Tanya and the student; he was certain Nadia had used magic as part of her decoy deception. Her stealth knocked him off balance.

He blurted, "I have something inside me."

His voice echoed. The few others strolling in the shadow of the basilica turned to stare. The three spies strolled in silence past the graves of Czech national heroes until the awkward moment passed.

"Hear me out, okay? It's a long story."

Tanya studied his face, his bearing, for a long beat before gracing him with a microscopic nod. Magnanimous.

"It started in Cairo," he said. He outlined his Egyptian misadventure for them, skipping over the part about surveilling Mossad officers (no reason to give the KGB information about the CIA's capabilities in the Levant) and instead emphasizing Jordan's hypothesis that he'd disrupted a major sorcerous work by Flame magicians. He figured that should win him some points with the Ice witches.

By the time he got to the mercury, Tanya was staring at him as though he'd grown a second head. Nadia took her elbow and pulled her a short distance away. They consulted in low voices. The consultation quickly turned into an argument, both women taking turns to flick glances in his direction. It grew heated; their hissing at each other sounded like Medusa's worst hair day.

"I'm not jerking you around. You wouldn't believe what it took to ditch my partner this morning."

Nadia turned from Tanya to look at him. "Oh, yes, Mr. Toms. And how is Joshua enjoying his first overseas posting?"

Oh, you slimy commie. Gabe played along, though. If they hadn't yet pinged to Dominic's arrival in town, he sure as hell wasn't going to tip them off. "Josh hasn't forgotten the way you led him on a wild-goose chase, if that's what you're wondering. He's eager to catch up with you sooner rather than later."

He didn't know if their English was good enough to catch the double meaning. All the better. Let them chew on it a while.

Tanya looked unconvinced, too. He looked her in the eye. "The hitchhiker," he whispered, "sometimes makes me feel as though I'm *floating.*"

Her eyes widened. She got it: The hitchhiker had led him to the barge. And then she flicked another razor-sharp glance at her comrade.

Interesting. So the Ice's cozy little barge is part of your tiff, eh?

Nadia said, "If what you say is true, then you should come with us right now. We can protect you."

"Does your offer come from the KGB or the Ice?"

"That depends," she said, touching a charm bracelet. It reminded him of Jordan's trick for discreet conversations. "Are you an American intelligence officer or a man suffering a magical illness?"

A false dichotomy. He conceded the point.

"This thing is dangerous," he said.

"So are we," said Tanya. "So are you."

"Not like this." And he told them about the golem.

This time the Russian invective was aimed at him. He got it in stereophonic hi-fi. Tanya looked ready to kick him in the nuts. Nadia—a boxer, according to her file—clenched her fists. He kept an eye on her. He was slightly taller, but she carried herself like somebody with a mean left hook.

Nadia scowled. "Have you any idea how much trouble your experiment has caused us?" That was the KGB officer speaking, he knew.

"No, of course I don't. Because nobody in *my* office cares about a string of dead policemen. How could that possibly bother *us*?"

"If we help you rid yourself of this encumbrance," said KGB-Tanya, "you'll become a more efficient officer. We do not benefit."

"What about the Ice? What about sticking it to the Flame?"

He could see the gears turning. She twisted her head aside, concentrating. She was nibbling the hook. *Come on,* he thought, as though he could mentally nudge her. But then her eyes focused on the distance, and just like that the twist turned into a hard shake. The glazed eyes were those of somebody looking inward, not outward. She was seeing something he couldn't. But it scared her, and that he *could* see.

"No. I cannot."

The spy in Gabe, the part of him that didn't care at all about magic and elementals and golems and secret sorcerous factions, sat up straight. He'd just glimpsed a vulnerability. Her Achilles' heel?

One fingerhold. That's all it took. That, and patience. If, over enough time, he could subtly exploit that weakness, like rain eroding a mountain . . .

Let Josh have Drahomir. Maybe I can flip this KGB witch.

But that was a vision in some distant future. He needed her help sooner than that. So he went for simple honesty.

"Please. This thing . . . it's destroying me. Maybe we can help each other?"

3.

Sasha abandoned the voltmeter. It was the wrong line of inquiry. The exact purpose of the mineral circuit inscribed inside the case still eluded him. But, like a broken pawn chain, it was the watershed. Now he understood the *true* nature of the problem. Tanya's radio wasn't an electrical puzzle. It required a very different approach. An approach he didn't dare attempt in his office. One that nobody could witness.

He lived alone in his two-bedroom khrushchyovka, but the second bedroom was not for sleeping. It had no bed—just shelves, cabinets, a workbench, and several very old books. And a series of wards he'd installed by himself.

He set the radio on the bench. Then, from one of the cabinets, he produced an eclectic collection of crystals, flower blossoms, and tarnished silverware. These he arranged in the corners of the room. Some he laid inside special chalk marks on the floor; others he placed in iron baskets suspended from the ceiling. Then he placed a thumbnail-size piece of patinaed copper mesh on his tongue and spoke the appropriate incantation.

The room instantly went from merely quiet to utterly still. It was as though the outside world had disappeared.

He removed the copper mesh from his mouth and set it on a towel. Only now, with the magical Faraday cage hermetically sealed, did Sasha turn his full attention to the radio. First, he removed the case again. He studied everything not with a technician's eyes but with a sorcerer's inner sense.

He plugged it into the outlet. As in his office, it functioned like a perfectly normal radio. When he twisted the dial, the speaker hissed nothing but static. Remembering how the circuitry had taken so long to de-energize, he unplugged it again . . . and now, with his inner eye wide open, he felt a tingle.

Such magical craftsmanship! So orderly. So precise. Almost crystalline. This was the work of an Ice sorcerer.

But to what end? He'd find out sooner or later. What one sorcerer could do, another could undo. What one spell could weave, another could unravel.

Sasha's magic could melt this Ice. That's what Flame did.

He touched the tuning dial; the static hiss grew stronger. The static took on a strange warble, as though the radio were pulling down a signal from very far away. He kept turning the dial. Slowly. Slowly . . .

The tingle became a spiritual jolt that almost knocked him from his chair. The static disappeared. And then the unplugged radio spoke in an old man's voice. "Tanushka? Are you there, little bird? What matters must we discuss?"

Tsk-tsk, Tatiana Mikhailovna.

The construct prattled, "Why won't you speak to your lonely grandfather, little Tanushka?"

Sasha smiled. "I'll speak with you, dear *Dyedushka*."

A staticky pause. For a moment Sasha thought the spell was broken. Then the construct said, "You're not Tatiana."

"No," Sasha said, "I am not. But tell me something, Grandfather. Do you play chess?"

She'd come to hate this time of night.

The darkest, quietest hours were when visions of Andula Zlata infiltrated Tanya's dreams. The student she'd worked so hard to save, she and Nadia. Her trusted partner . . . or so Tanya had thought. But Nadia had deceived Tanya, and now poor Andula was stacked and stored like frozen cargo on the Vltava barge.

When the clock ticked three and her nerves still thrummed, as they had all day, Tanya threw off the blanket.

It was Gabe's fault. *Damn you, Pritchard.*

His story, his pathetic appeal, was too ludicrous even for the most desperate CIA dangle. Yet somehow he had found the barge, a moving site virtually invisible to scrying, while a complete new-comer to the secret world of Ice and Flame. But what kept her awake all night was the look on Nadia's face when Gabe spoke of the hitchhiker.

Like a starving wolf glimpsing a lame caribou.

Hiding her disgust had been one of the hardest things Tanya had done in recent days. It was like trying to swallow broken glass. And now here she lay in the middle of the night: jaw clenched, mind racing, stomach roiling.

The foolish American might as well have begged Nadia to abduct him and put him under stasis. Maybe he'd land on the cot next to Andula. Tanya should let him. He was a Western intelligence officer; she benefitted from his troubles. If only it were that simple.

Because as much as she hated to admit it, she needed Gabe's help as much as he needed hers.

She needed to get her radio back. Every day Sasha held it—every hour—the danger grew that he might uncover its true significance. If Gabe had stumbled into their secret sorcerous world, surely others could too. And Comrade Komyetski was *already* looking for reasons to question her loyalty: Nadia had warned her, weeks ago, that he expected her to monitor Tanya. Her own safety, and her grandfather's, depended upon keeping the radio secure. Meanwhile, she desperately needed the counsel of her grandfather's construct. To tell him what she'd learned about the Ice, to ask him what it meant. She needed his reassurance.

She needed that damn radio.

She didn't dare enlist Nadia in a move against Sasha. So she couldn't trust anybody in the Ice, which was a new and startling truth, nor could she trust anybody in the KGB, which was a truth of the familiar but wearying kind.

At least Tanya knew where she stood with Gabe.

And in the end, she preferred the devil she knew.

The trick would be in taking the radio back from Sasha without his realizing they'd taken it. Which meant they had to replace it with a replica.

First problem: They didn't have an exact replica.

"I'll sell you charms," said Jordan, "at the regular price. Which you should consider generous, given what you owe me."

Gabe placed his empty glass on a handful of neatly folded korunas and a slip of paper. He slid it all across the bar. "No charms. I need something else."

"You really know how to push your luck, Pritchard."

"I thought you'd enjoy a fun challenge. I'm paying for it, aren't I?" Well, he and Tanya together.

Jordan moved his empty glass into a bus bin beneath the bar in one smooth motion. The money disappeared almost like a magic trick. She glanced at the note. Frowned. "Give me a few days."

Three nights later, two spies sat in a dark car. To any passersby peering through the steamy windows, they'd look like a couple having an illicit rendezvous.

But there was nothing sexual about the tension filling the space between them. It was the uneasy thrum of being vulnerable, of willingly opening the door to one's enemy. The tension of unwanted symbiosis.

Nothing would save Tanya if she were discovered in a car with a known CIA officer. Proximity to Gabe put a queasy lump in her stomach.

"Show me."

Gabe whisked a blanket from the replica on the backseat. "Ta-da." He watched her expression in the moonlight. "Please tell me it's a match."

She shook her head. *"Nyet."* And then she reached into her pocket and flicked open a knife.

He raised his hands. "Hey! Hold on a second."

She twisted in her seat, reached past him, and hauled the radio onto her lap. His aftershave smelled of lemongrass. She clenched her eyes and concentrated.

Several minutes passed. Gabe broke the silence, startling her. "Whatever you're trying to do, the spell isn't working. Otherwise the hitchhiker would be rattling its cage right now. And by 'cage' I mean 'my skull.'"

Americans. They loved the sounds of their own voices.

"Do you always talk this much?" She opened her eyes again. "I wasn't casting a spell. I was remembering."

She pressed the tip of the knife into one of the knobs and, very, very slowly, carved a small chip out of the plastic. Next, she dragged the blade over the metal case, which elicited a toe-curling screech as she did her best to reproduce a distinctive scratch.

"There," she said, folding the knife away. "Now it's a little better."

"A little?"

"The plastic trim is yellowed here," she pointed, "and here. But I don't know how to replicate that."

"I do." Now it was his turn to reach into a pocket. He produced a small vial of topical iodine, the kind used to disinfect minor cuts and bruises, along with a handful of cotton balls. "I stopped at a pharmacy on the way home this evening." She frowned at him; he shrugged. Almost apologetically he added, "Cheap Soviet plastics aren't known for their durability."

Half a dozen "what about"s leaped to mind. But she bit back on her retort. She sighed. "Resourceful."

"The iodine takes about twenty minutes to soak in. It'll set semipermanently if we let it sit overnight." He cleared his throat. "Or so I'm told."

She took the bottle. When she broke the seal, a faintly oceanic scent filled the car.

Second problem: Tanya didn't know where Sasha kept the original. It was possible he'd taken it home. That would require a team of lamplighters. But Gabe wasn't about to request that Frank authorize a penetration of the home of his own counterpart in the local KGB. Merely broaching the subject would be professional suicide. It would be even worse if Komyetski were keeping the radio in his office in the Soviet embassy. Authorization for an operation like that would have to go through levels so far above Frank's head one would need a telescope to see them. They would have to lure Sasha out, radio in hand.

A timid knock pulled Sasha from his contemplation of the transcript of a recent Komsomol meeting. A welcome diversion. Unless it was Kasimir coming to reiterate, yet again, his theory about NATO conspiracies to manipulate wheat prices.

"Enter, please."

It wasn't Kasimir. It was Tanya. "Sir, may I speak with you?"

"Of course. Always." He set the transcript aside, giving her his full attention. She closed the door. "How may I aid your struggles in defense of the motherland?"

She fidgeted. She kept her eyes on the floor, on her shoes, as though she couldn't bear to meet his eyes.

Finally, she said, "Recently, you . . . found something."

Aha. The strategic approach had worked. He'd been right to keep the zwischenzug in reserve. Sasha concentrated on keeping his expression clear of anything but the utmost sincerity. When a smile threatened to tug at the corners of this mouth, he deported it to the endless steppe.

"Why so despondent, Tatiana Mikhailovna? I told you I would take care of the problem, and I have. You needn't worry about others misconstruing what was surely an innocent misunderstanding."

"Of course, sir. And I'm very grateful to you." With visible effort, she stopped fidgeting. She looked up. "Soon after his arrival, General Bykovsky approached me privately. He wanted to verify the item was safe. I thought—well, I remembered what you had told me, so I reassured him. I let him believe I still had it."

"How did he know you held it?"

She shrugged. She looked ready to cry. "Moscow Center ordered me to take it to Prague, where somebody would retrieve it, and to tell nobody. I didn't know I'd have to wait so long. At first I thought it was meant for you. But then he asked . . . I was afraid to tell him I'd lost it."

He tented his fingers. Leaned forward. Nodded slowly. He was every inch the attentive listener. It encouraged her. She continued.

"A few days later he told me we would together deliver the item to a particular car parked near the *Prašná brána*." The Powder Gate. "A green Moskvich. I started to panic. I didn't know what I was going to do."

Is this why you sped along my old friend's departure, Tatiana Mikhailovna? Or have you finally joined me in a game of chess?

"I see," said Sasha. He stroked his chin. "What did you do, Tanya?"

"Nothing. That was the day of his . . . unfortunate circumstances." She looked down again. "I'm ashamed to say I was deeply relieved by his misfortune. I chose to pretend he'd never had a chance to tell me about the delivery."

Sasha nodded. "I understand. You were caught in a difficult situation. But why are you telling me now?"

"I passed the Prašná brána this morning. The car is there, sir. A green Moskvich, just as he described."

Oh, Tanya. He stroked his chin, watching her. The tears were a nice touch. *Is this your gambit? You'll suggest the errand should be completed, yes? That we should deliver the radio? And soon after that, when old Sasha considers the matter settled and the item long gone, it will secretly find its way back to you.*

"What do you suggest we do?"

"I don't know." She took a steadying breath. "But given his manipulation by that Westerner, I worry. Sir, what if this errand was orchestrated by our enemies?"

Sasha couldn't help but smile. No transparent gambits for little Tanya. She had played her own zwischenzug. He hadn't expected this. Clever.

He willed an avuncular gleam into his eyes. Still smiling, he said, "You think we should use the radio as bait and see who takes it."

She shrugged. "If I were not personally involved, I know it is the course I'd recommend. In this matter . . . well. I must rely on your judgment, sir."

The worst thing about hiding inside the trunk of a parked car wasn't the painful contortion. It wasn't the tire iron jabbing his ribs. It wasn't even the cold. It was keeping the hitchhiker in check while the liquid metal in the mercury switch just inches from Gabe's head kept sloshing against its glass bulb like a tiger trying to leap through the bars of its cage. If it broke free and tried to join with the hitchhiker, he'd have no good options. He could leap from his hiding place in plain view of two dueling (and unforgiving) agencies or he could lie there and let the poison wriggle up his nose and, probably, drill into his brain. Alestair's relaxation and meditation techniques were no help in this situation.

At least the iodine smell had finally dissipated.

He did his best to endure the cold, the discomfort, and the

incipient migraine. Just a little longer. If he could put up with this, then Tanya would get her stupid construct back, and then she'd help him get free of the hitchhiker once and for all.

He hated this plan. The hitchhiker loved it.

But just when he thought he'd have to give up and creep through the access panel in order to shake off the seizures, he heard footsteps. He froze.

A rear door opened. Somebody placed something on the back-seat and closed the door again.

Tanya wanted to warn Gabe that she wasn't alone, that Sasha was watching, but she didn't dare speak to the empty car. So she turned on her heel and strode away from the ancient city gate. She took a serpentine path back to Sasha's auto, parked at the edge of the Old Town. Partially because she knew it was important to demonstrate good tradecraft, but also because she dreaded getting back in the car with him.

It was a special kind of torture, pretending to enjoy the rumi-nations of a man who'd threatened, ever so subtly, to have her grandfather killed. If she had to hear one more Japanese poem she'd shoot herself.

To her immense relief, they didn't have to wait long. A man slightly older than Sasha crossed the square and went straight to the Moskvich.

"I've seen him before," she said, because it was true. "I saw him speaking with Haakensen, the Norwegian." Which was also true, of a sort. They'd exchanged a greeting.

"Your instincts were right," said Sasha. He folded his news-paper. "We'll follow him."

She started the car, acutely aware that she was being graded on everything she did.

"I'd forgotten how thrilling this could be," said Sasha. "You and Nadia must have such fun."

Gabe waited until Arnie had the car in gear. By agreement, they didn't speak. But Arnie did as they'd planned and drove as loudly as he could, which meant grinding the gears, gunning the engine at intersections, and driving over the bumpiest cobbles in Prague.

He'll plant a bug, she'd warned. *I'll suggest it if he doesn't.*

Once they were underway, Gabe opened the access panel into the noisy backseat. Arnie met Gabe's eyes in the rearview. He scratched his left ear. *We're being tailed.*

Gabe swapped Tanya's radio with the decoy. It was a decent match. He'd been skeptical about artificially aging the plastic, but it'd worked better than he'd hoped. Judging from her re-creation of the original discolorations, Tanya had quite a memory. He'd have to step lightly around her.

He left the replica on the seat and, suppressing a groan, retreated into the trunk with the construct.

Tanya followed the car from the Powder Gate all the way to a park on the edge of the city. By the time the driver of the Moskvich pulled over, she'd fallen back more than a hundred meters, as the traffic here was thinner than in the heart of Prague. The driver, Gabe's acquaintance, exited the car and walked into the park.

She endured another several hours in the car with Sasha. He smoked. When she wasn't wondering how long it would take to wash the smell out of her hair, she pondered whether Gabe had frozen to death. As they'd arranged, nobody came to collect the radio and the driver hadn't returned. The radio was unguarded.

But, to her surprise, Sasha didn't suggest retrieving it. Instead, he yawned, stretched, and winced.

"I think I am too old for these stakeouts," he said. "Now I remember why I no longer yearn for fieldwork. This is a young person's game. I'm a cold, hungry old man. Let's return to the office."

She coughed. "But . . . sir! You saw the Westerner just as I did. Something isn't right about this."

"You've delivered the package, as ordered. And those orders came from Moscow Center, yes?"

"Yes, sir," she lied.

"Then you have done your patriotic duty, and I have witnessed this." He turned to her with that dangerously innocuous smile. The one laced with barbs she could not see. "Don't worry, Tatiana. I have your best interests at heart."

Heart thumping like a *treshchotka* played by an overenthusiastic five-year-old, she turned the car around and drove home. Had he fallen for it? Under the guise of scratching an itch, she wiped beads of sweat from her forehead. She wanted to believe it had been so simple, but then she pictured his office, littered with chess pieces.

And now Gabe, and by extension the CIA, had her grandfather's construct. Could she trust him to return it, or had she just traded one problem for another?

The trunk opened.

"Hello, chum. Comfy?"

"Hi, Arnie. No."

Arnie offered a hand. Gabe needed it; he was numb from toes to scalp. He shivered. Arnie had thoughtfully brought a blanket. Gabe wrapped himself like a burrito and jumped up and down to restore the circulation to his feet.

The other man lit a cigarette. "Who was the bird? I've seen her at the Vodnář."

"She's been a pain in my ass for weeks." Gabe spoke with conviction, because it was true. "It helps me greatly if she's associated with you, because you're associated with Haakensen."

"You really know how to make a guy feel like a leper."

"Yeah. But you're my favorite leper, Arnie."

They shook hands. "Thanks for the favor," said Gabe. "I owe you one."

"I should be thanking you." The older man inhaled, swelled his chest until his ribs creaked. "God, I miss this work."

Gabe let the other man finish his cigarette. He waited until Arnie had disappeared before getting back into the car to study Tanya's construct.

Gabe's invisible pal was unusually quiescent. Gabe had been prepared for a tantrum from his ethereal Siamese twin. Proximity to the golem had had Gabe speaking in tongues, and before that, the hitchhiker had nearly given him an aneurysm the night it sensed the construct chasing Andula Zlata. Gabe had spent the evening in a preemptive mental cringe, dreading the moment when the hitchhiker detected the special nature of the radio.

But having failed to absorb the mercury, it was almost as if the hitchhiker had gone into hibernation and hung a "Do Not Disturb Until Summer" sign on the cave door. Like it couldn't care less about the radio construct. Almost as if—

Oh shit.

This wasn't Tanya's radio.

Sasha had made a replica too.

No wonder the plastic had seemed such a good match: Sasha had probably used the same iodine trick.

Gabe pulled out his pocketknife and, working quickly as he dared with shaking hands, removed the screws that held the case together. But when he opened the radio, his breath snagged in his chest like a sweater caught on a bramble.

The VHF transmitter was inconspicuous as a tumor. In his imagination, the tracking beacon pulsed relentlessly as a telltale heart.

Aleksander Komyetski, head of the Prague KGB, was toying with them.

And if not for the hitchhiker, Gabe would have bumbled straight into the trap.

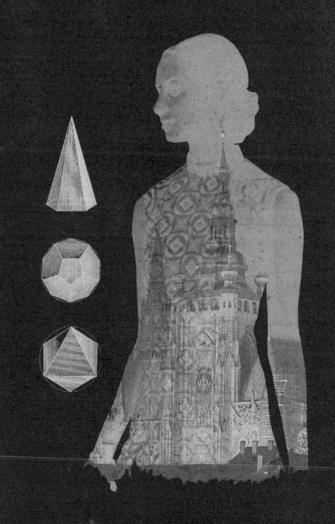

EPISODE 8

COVER THE SILENCE

Cassandra Rose Clarke

Prague, Czechoslovak Socialist Republic
February 23, 1970

1.

Zerena Pulnoc strolled across the Malostranské Square, her heels clicking against the stones. A basket with the first of the day's purchases was tucked into the crook of her arm. Most of the preparation for tonight's party she had delegated to her battalion of servants, but there were certain items that required a more refined taste, and these she bought herself. Already in her basket were two bottles of imported wine to be saved for the Indian ambassador, a new necklace—purchased discreetly on the black market—that would look stunning with her gown for the evening, and an assortment of French cheeses. She was on her way now to pick out the flowers. She hoped to find something that suggested spring. That would be a lovely touch, wouldn't it, even as the Prague winter dragged on? The right flowers, the right combination of colors for the linens, and her guests would almost feel a hint of warmth in the brisk air.

She'd always thought the neighborhood flower shop had the best selection, and the owner, Aleksander Hruška, was an elegant man with an impeccable sense of taste for someone with his background and breeding. But the shop was also conveniently located a few blocks away, and when people saw her coming and going, they would never question it, because why wouldn't Zerena Pulnoc, wife of the Soviet ambassador and hostess of all the *best* parties in Prague, frequently visit a flower shop?

She clicked along the sidewalk until she came to the little park, which wasn't really a park at all, but a courtyard, tucked in between two of the heavy stone buildings. In the summer it was lovely, a verdant patchwork of green doused in the sweet scent of roses, but now it was just a plot of cold mud punctuated by thorny shrubs.

Zerena followed the stepping-stones to the bench in the corner, where she sat delicately, setting the basket at her side. She reached into her purse and pulled out her cigarettes and lit one, the smoke twining up to the steely sky. Pedestrians passed by on the sidewalk, but they paid no attention to her, this woman taking a break from her shopping. As she smoked, she slid one hand along the back fold of the bench. There had been an advertisement for Russian dolls tucked into her newspaper this morning. A bit of a joke, really—who would buy such a thing these days, in this place? But that was the sign, the secret code. *I have a message for you.*

Her fingers hit the bit of paper stuck into the bench's wirework; she enclosed it in her fist and brought her hand into her lap. She kept her hand there as she smoked. When she finished, she dropped the cigarette into the mud, gathered up her basket, and continued on her way.

She did not look at the message until she had nearly reached the flower shop. The shop's bright, hand-painted sign swung back and forth in the wind. There were ferns in the windows, feathery and prehistoric. Zerena unrolled the paper with her thumb

THE WITCH WHO CAME IN FROM THE COLD

and glanced at the text, taking it in quickly before crumpling it into a ball and tossing it into a patch of lingering snow, where she stepped on it, puncturing and ripping it with the heel of her shoe, before breezing in through the doors of the shop.

We must meet, the message had read. *11 a.m., Rousseau's Bakery.*

It seemed Mr. Komyetski had taken her party preparations into consideration. It was a small consolation.

2.

Jordan ran a rag over the inside of a beer glass, giving it one last polish before setting it back in the cabinet. The bar wasn't going to open for another couple of hours, but she liked getting the easy chores finished early, before she started in on some of the orders for charms and potions and other bits of magic that were still outstanding.

She draped the rag over her shoulder and gazed out at the room, checking over her domain. Everything looked good: The floors were swept and mopped, the chairs straightened, the mirror behind the bar polished to gleaming. Cleaning was mindless work, but that was what she liked about it—magic forced her to dive too deeply into her own thoughts sometimes, like she was pulling herself inside out.

The air tightened, squeezed, and exhaled. A prickle of energy rushed over Jordan's skin. She cursed under her breath.

Something had tripped the protection charms.

Such charms were strewn all over Bar Vodnář, a hodgepodge of magic that Jordan had assembled over the years. Some were twisted into the walls of the building itself, family heirlooms that had been here since the beginning. Others, less permanent, were made to look like decorations: bunches of dried herbs in a chipped vase, polished stones scattered around the tables. She used a blend of some staid Ice magic and a few select Flame spells, as well as some of the homey folk magic she'd picked up in her travels. It was an effective arrangement, and it didn't miss much.

It was still thrumming. More strongly now, more insistent.

Jordan sighed and slapped the rag down. She sidled up to the window and peered out, catching a glimpse of a pair of men strolling down the sidewalk. She frowned. Then she reached into the cabinet below the bar. She pulled out a strand of wooden beads, each one carved with a different alchemical symbol, and draped it around her neck. Then she grabbed the little velvet bag of offensive charms and tucked it into her pocket. It wasn't much, but she wasn't going out there completely unarmed.

The air buzzed and sparked against her skin: an eerie sensation, but not exactly unpleasant. This wasn't Gabe's damned golem, at least. Something smaller. Something she could probably handle.

She did a quick reconnaissance of the inside of the bar, checking the upstairs seating area and then the labyrinthine back rooms. Nothing. She assumed whoever it was hadn't gotten inside yet—the charms would have been screaming if that were the case—but Jordan was a cautious woman, and sorcerers, whether Ice or Flame, were slippery sorts. They found their way through the cracks.

Jordan approached the alley exit tucked away in the corner of the bar. She put one hand on the doorknob and gathered the wooden beads in the other, tugging the necklace against the back of her neck. She closed her eyes and murmured ancient words very softly. Magic bolted through her. If anyone tried to attack her unawares, they wouldn't get her on the first shot. Maybe not the second, either. No guarantees on the third.

She pushed the door open.

Cold February wind swept inside, blustery and still holding on to winter. Jordan let go of the beads and stepped out into the street.

"Who are you?" she shouted. "I know you're here. I can feel you."

Voices. A whiff of cigarette smoke. Jordan followed the building up the alley to the main street. A pair of men leaned against the lamppost in front of the bar. They glanced up at the sound of her footsteps but didn't say anything. The smoker lifted his cigarette away from his lips and blew out a cloud of smoke.

The protective charm pulsed. Jordan stomped forward. "Bar doesn't open till noon."

The two men glanced at each other. Jordan had never seen either of them before, but they had a toughness to their features that you didn't usually find in the Ice. The Flame selected by talent and skill and loyalty to the cause; the Ice selected by pedigree.

"We heard good things about this place." The smoker gestured toward the front entrance with his cigarette. "Wanted to see it for ourselves."

"I told you," Jordan said. "I'm not open." She didn't reach for her charms. Not yet. If they were just scouts, she didn't want to start anything she didn't have to. She'd try to chase them off the mundane way first.

"Great location." The second man peeled himself away from the light pole and ambled toward her. Jordan tensed. "An excellent intersection, don't you think?"

The bar's location was shit, actually, tucked in between ornate buildings housing government bureaucracies. Most of the people around here weren't the sort to frequent a place like Bar Vodnář.

But there was another reason you might say this place had a great location, and it was burning in invisible rivers beneath their feet, a nexus of power that converged directly under the room where the lonely and downtrodden and desperate of Prague sat down to have a drink every night.

These two *gazma* were Flame, then.

"I told you, we're not open yet." Jordan took a step forward.

The smoker flicked his cigarette out into the street.

"And I'm not letting you in until noon," she continued. "You want to drink, you come back then. You want something else from me—" She fixed them both with a stone-cold stare. "Don't bother. I don't have what you're looking for."

The smoker grinned. "I don't know about that, Miss Rhemes."

"Well, I'm not offering it. That better?" Jordan jerked her head down the street. "Leave. If you stick around out here, you're gonna freeze to death before we open."

The two men exchanged glances, and then they shifted, their movements slow, casual, vaguely menacing. Jordan stared at them, chin lifted. These two were low on the chain; she could take them if she had to.

They shifted their weight, kicked at the old ice in the snow.

"We don't freeze," the smoker said as he walked past. "You'd do best to remember that."

Jordan watched them go. They meandered down the sidewalk. The smoker kept throwing glances her way, but they eventually rounded the corner and disappeared. Off to report to their Flame bosses, no doubt.

Jordan went back inside through the alley entrance. The protection charms had quieted and stilled. For a moment she stood beside the door, breathing in the scent of sage from her charms and the lemony glow of her cleaning solutions. It was difficult to do serious magic without support from the two factions, but Jordan had managed all this time because of the ley lines converging under her bar. She could feel them now, like lines of electricity.

The Flame was up to something. First those two university professors had stopped by, and now there were men skulking around like a pair of hungry dogs. This was about the ley lines, about the kind of magic you couldn't do alone.

She did not like it.

Jordan double-checked the lock and then stepped into the first of the back rooms, past the storage shelves, and into her office. The familiar scent of dried herbs washed over her, and for a moment she stood and considered her options. The Flame had approached her before about access to Bar Vodnář, but this encounter made her nervous in a way the previous one hadn't. Before, they'd at least pretended to be genteel. This aggression had the stink of desperation about it.

With quick, practiced movements, Jordan began pulling supplies from the shelves. Bits of stone, boxes of matches, twists of twine—she selected each item from memory, then laid them out on her desk. Studied them. Then she unlocked the bottom drawer of her desk and pulled out her grimoire, a book she had sewn together herself many years ago, chanting softly as the thread wound through the paper. Now she thumbed through the pages until she came to the section she needed.

For Fighting, it read in Arabic, written out in the looping handwriting of her youth. She hardly recognized it all these years later, hardly connected that writing to the person she'd become.

She selected a charm from the table of contents, and then she set to work.

3.

Sasha was waiting near the entrance to Rousseau's Bakery. He leaned against the wall, eating from a bag of roasted nuts that he must have purchased from the street vendor two blocks away. As Zerena walked over to the entrance, he pulled himself upright, then walked with her into the bakery. It was empty save the girl behind the counter, dull faced and covered in flour. She was laying out pastries on a display sheet, her brow furrowed in concentration.

"Would you like one?" Sasha asked, holding out the greasy bag.

Zerena shook her head and gently pushed the bag away, wrinkling her nose with disgust. "Not right now, Sashenka."

Sasha chuckled and tucked the bag into his coat pocket. Zerena walked up to the counter, where the girl looked up from her work, blinking.

"I put in an order," Zerena said. "For Zerena Pulnoc. I'm here to confirm."

At first the girl gave no indication that she understood anything Zerena had said, but then, as if she had only needed the time

343

to mull things over, she turned and vanished into the back. As the door swung shut, Zerena heard her call out the owner's name. Zerena crossed her arms over her chest.

"What do you want?" she said, looking ahead at the rows of delicately iced pastries.

"Information," Sasha said.

"You'll have to be more specific than that."

The door flew open and out stepped the owner, Rémy, holding up his hands in greeting. "Madame Pulnoc!" he cried, rushing to Zerena so he could kiss her on the cheek. Rémy had been born in Paris; he'd moved to Prague to be with a girl he loved. A sweet story, yes, but not of any real interest to Zerena. Although his pastries were magnificent.

"You will adore what I've done for you," Rémy said in French. "A perfect selection for your party tonight."

"I have no doubt of that, Monsieur Rousseau." Zerena beamed at him, but really she was thinking about Sasha and his unhelpful little request. *Information*. What else would he come to her for?

"You said you wanted something classic," Rémy said, "and I took that to heart. Have a seat"—he gestured toward the bakery's single tiny table—"and I'll bring out the samples for your approval."

"That sounds lovely. Thank you." Zerena gave him one last bright smile before moving over to the table. Sasha trailed behind her. He'd known about this, her little pre-party ritual at Rousseau's, but only because she'd let him know. Information was her true currency, and she managed it as she did her husband's wealth, doling it out whenever it was advantageous for her to do so.

"I imagine you're regretting those awful nuts now," Zerena said in Russian, tucking her napkin into her lap.

"French pastries?" Sasha waved his hand dismissively. "Bourgeois decadence. Give me a Kiev cake any day."

"Your patriotism is admirable. Now, what is this information you need?"

Sasha glanced back at the counter, where Rémy shouted at the girl to hurry, hurry, the madame was waiting.

"You do that every time we meet here," Zerena said, leaning back in her chair. "Think the girl is listening in. Speak Russian. You know there are no ears here."

Sasha grinned easily at her. "I remember. But it's an old bureaucrat's paranoia. Forgive me."

Zerena shifted in her seat, irritated. Sasha always did this, flitting around the conversation like a butterfly. This was not the day to sit at the table in Rousseau's and circle around each other.

"I don't have much time," Zerena said, "as you well know. Tell me what you need."

The girl was approaching, balancing two plates of pastry samples on outstretched hands. Sasha fell silent, watching her, and Zerena rankled at the interruption, uncomfortable that she still did not know what Sasha wanted.

"Monsieur has prepared three pastries for you: a mille-feuille, a Saint Honoré cake, and a petite madeleine," the girl murmured, not making eye contact. She set the plates down on the table and shuffled away, her hair hanging in strings over her eyes. Zerena sniffed, turned to the pastries. They looked like tiny eighteenth-century sculptures, delicate and shimmering.

"Perhaps I can be bourgeois for the afternoon," Sasha said, picking up a cake. Zerena peered up at him.

"What," she said, "do you need?"

He bit into the tiny cake and chewed, closing his eyes and

letting out a delighted *mmm*. Zerena didn't need to try the pastries to know they would be perfect. She trusted Rémy. Sasha, she did not trust.

"I told you," Sasha said, "information." He looked at her. "In exchange, I will give you information. You'd like that, wouldn't you?"

They were alone; Rémy and the girl had ducked into the back room. Zerena tilted her head—interested, perhaps, but not terribly so. "I always have need for information."

"It's about one of my officers." Sasha licked at the cream on his fingers. "Tatiana Mikhailovna."

Zerena considered this. She knew Tatiana, who always dutifully attended the cultural events required of her cover. No real sense of fashion, the poor thing, but she came from an important family, highly ranked in the Party.

"And what information do you have about her?" Zerena picked up the madeleine and weighed it between her fingers.

"I think she may be speaking with the West."

At that, Zerena laughed. "That little mouse? Don't be silly, Sasha. Her family's loyal. She's loyal." Zerena nibbled dutifully on the madeleine and then called out in French to Rémy, who had emerged from the back room, "Marvelous work, darling! They'll be the hit of the party, I'm sure."

Rémy pressed a hand to his heart, his way of saluting good taste. Zerena turned back to Sasha. He was scowling at her.

"What's the matter?" she said sweetly.

"She has access to a radio," he said.

"Don't we all?"

Sasha sighed. "Not that sort of radio. One used for communication." He shifted his weight and leaned forward, pushing the pastries aside. "I have reason to suspect she's using it to contact the Americans. There was an—incident."

"Oh?" Zerena kept her expression neutral.

"I replaced the real radio with a plant, which was stolen out from under me. It had a tracker on it, of course." Sasha's eyes glittered. "And I tracked it to an alley near the American embassy compound. An unusual coincidence, don't you think?

Zerena gazed at him. This *was* an interesting development.

"And of course you know she's been dallying about with that American security man. Pritchard."

"Ah, yes, I had heard something about that." So Tatiana Mikhailovna Morozova was flirting with the other side. Very interesting, indeed. Despite her protestations to Sasha, Zerena had, in fact, been considering this possibility herself—she wasn't going to let him in on *everything*. But her little whisperers throughout the city had begun to talk of Morozova and Pritchard being seen together on a handful of occasions. Zerena didn't care about treason; she found it a pointless concern—whose alliances remained steadfast throughout their lives? But to the Party, and to the West, such betrayals mattered deeply, and knowing of one was a treasure indeed.

Still, she wondered why Sasha brought this information to her—Sasha, who played his own intelligence games in between those endless rounds of correspondence chess.

"You understand my concern, then," said Sasha. "My need for information—anything you have about Tanya, about the American, that might explain why she'd take her radio to such a—peculiar place."

And here Zerena saw the opportunity to vault herself back into her preferred position of power. Convince Sasha that the girl's actions were of no concern to him, that this radio and this incident with the American embassy were part of an assignment he was not privy to—and then Zerena could tuck the knowledge of Tatiana Mikhailovna's betrayal away, where she could make better use of it than Sasha, or the Party, ever could.

"The information I have to give you won't make this the story you want." Zerena took another small bite of her madeleine. "The radio itself is nothing of concern. It's a decoy. A means to an end."

"A means to an end?" Sasha's eyebrows drew closer together. "And how would you know that?"

Zerena smiled at him. "How do I know anything? Your Tatiana is only doing what Mother Russia has asked of her. An assignment for my husband. Quite secret. I'm afraid I can't say more than that." She leaned forward and placed a hand on top of Sasha's; he glowered at her. She was winning now. "I can assure you she's not a traitor."

"You don't really expect me to believe that."

"Believe what you want. Just remember that in a place like Prague, we can't always be open with one another. Although I must say it's a good thing the *real* radio was of no value either—there are people who would be very upset to hear that you meddled in their affairs, swapping out plants when you had not been ordered to."

Sasha gave her a cool look.

"I can ask my husband to verify for you, if necessary."

Sasha did not believe her. She could tell by the way he was glaring at her over the crumbs of his pastries. She could see him working up protestations behind his angry expression. Zerena leaned across the table, pushing her plate aside. She rested her chin on one hand and gazed at him. He looked back at her, still angry, but now also cautious.

"Of course, I can't honestly say the ambassador would be *happy* to verify. As I understand it, the business with the radio is rather important, and for the KGB chief of station to intercede without permission . . ." She clucked her tongue.

Sasha's eyes narrowed. "What are you saying, Zerena?"

Zerena smiled at him. "Simply that my husband will not be happy about this situation. And I should remind you, Sasha, my friend, that my husband has very powerful friends back in Russia."

Sasha stared at her. He kept his expression blank, old spy that he was, but Zerena thought she saw a quiver of fear skipping across his features. It wasn't just her husband's powerful friends Sasha had reason to fear; Zerena had powerful friends of her own.

"What are you saying?" Sasha asked again in a low voice.

A crash came from the bakery counter—the girl had dropped a mixing bowl, and it clattered and spun across the tiles. Sasha tensed at the sound, his hand curling around the edge of the table. When he saw Zerena looking, he dropped his hand to his side and leaned back easily. But it was too late. She had seen that tension, that anxiety.

Rémy berated the girl in rapid French. Zerena beamed at Sasha. He did not return the smile.

"Only that this radio was always meant to be worthless to the Americans, so you didn't muck things up *too* badly." Zerena laughed, a sparkling, champagne-fizz laugh, and Sasha glared at her. "Now, let your girl do as she's been commanded, and let my husband have his peace of mind."

Sasha kept staring at her, and she knew she had him, at least for the time being. If she could string this deception along for another few weeks, and keep Sasha fearful of doing his own investigations, it would be enough time for her to learn who, exactly, had been speaking to Tanya through that radio. A delicate piece of information, but an important one. Information that could do the right damage, if she laid it out at the right time, and for the right people.

Sasha Komyetski was not the right person.

4.

The agents from the Flame were back. Jordan felt the air tighten with their approach, her charms lighting up in agitation. She glanced out the window to be certain, and, sure enough, it was the two men from earlier, the smoker and his friend.

Neither was smoking now. They stood conferring with each other on the sidewalk in front of the bar, heads bent together. Jordan pulled the curtains farther back and peered out at them. A pile of old leaves smoldered in an ashtray on the windowsill; the smoke was a curtain, and when the two men glanced her way, they'd only see an empty window.

"What are you up to?" she whispered. The smoke burned at the back of her throat. The leaves had been soaking in a certain chemical compound for years, and the smell of it wrapped around her: the acrid toxicity of the chemicals, an undercurrent of magic. It was one of many charms she had prepared earlier this morning, down in her office.

The two men pulled apart, turned, and paced the length of the sidewalk. Jordan counted their steps with them, her breath creating little white puffs on the glass. With each step her chest grew tighter. *Ten . . . eleven . . . twelve . . . thirteen . . .*

She willed them to take one step too many, to ruin their spell's foundation so she wouldn't have to fight. But they didn't. At the thirteenth step, both men turned around, as if preparing for a duel. The smoker pulled a rolled-up scroll out of his pocket. The protection charms thumped in time with Jordan's heart.

The smoker unfurled the scroll, and it dropped to the sidewalk. Jordan yanked away from the window and bolted over to the bar. She flung open the cabinet and grabbed a handful of the prepared charms, shoving them in her pockets. Then she pulled out a stone box, figures carved into the lid and sides and stained red with ancient blood. She had taken it out of the safe in her office. Just in case.

Beneath her feet, the ley lines hummed.

Jordan hurried across the empty room, up to the front door. She could hear the men's voices chanting softly on the other side. Stupid of them, doing a spell like that where anyone could walk by and see. They must be getting desperate indeed.

She kicked the door open and stepped out into the cold.

The men didn't see her. They were deep into the spell, their eyes closed, voices rising up together as they reached out to the ley lines running beneath the bar. A pop came from inside: one of her charms disintegrating into ash.

Jordan ground her teeth and held the box overhead. Damn the Flame, forcing her to do this out in the open. She began to chant too, a different chant, in an older language. The thing inside the box rattled, thrashing against its confines. The man without the scroll glanced over at her, his eyes going wide. She glowered at him.

No one stopped chanting.

Her box began to glow, the figures turning molten, though they didn't give off any heat. Her fingers tingled. The box cast a neon glow over the street, over the two men, and the one without the scroll stumbled in his chant and then stepped backward. The smoker's eyes flew open.

"Damn you, Ivan!" he roared, before his eyes found Jordan and her box, and he let out a string of frightened profanity.

"Get away from my bar!" Jordan shouted. She didn't lower the box, but she didn't open it either. She wasn't about to let the thing inside loose on the streets of Prague—she wasn't Gabe, for God's sake—but the two Flame men didn't know that. Let them think she was crazy enough to do it. She'd left the Ice, after all.

"You wouldn't dare!" The smoker stepped toward her, his scroll fluttering, useless in the wind. Jordan jerked the box so that it pointed at him, and it released a jolt of magic that knocked his head back.

"Try me!" she shouted.

And then a hot burst of power slammed into her back.

For a long, stretched-out moment, Jordan was flying, her feet lifted nearly a meter off the ground. Cold air rushed around her. *The box,* she thought, and she curled it to her chest just as she went sprawling. The impact of her landing sped time up to normal. The box was still shut tight, although her magic had faded from it, and the thing inside had gone quiet.

Chanting behind her, low and guttural. She recognized the spell and without thinking rolled to her left, into a patch of dirty snow. A ball of fire arced overhead and landed a few paces away. When it hit the ground, the flames erupted, shooting straight up to the sky. They were tinged in green, not red, and they smelled like incense and spices.

Jordan scrambled to her feet, feeling around in her pocket as she did so. The two Flame men were moving toward each other. One of them shouted, but Jordan's hearing was muffled by the haze of magic drifting off the flames. She pulled a tangle of metal out of her pocket. Wollaston wires from an old telescope twisted around a bundle of matches. Platinum and phosphorus. If they wanted to fight with fire, so could she.

"Hey!" she shouted, her voice hoarse. The two men ignored her. They were facing each other, lips moving. Shit. *Shit*. She didn't recognize the spell.

Jordan tucked the box under her arm. She twisted the tail of wire in her charm into the shape of an ancient rune, then held the whole thing to her forehead and closed her eyes. She murmured the sound of the rune three times under her breath, and then she hurled the charm onto the street between herself and the men.

It exploded in a shower of golden sparks. Jordan flung herself back into the snow, arm up to cover her head. The box slipped out of her grip and landed hard on the frozen dirt. Her heart skipped a beat, but the box was still closed, thank God. She was deeply regretting bringing the thing out here, regretting her attempt at a bluff.

Her charm continued to spew sparks. From this angle, they were harmless, but on the other side, the side that faced the two Flame men, the light would be like staring straight into the sun. She pushed herself up to standing. Her back ached where the Flame agent's charm had struck. She lurched over to the golden sparks, one hand shielding her eyes. Behind the fountain of light, the shadows of the two men were scrambling toward her, away from the burning brightness of her spell.

"You can't take the hint?" she shouted at them. "I don't want you here."

One of them flashed into view between the sparks. His eyes were squeezed shut.

"Just wanted to talk!" he shouted back at her. "And then you had to bring out the Box of Cosstad."

"The Flame never just wants to talk," Jordan shot back. She had a decision to make. The two men weren't giving up, and they'd already done enough damage fighting out here in the street. These two spells would burn down eventually, leaving mysterious charred spots on the road, but God knew what other weapons these Flame bastards had brought with them. And anyway, Jordan's full arsenal was inside, tucked away in the restocked cabinet beneath the bar.

That didn't mean she wanted to let them in, though. Not with the confluence underneath their feet. Not with that suicidal determination both of them seemed to possess.

The one named Ivan was inching his way toward her. She took a step backward. She had two weapons remaining in her pocket. Two chances to get these men the hell out of there.

Ivan slunk past the curtain of light. The skin of his face was red and peeling away in long strips. His eyes flew open. He snarled at her. Lifted one hand. Something glowed in his palm.

Jordan didn't have time to think. She pulled out both of her remaining charms: a vial of salt water dotted with flakes of gold, and a circuit board she'd designed herself, the copper wiring twisted into the language of the ancients.

Ivan gave a cold grin when he saw her two weapons. "You think you can defeat the Flame with those handmade baubles?" He lifted his glowing palm. The light was a sickly red. Jordan could feel the magic staining the air around her.

"I do, actually." She flipped off the lid to the vial of salt water and threw it straight up. The gold-flecked water spilled out, fusing with the air. The ley lines thrummed. The area around her bar was the only place this charm would work, she'd seen to that. Within seconds, the water had turned into a cloud, which turned into a storm, a tiny, person-size storm that rained concentrated energy over its victim. Ivan shrieked and dropped his own charm, which landed on the cement and shattered, the magic having flown out of it as soon as it left contact with his skin.

Jordan reached into the storm and yanked Ivan out into the clean air. He gazed up at her, eyes wide with fear and panic, his skin glowing from the sudden influx of energy.

"Whatever the Flame wants to do with my bar, they can't have it," she said.

"You don't get to make that decision," Ivan snarled.

Jordan shoved him back into the energy storm. He howled, tried to move away—the cloud followed him. It wouldn't kill him, it just stung like peroxide on an open wound, and it would wash the magic out of him for a day or so.

"Send word back to your masters!" she shouted at him. "They're not getting my bar."

The sparks from her first charm were dying down, and she could see the other Flame agent curled up on the ground behind them, his arms wrapped around his head. Jordan walked over to him. She could feel the heat from the sparks against her back, as hot as the Egyptian sun. The man dropped his arms at the sound of her footsteps and gazed up at her. A heat blister bubbled over his left eye.

"You'll live," Jordan said, and she held up the copper circuit board. "Look at your friend over there."

The man glanced over his shoulder. His eyes widened. "What did you—"

"That's a charm of my own design. So's this." She lifted the circuit board. "I guarantee that what it does is worse than that." She tilted her head toward Ivan. "So you get the hell out of here before you find out what it is."

The man's head lolled. His eyes rolled up toward her. "You're going to regret this," he said.

"I never regret kicking the riffraff out of Bar Vodnář." She stepped back, keeping her eyes on him. Didn't trust him not to try something desperate on her at the last minute. Her little energy storm was dying down, and his partner would be free soon, although he would be stripped of his magic. "Whatever the Flame's got planned, they can do it elsewhere."

"You're supposed to be neutral," the man croaked. He forced himself into a sitting position.

"You've got a strange idea of neutral if you think it means I'll just give the Flame whatever they want." Jordan gazed down at the magic burning itself away in her street. This was ostentatious, even for the Flame. It was a quiet, sleepy morning, to be sure, but they hadn't even tried to keep things hidden.

"Get the hell out of here," Jordan said, and the man lifted his hands in surrender and climbed to his feet. "You too!" she shouted at Ivan, glancing over her shoulder at him. The storm had evaporated completely. He scowled at her, slick with residue from the energy.

"You'll be sorry you did this," he hissed.

"You've made that clear. If I see you hanging around here again, I'm sure I'll be even *more* sorry."

Ivan shuffled over to his partner, and the two glared at her. She flicked her hand at them. *Bye-bye.* They slumped in defeat, looked at each other, and then trudged away, the scent of spent magic rising off them into the air.

Jordan was suddenly very tired. The pain in her back throbbed. She had work to do: cleanup, reinforcing and repairing her protection charms. But she didn't move. She watched the men stagger away, her head swirling with magic and questions.

5.

Zerena descended the stairs, one hand sliding over the banister, a slight smile fixed into place. The ballroom was already half-filled with guests. Zerena always made certain to arrive at least half an hour late to her own parties—the caterers and hired staff could take people's coats and direct them to ballroom, and she knew the importance of making an entrance.

She was making an entrance now, just as she'd calculated: Heads swiveled toward her; someone called out her name. Zerena lifted one hand in greeting. "Hello, Jakob, darling," she called out over the stair's banister, and then breezed the rest of the way down. Her Givenchy gown was perhaps a bit too formal for a cocktail party such as this one, but Zerena preferred to be overdressed. Clothing was one of the clearest expressions of power—something the bourgeois West understood well. Tonight, her silver gown hung in sharp, cruel angles, and her new necklace glittered at the base of her throat. She was a knife, primed to cut.

"Marco," she said, floating over to a group of agricultural

secretaries from the Italian embassy. "I'm so glad you could join us this evening."

"I'm so glad *you* could join us this evening," Marco replied. He plucked a wine flute from a passing drink tray and offered it to Zerena with a twinkle in his eye. "I wanted to congratulate you on the party. It's been absolutely sublime so far. Love the ice sculpture."

"I'm glad to hear that." Zerena touched the wine to her lips but didn't drink. She glanced at the others. "Renato, Pietro, Cesare—thank you all so much for coming."

"I wouldn't miss a Zerena Pulnoc party if the embassy were burning to the ground," said Pietro, and they all laughed uproariously. Zerena only smiled. What a sweet thing for him to say, said the tilt of her head, the idea that treason was worth an evening of cocktails and hors d'oeuvres.

"I was wondering," said Renato, the oldest of the four and the most seasoned at the diplomatic circuit, "if your husband would be joining us."

The other three men looked toward her expectantly, and Zerena put on an expression of carefully cultivated disappointment. "I'm afraid the ambassador is not feeling well this evening. And you know how he is with parties." She touched Renato's arm softly, a gesture of calculated intimacy.

He chuckled. "Never had the patience for them. That man. How he manages as a diplomat is beyond me."

"Now, now," Zerena said. "There's more to diplomacy than just parties."

Renato swiped one hand dismissively, and the others laughed. Zerena took this moment to make her departure—"Oh, I'd love to talk a bit more, but I need to make the rounds; you know how it is.

Shall we chat later?"—and then she was on her way, flowing slowly through the party, scanning the faces for anyone of interest. The lights in the ballroom were dimmed, hiding the worn shabbiness of the wood paneling in the walls, the faded spots in the silk curtains that cascaded down from the soaring ceilings. Zerena knew how to capture the opulence of her fading estate, even if its bright gleam lasted only a moment.

She stopped and chatted with a few more clumps of guests, going through the motions expected of her as the Soviet ambassador's wife. She air-kissed and pretended to sip her wine and asked about Leandro's daughter, away at boarding school in England. And then she moved on, gliding like a shark through the eddies of guests.

She had been circulating for about fifteen minutes when she saw Tatiana Mikhailovna and Nadezhda Fyodorovna speaking with an attaché from West Germany. They did not see her, and they were involved enough in the conversation that it was acceptable for her to breeze past. Here at the party, muffled by her drab Soviet clothes, it seemed impossible that Tatiana would have given an illegal radio to the Americans. She was a perfect little Party girl, Zerena knew, and hard to find good gossip on. This radio was good gossip. Weaponized gossip. Zerena had no doubt it would come in handy sometime in the future, assuming she could uncover the truth, and then keep Sasha distracted from learning it himself.

"Oh, Zerena! Over here! I haven't seen you in *ages*."

Zerena turned in one liquid motion, following the sound of the voice to Martyna, wife of the Andorran representative and a dull woman who fancied herself one of Zerena's friends. Zerena hadn't yet disabused her of the notion; she was still too useful. Zerena threaded her way over to her.

"Hello, lovely," she said, and they kissed the air around each other's cheeks. The scent of alcohol was already seeping through the heavy floral curtain of Martyna's perfume. Tacky, yes, but she was notoriously chatty when she drank too much.

"Are you having a good time?" Zerena asked.

"Of course." Martyna giggled. "I think it's impossible to have a bad time at one of your parties, Zerena."

"Oh, that's kind of you to say."

"Have you seen Luisa? She wasn't sure she would be able to come; she's been sick with the flu the last two weeks—I do wish this weather would just warm up, don't you?"

Zerena gave a sharp smile. "Oh, darling, I'm used to it."

Martyna's cheeks pinked, and she made a flustered noise in the back of her throat. "Oh, yes, of course, I know, I just find the cold so dreadful. I'm looking forward to summer. I tell Sebastian that he needs to be stationed someplace warm, the Philippines or Algeria or some such place, and he tells me I should be grateful that we're here in Prague—"

She blathered on. Zerena's irritation tightened into a coil inside her. If only she would blather about Tanya's radio. Not that the wife of the Andorran representative would know anything about that.

Zerena angled her body toward Martyna as if listening closely, but her gaze turned out upon the sea of party guests. More people had arrived, and the party was beginning to form its own eco-systems, its own bureaucratic channels, the way parties always do. Zerena took note of it all, watching who toasted with whom, and who gathered together near the bandstand, and who stole away into the smoking room together.

And then she saw someone she had never seen before.

"Martyna," Zerena said, and tapped the woman on the arm to

get her to shut up. Martyna glanced over at her expectantly. "Tell me, who is that man there? The handsome one." She gestured discreetly. The newcomer was stocky, dark haired and brown skinned, but he had an easy smile and a glimmer in his eye that she found appealing. Something about him seemed familiar. She hated this feeling, that there was information out there she should know and yet it had somehow slipped by her.

"Oh," said Martyna. "That's the new arrival at the American embassy. Dominic Alvarez. He *is* rather handsome, isn't he?"

"I should go introduce myself." Zerena looked apologetically at Martyna and then whisked herself away. *Dominic Alvarez.* She rolled the name around inside her head. *What secrets can I get you to share?*

Dominic sipped at a whiskey, watching the room with keen eyes. Zerena floated over to him, and he glanced at her, smiling in a devastatingly charming way.

"Hello there," he said, as if she were a surprise.

"Hello." Zerena held out one hand, and Dominic gave it a firm shake. "I always introduce myself to new faces. I'm—"

"Zerena Pulnoc," Dominic said, eyes bright. "I saw a picture of you in the embassy, with your husband. I'd never forget a face like that."

Zerena pretended this kind of flattery worked on her. "Oh, you're too much, Mr.—?"

"Alvarez. Dominic Alvarez. I just arrived at the US embassy."

"Ah, of course." Zerena smiled at him, taking in the details of his person: his suit fit him well, but it was shabby, the fabric worn and shiny in places. He smelled faintly of cigars. His hands had been rough to the touch—an outdoors man. A military background, Zerena guessed, and she wondered what job he could have at the American embassy. It did not escape her notice that he hadn't offered the information freely.

This was her project for tonight, she decided. Finding out all she could about this stranger.

"Tell me, Mr. Alvarez, how are you liking Prague so far?"

"It's cold as shit." He winked at her. "But it's getting warmer. And please, call me Dom."

"Dom," Zerena said. "I think I can do that. Shall I show you around the party? If you're a new arrival, I can think of quite a few people who'd be interested in being introduced."

"That would be fantastic, Mrs. Pulnoc."

She tittered, the lilting little laugh that set men like this at ease. "Oh, Zerena, *please*."

"Zerena it is. Shall we make the rounds?" He offered his arm to her, a proper gentleman underneath those threadbare clothes. Zerena looped her arm through his and led him into the crowd. She leaned in close as they walked, talking to him in a low murmur, pointing out certain people. She wanted to know if he already recognized them or not.

"And that's Lars Janssens, the Belgian ambassador." She pointed her head toward a tall, rather lanky man dancing with a voluptuous heiress. "And the woman he's dancing with is Simona Fiala. She's a socialite here in Prague. You'll encounter her often enough, if you attend the right parties."

"I never miss a party," Dom said, grinning. He didn't seem interested in the ambassador or the heiress, and Zerena filed that information away. They drifted on, a pair of feathers twisting together on the wind.

"Oh!" cried Zerena. "There's Oliver and Marianella Haik. Have you met them yet? It would be dreadfully useful for you to know them, since you're connected to the American embassy." She gave him a shining smile, and he returned one just as bright.

"I'm afraid I haven't had the pleasure."

She guided him over. Oliver and Marianella were part of a ring of conversation that fell silent as she approached. Oliver lifted his glass in greeting. "Zerena!" he said. "Lovely party."

"I'm so glad to hear that." She gestured at Dom. "This is Dominic Alvarez, the new arrival at the American embassy. I wanted to show him a taste of our hospitality here in Prague."

This statement was greeted warmly, and Zerena made the rest of the introductions, pointing to each person in turn as she spoke their name and offered a bit of background, for Dom's sake. She watched Dom's face as she performed, looking for a spark of recognition, a recoil of suspicion. Any break in his facade could be useful to her. But he was good. Charming to the last, and he gave nothing away.

"You're stationed in Prague at an interesting time," said Oliver, who drained his glass and then gestured for a nearby waiter to bring him another. Zerena could tell he was already drunk. "We don't usually find ourselves with murdered StB officers in our cemeteries."

Marianella looked over at him in alarm, but Oliver just laughed and slapped Dom on the shoulder. "I wanted to be honest, that's all!"

"I assure you I'm not an StB officer," Dom said smoothly, "but I'll avoid cemeteries for the time being, just in case."

Zerena considered this. Such a classic American, entirely unflappable. This coolness under pressure made her even more intrigued, more curious to peer into his closets.

And so she politely excused Dom and herself from the Haiks and angled him back out to the party.

"Don't mind that talk about murdered StB operatives," she said, scanning the room for their next target. "The gossip hounds are making it out to be more than it is."

"Sometimes the gossip hounds learn the truth before the rest of us."

Zerena looked over at him sharply.

He was smiling down at her, eyes twinkling. "Surely the wife of the Soviet ambassador would understand that."

"I'm not a politician. Just a housewife. I couldn't say."

They wove through the party. Tension crept into Zerena's shoulders, but Dom seemed as loose as the first moment they'd spoken. She hated being in this position. It was not the place for her. She was used to being in control.

And then, across the room, she caught a flash of something interesting.

"I see one of your colleagues," she said softly, watching Joshua Toms, another member of Prague's CIA office. She knew all about this one, had been slowly cultivating scraps of information about him since he first arrived in the city.

Tonight, he was speaking with Alestair Winthrop.

Curious.

"Shall we go say hello?" she asked Dom. "The man with him might be a good contact for you, as well."

"You lead the way," Dom said, pointing to the crowd.

Zerena kept her eyes on Alestair and Joshua, squeezing her fist in frustration whenever a crowd of guests passed in front of them. The two men were leaning in close. Joshua's head was tilted toward Alestair, and Alestair rested his hand on Joshua's shoulder and smiled to himself whenever Joshua spoke. *Very* curious.

Zerena knew quite a bit about Alestair. He was from an old

British family—in the way of such families, they were more proud of their past than their present. But that had only made Alestair more interesting to her, and so she'd sent her whisperers out. They'd come back with stories about his career in MI6, about his absurd tales from his time spent abroad, about his preferences for sweet-faced young men who spent too much time poring over books.

Young men very much like Joshua Toms.

Zerena approached the pair, Dom trailing alongside her. Alestair glanced up as she approached, and although he did his best to keep his expression flat, she saw a darkness pass over his features. A flicker, a shadow. She smiled brilliantly at him.

"Alestair, how *are* you?" she cooed, and he held out his hands as if to embrace her as she rushed up to him. They kissed the air—once, twice—all the usual rituals.

"Wonderful, as always, Zerena. Absolutely smashing party, by the way."

Joshua had jerked away, his gaze fixed on the floor, cheeks tinged with pink. *Naughty boy!* Zerena thought, and she glanced at Dom, who seemed to have taken no notice of it. Of course. Men like him never saw the obvious.

"Alestair, I'd like you to meet the new arrival at the American embassy, Dominic Alvarez."

"Ah, yes," said Alestair, striding forward, not missing a beat. "I've heard about you."

"Have you, now?" Dom wasn't so keen to employ his charm on Alestair, it seemed, and Zerena wondered if this was because he knew of Alestair's preferences after all, or because Alestair was British, or both. An American like Dom, he probably thought the two were interchangeable.

"Nothing but good things, old boy. No need to worry." Lines

crinkled around Alestair's eyes. It wasn't exactly a smile. "I know you and Joshua already know each other."

Dom nodded at Joshua, who had managed to collect himself from his earlier embarrassment. "Dom," Joshua said. "Are you enjoying the party?"

"Sure." Dom gave a shrug, then glanced at Zerena. "Can't complain about the company."

Zerena laughed and swatted at him. She knew her cues.

"Well, Dom, I was just telling Josh about an old colleague of mine back in London. I think you'll like this one." And he launched into his story, one Zerena had heard at least twice before, about an old Eton chum of Alestair's who had gone on to become an important figure in British intelligence. Zerena used the story as an opportunity to study Joshua, who was shifting his weight from foot to foot, brushing at his hair, giving a strained smile at the droll moments in Alestair's story.

Joshua, Joshua, Zerena chided him silently, *you're a better spy than that.*

It amused her, seeing his discomfort. The party was running smoothly, like all her parties. All tasteful and glamorous and very, very dull. But Joshua and Alestair had added a wrinkle to its glossy finish, an intriguing imperfection. Standing so close together, at a party like this! Practically flirting for all to see. They should have known better.

Alestair finished his story, on the same ridiculous note he always did—"And then we splashed down into the Thames!" Dom let out a roaring laugh and slapped Alestair on the back.

"And that's why you never trust a German," Dom said, which made Alestair laugh in turn.

Joshua smiled, too, a little calmer than he had been before.

The music swelled, then: "Dance of the Hours." Ah, here was

Zerena's chance to make a little trouble, to scratch at that imperfection and see what she could find underneath. She slipped her arm in Dom's and purred in his ear, "Oh, would you dance with me, darling? I've always loved this song."

Dom smiled down at her, looking pleased with himself. "Well, if you've *always* loved this song." They spun away from Alestair and Joshua and into the whirlpool of dancers. Dom straightened his spine, lifted Zerena's hand, pressed his palm into the small of her back. They swirled off, moving in slow, elegant strides.

"You're a talented dancer," Zerena told Dom. Her skirt flared out behind her, a silver gleam in the lights.

"My parents are Cuban," he said. "You can thank them."

"Cuba?" Zerena smiled. "And yet you work for the Americans."

"I *am* American, sweetheart." He led her into a turn. She smiled at him across the sudden distance.

"Of course," she said.

He pulled her back to him.

"I see Alestair and Joshua are getting along quite well." She pressed herself into him, tilting her head so that she was murmuring into his ear. "It's always gratifying to see that sort of interagency cooperation."

"Sure."

They swooped around in time with the music, with the other dancers. The trajectory of the dance was bringing them around to Alestair and Joshua again. Alestair said something to make Joshua laugh, and he peered up at Alestair, his eyes shining.

"There they are," Zerena said. "Britain and the United States are working *very* closely together, don't you think?"

Dom gazed across the room. His brow wrinkled. His mouth worked into a frown.

Zerena knew he saw it.

"They should be careful," she said, watching Dom as she spoke. "Even allies can get too close. Don't you think?"

Dom gave a grunt of disapproval. "Yeah." He swung her around, into the main current. Alestair and Joshua disappeared behind a wall of guests. Zerena let herself fall into the dance, even as Dom became inattentive, his steps too short and off rhythm. A seed planted, then. Zerena didn't know what it would grow into, but that was the joy of gardening, wasn't it? Laying future plants in the soil, coaxing them out with water and sun, and waiting, watching, as seeds became a work of art.

The music died, and Dom and Zerena stepped away from each other. Dom pushed his hair back. Gave her a little smile. He was distracted. Good. Zerena had nothing *personal* against Alestair or Joshua, but she never let an opportunity go unused.

"It's been fun," Dom said. "But I should make some of the rounds myself." He gave her a little salute. "You're a hell of a dancer."

Zerena watched him go. He didn't walk over to Joshua and Alestair, and she wasn't certain with whom he hoped to speak—she lost him in the crowd before she got the chance to see. And then she caught sight of Tanya again, weaving her way through the crowd as she spoke to one of the Russian attachés. Tanya and her radio.

Zerena still had mischief to sow tonight.

6.

Jordan swept the remains of a protection charm into a haphazard pile near the door. Then she leaned against her broom and surveyed the bar, taking in the day's handiwork. She had kept Bar Vodnář shuttered after the morning's battle. The loss of a day's income was a fair trade for keeping the Flame out.

She had spent all evening reinforcing her protection charms. Down in her spell room, she'd built new ones out of scraps of string and broken twigs and dried vines. She'd sat with her eyes closed on top of the confluence, feeling its energy vibrating through her as she hummed and chanted until the magic rubbed her voice raw. She had been weak from the fight, the muscles in her body trembling from the strain, but she forced herself to finish the spells anyway. If the Flame was willing to fight like that, she had a very serious problem on her hands.

Jordan picked up the dustpan and swept the charm dust into it. Half her old protection charms had been shattered by the Flame's magic as the men had tried to force their way in, and the detritus lay scattered around the bar, ash and dust and burned-up chunks of metal. As exhausted as she was, Jordan didn't want to stop cleaning. The rote mechanics of sweeping and dusting and wiping cleared the way for more complex thoughts. She'd sleep later. Right now, she needed to figure out what the Flame wanted.

Jordan moved around the tables, gripping the broom tight. What could they possibly be planning? And did the Ice know about it yet? Because once they learned, they'd be sniffing around her bar too, trying to get at the confluence. This space had been in Jordan's family for decades, and she'd always pretended that she'd turned it into a bar solely for her own purposes, her own access to magic—a renegade practitioner like herself needed all the assistance she could get. But really she had moved in because she wanted to keep *them* away from it. The Flame. And the Ice, too.

They thought they were so different, Flame and Ice. Enemies always do. The Soviets and the West, they were the same. They looked at each other and saw monsters; they looked at themselves and saw men. But Jordan stood on the outside and knew them each for both monsters *and* men, the good and the bad bleeding together. They were only villains and heroes in their own stories.

Jordan swept more furiously, the dust billowing up into clouds. She could feel the ley lines buzzing beneath her feet, and she remembered the first time she had ever experienced the power of a ley line. She had been a little girl living in a big house in the middle of Tehran. The courtyard had been filled with flowers that loved the heat; there had been servants, a maid who brought her rose water and ice cubes in the sweltering afternoons. Jordan's parents were important people, with important friends. She hardly saw them. But then, one evening, the maid had put Jordan in a silky dress and told her she was going out with her mother.

The ley line had been in the desert, running parallel to the city.

It felt like starlight settling over Jordan's skin, a thrumming, silvery prickle. Her mother had crouched down beside her and said in a low voice, the voice Jordan would later hear her using for spells and incantations, *This is our family's legacy.*

Jordan hadn't understood at the time; she thought her mother was referring to the strange, prickling energy. Later, though, she learned what her mother had really meant: neutrality. The in-between places, her family believed, were the most honest, the most true. They created the best magic.

Someone knocked on the front door of the bar, dragging Jordan out of her reverie. She shook her head, loosened her grip on the broom handle. She was too wrung out for this. That was the cost of neutrality, she'd learned in the years since she had first set eyes on that ley line: It was much more tiring, working on your own.

The knocking came again, a little louder, a little more insistent. Jordan sighed.

"We're closed!" she shouted. "Come back tomorrow."

She held her breath, listening. Her protection charms were all still and silent around her, but she stayed alert, aware of the potential for danger. Had the visitor left? Jordan glanced at the clock ticktocking above the bar. Almost one in the morning.

Jordan picked up the broom. She really should stop for the night. Sleep. She'd have a better sense of what the Flame was after in the morning—

Over at the door, something snapped, like a piece of wood breaking in half.

Jordan's exhaustion vanished in a flood of adrenaline. She let the broom fall with a loud, cracking *bang* and darted behind the bar. She still had some charms in her cache there. Weak ones, but they would do.

The doorknob turned; the door sprang open. The charms rippled, as if disturbed by a breeze, but there was no overwhelming force of magic like Jordan had felt that morning.

"I told you!" Jordan shouted, squeezing one charm in her hand, fingers poised to snap it in half for its activation. "We're closed."

Zerena Pulnoc breezed through the door and blessed Jordan with a smile as cold and shimmering as a frozen lake.

"Jordan," she purred. "Surely you can make an exception for me?"

Jordan didn't move. She didn't break the charm. Just watched as Zerena strolled into the bar. She was dressed for a party, her long silver gown trailing behind her, the jewels at her throat blinking in the bar's dim light. Her gaze fell on the fallen broom, the piles of ruined charms.

"I heard you had a bit of trouble earlier." She nudged the broom with the pointed toe of her shoe. "Some delinquents saw fit to bother you." She lifted her gaze and caught Jordan's eye. "I know you have a charm behind that counter, Jordan. Don't bother activating it. I have my own charms tonight." She fingered her necklace, which sent a pulse of energy through the room. The ley lines flared. Jordan dropped her charm to the floor.

"What do you want?" Jordan hissed. "I already told your two dogs no."

"Yes, you burned poor Ivan quite badly." Zerena clucked her tongue and shook her head. Then she pulled one of the chairs off the closest table and sank down into it. "I'll have a sidecar, if it's not too much trouble." She wrapped the necklace around one finger. Energy rumbled.

"We're closed." Jordan's heart thudded against her ribcage.

The Flame *was* desperate. A fight outside, and now Zerena

Pulnoc herself, in the flesh. The ambassador's wife and the Flame's mistress.

"You can still fix me a cocktail." It was not a request. "I'm not here to fight. I want to speak to you. That's all."

She looked up, eyes glinting. Jordan pulled a bottle of brandy from the shelf. Getting Zerena her drink would be the fastest way to get her out of here. That, Jordan knew from experience.

"Extra lemon?" Jordan said.

"Ah, you know me too well."

Jordan added the lemon juice, rattled the shaker, and poured the drink. The motions came easily, a distraction from the pounding in her chest. She poured herself a glass of brandy as well, then carried both drinks over to the table where Zerena sat watching her.

"Perfect," Zerena said as she reached for her glass. "I had a party tonight, you know. One of those diplomatic circuit things. Dreadfully boring." She took a sip. Jordan watched her warily, fingers tight around her glass. "But I couldn't have a sidecar there. I had to remain alert." She smiled over her drink.

"Why are you here?" Jordan asked.

"Let's finish our drinks before we talk business," Zerena said.

"No." Jordan took a long gulp of her brandy and slammed the half-empty glass on the table.

Zerena didn't even flinch, just gazed at her with an expression like a winter night, cold and clear and unfathomable.

"I've had a long day, Zerena. I don't want to fight you, but I will." Jordan jerked her chin toward the front door. "I took out your two boys earlier, and I can take you out too. Don't test me."

Zerena laughed. There was no mirth behind it, though, and the sound stabbed at Jordan's chest. "I'm not here to *fight*, Jordan.

My God! That's what people like Ivan and Edvard are for, are they not?"

Jordan drained the rest of her glass. The alcohol burned in her belly.

"It's true that my *organization*"—Zerena stressed the word— "would like access to your bar. It's selfish of you, keeping all this power to yourself."

"It's a family property," Jordan said. "I'm not handing it over to the highest bidder."

Zerena sipped her sidecar. "All we want is access. You occupy a strange place in our war. There's no reason for you to deny us help."

"There's no reason to offer aid," Jordan snapped. "If the Ice came sniffing around, I wouldn't let them have it either."

Zerena narrowed her eyes at the mention of the Ice. "Yes," she said slowly. "I suspected as much. It still doesn't help me."

Jordan shrugged. She eyed Zerena's drink. Not even half empty. She hated this kind of shit, this waiting-and-watching, this spy nonsense. This was Gabe's realm, not hers.

"At any rate," Zerena said, lifting her glass to her lips, although she did not drink, "I'm not here on behalf of my organization."

Jordan's body went tense. "Then why—"

"It's a personal matter." Zerena set her glass down. "Although I admit I did wish to compliment you on the impressive magic you used on poor Ivan and Edvard. Phosphorus and platinum! A classic."

"Why the fuck are you here?"

Zerena sighed and arranged her hands in her lap. "I need a charm. A small thing, nothing you haven't sold a thousand times over."

"Which one?" Zerena and her stratagems. Jordan was sure

that's what this was—some kind of trick, some elaborate, under-handed way of getting to the confluence under the bar.

"A source charm." Zerena leaned back in her chair. "One of the Russian officers has access to a device that I suspect is magical. I want to see who created it."

Jordan softened a little. This wasn't a wholly unreasonable request, and rooting around for magic in the KGB had always been one of Zerena's hobbies. Moreover, a charm like the one Zerena wanted was difficult to create without a strong power source—which Jordan had access to and the Prague Flame did not. Such charms took more than a month to make, even with the help of the ley lines, but Jordan kept a stash of them in her office. They were a common enough request that on the new moon she usually set aside time to start the process of creating one. If she sold Zerena her charm, she could get the woman out of her bar that much sooner. Even if she was telling the truth and wasn't here on Flame business, Jordan didn't like her hanging around. You could never know for sure what Zerena was up to.

"All right," Jordan said. "If I sell you one of these charms, will you get the hell out of my bar?"

"Where's that Bar Vodnář hospitality I hear so much about?"

Jordan glared at her.

"Fine." Zerena gave a bored shrug and took a drink. "I'll leave, just as soon as I have the charm." She appraised Jordan for a moment, looking thoughtful. "But Jordan—and I say this as an admirer of your work—you really ought to consider the Flame's offer."

"Offer?" Jordan laughed. "What offer? You sent a couple of toughs to my front door armed with magical weapons."

Zerena didn't say anything.

Jordan sighed: in frustration, in anger, in fear. She shoved away from the table and stood up.

"Wait here." Jordan didn't want to let Zerena anywhere near the supplies in her office. "If you touch anything while I'm gone, I will know."

"I would *never.*"

Jordan stumbled into the cool, dark hallway. Her palms were slick with sweat; she hadn't noticed until she was alone, away from Zerena. As she made her way down to the basement, she was painfully aware of Zerena sitting overhead, sipping her sidecar and scheming.

Jordan had no doubt that this source charm was tied in, some-how, to the Flame's over-arching plans. She had no doubt that when she handed the source charm over to Zerena, she would be aiding the Flame in some way. Not as much as if she gave them access to the ley lines. But enough that her tenuous position of neutrality would wobble and shift, leaning toward the fire. She hoped she was making the right decision.

The source charms were in a cabinet, locked and enchanted. Jordan pulled them out and picked them up one by one, feeling the ley lines thrum beneath her feet. Some of the charms were weaker than others, and when she found the weakest one, she dropped it into her pocket and shoved the basket of charms back into the cabinet. Then she made her way up the stairs.

Zerena waited where Jordan had left her. Her tumbler was empty. She stood up as Jordan approached, one of her arctic smiles frozen across her face.

"Here's your charm." Jordan tossed it into the air between them. Zerena didn't even blink; she caught it easily and turned it over in her palm.

"Thank you." Zerena looked up, and Jordan felt a sharp pang of fear when Zerena's eyes met with hers. She looked away, her breath short.

"You'll find your payment on the table," Zerena said. "Seventy-five should be enough, yes?"

"It's fine."

Footsteps, high heels clicking across the wooden floor. Jordan looked back over as Zerena stalked out of the bar, her long back taut and straight as a bowstring beneath the silver of her dress. She pulled the door open. Jordan watched, holding her breath.

And then Zerena stepped outside, vanishing into the night.

Jordan let out a long exhalation, slumping down at the table where Zerena had been sitting. A stack of bills sat neatly beside the empty glass. Jordan picked them up and ran her thumb along the edges, although she didn't bother to count.

She dropped the bills with a sigh and stared at the door. She could feel the power of her charms chiming around her, could feel the strength of the ley lines bubbling beneath her feet. They were calm right now. Just shimmering a little, waiting to be plucked, waiting for the music of enchantment to be unleashed into the world.

And Jordan was terribly afraid it would be the Flame's eager fingers picking those strings.

22
35
32
15
33

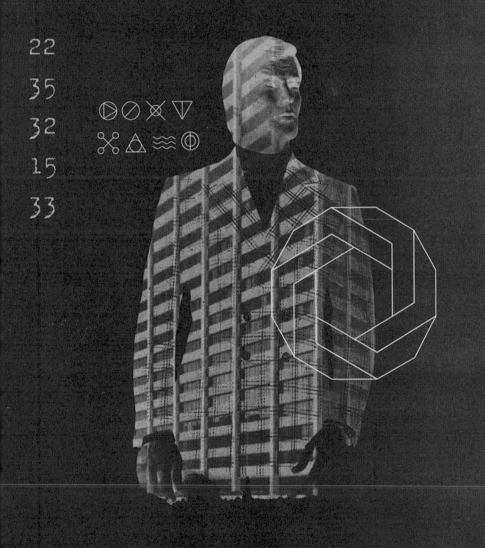

EPISODE 9

HEAD CASE

Max Gladstone

Prague, Czechoslovak Socialist Republic
February 24, 1970

EPISODE 9

1.

Even the finest hotel goes mad before a big event, and the Hotel International Praha was no exception. Gray-clad staff swarmed the back stairs and choked service elevators. Representatives from the Ministries of Culture and Science toured frieze-lined meeting rooms, hands clasped behind their backs, reviewing plush carpets and sparkling chandeliers with the couched disapproval of bureaucrats angling for a bribe. Everyone watched everyone else: Soviets watched Americans, Americans watched Soviets, Brits watched both, and everyone watched the Czechs.

But few people watched the maids.

"It's a wonder," Nadia Ostrokhina said as she pushed the cleaning cart into a fifth-floor room and closed the door. Once inside, she switched from Czech to Russian. "Even in our line of work, where you would expect more vigilance, people tend to overlook serving staff. As if rooms clean themselves."

Tanya Morozova shrugged, and lifted the top layer of folded bedsheets from the cart to reveal a stash of transmitters, which she then seeded around the room. "At least the uniforms matched this time. Not like the Berlin job."

Nadia laughed. "The Berlin job! Those girls will drink on that story for years. But this fabric feels cheap enough to be real." She flicked her overstarched collar, then grabbed another transmitter and headed for the bathroom. "I love this part of the work. Don't you?"

Tanya frowned at the transmitter she was trying to attach to a dresser's underside; it would not stick. She pressed its back harder against the wood. "Forty rooms to check on this floor, bugs to plant, then surveillance to make sure no one removes them. There's a fine line between impersonating menial laborers and performing menial labor."

"Oh please." Tanya heard a clatter from the bathroom—Nadia, climbing onto the counter. "For once we get to do clean, normal spy work. No magic, no ancient struggle between Flame and Ice, only comrades and their enemies playing at a shadow war. Think of it as a vacation."

The damn transmitter still would not stick. Tanya licked her thumb and rubbed the wood clean. "For this to be a vacation, we'd have to give the other world a rest." Again the transmitter fell. "It won't leave us alone just because we're ignoring it."

"Magic can take care of itself for a week or two." Tanya heard Nadia climb down from the bathroom sink, followed by the sound of running water. "We have a building of biologists on whom to spy, quite possibly *Amerikanski* schemes to thwart. Our comrades in the Ice will understand a slight shift in priorities."

"I'm not certain what to believe about our comrades in the Ice anymore." Tanya clutched the transmitter in her fist as if to snap it in half. She remembered frozen bodies arrayed on narrow beds on a barge. She remembered Andula's wide eyes before the safe house door closed, and imagined those same eyes, frozen shut.

Tanya sat back on her heels and glared at the transmitter in her palm. Nadia was standing beside her. Tanya hadn't heard her move. She followed the line of stockings and skirt up to her friend's—her partner's—face.

"Tanya. I understand your misgivings, but you need faith for now. We're doing good." The last word seemed very hard for her to say. "Focus on the job. This is fun. If you don't let yourself smile a little, you'll crack."

"Fine," Tanya said, and slapped the transmitter back against the wood. This time it stuck.

For now.

"Not much of a safe house," Dominic Alvarez said through his lit cigar.

Gabe Pritchard, hands in pockets, reviewed the alley. They hadn't been followed, as far as he could tell, and even with all the secret magic crap he'd dealt with in the last few weeks, he remained confident in his ability to spot a tail—but there was always the chance he'd missed something, especially with Dom along. The man was distracting, and not exactly subtle.

"Christ, keep your voice down," Gabe said. But the alley stayed still and cold and dark. No snow for once—a nice change—but enough left over from the last night's fall that Gabe should have been able to hear footsteps, or a silent observer changing position. Nothing.

Not that a prospective tail had anywhere to hide: no obstacles or shelter here, unless you counted those few trash cans. Dom tipped cigar ash into the snow by the basement door and kicked more snow to cover it up.

Gabe frowned. "They'll see your footprints."

"You CIA guys." Dom didn't quite laugh. "Always jumping at shadows. We would have seen a tail, and, Christ, do you really think some Soviet stooge will give a shit about one more ash pile in this city?"

Maybe, Gabe thought—*if there were magic involved.* The KGB had Ice moles—so why not Flame as well? Both mystical factions seemed to have a pretty damn wide sense of their own territory. Either way, might as well get on with it. If he started second-guessing himself about magic, he'd be here all night. "The space looks good to me. Clear lines of sight, off-street door, drop a sniper in the window up there and a guy on the roof, and nobody's getting in or out without our say-so. What am I missing?"

Dom shrugged.

Gabe resisted the urge to hit him. "ANCHISES starts in forty-eight hours. Our"—he stopped himself from saying *defector*—"guest arrives the day after tomorrow, and if we have to find a new safe house to stash him in, I'll need more than a hunch to justify it to Frank."

Dom went very still. The ember at the tip of his cigar flared. Then he moved. One arm darted out across Gabe's back, and the blunt, strong fingers of his hand bit into Gabe's shoulder. Gabe tensed, body calculating options and outs: dart inside, elbow to the throat, drop weight, don't go to the ground, where you'll lose the use of your height and Dom's dense strength will work to his advantage—

Then he realized Dom was laughing.

"Mother—" Gabe said, but didn't finish.

"Gabe, you're all right. High strung, but I like you." Dom

grinned around the cigar. "This place looks great. I was just fucking around. Come on. Let's check her out from the inside."

The padlock looked rusted but opened without protest, admit-
ting them to the bowels of the safe house.

This, too, looked defensible: a wide-open basement chamber,
lines of sight interrupted only by a few pylons, wooden pallets
piled to one side. One door led into a narrow hall, stairwell door
to the left, easily securable, storeroom to the right. Dom checked
exits and airflow. "Seems good."

Upstairs, a warren of rooms tangled around the central stair,
all unoccupied and in various stages of decay. This place had been
elegant once, before some revolution or another got to it. "Why's
no one here?"

Gabe shook his head. "Whole place is marked for demolition
come spring."

"Structural problems?" Dom asked, peeling away a long strip
of plaster.

"Nothing like that," Gabe said. "Just building something else
in its place."

"Make-work shit. Shame, beautiful old piece of junk like this."

The hitchhiker in Gabe's head twitched.

"You okay?"

Months ago, Gabe wouldn't have been. Months ago, even that
little twitch would have doubled him over in pain. Much as he
hated to admit it, he seemed to be learning how to deal with the
bastard. Either that or the hitchhiker, this dumb elemental stuck
half in and half out of his head, was finally on board with the
whole "don't get Gabe reassigned for mental health reasons" plan.

Still, no sense ignoring the thing. "I'll go check the roof, in
case the advance team missed something."

Dom stuck his head back out through a cracked doorframe. "You want me to come with?"

God, yes—he could use some cigar-chomping, well-armed backup. But if there was something magical up there, Dom would demand an explanation, which would mean explaining to the brass, and if he did that . . . well. So much for Gabe Pritchard, CIA officer.

"Nah," he said. "I can handle it."

Stairs creaked underfoot. Dust filtered through the faint gray light. The twitch in Gabe's skull intensified as he climbed, but reciting Alestair's formulas kept it contained. As to what Gabe would find on the roof, he had no idea. Another Host, maybe? Could the captives on the boat have worked their way free? Someone hostile, or hunting him?

He opened the door onto the roof and exhaled, caught in a fist of cold air. After the tight stairwell, the Prague rooftops seemed to unfold forever on all sides, slate tile and spires of disused churches.

The golem stood at the edge of the roof.

It didn't move, at first.

The golem had chased Gabe through the nights of Prague, clattering after him down alleys; he'd felt its clay hand close around his leg, but always he had seen it out of the corner of his eye, or racing from shadow to shadow. In movement and nighttime shadows the—"creature" was the wrong word—the thing seemed unfinished, made in haste by a rushed sculptor, but in the chill, sourceless light of this late afternoon, it did not look unfinished at all.

Human fingers had left loving tracks upon the roughness of its face. The curve and edge of a palm had shaped the swell of muscles; nails had carved the whorls of the golem's fingerprints.

THE WITCH WHO CAME IN FROM THE COLD

The golem had not been built to pass for a human being, Gabe thought, in that frozen rooftop moment. The golem had not been built to pass for anything save itself.

In the rough beauty of those features Gabe recognized himself, and Tanya Morozova, and Josh Toms and Alestair Winthrop and Nadia and even Dom, down below.

He was surprised how still it looked; he hadn't realized until he saw the monster waiting just how much real people moved, legs shaking, shoulders rising and falling, eyes darting as focus shifted.

He was even more surprised when the golem lunged.

It did not need to shift its weight—no muscles tensed before that hunk of clay sprang. It caught his arm in one massive three-fingered hand and slammed him against the wall. Its mouth opened, revealing crystal teeth and a long, dark gullet. A wind colder than the wind of rooftop Prague hit him from behind somehow, and he was drawn down and down into the pit between those teeth. His hitchhiker screamed.

He tried to pull free of the golem but could not shake its grip. His free hand clutched inside his trench coat for the flask of Vltava River water he kept there—Alestair had used it against the golem last time; he'd collected some himself by moonlight—he felt stretched, pulled, in and down the golem's throat—

He fumbled the flask open and splashed the golem in the face.

The golem did not roar. It had no lungs. But it fell back, flailing, and Gabe fell too, skidded on the tile roof, almost tumbled over the edge but caught himself. He lunged for the fallen flask. There were a few drops left, maybe enough to save him.

The golem staggered to the roof's edge and leaped away. As it arced over the alley, its head spun a half turn on its neck and glared back at Gabe—glared with Gabe's own eyes.

Prone on the safe house roof, Gabe told himself he was imagining the resemblance. The golem had been vague at first, its features an artful meld. But that had been his own face staring at him as the golem scuttled over rooftops out of sight, his own face in clay. The thing had tried to draw him down, to swallow him into itself.

He'd hoped the golem would keep to the shadows for another couple weeks, a string of unsolved crimes pestering the Prague police, but it was coming for him now, on the eve of ANCHISES, when the Company needed all hands on deck, when the slightest mistake could tip their hand to the Russians. When he could least afford goddamned distractions and goddamned magic.

"Hey!" Dom's voice issued from the stairwell. "You okay up there? "

"I slipped," Gabe said, forcing himself to his feet. "There's ice, but the roof looks . . ." He searched for the right word. "Clear. We're good to go."

He climbed back down, carrying the empty flask, but the rooftops and the cold lingered in his mind.

2.

That's the shape of it," Dom said in the meeting with Frank the next morning, and tapped his cigar into the ashtray. "Safe house secured, retreat lines scouted. We're good to go once the eggheads get here."

Frank sipped his coffee and reviewed the troops: Dom, relaxed as ever, smoking; Josh, controlled, pale, with an eager edge Gabe remembered from his own first big op; and Gabe himself.

"Like he said." Gabe had picked up a limp during his near tumble off the roof, and he hoped he was hiding it well. "We'll have the safe house locked up nice and tight."

"Glad to hear it, gentlemen." Frank flipped two pages on his clipboard and did not frown with his face so much as with his entire body. "The conference starts next week, but the first delegates arrive tomorrow night—Dr. Sokolov among them. There's an arrival ceremony the day after, but most everyone's bound for bed as soon as they touch down. That makes tonight our best opportunity to rendezvous with Sokolov."

Gabe tried not to tense. He'd be the logical choice for the

rendezvous, given his field experience, and under any other circumstances he'd have happily made the play, but not with the golem gunning for him. Frank watched him for a pause that lasted far too long, and Gabe scraped for some legitimate reason to beg off.

"Josh," Frank said without turning, "you'll make the contact."

Relief tasted sweet as honey. Yes, Josh getting the tap probably meant bad things for Gabe's own career—it likely meant Frank hadn't forgiven Gabe's earlier magic-induced fuckups with Drahomir and the Russians—but at least the op would roll off smoothly. He covered, though: "Toms doesn't have the field experience."

"He has to get it somehow." Frank held a piece of paper from the clipboard out to Josh, who didn't move. "Son, you handled the Milovic approach just fine. Gabe's overexposed for this sort of job—we can get you in with the bellhops, give you a solid approach vector for Sokolov, and a script. It's an easy run." *So long as you don't fuck it up,* Frank very pointedly did not say. "How's that sound?"

Josh's hand didn't shake when he took the paper—or at least, didn't shake much.

Gabe caught up with Josh in the closet that passed for the office kitchen. Josh didn't notice Gabe's approach at first—he was drinking coffee from a mug he held with both hands and staring at a blank yellow patch of wall. Gabe reached for Josh's shoulder, but stopped himself. The slightest touch might send the kid to the rafters. Instead, he leaned against the counter and waited with his head down and his arms crossed.

"I'm that obvious?" Josh asked after a while.

"You'll be fine."

Josh uncurled one hand from the coffee mug, drew the folded paper from his inside pocket, and passed it to Gabe.

"You shouldn't let me read this."

"None of this should be happening in the first place."

Gabe skimmed the paper, folded it again, and offered it back. "Easy liaison. Winthrop's in with the bellhops is solid, no risks there. It's not the easiest job I've seen, but you could do a lot worse. No running, no gunning, hardly any risk. Get a full night's sleep and you'll be good to go."

"I've never done anything like this before."

"Back when we were stalking Morozova, you took a flying leap out of a car to chase a lead."

"That was a mistake."

"Whatever you want to call it, that's what we need right now."

Josh took the paper back.

"I'll see if I can get any more intel on the Russian counter-ops, in case they're playing a new game. You'll be fine."

"Are you sure?"

They stared at opposite walls, painted the same horrible yellow. "Hey," Gabe said. "You can count on me."

"I," Gabe confessed to Jordan Rhemes over beer that night at Bar Vodnář, after she'd chased the other customers out, "have no god-damned idea what I'm supposed to do. I thought learning about the Ice and the Flame was supposed to make my life easier—get this madhouse under control, figure out what's going on inside my head, and push myself back to work. Now I have a golem hunting me through Prague, and—" He cut himself off. Jordan wasn't Ice or Flame, exactly, but she wasn't CIA, either. "It's getting in the way of my day job."

She tossed back the last of the two fingers of bourbon she'd poured for herself and glanced a question at him, which he answered with a tired nod. More bourbon for him, a splash for her, and she returned the bottle to its shelf. He started drinking. She pondered him, and the glasses, and the bourbon, and did not. "You say the Vltava water did nothing."

"It worked. The golem ran for the hills after I splashed it."

"But it didn't stop the thing—our monster didn't calm."

"More like the opposite."

"And after you experienced what you called a 'sucking' feeling, it began to look like you?"

The golem's face had changed when it tried to draw him into its mouth. It *had* looked more like him. Or was that only a well-placed shadow, mixed with fear? "I must have made that up."

"If you want to survive while working magic, Gabriel, you need to resist self-doubt. Trust your own eyes, your own ears, more than your judgment."

Gabe shifted in his chair and stared into his glass. "Eyes lie all the time. Ears too."

"No," she said. "Eyes never lie. The judgment lies—it leaps to false conclusions, it embraces easy answers."

"But if I trust my senses more than I trust my judgment, how can I tell if I'm going mad?"

"There's a thin line between magic and madness," she said, and took a drink after all.

"You're not making me feel better."

"You don't come to me to make yourself feel better. You come for help. And you need more of that than usual."

"So you think the golem's going to stay a problem."

"Don't you?"

He tilted the shot glass and stared through its amber lens down at the bar. "My luck's not been that good recently."

"I believe," she said, "the golem wants to stay alive. All living things do, and it was made to simulate a living thing. When you drew near in the graveyard, your 'hitchhiker'—the elemental—gave it power. Perhaps now it seeks to draw the elemental into itself. Unfortunately for you, the elemental is too deeply fused with your body, your soul, to slide from you so easily."

Because anything else would be too damn simple. "I die if it goes."

"Or you may be ripped from your own body, and bound into the golem's."

"Do you see much difference there?"

"Death or eternal imprisonment." She shrugged. "They seem different to me."

"So what do we do?"

"Alestair says—"

"God, I don't want to go to the Brit about this. I'm in deep enough with him already."

"Even with your soul on the line?" Jordan leaned the bar's ladder against the topmost shelf and climbed up. "At any rate," she said as she groped among the bottles and casks and wrapped packages there, "I only mentioned him. You don't need to be so defensive."

"Long day, I guess."

"Alestair says every time someone's woken the golem in the past, it wandered until it ran out of power."

"So where's the power coming from?"

"Maybe it's feeding off your elemental—like a moving magnet starts a current in a wire."

"It's not *my* elemental."

"It *is* your elemental—it's just not completely inside you. Maybe the golem can draw off the part you're not using. That explains why the Vltava water didn't work—the water tries to force the golem to sleep, but your presence wakes it up."

"What if we drown it in the Vltava? Or dump it in?"

"You'd end up with a very wet, very angry golem. Catch." A red flash floated down from the top shelf, spinning and sparking in the taproom lamplight. He caught it: a long quill, blood-red from tip to farthest barb. Jordan descended, bearing a bottle that contained only a yellowed scroll.

"What's this?"

"Golems run on scripture in their heads, written on vellum or leather—that's the myth, anyway. I've never had a chance to play with one myself. But if tales are all we have to go on . . ." She uncorked the bottle and tipped the scroll into her palm. It was smaller than he'd thought. She unrolled the scroll an inch, drew a knife from her belt, and sliced off a piece. The way the knife parted the scroll seemed familiar. His stomach turned.

"Is that skin?"

"Yes," she said, and took a silver bowl from beneath the bar. "I'll write 'stop' on here, in Hebrew and a few other languages just in case. When you see the thing next, get this into its head. It might not work, but if it doesn't, I don't know what will."

"It almost crushed me."

"So find someone to help. Maybe your friend in the Ice."

"Morozova's not my friend."

Jordan shrugged. "This is what I can offer. And you should be grateful." She slid the scroll back into the bottle and replaced the cork. "You have no idea what this stuff is worth."

"What will you use for ink?"

She slid him the bowl and the knife, which was not quite as sharp as her smile. "Guess."

3.

Josh had spent all afternoon talking to himself in the mirror in his apartment, practicing his walk, the angle of his shoulders, picking up and putting down suitcases. He expected, based on his brief, unsuccessful stage stints in college, that even so simple an act as carrying luggage would become, conservatively speaking, a million times ganglier and tanglier when performed. The first time he'd learned to walk had taken a year or two, depending on how one counted, and considering that, he made remarkable progress in a single afternoon. He was almost feeling positive about the evening's operation, at least until he entered the embassy briefing room and found Alestair waiting.

"My dear Mr. Toms!" The Englishman uncurled himself and leaned across the table, one hand extended. "I didn't expect you would be the one our dear friends dispatched for this rendezvous." His hands looked spindly, his fingers long and narrow, but his grip could have pulped wood.

"I'm as surprised as you are," Josh said. The room's bad lights cast a sickly green over everything, but somehow Alestair's eyes stayed bright, pale blue.

"Let's not all get too chummy." Dom sauntered in, thumbs hooked through his belt loops, suit jacket flared, smelling of cigar smoke—though thankfully, for once, not smoking. "Your people can get us into the hotel, Winthrop?"

"Our staff contact, Baračnik, can outfit Josh with the needed uniform and place him. Josh, you will be directed to Sokolov and will escort him upstairs, do your business, and exit. Baračnik will meet you beforehand in the restaurant two blocks south and three east of the hotel; you'll identify yourself by carrying this folded newspaper." Alestair passed it across the table. "He'll approach you with a question about opera, an article about which he will recognize in the paper. Claim that you are not a follower of the form. He'll take you to the hotel and instruct you—all very straightforward. You won't be in public until the proper moment. Acceptable?"

"He gets the picture," Dom said.

"While I share your confidence, I'd prefer to hear him agree in his own voice."

"I can do it," Josh said. "Thank you for setting this up." His mouth felt dry.

"My dear friend, it's the very least I can do. Feel free to call upon the services of, ah, Her Majesty's government whenever you have need. Anything for the colonies, and so on and so forth."

Gabe spotted Morozova across the International's crowded entrance hall—wearing a name tag, even, and talking with a uniformed woman who must have been a member of the hotel staff. Here on cover business, probably. He waited, buzzing with adrenaline and whiskey, as Morozova's conversation swelled to a full hand-waving argument. Which woman would stab the other first? Neither, it turned out. They shook hands, and the staffer marched away as if to the trenches of a lost war. Morozova remained, staring into an explosion of hothouse roses in an ugly vase by a window. Behind the roses, snow fell.

"We have a fairy tale about that," he said, in English, when he joined her. "Roses and snow. Sometimes there's blood, and a raven or something."

She'd given no sign that she'd noticed his approach, but neither did she seem surprised when he spoke. "So do we. Yours probably comes from ours."

"They let you tell fairy tales?"

"Have you ever tried to stop someone from telling tales?"

Gabe shrugged and let her have the point. "You here in character tonight?"

"An embassy cultural attaché has her duties, among them overseeing the organization of this conference and assuring the delegates' comfort."

Bullshit. "That why you were arguing? The delegates' comfort?"

"Comfort," she said, "and security."

"That's what I wanted to talk about." He was drumming his fingertips on the table and made himself stop. Outside, wind swirled snowflakes against snowflakes. Rooftop shadows cut strict lines over fallen white. Nothing moved but the snow. "Delegates arrive tonight."

"Yes."

"And the golem's still on the loose."

A car rolled past outside. Headlights lit her ivory. "What are you saying, Pritchard?"

She looked so honest and interested, and so alone, that he

almost told her everything: the golem, the risk, and how alone he felt too, unable to confide in Josh or Dom or Frank or even Jordan completely, how it felt to be pulled from your own skull and dragged down a gullet lined with glowing teeth. But Tanya Morozova was an acolyte of the Ice, which he barely trusted, and an officer in the KGB, his—what did you call it? Mundane? "Secular" was the word the nuns would have used. Either way, his enemy.

He could not trust her, or tell the truth. But he could ask for help.

"The golem hasn't been a problem so far, because it's preying on locals. But what if it takes one of the delegates?"

"It wouldn't try. There is too much security." Too quick an answer: She wanted that to be true but wasn't sure.

"Maybe the golem isn't afraid of guns. If it gets the notion it wants to kill one of the delegates—that would make a lot of headaches for both sides. For all sides," he corrected himself.

He told the truth, because you always did in this business if you could. Telling the truth cut the chances of being caught in a lie to just north of zero. Don't tell the whole truth, no, just enough to let your target draw her own assumptions. Morozova wanted the golem gone as much as he did, and the more she directed her attention toward it, the less she'd be focusing on the International, and on Sokolov.

"Do you have a plan?"

He checked the reflection in the window glass. In the lobby behind him, two clerks annotated registers behind the front desk. A bellhop escorted a late arrival in a wheelchair to her room, and another followed, struggling with bags. A fat man lay asleep beneath a newspaper. If he was faking, he faked more convincingly than anyone Gabe had ever seen.

He took, from his inside pocket, the slip of skin-paper. "If the thing shows up, we need to get this inside its head somehow. I'm not sure if it will work, but it's all I've got. I'd do it myself, but the thing's big, and fast. Many hands make light work."

She touched the slip. "Where did you get this?"

"Jordan."

"Rhemes wouldn't have just given you something like this. She would have demanded more payment than you could afford."

"She's a friend," he said. "She wanted to help."

"You're hiding something." He never would have described her as open, but she closed before his eyes.

That's what we do, he almost said. "I'm not."

"Rhemes would not have given you this without reason. She's not enough a part of our world to care about this conference. She thinks you're in danger. I don't know why, but I'm tired of being kept in the dark."

He remained alone by the window, watching the snow, after she left.

Josh finished his prep in good time, filing cases beneath rows of ticking clocks, each showing a different time in a different city. By Tokyo this whole thing would be over, one way or another.

A shadow crossed his desk, and he smelled cigar smoke. He closed the folder. "Alvarez."

"Josh, I know you've got your panties in a twist about this, but really, you'll be fine. It's like the first time you shoot a guy. Seems a lot worse when you're thinking it through than when you're doing it, or when it's done."

Josh locked a stack of folders in his desk drawer, pulled on his greatcoat, and picked up his suitcase. "Going my way?"

"No one's really going your way, Josh," Dom said, "but I'll walk you out."

They wound down three flights of stairs in silence. Josh barely felt the carpet beneath his feet. A gust of wind could have blown him away. Dom's footsteps echoed, even muffled by the carpet. The guy moved as if testing the ground beneath for weaknesses. Josh couldn't imagine him sneaking up on someone. Different training, maybe. Different tools for different tasks.

Dom didn't speak until they reached the ground floor. He slid one hand from his pocket and settled it on Josh's shoulder. Emily, Frank's secretary, rushed past them up the stairs, bearing a mug of coffee and a thick accordion file; Dom followed her skirt with his eyes.

If Emily noticed, she didn't acknowledge. Dom didn't seem to care whether she had.

"Just wanted to talk to you," he said, in a tone of voice Josh knew too well, had heard too many people use in his direction, half-cautious, half-dismissive, as if the subject under discussion was barely worth mentioning. "We're all friends here, and because we're all friends, I can say: You know about Winthrop, right?"

"I know he's"—*don't say MI6; the area's not secure*— "a culture guy for the UK."

Dom's hand tightened on Josh's shoulder. "That's not what I'm talking about, understand?"

"I don't think I do." But you had to be careful, of course, because if you came off as too dense they'd peg you for defensive, ask: *What do you have to hide?* "Is there a problem?" Which could mean: *Is there something wrong with the mission? Is he a double agent? Treacherous?* But could also mean whatever Dom wanted to hear.

"Not really," he said. "I mean, he's not, let's say . . . he's not unreliable"—with weight on that last word. "But if I was you, I wouldn't let him get too close. Might give some people the wrong impression. Nothing to worry about, nothing I've heard specifically, nothing you need to trouble yourself with. Just—watch out, all right?"

Josh nodded but couldn't bring himself to say *all right*.

On his way to the meeting, switching from van to bus to van again, doubling back through narrow streets in snow as the gray night deepened into dark, he rewound the conversation in his mind. His reactions seemed so obvious in retrospect: the way he'd tightened under Dom's hand, the slight lean forward in his conversation with Winthrop, and he'd certainly, for all his care, overplayed perplexity with Dom. No one would have missed that implication, and most, having caught it, would laugh, deflect, make some crude joke. He'd exposed himself. He rehearsed the old arguments he hoped he'd never have to make: Liking men wasn't a security risk any more than liking women; hell, there were women in the agency these days, and some of them presumably liked men just fine. Blackmail? Sure, but blackmail only worked if you feared discovery. Which he did.

Dom thought he was looking out for Josh. Gotta warn people about that Alestair Winthrop. Who knows what reputations he might sully, what insinuations he might slide into the old boys' networks, close and vicious as any quilting circle.

Fuck, the gall of the man. Like Josh couldn't take care of himself. Like he didn't know what Winthrop was about. Like he hadn't been thinking about it for . . . well.

He dreamed sometimes about those eyes. Not often, but enough.

I'll be fine, he told himself as he entered the narrow corner restaurant with its low Formica tables. *Fine,* he repeated in his mind when the tall blond man with the double chin approached, examined his folded newspaper with grim earnestness, and asked if he planned to read the review of Arroyo's new album. *Fine,* he prayed earnestly as he'd ever prayed to any god before, as Baračnik excused himself, having established by code that Josh should meet him at the hotel loading dock in forty-five minutes.

Fine, as the hotel door opened, exhaling steam into the snow-swirled dark, and Baračnik beckoned him into reddish light.

He'd never done this before, but Gabe was there, and Gabe would watch out for him.

The doors closed with a clang, and Baračnik snapped the lock shut.

Gabe spent an unprofitable few minutes watching snow and trying to talk himself out of his funk. He'd misplayed Morozova. Rookie mistake—come on too strong, too fast, lean on her loyalty to the Ice and her self-regard and expect her not to ask your angle. He needed help with the golem, yes, but he'd hoped to parlay that into information about her KGB masters' security plans.

So much for that. Might as well handle things the old-fashioned way.

When the lobby behind him was clear, he reached into the rose vase, past the thorns, and found the folded piece of paper pasted inside the vase neck, right where Winthrop's contact had left it. Blood beaded on the back of Gabe's hand. He hadn't felt the thorn go in. He sucked up the blood and unfolded the paper: room 618, Sokolov's berth. They didn't have time to screen the whole hotel for bugs again, but he could look over the scientist's room one last time, in case Morozova or her pals had bugged the place after the embassy team's sweep.

He checked his watch. Delegates would arrive in an hour and a half. Plenty of time. Run a thorough search, drop by the lobby, catch Josh's eye, and give him the all clear. Easy.

He walked past the elevators to the service stairwell. Six flights would do him good, after a winter stuck in too-cold offices. In Cairo, he'd promised never to complain about cold weather again. So much for promises.

The door slammed behind him, so loud Gabe almost convinced himself he'd imagined the twitch in his skull. But the twitch did not fade with the echo. It remained, pulling down toward the basement, to the center of the world. Not the clear bell-throb of a Host's presence, either—this was the same squirrely tug he'd felt in the abandoned safe house.

The golem had come.

Shit.

He must have led it here—the golem wanted his elemental, and he'd dragged it into play on the night of Josh's op. Should have known better, should have stayed away, asked Dom to check the room—no. Shoulds were for after-action reports.

Consider the situation.

You're in a conference hotel in Prague. There's a golem in the basement that will track you down wherever you run. You have no backup. But then, it has no escape.

A smart man would have run, or found help. Winthrop, maybe; Gabe hated being in the man's debt, but there were worse fates.

Gabe, at the moment, was not feeling smart.

He descended into the bowels of the hotel.

4.

Tanya trailed storm clouds through the International's conference level, reviewing meeting rooms and coffee services and posted schedules for some damn thing she could argue about. Pritchard. She didn't like the bastard, couldn't forgive him for wasting her time and—what was the American expression?—yanking her chain. But she should not have turned him down flat and marched off. The American was an asset, however reluctant, and she'd ignored a chance to reel him in.

Why?

Trace the causes. Especially in magic.

The rage welling up at Pritchard was the same fury she'd felt when Nadia had joked (joked!) about the *comfort* of spy work. Tanya was tired of being kept in the dark. She was tired of bodies on barges and of other people deciding her ignorance was necessary.

She was tired of being used.

Pritchard wanted help but wouldn't say why. His notion that the golem might disturb the conference seemed far-fetched.

The thing had kept to the shadows so far. But Pritchard might know something she did not—about the golem, or about the conference—which had no magical significance so far as Tanya knew. What if he wasn't worried about magic, though? What if his masters in the CIA had their own plans for the next week?

She could have played him out, learned his secrets, but she'd let her pride chase him off.

Damn.

To persist in a mistake, her grandfather always said, was to repeat it.

She closed her eyes and exhaled some of her anger. She no longer felt imminently murderous. Good start.

She ran downstairs from the mezzanine to the front hall and crossed to the bellhop's desk. "Did you see which way the American went when he left?"

"Didn't leave." He pointed to the stairs.

"Thanks, Comrade," she said with a wave, and walked as fast as decorum would allow toward the stairwell. Concrete up and down, no footprints anywhere. Might he be searching the hotel? Meeting a contact?

She heard a muffled cry from the basement, and started running.

Gabe came to and found himself being dragged along a cracked concrete basement floor. This was why you went in with backup, with a partner: so when you were proceeding down an ill-lit basement hallway with a bottle of Vltava water in each hand, someone would shout a warning when the golem you'd thought was in front of you turned out to be hanging from the ceiling.

He blinked his eyes clear and focused on the hand that held

his leg. The golem seemed thinner than he remembered, and when it glanced back over its shoulder, it looked even more like him. He kicked at the golem's hand, but the clay seemed impervious to size-eleven oxfords.

He inventoried his assets and outs. Vltava water, gone—he'd brought his flask and a fresh wine bottle full of the stuff; the wine bottle had fallen in the attack and was likely broken. Not that it would have been much use anyway. He groped for his inside jacket pocket—the scroll was still there.

The golem turned a corner and tossed him against a wall.

The impact knocked the breath from his lungs. He heard something tear and hoped it was his jacket. *Okay, okay, get it together. Stand up. Find an escape.*

He lay in a nook in the hotel boiler room. Pipes knocked and steam hissed. The golem loomed above him. Reddish light played off its features, rough clay echoes of Gabe's own.

He forced himself to his feet, one hand stanching the blood from his split lip. The golem stretched out its arms. Gabe breathed twice, then leaped forward and stabbed the golem in the forehead with the scroll—but the scroll did not go in.

He had just enough time to watch mirror-familiar confusion play across the creature's face before it caught him by the throat, lifted, and opened its mouth.

Tanya found the fallen bottle in the reddish shadows of the hotel subbasement and followed rough, muddy footprints through a maze of pipes.

She almost ran past the alcove where the golem stood, back toward her, strangling Pritchard. The American pried at the clay

THE WITCH WHO CAME IN FROM THE COLD

hand's grip, kicked nonexistent genitals at the clay legs' fork, and, generally, seemed about to die. His face looked wrong, blurred like smudged film and stretched toward the golem's mouth.

She threw the bottle at the golem, and the glass shattered on its head.

The golem turned.

Tanya ducked an arc of clay. A fist clanged off a pipe, and superheated steam hissed into the narrow hall, darkening and softening the golem's skin. The thing lurched toward her, flailing, blind. In the dark, its face looked just like Gabe's.

The American lay groaning on the floor.

"Pritchard!" she cried. "The scroll!"

The golem lunged for her again, and again she dodged; one clay arm tangled in pipes, and she struck its elbow, to no avail. The golem glared at her with Pritchard's face and tore its hand free, breaking more steam pipes. Some people would miss their hot showers the next morning. The thought was absurd, but she didn't laugh.

She dodged the golem again and bared her teeth. The top of the broken wine bottle lay on the ground, some water still within. She grabbed the bottle by the neck and crouched low. The next time the golem came for her, she ran into its arms.

The golem crushed her to its chest. Her ribs creaked. The golem's body felt warm and smelled of sunbaked mud and warmer places than Prague.

She drove the broken bottle into its face.

Glass bit and cut. Clay features twisted in pain. She flew back into bent metal, fell. Her ears rang. The golem raised its foot to stomp on her chest, crush her skull—and through the reddish bloom of her vision, she saw Pritchard clinging to the golem's back with one arm, saw him thrust his fist into the golem's head and draw it out again, fingers clotted with wet clay.

The golem stilled.

There was no sound in the International's boiler room but escaping steam and the creak of broken things. Waves of pressure and terror rolled through Tanya, rolled out, rolled in again. The basement throbbed.

Gabe offered her a hand. She accepted it and pulled herself up.

Hiding the golem was easier than Tanya feared. The golem weighed much less than it seemed it should. Perhaps it was hollow on the inside; perhaps animation gave it weight. Either way, they could lift it together, Gabe at the feet and Tanya at the shoulders. There were many storage lockers and closets in this subbasement, some of which obviously had not been opened in years, but none of which she trusted to remain undisturbed when the International sent staff to fix the broken pipes. In the end, they lugged the golem to the furnace and hid it among piled junk and spare parts.

They watched each other in the reddish shadows, torn and bruised. Blood from Pritchard's lip smeared his jaw. He looked like a wild man caught feeding. Tanya did not imagine she looked any better. They needed to clean up. They needed to talk. "Come on."

She led him up the back stairs to the fourth floor, slipped a lock on a randomly chosen hotel room—they'd all be empty here, none of the delegates having yet arrived—led him in, and closed and locked the door behind herself.

"Thank you," he said, the idiot, but at least he shut up when she glared and pressed a finger to her lips. He stayed by the door, out of sight, as she closed the window blinds and deactivated the bug under the windowsill and the bug under the dresser, as she climbed onto the bathroom sink—saw her reflection, bruised and

410   THE WITCH WHO CAME IN FROM THE COLD

dirt caked, her face and blouse smeared with rusty mud—and turned off the bug there too. She washed her hands, wet a towel, wiped her face clean, wet another, and threw it toward him.

"We can talk," she said, "for a few minutes."

"They won't notice?"

"They're not expecting to hear anything," she said. "Tell me the truth."

He dabbed his chin with the towel and frowned at the blood.

"You missed some," she said.

"Where?"

"All over."

He shouldered past her to the mirror and scrubbed the mud-mixed blood away. In that moment, leaning forward, frowning critically at lip and jawline, in spite of the divides of ghosts and golems and gender and the Iron Curtain, he reminded Tanya of Elena Petrovna, her old roommate back in the Moscow International School, cleaning off the wreckage of a successful night. Golem makeup. She caught her laugh in her palm before it could form.

"What's that?" Pritchard turned from the mirror. She tapped her own chin, and he swiped away the last of the blood.

"Tell me the truth," she said. "Why did you come to me?" Best sort of question to ask in an interrogation, which this was, after a fashion: a question to which you already knew the answer.

"The golem was hunting me," he said. "Hunting this thing in my head." He tapped his temple. "It wanted to eat me. If you hadn't come along when you did—I don't know what would have happened."

He did know. He just couldn't say it. Americans did not like thinking about death, especially their own. "But if it was hunting you, why would it start now? It's been awake for weeks. Surely it could have tracked you down earlier."

"Search me."

She raised an eyebrow.

"I mean, I don't know. I don't know anything about this. You people have your rules, your stories, your magic, and I don't want anything to do with it. I just want to do my job. Live my life." He exhaled. "But here I am. I was in trouble."

"And you came to me. Why?"

"It was the right decision, wasn't it? You saved my life."

She had, was the damnedest thing.

"Winthrop." It was not a question, but it was all she could manage at the moment.

"Knows what he's doing, but he's an operator."

"So am I."

"I know," Pritchard said. "And you don't even really like me. We don't see eye to eye on much." He ran a hand through his hair, which he hadn't cleaned; mud and sweat made it stand up like a sad clown's wig. "That's an understatement, I guess. But I don't trust Winthrop at my back. And I do trust you."

The words bit. She remembered Nadia's extended hand. Fire couched in her throat. "Get out of here," she said, and showed him her watch. "We don't have time."

He did not need to be told twice.

Josh, feeling ridiculous in the scratchy, gold-corded bellhop uniform, followed Baračnik from the break room to the lobby. A row of blocky gray vans pulled up outside. He did not gawk or speak, just kept to Baračnik's heels, eyes on the carpet. Some of the other bellhops were also new: busy night, it seemed.

Discipline be damned, he couldn't stop himself from checking the front hall for Gabe. He'd be reading a newspaper, perhaps, or savoring a glass of something amber and not entirely unlike whiskey at the bar.

But Gabe wasn't there.

No arrival ceremony tonight, Baračnik had explained: The delegates were tired from their long voyages, missing homes and families—none, of course, having been allowed to bring wife or children. One more layer of security. Sokolov's wife had passed away of cancer two years before; his son was an army officer, fiercely loyal—his career would be hurt if the old man's defection ever became public, but not destroyed. At least, that's what the initial contact had tried to persuade Sokolov to think.

Such were the ways of the world.

Bellhops assembled in a gauntlet by the doors, two lines facing each other. Baračnik took point—if someone else angled for Sokolov, Baračnik would block him, ensure the scientist ended up with Josh instead.

Scientists emerged from the bus, swaddled in snow-frosted furs. Steam wreathed them. They seemed anonymous and interchangeable in the mist and dark, and though Josh that afternoon could have drawn Sokolov's picture with a Dutch master's precision, Josh standing in the International's front hall at night felt a brief stab of panic. Maybe he'd get it wrong. Maybe Sokolov would miss the sign. Maybe he'd screw it up.

Josh tried to swallow. His uniform felt too tight. He thought about Alestair Winthrop's soft skin, and then, because the world was a sad, sick place, he thought about Dom Alvarez's warning by the embassy front door.

Where the fuck was Gabe?

A jowly apparatchik in one of those big round fur hats Josh

could never quite believe anyone wore outside a Rocky and Bullwinkle cartoon gathered the scientists, shivering, into a line, paired with their luggage.

He didn't need Gabe, Josh told himself. He didn't need anyone. He could do this on his own. In the end, you always had to, anyway.

Someone tapped Josh on the shoulder and said, with Gabe's voice, in heavily accented Czech, "Excuse me? Can you tell me how this address?"

There was nothing dignified or professional about Josh's relief. With what he later considered the best acting of his life, he kept his face impassive, turned, and, looking at the note in Gabe's hand rather than at his friend's face, answered, in clipped English, "It is left out the doors, down the road four blocks, take a left, and then two blocks."

The note read: *Over bathroom mirror, under dresser, under windowsill.* They must have seeded another round of bugs after the security sweep. And he would have walked right into it, maybe spoiled the whole mission. An electric chill climbed his spine and spread through his shoulders, like water working up a tree from taproots to leaves. A surprise, noted for later review: He hadn't expected near-miss disaster to feel quite so exhilarating.

"Thanks, buddy," Gabe said in English, and brushed past him, overcoat collar up, hat in place, limping into the night.

Bathroom mirror, Josh repeated to himself. *Under dresser. Under windowsill.* Not much of a prayer, but then, he'd never been a praying man.

The apparatchik finished his speech, and the scientists filtered in. Josh watched their faces like he'd seen gamblers watch roulette wheels. Not Sokolov—not Sokolov—not Sokolov. Or was it? Had that first one been—maybe if the good doctor put on weight, or lost some—but the pictures should have been recent—

And then there was no question: The man himself walked in out of the rain, perfect from the tufts of pale hair on his earlobes to the slight inward turn of his left foot, the reddish bulb at the end of that narrow nose, the long thin skull bobbing on the long thin neck, the most beautiful man Josh had ever seen, at least for the next few seconds. He wore reddish-brown shoes, as promised, and he carried his bag in his left hand, and after three steps he stumbled under its weight.

Josh was there to catch him. Baračnik didn't even need to move. Josh lifted the suitcase and walked the good doctor upstairs.

5.

Tanya found Nadia working the heavy bag alone in the embassy gym. Gloves pounded white dust from the canvas. Nadia danced as she struck, weight on the balls of her feet, three blink-quick jabs followed by a hook that rocked the bag against the chains binding it to the floor. A sculptor had chiseled those lines into Nadia's calves, pressed out the planes of muscle on her back. Sweat covered her. She snarled as she struck. She grunted. After one sharp hook that would have broken a jaw, or else Nadia's own hand, she screamed in rage and triumph.

Tanya approached. Nadia did not stop. The gym was empty but for the two of them. Dawn wasn't yet done dawning. At last, Tanya tried: "Hi."

Nadia stopped. "What are you doing?"

Tanya gestured down to her own trunks and her T-shirt and shoes, suddenly aware of how little she resembled Nadezhda Fyodorovna Ostrokhina. "I thought we could spar."

Nadia blinked. The bag swayed.

"Sure," she said.

Nadia threaded through the ropes into the ring. Tanya tried to follow, but caught her foot in the process, then, hopping, freed herself. She was bruised from the golem, sore all over. She'd barely slept. She didn't care.

They touched gloves.

Tanya circled, and Nadia circled her in turn. She kept her guard up—remembered school classes, habits of exercise long abandoned. Work combinations: one, two, body blow—

Nadia slipped away from Tanya's punch and tagged her lightly on the jaw.

Tanya's eyes stung. She circled more, tested the air with jabs, none of which landed. Nadia slid a second punch through her guard, but her next two blows hit Tanya's raised forearms. Tanya's heart began to beat faster. Breath came in swimmer's gasps, down into the deepest core of her. She swung at Nadia again, and again, but the woman was a dancer mixed with a brick wall. Tanya had reach, should have had, but Nadia knew how to use that reach against her.

At last, exhausted, furious, Tanya spread her arms and dove for Nadia, trying to catch her around the waist.

Nadia didn't register the least surprise. She met Tanya's rush with open arms. The world turned on its axis, and when it stopped, Tanya lay on the ground, staring up into the rafters and Nadia's eyes, with Nadia's knee and glove pressing her shoulders to the mat. Nadia felt strong—real. "What is wrong with you?"

Tanya's breath was wet, and so were her eyes. She could not speak. She hadn't realized how hard she'd driven herself, how much she'd needed to wear herself down to manage this. "Can I trust you?"

"Of course," Nadia said, confused.

"That's not what I mean." Everything Tanya meant to say gathered in her throat. "I can't trust the Ice. Not the way I used to. I'm fighting on their side, I'll stop the Flame, it's the only choice we have, but that's not enough. I need someone—not my grandfather, not a superior—I need a real person, or else I'm just as frozen as that girl on the boat. I need a friend."

And after all they'd been through together—partnership and secret machinations, Host tracking; after all the trust they'd traded and all the numberless ways each could have dragged the other before a firing squad—that last admission still made her feel like she lay naked in the ring.

Nadia let go of Tanya's shoulder and sat down by her side. The hard lines of her softened, but she remained herself. She undid her own gloves with her teeth, then pulled off Tanya's. Their fingers met and meshed.

She did not speak. Neither of them did.

That was all the sign Tanya needed.

For some diplomatic reason Josh hadn't been able to determine, the French embassy hosted the conference kickoff soiree, which meant, on the one hand, an overabundance of speeches, but on the other (far more fortunate) hand, a plentitude of actual champagne. He avoided looking at, or for, Sokolov—during their brief conversation in his hotel room, the man had seemed eminently capable of the limited acting their scheme required, but Josh had no interest in testing either of their covert abilities. His own few recent brushes with fieldwork, no matter how successful, had been more than sufficient.

But it felt good, after all this madness, to drink a glass of champagne and wander through a party in control of his own destiny. Drinking a goddamned glass of champagne in a goddamned embassy to celebrate. Okay, so maybe nobody would confuse Josh Toms for James Bond, but he had done the work, and when Sokolov was safe across the Iron Curtain two weeks from now, he, Josh Toms, skinny geek from Brooklyn, would be the one responsible.

They were winning, dammit. As for Dom's sly not-smile and his sideways accusations (*I'm just looking out for you, buddy*), the hand on the shoulder—to hell with him, and to hell with all that.

Across the hall, Alestair Winthrop accepted a third glass of bubbly from a waitress in a cocktail dress and toasted thin air.

Josh slid toward him through the press. "Can we talk in private?"

"This is hardly my estate," Winthrop said. "But Monsieur Dubrueil owes me a favor or three, I should think. After you."

Whatever favors Winthrop was owed, he seemed to enjoy free run of the embassy: Security stepped aside, doors opened, and after two flights of stairs they stood in a small conference room with a topological map of Europe on one wall and thick curtains drawn across the windows. The latch click echoed. Winthrop leaned back against the closed door. "If you have business to discuss," he said, "we should find a more secure facility—and perhaps a time when the both of us have had somewhat less to drink."

"This isn't about business." Josh stepped close to him. Too many "never"s tangled in his blood. Winthrop radiated through that perfect slender charcoal suit.

One corner of the man's mouth crooked up, all arrogance and wealth and at least a thousand years of royalty. "What, then?"

Josh kissed him. He tasted right.

"Well," Alestair said, and kissed Josh back.

The Department of Commerce, Gabe reflected as he stared into his disastrously empty champagne flute, offered the perfect cover in all cases save when you actually had to pretend to care about agriculture tariffs. This was, and had always been, his great weakness as an intelligence officer: He had a hard time faking enthusiasm for a cover. He knew a guy back in Iowa who, if the Company asked him how he felt about paper or women's hand lotion, say, could, at the drop of a dime, enthuse about the subject with a lifelong devotee's passion. Not so Gabe. Oh well—to each his own.

Meeting conference bigwigs in the guise of Gabriel Pritchard, DoC, then, was—to put it mildly—one of the less satisfying parts of his job. The booze was good, the music fine, and the French knew how to cater, but if it hadn't been an opportunity to meet the defector in person, he'd have long since told this squat Soviet goofball who'd spent the last half hour babbling about crossbreeding corn to go jump in the Vltava. Gabe had had enough of corn back in Iowa.

At least he didn't have to worry about the golem crashing the party—though the hitchhiker had stayed on a wary alert since their fight in the basement. He'd started to wonder if the golem had dislodged it somehow. That would be a pleasant parting gift: a way to work the elemental free. Maybe Jordan was wrong about how extracting the hitchhiker would destroy his mind. Stranger things had happened, some this week.

So, bored or not, Gabe was feeling pretty good until the Soviet goofball stepped aside and introduced him to Dr. Maksim Sokolov, a skinny, horse-faced man with a narrow, red-tipped nose, brilliant eyes, and an affable smile, whose handshake set Gabe's hitchhiker pealing like a bell.

Thanks to months of practice, to careful self-discipline and chanted spells and mercury experiments, Gabe did not collapse. He did not even wince. He shook Sokolov's hand back, and smiled, and looked him in those bright eyes, and felt a stab of panic entirely separate from the clamor the hitchhiker raised inside his skull.

Maksim Sokolov, the object of ANCHISES, the defector they'd spent most of this year preparing to extract, was a Host.

52
77
48
74
59
57
26
89
26
85
56

EPISODE 10

ANCHISES

Lindsay Smith

Prague, Czechoslovak Socialist Republic
February 26, 1970

1.

Maksim Sokolov was a Host.

Gabe rubbed at his temples, trying to soothe away the volatile mix of hangover, stress, and elemental excitation that gripped his skull. Their defector was a Host, and now Gabe had to worry about far more than just the KGB trying to foil his plans. Did the Flame know there was a Host free and running around Prague? Just what he needed—a bunch of megalomaniacal witches interfering with his exfiltration op.

And then there was the Ice.

Gabe gripped the Moskvich's steering wheel, hands squeaking against the cheap rubber. Alestair, Morozova, and whoever else the Ice had lurking around Prague were all ready to toss each and every Host into cold storage. Alestair certainly presented a challenge. He was far more observant than he let on. Though MI6 had helped facilitate their work with Sokolov, they weren't involved in the actual exfiltration; these sorts of missions needed all the secrecy they could get. Sure, it always looked good for British-American relations if they could pull off a win together. But too often, the Brits only managed to gum up the works.

Now Gabe had a whole new reason to keep Alestair in the dark. The minute that swaggering prick found out what Sokolov really was . . . Gabe grimaced. Would Alestair really endanger a major win for the West just to help out his little secret society? Alestair had acted like gathering all the Hosts under Ice protection was a matter of life and death. But this was life and death too, this mundane world of rocket science and political maneuvering and nuclear stockpiles. America needed Sokolov. The Brits needed America to have him. Surely Alestair would see that. He wouldn't risk his country's standing—and more importantly, his own standing within his country—over one Host.

That left the question, then, of Morozova. The woman had readily sent that poor student girl into Ice custody. True, Morozova hadn't known what the Ice would do with her, but Gabe couldn't be sure she wouldn't consign Sokolov to deep freeze, thinking there was no other way to keep him out of the Flame's grasp. Bad enough that he was trying to whisk away another Host, away from her protection and the Ice's. That alone would bring out her claws. But as a *KaGeBeznik*, determined to prevent Soviet citizens from defecting at all costs . . .

That settled it, then. Gabe didn't want to leave Sokolov vulnerable to the Flame, that much he was sure of. But he couldn't count on the Ice to help him. The only Ice agents he knew were Morozova, Ostrokhina, and Alestair. If Tanya found out that Sokolov was a Host, it was as good as marching right up to the Soviet embassy and announcing the man's plans to defect. It would end in a bullet in the back of Sokolov's head, and another one in the shambling corpse of Gabe's career.

Gabe took a deep breath and turned toward Josh. "How're we looking?"

Josh glanced toward the far corner of the Hotel International Praha, but there were still no signs of their scout. "Waiting."

Gabe smiled and drummed his fingers on the steering wheel. Already he felt lighter, having made up his mind. The defector's status as a Host was just another secret for him to keep. And Gabe was damned good at keeping secrets.

He hoped Maksim Sokolov would prove just as good.

"Here we are." Josh closed the newspaper he'd been pretending to scan and folded it up. "He's walking out now, heading toward the corner . . ."

Gabe fixed his eyes on the person strolling along the sidewalk in front of the hotel, catty-corner from the parking lot where they sat partially obscured from view by a hulking construction truck. Their scout was dressed like every other man in Prague these days: black turtleneck, dark plaid flared trousers. He had the hollow-cheeked, suspicious stare of the Czechs, but his US embassy paycheck was sure to lift his spirits. He leaned against the streetlamp, paused, then pulled a cigarette from the pack in his pocket. Lit it.

"Come on," Gabe muttered.

The man closed his eyes and tilted his head back against the post. Tapped the cigarette twice. Then took a slow drag.

"Excellent. Just two guards, south side. We're set."

One good day. That was all Gabe needed to keep the defector's identity hidden. Then he wouldn't have to worry about the Ice, the Flame, or even the KGB. Gabe could hold out for just one day. Hell, even the hitchhiker was behaving itself. This would be a piece of cake.

Gabe slid out of the car and turned toward Josh as he did the same. "It's your show now."

Joshua Toms straightened his corduroy blazer and pushed his way toward the registration table in the foyer of the Hotel International Praha. Excitement crackled through him, fortifying, like a good shot of whiskey. His show. Today, at the conference proper, was his show.

He flashed a quick smile toward Gabe. It felt so good to be on the same page again, working together like a well-oiled machine. Spring was blowing into Prague, and whatever darkness had muddled Gabe's actions before was burning away.

Maybe it had just been the long winter days, hardening around Gabe's psyche like a shell of ice. Gabe had come from Cairo Station—hot, dry, equatorial. The change would jar even the toughest operative. He felt a little embarrassed, now, for second-guessing the guy. ANCHISES was going to be a huge win for both of them, and all that nonsense from earlier this winter—the KGB woman, the missing student, and everything else—would fade away.

"Toms," Josh told the secretary. "United States Department of Commerce."

"Of course, Mr. Toms. Here's your name tag and your conference schedule."

Josh pinned the card to his breast pocket and headed into the lecture hall with Gabe.

"Wheat," the lecturer intoned, gripping the podium like it might try to escape. "Without wheat, we have no society. Without society, we are darkness."

Josh settled into his chair next to Gabe. It was going to be a long day.

He didn't find Sokolov in the crowd until the end of the third speech during the morning session. Thick bags bunched under the scientist's eyes, and his suit was threadbare, straining to fit around his shoulders. He was sweating, even as the conference hall seemed to radiate the last of winter's chill from its granite floors and walls.

Pull it together, Maks. Then Josh looked down and found his own knuckles clenched, bone white, around his conference folder. He drew a deep breath and slowly loosened his grip.

His gaze came to rest on Alestair Winthrop. The British agent was a few rows over, chatting animatedly about corn-pricing inflation, but then his eyes caught Josh's—for the faintest of moments—and the corner of his mouth twitched in a grin.

Josh glanced away, unable to wipe the smile from his own face.

"It's almost time. Is everything ready for our information session?" Gabe asked.

Josh checked the folder. Twenty fact sheets on the United States Department of Commerce and Department of Agriculture joint international ventures, neatly typed and mimeographed, smeared with faint purple. And tucked in the stack, a thin strip of paper covered in tight, cramped handwriting.

"I believe we're set."

Gabe nudged him on the shoulder. "Thank God. I can't take another minute of lecturing about capitalist wheat manipulation. Let's go."

They'd been granted a small conference room for their

information session, and already the other Commerce men—the ones without side jobs in the embassy's bowels—were waiting inside. Gabe greeted them with his usual ease, joking about the agency politics he was expected to know, agreeing about what a real hard-ass the new labor secretary was. Josh just hoped he didn't look too stiff beside Gabe.

And then the attendees began to file in.

Russians, Czechs, Brits, Germans—but the Russians lingered the longest, asked the toughest questions, crinkled their noses at Josh and the fact sheets he tried to hand them. Maksim Sokolov fit the type, for which Josh was eternally grateful. He strode right up to Josh and snatched one of the mimeographed sheets out of his hands.

"You did write this?" Sokolov asked, his English gruff and brutal.

"My department did, sir." Josh swallowed and tucked the thin strip of paper in the palm of his hand. "Joshua Toms. I'm a secretary of commerce at the United States embassy. . . ."

Maksim stared down at his hand. For a moment, Josh was afraid he wouldn't shake it. None of the other Russians had shaken hands with them so far. Would it look too suspicious? Maybe he could wrap the paper around a mug of coffee, or tuck it in Maksim's pocket as he walked past—

Then Maksim took his hand for the briefest of shakes. Crunched the paper in his fist. Withdrew. All before his minders—the broad-shouldered thugs lurking around the room's perimeter—had a chance to wave him off.

"I must congratulate you on your propaganda skills," Maksim said. "I believe each word on this sheet is a lie, and yet you tell it so well."

"I assure you, we're committed to the international cause of agricultural aid—"

"Pfffah." Maksim stuffed his hands in his pockets. "Words are one thing. Action, Mr. Toms, is something else entirely."

Maksim sauntered off. Josh looked down at his stack of papers, then slowly, subtly, glanced toward Gabe.

Mission accomplished. Maksim had his instructions.

Once the meet and greet wrapped up, they pushed their way through the crowded foyer. "Taking off already, gents?" Alestair Winthrop asked, blocking their path toward the door. Josh sucked in his breath, smiling, but took care not to look at Alestair directly. The Reds had eyes everywhere here.

Gabe shrugged his shoulders. "Yeah, you know, the office calls. See you at the party tonight?"

Alestair's eyes glittered in the chandelier light as he glanced toward Josh. "Wouldn't miss it for the world."

"See you then, Winthrop," Josh said.

And executed his second successful brush pass of the day—fingers grazing together, warmth there and gone, shielded from the rest of the world in the churning crowd.

Everything was going exactly according to plan.

Gabe leaned against the concrete pillar of the embassy's loading dock while the truck took its sweet time backing up. The closer the truck came, the tighter a screw seemed to turn inside his skull. The hitchhiker was, understandably, upset. Gabe didn't feel too far behind.

"You ever done something like this before?" Dom asked him, tapping away the ash of his cigar.

Gabe pressed his lips thin. "Can't say I have."

Dom snorted. "You're in for a treat, pal. It's a special kind of art, you know, doin' a job like this. It's like . . . magic. Like wizardry. Right?"

The blunt corner of his elbow landed in Gabe's ribs.

"That's it!" Dominic shouted to the truck driver. "Perfect."

The truck stopped, and Dom waited, smoking, smiling, while the workers unsealed the back. Inside, boxes and boxes of feminine hygiene products were stacked floor to ceiling; the workers seized the boxes and began tearing them away.

Gabe forced himself to adopt a pleasantly neutral expression. But he could feel the hitchhiker strumming a vexing elemental chord as it sorted through the elements nearby. Blood—yep, Gabe expected to sense that one. Water, tasting cold against the back of Gabe's throat. And was that a faint feeling of—fire? A dried-out, bitter taste like ash clung to his tongue.

The workers finished tearing down the front stack of boxes and unveiled their real cargo: a heavy metal container. Coffin size. They hauled it onto the dock, placing it on a waiting trolley with an ominous clang.

Dom's smile widened, carnivorous, and he elbowed Gabe again.

"Sign, please," the worker said, shoving a clipboard at them. Custody chain. Everything so formal and bureaucratic for the grim business they were about to undertake.

Dom scrawled his signature and shoved it back at the worker. The hitchhiker was strumming, strumming, but Gabe had no reassurances to offer it. At least there was no magic involved in this affair. At least, not yet.

Gabe held the doors open, and Dom steered the trolley into the embassy's bowels.

"Now," he said, "the real fun begins."

✦ ✦ ✦

The blue scrim of twilight was beginning to settle on the streets of Prague. The conference at the Hotel International Praha had concluded for the day; the bugs Nadia had placed with Tanya were yielding nothing but tipsy chattering and the sounds of men preparing to hit the town.

Nadia's job was to ensure that none of them were preparing for anything more.

Tanya had been right. The Americans were interested in the conference. But why remained unclear. Hoping to court new assets? A reasonable assumption; even with the KGB's minders looking about, they'd have a much easier time approaching potential conspirators here, in Europe, than back in Moscow or Arkhangelsk. Yet the Westerners had, annoyingly, kept to themselves thus far. That information session she'd attended, with its pathetic fact-sheet propaganda, seemed hardly worth the effort.

But, Nadia supposed, there were always the diplomatic parties. Nadia had always shined at those—she spoke the Western language of jazz and boxing and cold, dead consumerism. But tonight that was Tanya's burden. Tonight, Nadia was left to the thrill of another sort of hunt.

"May I offer you any more coffee?" the waitress asked, stumbling over her Russian.

Nadia looked up from her window seat at the café and smiled. The waitress was a pretty thing, brunette, a little skittish, but then, the sound of homegrown Russian in Prague tended to have that effect on people who hadn't welcomed the tanks. The girl was probably one of Dubček's fans, then. A pity. All the same, Nadia flashed her a bright smile and leaned over the cup.

"You make an excellent brew. Did you learn this style in Paris? Rome, perhaps?"

The waitress's wan cheeks flushed red, and she crossed her arms over her apron. "Oh, no, I've never been outside Czech—well, outside of the Soviet republics."

Good girl, Nadia thought. *You learn quickly.* She lowered her lashes and peered up at the girl through them. "Well, it's excellent. I'd love another one."

When the waitress returned, Nadia gestured toward the empty chair opposite her. "Please. Have a seat. You're hardly busy."

The girl's mouth twisted; she glanced toward the cash register, but her boss was cramming an early dinner into his mouth. "I suppose it won't hurt."

Nadia pursed her lips to blow on the coffee, then stretched one hand on the table in front of her, toward the girl. "Awfully busy across the street, aren't they?"

The waitress nodded. "Scientific conference of some sort, I think. I heard a few of them talking when they stopped in for lunch."

Very good girl. Nadia stretched her legs out beneath the table, and when her feet brushed the girl's leg, she made no effort to withdraw them. "Curious. English speakers too, or only Czech?"

"All kinds." The girl hesitated, leg trembling, but, ultimately, she didn't pull away.

Nadia leaned closer. Eyes sparkling. Freshly applied lipstick just the right shade of rosy—one part innocent and three parts wicked. "Very interesting." She cocked her head to one side. "These English speakers. Did you understand what they were saying?"

Realization seemed to dawn on the girl's face, but she didn't back down. Whatever trap she was being pulled into didn't concern her too much. Just as Nadia had hoped. "Well . . . my English is a little rusty, but . . ."

Something twinkled around them, a faint sound, delicate like wind chimes.

The waitress blinked and furrowed her brows. *Shit.* Nadia plunged one hand into her satchel and snapped a charm for distraction while whispering, "I'm so sorry. I must be off. Hope to see you again soon." Tossing out a few bills, she stood, shrugging on her jacket, and trailed her hand over the waitress's shoulder as she bustled out the door.

As soon as she was on the sidewalk, she ducked into a doorway and hunted through her charms until she found the culprit: a multifaceted charm studded with raw crystals. She turned the charm around in her palm, examining each crystal until she finally spied a faint glow.

It wasn't the one she'd expected.

Four cups of coffee and Gabe still couldn't burn the smell of rot away.

"You're absolutely certain?" Frank asked. "No identifying features, no nothing."

"No sirree," Dom answered. "Knocked out the teeth myself. And your boy Pritchard here . . ." He regarded Gabe with flinty eyes. "Well, let's just say he's a wizard with a paring knife. Not a chance anyone could piece together fingerprints from that."

Gabe swallowed, hard, but he felt the sting of bile reaching up his throat.

Frank looked from Gabe to Dominic, twirling a ballpoint pen in his fingers. "I don't know. Sokolov is pretty damned distinctive."

Dom chuckled. "No one looks distinctive after a few weeks feeding the catfish." He hiked his trousers up and perched on the corner of Frank's desk, earning him a cocked eyebrow from Frank. "Look. I've done this switcheroo five times now. There was a guy in Havana, needed to evaporate real fast when his mistress caught wind he was working for us. Figured there was more money in turning him in than convincing us to take her, too, right?"

"Right." Frank held his jaw tight.

"You tie the weights right, even the fucking KGB can't dig him up. He won't surface until we're damned good and ready, and by then . . . nothing but a waterlogged mess." Dominic slapped his hands against his thighs. "Now. Pritchard? You still feeling a little green, or can I count on you tonight?"

Gabe thrust his shoulders back. "I'm set. I've got Toms for backup. We'll run over the plan one more time before we head out, but trust me, I can recite it backward in my sleep."

Frank cleared his throat. With his reading glasses perched, schoolmarmish, on his nose, the chief might have been mistaken for a soft touch, a prim desk man. But only by a fool. Gabe glanced at Dom and wondered if he was the right kind of idiot to cross a man who only needed a rusty shovel to take out an entire trench of enemies.

"Dominic, with all due respect," Frank said in a tone that offered no respect at all, "my men know this op's history. They know the importance. Sokolov's been one of our best producers out of Moscow Station. Hell, at this point he's probably responsible for damn near half of what we know about the Soviets. Everyone wants to make sure he's treated well. The president will probably pin a medal the size of my hemorrhoids on his chest. At the very least, we're gonna give him a comfortable retirement. Tampa, maybe. A summer home on Nags Head. This is the biggest op anyone on my team has ever seen, possibly *will* ever see. They're taking it seriously."

"Look, I just want to ensure that Mr. Pritchard is up to the task—"

"I wouldn't have recommended him if I didn't think he was." Frank snapped a stack of papers against the edge of his desk.

"I know the plan," Gabe said. "I'm ready."

"Not good enough, Pritchard," Dominic said. "I want it tattooed on your eyelids."

Gabe sighed. The worst part of these kinds of ops was having to answer to two bosses, neither of whom wanted to answer to the other. "I assure you, I've got it down—"

"And I'm sure you thought the same thing recruiting . . . Drahomir, was it?" Dom tossed a grin toward Frank, but the chief's expression stayed guarded. "Or that antiques dealer back in Cairo? I've read up on you. I know what you're capable of. But also what you aren't."

Gabe shoved his hands into his blazer's pockets, and his fingers brushed a stray charm tucked within. He grazed his thumbnail against it, weighing, considering . . . But no. This grandstander wasn't worth the effort. Something loosened inside him, like the hitchhiker was standing down, and he pulled his hand away.

"I can do this." He squared his jaw. Forced the smell of searing, soggy flesh from his mind. "He'll be right on time. Just make sure you're waiting."

Dominic looked toward Frank, still grinning like he'd told a joke, but Frank crossed his arms and gave him a stern nod. "If my man says he has it handled, he has it handled."

"We'll see about that." Dominic slipped off the desk. "Once Sokolov's safely in the air, then I'll buy you all a drink."

2.

The West German embassy didn't know it, but they'd selected an ideal venue for ANCHISES when they arranged the conference reception: the Lichtenštejnský Palace, a stark Georgian block of stone and plaster mounted right along the western bank of the Vltava. Gabe waited patiently while the security guards frisked him, then Josh, and then headed into the soft amber glow of the grand reception space. Cherubs smiled down on them from the frescoed ceiling overhead as Josh and Gabe snagged appetizers off the waiters' trays; stern oil paintings watched them from the wall with long-suffering stares.

Gabe studied the ceiling for a moment. At least the Party hadn't redrawn the cherubs as Marx and Lenin. Yet.

"Our friends are fashionably late," Josh said, fidgeting with his glass of club soda. No whiskey tonight.

Gabe shrugged. "They run on their own timetable."

But his mind was whirring over the potential ways they could be getting screwed right now. The Russian delegation's minders could have decided that the dinner away from the hotel presented

439

too great a security risk. They might have caught another delegate prowling the red-light district without his minders and decided to punish the whole team. Or they could just be postponing— laying the lectures on thick about the danger of speaking with Westerners, for instance.

Gabe and Josh had to be prepared for the distinct possibil- ity that all their well-laid plans for tonight had been for naught. That, at any moment, a minder's suspicions could be tripped, and they'd blow their best chance at nabbing Sokolov. Surely Frank and Dominic couldn't fault Gabe for it—these things happened. Spooks got spooked. But, God, it sure would be nice to have some- thing go right, just this once.

Gabe's gaze slid across the cloth-covered tables toward the entrance just in time to catch sight of Tanya Morozova entering the reception.

Shit. It had been too much to hope that he wouldn't cross paths with her again until Sokolov was safely in US airspace. So much for an easy night.

Tanya held a small clutch close to her chest as she scanned the room. Her dark blond hair had been swept up and fastened with some sort of elegant jeweled device Gabe couldn't name, and she wore a gauzy, shimmering gown that surely came out of the KGB's costume closet. It bared her sharp Slavic collarbones and softened her hips and brought out that glimmering something in her expression that he'd only seen in flashes before. She looked . . . *good*. Fresh faced, shy. Hopeful.

It immediately set off every alarm bell Gabe had.

Gabe turned back toward Josh before Tanya could catch sight of him and gripped the edge of the standing table. All right. So that's how she wanted this to play out. Tanya thought she'd made a mark of him—that had to be why she was here. They'd had a moment in the hotel basement, their magic working harmoniously to stop the golem's rampage. And in that moment, she must have seen something in him. An opportunity. A weakness to exploit. An open door to wedge her foot into. An unhealed wound that she could dig at with her wicked little nails—

"Gabe?"

Gabe blinked and looked up. Josh was frowning at him, that damning mixture of fear and concern from before Gabe had managed to get the hitchhiker under control.

"What's the matter?" Josh asked. "You looked . . . angry, all of a sudden."

Gabe exhaled, breath whistling through his nose. "More eyes here than I'd anticipated."

Josh peered over Gabe's shoulder, then nodded. "I see."

Josh twisted his glass in his hands, like he was screwing up the courage to say something. *No,* Gabe thought. *Please. No. It's what she wants—for you to think that maybe there could be something between me and her. It's nothing like that.*

It's so much worse.

"Well, she shouldn't be a problem." Josh forced a smile and elbowed Gabe. "Should she?"

Gabe smiled back, hand slipping into his pocket again. The braided bits of copper and tin soothed him. They sang to the hitchhiker like a lullaby. "Not once the show starts."

A pinched-looking diplomat appeared at the base of the staircase and silenced the reception with a spoon against his glass. "Attention—might I please have your attention?"

He introduced himself as the special assistant to the West German ambassador and launched into a lengthy speech about his country's deep and abiding interest in promoting scientific progress and agricultural advancement. After a morning full of such talk, Gabe could feel his eyelids starting to droop. He'd already pledged to stick to water and soda tonight—this op was too important—but he started scanning for a waiter to bring him a coffee.

"Our friends from the Russian delegation are already waiting for us in the dining hall, so please, let us join them. After we eat, then we shall present the awards."

Josh and Gabe looked at one another. The Russians were already here? Their minders must have brought them up a rear staircase. The ice in Gabe's glass rattled as he took a slow sip and followed Josh toward the dining hall. "Well," he said quietly, "they always know how to keep it interesting."

Dinner was the usual rubbery chicken Kiev and wilted sides of cabbage and beets. Gabe and Josh wound up at a table with a couple of agricultural scientists who spent the entire awards ceremony whispering their disdain back and forth in rapid-fire French. Sokolov was stationed at the far side of the room, at one of the tables closest to the podium. He never looked toward Gabe, but he did seem unusually fascinated by the long row of French windows along the eastern wall of the ballroom, which opened onto a series of balconies.

"Beautiful night," Gabe said to Josh. "Want to see if they'll let us get some fresh air once the dancing starts?"

Josh smiled. "I'll go have a word with the hosts."

The Russians had moved, en masse, to the bar, the handful of scientists encircled by an arc of minders as they crowded the long wooden counter. Gabe reached into his pocket as he stood. Morozova wasn't with them—it looked like she'd gotten trapped in conversation with the insufferable Hungarian secretary who'd become something of a hazing ritual for the Western officers. Gabe smiled to himself as Tanya squirmed, looking about ready to gnaw her arm off to escape whatever night at the symphony the secretary was recounting right then.

The hitchhiker shifted, stirring, as Gabe closed his hands around the first charm in his pocket and approached the bar.

Copper and crushed Czech wildflowers; ashes from a burned birch tree and a few dabs of blood. Gabe tasted it like an early spring awakening, blossoming on his tongue. This was how he'd imagined magic should feel. A current that he could harness, not a live wire threatening to burn him to a crisp. This was exactly what he needed—magic that supplemented his work, not magic that got in the way.

The hitchhiker approved. And, from the middle of the pack of minders, he sensed the elemental inside Sokolov awakening as well.

"Omluvte mě," Gabe said, intentionally using thickly accented Czech instead of Russian as he shouldered his way past the goons up to the bar. In his pocket, the charm began to vibrate.

The monitor whose personal space Gabe was currently invading curled his lips back to reveal a gummy sneer. "I am not Czech."

"Oh? My apologies." Gabe jabbed out one hand. "Gabriel. And you are . . . ?"

"I am not interested in speaking with you," the ape replied.

A second monitor peeled away from the crowd and sauntered over to them. "Dima. Who are you talking to?"

"American man. Sounds like he is lonely." Dima narrowed his eyes at Gabe. "Is trying to make Russian friends. Does not seem wise for someone in his position."

As soon as the second minder approached, Gabe activated the second charm. Through the thicket of Russian shoulders, Gabe noticed Sokolov wince—he, too, felt the power Gabe was drawing, whether he understood it or not.

"Is easy mistake," the second minder said. "Also easy to fix."

Gabe smirked. "Oh? And how's that?"

Come on, Gabe thought. *One more.* There was just one last minder who hadn't approached him yet.

"You buy us round of drinks," Dima said. "Then, maybe then, we forget to tell people you talked to us, yes? Could be most embarrassing for you."

The other minder folded his arms. "I am sure your friends at embassy would not like to hear the treasonous things Mr. Gabriel Pritchard, commerce secretary for the United States embassy, said to me."

Gabe's smile widened. He could always count on the Russians to do their homework. And he could always, always count on them to assume their boldness would give them the upper hand.

"Very well." He waved to the bartender. "A round of Goldwasser for my friends. In honor of our German hosts, yeah?"

Dima and his beefy companion nodded after a moment's beat.

"Oh, but, uh . . . what about your other friend?" Gabe gestured toward the third monitor. "Wouldn't want him to feel left out."

The second nodded. "Kostya! Come. We have drinks."

Gabe smiled and, as Kostya approached, thumbed the third charm in his pocket. The bartender poured out four shots of Goldwasser and Gabe plucked his up with a quick whisper under his breath.

The whisper was only a single word. Amharic, probably. Ancient, definitely. He'd most likely botched the pronunciation. But Jordan had drilled him over it, again and again, and he knew exactly how it should feel, pouring out of his mouth. Exactly the golden rush that would cleanse through his nostrils and wash over his vision, if only for a moment's time.

The energy arced through him, fed by the elemental half

lodged in his skull and by the not-too-distant ley lines that coursed beneath Prague. Filtered through the charm, the charge of his spell dispersed over the shot glasses of Goldwasser and settled into the liquid and flecks of gold.

Gabe raised his glass in toast. "*Za zdorovie*, comrades."

"*Za zdorovie*," the minders echoed, and tossed back their shots. Everyone flipped their shot glasses and dropped them upside down on the bar. In such a mess, it was hard to notice that an entire shot's worth of liquid had failed to make it into Gabe's mouth.

Already the Russians were calling for vodka. Gabe took the opportunity to step away from the bar and let the spell do its work. This was almost too easy. A few minutes' time to set up something that might have taken him hours and several rounds of drinks to accomplish otherwise? Maybe there really was something to this whole "spycraft-via-magic" business.

Gabe reached into his pocket once more to rub the charms. For good luck, he supposed. And for a silent thanks that Tanya Morozova was keeping away.

Then a hand closed around his wrist.

"Well, my dear fellow," Alestair Winthrop said, looking up at Gabe with one eyebrow carefully raised. "I'm rather certain your agency doesn't provide *those* as standard issue."

"Now's really not the time, Al—"

"But is this for business?" Alestair asked. "Or strictly for fun?"

Nadia's boots slid across Staré Město, the cobblestones slick and gleaming from centuries of footsteps. Something was wrong. She sensed it in the warp and weft of the magic rising up from the ley line beneath her. Something was terribly wrong. Whatever had tripped her sensing charm was pulling way too much power off the line to be some simple incantation.

Ritual magic. Elemental magic. Deep, powerful, and—if it wasn't being conducted by the Ice—quite possibly dark.

Her boxer's muscles carried her quickly around the pedestrians out reveling in the precious extra hours of sunlight they'd snatched from winter's grasp. She bounced on the balls of her feet periodically to scan over their heads and darted down alleyways for a quick assessment. What the hell was the Flame brewing this time?

A sudden horrific possibility flashed through her. What if they'd found another Host? A dark rumor had been winding its way through the Ice channels of late—whispers and wonderings over just what the Flame intended for the Hosts they collected. Blood sacrifices, elemental harvesting, all sorts of gruesome possibilities that Nadia didn't care to dwell on for long.

But if the Flame intended anything of the sort—Nadia knew exactly *where* they'd need to go to accomplish it.

She crashed through the door of Bar Vodnář shoulder-first, a fistful of ashes at the ready and an ancient Slavic curse heavy on her tongue.

The babble of conversation stopped abruptly as all eyes turned toward Nadia. Hedgewitches, in their dirndls and piles of crystal pendants, eyed her over glasses of mulled wine; tweedy, shifty-eyed spies shrank back into their corner booths. A Czech worker drinking at the bar tugged his cap brim over his face and curled his lip back. The jukebox bleated out a cheerful chorus of "sugar, oh, honey, honey" as Nadia scrutinized everyone, and they, in turn, scrutinized her.

Finally, Jordan Rhemes broke the stalemate as she swept out from behind the bar. Her broom skirt twisted around her ankles and spun widely in rhythm with her steps as she approached Nadia at the door. She wore her usual bartending smile—amused but not enchanted—but the skin around her eyes had pulled tight.

"Hello, Miss Ostrokhina." Jordan's voice was low, threaded beneath the chipper jukebox song. "Is there something I can help you with?"

Nadia heard, too, what Jordan didn't say. *Because if there isn't, you'd best be on your way.*

Nadia moved slowly, deliberately, making her intentions known as she tucked the handful of char back into her jacket pocket. "Someone's pulling off the ley lines," she whispered. "Powering something big. Huge. I was worried . . ." She swallowed past a sudden tightness in her throat. "I thought they might be—be using the confluence—"

She broke off as Jordan's expression changed. The woman's lips pressed into a thin line, and she reached for Nadia's arm.

"Let's have a word around back."

Nadia let herself be steered into the Vodnář's storerooms. They ducked around dangling bouquets of dried and drying herbs, and Nadia narrowly avoided knocking a calcified lizard skin off a shelf. As soon as they were fully inside the back rooms, Jordan shut the door and uttered a few words of warding as she smeared a tincture from a nearby jar around the door's frame.

Nadia tilted her head, curiosity getting the better of her. Rhemes's magic had always seemed so wild to her, so haphazard and imprecise. But she saw now a certain elegance in it. A simplicity that the Ice's work often lacked.

"A couple of Flame scumbags came poking around last week," Jordan said.

Nadia folded her arms. One of the rare times she hated being right. "They wanted access to the confluence?"

"Tried to strong-arm me into giving it up. Started with the soft sell, then when that didn't work, brought out a few sick pieces of ritual work. Ugly stuff."

"You should have contacted us," Nadia said. "We could've helped you take care of them."

Jordan shook her head, a loose dark lock falling over one eye. "No need. They got run off by one of their own."

One of their own. Irritating, the way Jordan always sidestepped the most valuable bits of intel. Nadia was dying to know exactly *who*, but she'd been around Rhemes too long to expect anything more. Top-shelf bourbon and useful bits of knowledge—you always paid extra at Bar Vodnář.

"That doesn't sound like Flame," Nadia said instead.

"The giving up? Or the internal conflict?"

"Both." Nadia sighed. "Believe me, I'd love nothing more than for the Flame to tear themselves apart from the inside. Less work for me. But this pull of energy . . . it isn't us."

Jordan worried a strip of dried reeds between her fingers as she thought. "Could be that the Flame in charge didn't want to risk revealing that they were conducting something that powerful. If they seized control of the Vodnář, of the confluence, then people would hear. And people would realize that the Flame was working on something big."

Nadia nodded, ideas gathering speed. "Right. Better to conduct it somewhere safer, where they can control who knows about it, even if it means less energy to fuel the ritual."

"Fortunately for the Flame, they don't know about your sensors."

Nadia froze. Jordan was grinning at her, white teeth gleaming in the dim light. Slowly Nadia pulled her shoulders back. "I beg your pardon?"

"Oh, you know." Jordan gestured in the air. "Those charms you've hidden all along the main path of the southwest-northeast ley line to see where power's being drawn."

A number of choice Russian phrases ran through Nadia's mind.

"Spies aren't the only observant people in this city, Miss Ostrokhina." Jordan smiled.

"Be that as it may . . ." Nadia swallowed. A cold sweat was encasing her like a shroud. Rituals requiring utmost secrecy . . . Flame goons trying to gain access to the confluence. "I really don't like the way this is adding up."

"Then I suggest you use those sensors to find what's drawing the energy and put a stop to it." Jordan turned toward one of her shelves and dug around in a small cigar box. "And here—this might help."

Nadia pocketed the thin sheet of mica Jordan handed her, its edges wrapped in a slender thread of silver. "Thanks," she muttered. She had no doubt that, one way or another, Jordan would find a way to make her pay for it.

Gabe pulled his wrist away from Alestair and made a nervous scan of the ballroom. "Look, Al . . . Now is really not a good time. . . ."

"Nonsense. We're all friends here."

There was no mistaking the sudden sharpness in Alestair's sunny expression, the hard steel glint of his eyes. For perhaps the first time since they'd met, Gabe felt that he was finally seeing the slick operator MI6 was known for producing. That beneath the bespoke suits and Eton rhetoric, a cold-blooded spy was at work.

Maybe he had been all along.

"All right," Gabe said, lowering his voice. He eased back on his heels and donned the best bored, polite party smile he could. "It's business. But I thought I could . . . y'know. Practice."

Alestair snorted with something resembling a laugh. Gabe got the distinct impression the Brit was enjoying this way too much.

"I don't know which disappoints me more. That you haven't let me in on the fun of whatever you're hunting, or that you didn't ask for my help working those charms."

"They're nothing, really. An old gift from Jordan." Gabe lifted his shoulders. "Thought I should get more comfortable working with them."

"And the case?" Alestair asked.

Gabe sighed. "You know I can't talk to you about that."

Alestair cocked one eyebrow. "Now, now, what's the harm in a little chat among friends?"

"That." Gabe shook his finger at Alestair. "That's *exactly* the problem. Especially when you count people like *her* among your friends too."

"Everything okay?" Josh asked, sauntering up to them. He kept an easy pace, but his expression was strained. "Gabe? Shouldn't we . . ."

Josh's gaze flickered toward Alestair. Only for a second, but it was enough. Gabe suppressed a groan. Al was friendly with Tanya, and he was more than a little friendly with Josh, apparently . . . Alestair's loose lips might sink all sorts of ships.

Alestair's smile dimmed as he turned his attention back toward Gabe. "If you need my help," he said, "you need only ask."

Gabe shook his head. "I appreciate it, Al. Really, I do. But honest—I have everything under control."

At that moment, the shouting began.

3.

Tanya was conducting another perimeter sweep of the second floor of the Lichtenštejnský Palace when the screaming started.

An ancient Slavic curse rose to her lips. The West German security team—which had, until this point, been tolerating her obvious surveillance with bored indifference—hunched forward with coiled intent. Tanya paused, lipstick in hand, and stared a moment longer into the mirror she'd been pretending to use to reapply her makeup.

The ballroom. The shouting was coming from the ballroom. Two main entrances, plus the service entrance from the kitchen. Enough of the service staff was in the KGB's pocket that she had to trust they'd divert any escape attempts via the kitchen. Currently, the West German heavies were crowding the first ballroom entrance, forming a wall of well-carved muscle. That left . . .

She dropped the lipstick and sprinted down the corridor for the remaining ballroom entrance.

The doors around the corner were closed. Tanya slapped her palms against the metal bar—locked from the inside. She ran her fingers through her bangs, knocking some strands loose from her carefully swept chignon. What the hell was happening in there?

She squeezed her eyes shut. Somehow, Gabriel Pritchard had to be involved.

Blyad.

He'd been so slick, working with her to stop the golem. Like they really were members of the same team. She'd been hoping for that, if she was being totally honest with herself. That they might trust each other someday. They'd never be outright allies, she knew, but she'd hoped she and Gabe could find the sort of comfortable stalemate she'd settled into with other Western Ice members like Winthrop. Ice business was Ice business, and to bring up anything regarding their office work was just impolite conversation. It shouldn't even factor into their rapport.

But of course Pritchard couldn't ever see it that way. He was a red-white-and-blue-blooded patriot, and magic was only slightly more than a nuisance to him. Why had she ever thought it could be more than that? Why would she ever have wanted it to be?

And yet.

And yet he'd told her the truth about the Ice's stasis program for all of the Hosts. When Nadia wouldn't. When her own grandfather wouldn't—assuming his construct had even been created with such knowledge in mind. Gabe had nothing to gain from telling her short of the momentary satisfaction of rubbing her nose in her own ignorance. It was too temperamental an act, coming from a place of too much emotion, for him to even try to exploit it for something more.

That wasn't the behavior of a slick spymaster laying a trap. It was the desperate flailing of a wounded animal trying to strike back.

Tanya paced back toward the first entrance, where the guards still formed a protective barricade, and approached. *Leave a kopeck-size gap between your lips.* She worked through her mental repertoire. *Legs slightly narrower than shoulder width. Shoulders rolled back. Dewy-eyed. Peer through your lashes rather than tilt your chin up.*

"Excuse me," Tanya whispered, first in Czech, then, when none of them looked back at her, in German. "Excuse me. *Excuse me.*"

"Fuck off," the guard snarled. "No one's allowed in or out."

Tanya batted her eyes, but he wouldn't so much as glance her way.

Fine. We'll do it my way. She snapped open her clutch and gripped a handful of interwoven herbs and twigs in one hand.

"Pardon me," Tanya whispered. "I'm afraid it's very important that you permit me inside."

The guard turned around to scold her again, but his eyes unfocused, as if looking at her only presented a fun-house reflection back at him. His brows furrowed, but the gap had been made; any effort to look at her as she slipped past him would send his gaze skittering away. It only lasted a few seconds. But that was all she required.

Now she was inside the ballroom and staring at a full-blown bar fight.

"Don't think I've forgotten," Dima—one of the scientist team's minders—growled. His cheap wool tie dangled precariously from his neck like a noose; blood trickled down one side of his mustache. "I remember how you wronged me back in Piter."

One of the scientists under his care—Maks? Misha?—threw his arms in front of his face to defend against a blow. From the shiner swelling around his right eye, it looked like it wouldn't be the first of the evening. "I swear to you, I didn't mean it! If I'd known you liked her—"

"Enough! Dima, you are a pig with drink and women alike." Kostya staggered in between them.

But he was too slow to avoid the emptied bottle of *Sovyetskoye shampanskoye* Dima swung at his temple.

Tanya had mere moments to decide. Did she intervene and undoubtedly blow her cover in front of the substantial crowd that had gathered around the brawl? Or did she stand back and let these minders—these men the Communist Party had specifically tasked with shielding the scientist delegation from Western agents—have their brawl and risk leaving the scientists exposed?

And what the hell had gone so wrong that they were turning on the very men it was their job to protect?

She rocked onto her back foot, prepping herself to leap forward and try to talk some sense into the minders.

Then she recalled Sasha's smug face. The way his jowls pushed up when he was particularly pleased with himself; when he knew he had one of his operatives wedged under his thumb. Tanya was already serving a permanent posting in Sasha's thrall, thanks to his discovery of her elemental radio and her subsequent failure to recover it. An incident this huge, on her watch, would surely cost her even more. Far more than she could afford around the Prague *rezidentura*.

Tanya flinched as the cheap glass bottle shattered and sprinkled the onlookers.

"All right, that's enough." A contingent of security officers moved in to encircle the brawlers. Tanya gripped her clutch to her chest and shrank back. If the minders were busy duking it out, even dragging some of their charges into the melee, then where had the rest of the scientists gone?

Pritchard.

Tanya found herself in one of the rare situations in which her small stature actually hindered her. Even in heels, she had to bounce upward to search the assembled crowd. She'd spotted the American earlier, at the reception, looking bored, distracted, rubbing elbows with his puppy friend. Now, though, she was searching for him in the gaps between a heaving sea of faces contorted by drink and the dim chandelier lighting. She swore under her breath. Somehow, she knew, *knew* Pritchard had something to do with this madness.

The what and how, though, remained to be seen.

The crowd swept around Tanya like rapids, slowly but inexorably moving her toward the front. She looked up, and found herself suddenly exposed on the edge of the fray. The fight had spread, that alchemy of drink and violence catching alight and feeding on itself. The security grunts were flecks of water against the roaring flames.

Only KGB training and reflexes allowed her to dive out of the way as one of the minders crashed into the glass-topped round table beside her.

She threw up one hand, sparing most of her face from the spray of splinters and shards. Her scalp wasn't so lucky. Something warm trickled down her forehead and into the corners of her eyes.

Tanya dropped to her knees beside the shattered table—cover be damned—and seized the minder sprawled over the wreckage.

"Where," she said, spit spraying and blood dripping down her face, "are your scientists?"

The minder's eyes flickered an eerie shade of red and gold as he looked back at her. The only answer he gave was a bone-chilling laugh.

Nadia locked the rooftop access door behind her as quickly as she could and ran to the ledge. Sure enough, the bits of crystal hidden in the seams between the stone emitted a faint red glow. She permitted herself one moment to cringe, then, as the crystals flickered back and forth, fished in her bag for her binoculars and took up Tanya's usual post along the rooftop.

So it was going to be another one of these nights, then.

Briefly, she considered summoning Tanya to meet her, then remembered her partner was on duty for the rezidentura, watching over the scientific conference. Half the city's spooks were tangled up in that soporific sprawl. Winthrop too, then, most likely. And Metzen, her KGB double agent out of West Germany. Try as she might, Nadia couldn't think of a single member of the Consortium of Ice she could call on tonight without blowing a cover, crashing a banquet, or enraging a jealous husband.

Nadia dug in her satchel and laid her array of charms on the rooftop ledge. With a sad twinge, she recalled a night not so long ago when she and Tanya had surveilled this corner together, ready to intercept the construct the Flame had sent to hunt the Host Andula Zlata. Life was much simpler back then. Before Tanya learned about the Ice's stasis program when she wasn't ready for it. Before that smug American officer began to meddle in their affairs.

Now she didn't have to worry about disappointing Tanya with her grim calculus. The thought should have brought her some comfort. But she'd seen the real fear in Tanya's eyes, the kind of fear that quickly burned off and left poisonous rage behind. They'd tried to settle their differences. Reached a sort of agreement. But such truces weren't meant to last. Ask Molotov and Ribbentrop.

The first of Nadia's charms chimed once more.

She settled on her stomach and brought the binoculars up. Then, just as she was about to shift to her side to scan the square, she remembered the charm Jordan Rhemes had given her. Gingerly she pulled it from her pocket and removed it from its casing.

A soft kiss of blue filtered through one corner of the mica as Nadia held it out before her. She swiveled it left, then right, until she settled on the point where the blue glow was strongest. Then she took a deep breath, cursed the nonexistent gods, and whispered an old Amharic prayer.

She really hoped Jordan knew what she was doing.

Nadia sensed something like a thread pulling in and out of her body, stitching a line between her and the mica square. It wasn't an unpleasant feeling, not entirely, but a little unnerving, carrying a chill through her as the thread pulled tight. Then, all at once, the threading ended with a feeling like a snap. Nadia leaned backward, dazed, and dropped the square beside her on the roof. She blinked the constellation of stars from her eyes and pulled her binoculars up again.

Within minutes, the chiming sound grew in strength; the other charms joined it with a series of chirps and glows. Nadia squared her shoulders and watched the far end of Staré Město.

Out of the twilit alley, a hunkered, unnaturally squared-off figure emerged.

Nadia dropped the binoculars and brought herself to a crouch. The Flame had made another construct.

Which meant they believed there was another Host in Prague.

Someone at the Lichtenštejnský Palace had gotten the bright idea to turn off the overhead chandeliers. As Tanya would have happily told them, had they bothered to ask her opinion, the darkness did nothing to dampen the brawl. If anything, the fighting had grown even more heated—men grunting and shouting, no longer bothering to give reasons why before leaning into a punch.

Not that much of anything could tame that storm, now that Tanya knew that somehow, some way, magic was involved in the chaos playing out before her.

"You are hurt." A West German officer seized her by the arm—she thought it was a West German officer, as best she could tell in the dim light from the table candles—and yanked her upright. "The Czech police and paramedics are on the way. Please—allow them to tend to you."

"I'm fine." Tanya yanked her arm away. "You should be subduing those men. I am afraid they might be . . ." She paused for a moment, concocting a suitable lie. "Under the influence of some sort of drug. Perhaps your men permitted someone to enter the premises with drugs?"

The officer's tone hardened. "No. That cannot be possible."

"Are you certain of that?" Tanya asked. "If they take these men to the hospital, and learn they were given illicit substances at an event you were supposed to secure . . ."

The officer's scowl deepened.

"Well, I am afraid it could be rather embarrassing for you and your embassy. Do you not agree?"

"Step aside!" someone shouted in Czech. "Paramedics! Coming through!"

A squadron of Veřejná bezpečnost policemen shoved through the crowd, escorting paramedics with canvas stretchers. The policemen formed a tunnel of khaki uniforms while their commander subdued Dima, the sole Russian minder who had yet to crumple into a delirious, drunken, battered puddle on the ballroom floor. They hoisted the minders and a scientist onto the stretchers with

THE WITCH WHO CAME IN FROM THE COLD

brutal efficiency. Police escort to the hospital, then, before being taken into custody.

"Wait." Tanya pushed her way toward the commander. "You cannot arrest these men. They are representatives of the Russian Soviet Federative Socialist Republic—"

But Gabriel Pritchard looped his arm through the police chief's and turned him away from her. Tanya's mouth flapped open. This had to be Gabe's doing. He'd engineered this whole distraction—

"Thanks so much for answering my call," Gabe said, not bothering to conceal the American twang in his Czech. "These men are pretty banged up. Sets a piss-poor example for their motherland, don't you think?"

The police chief glanced over his shoulder toward Tanya before looking back to Gabe. "I am sure that will be for our Party representative to determine, after a complete investigation . . ."

Tanya's mouth worked, but no noise came out. He couldn't be so bold. But no—of course he could. "You can't take those men away. They are in the custody of the Soviet delegation!"

"Miss, please, you are in hysterics," the West German officer said, moving between Tanya and the quickly departing delegates. "I insist that you have a seat. Might I bring you a schnapps to calm your nerves?"

"I don't need your fucking schnapps!"

"Honestly, miss, there is no need to be upset—the situation is handled—"

Tanya reached into her clutch, hoping desperately that she'd brought her trusty flash-bang charm with her. No such luck. Only the invisibility charm she'd already depleted, and her favorite talisman for turning someone ever so slightly to her favor. But she suspected it would take more than an eyelash-bat and a limited talisman to get her way tonight.

She grabbed a wine glass off the nearest table and threw it in his face.

"What the fuck—" His words quickly dissolved into a snarl of multisyllabic Germanic compound swears. But Tanya didn't stay to hear it; she was too busy chasing the paramedics and VB officers down the stairs.

If Gabriel Pritchard thought he could sneak away with a Soviet scientist on her watch, he was about to learn he was sorely mistaken.

4.

N adia stuffed her charms and sensors and talismans back into
her satchel and moved toward the far end of the rooftop.
Beneath her was a short alleyway, crowded with garbage bins
and old crates. Nothing she particularly wanted to land on, but she
could use them to cushion her fall if absolutely necessary. With
luck, though, the construct had every intention of coming to her.

The square of mica magnified energy, cheaply, while the silver
wiring stored it and coiled it up long enough to sustain a decent
charge. Based on what Nadia had found in the creatures she and
Tanya had already dismantled, the Flame designed their constructs
to home in on power amplification—the telltale "heat signature"
of an awakened elemental. For a short while, at least, the construct
should fix on Nadia the way it would a Host, following its instincts
to pursue this new source of power and attempt to bring it to its
Flame masters.

At least Nadia assumed that's how it would go. She'd tried not
to let it get that far in the past. But then she'd never had a tool like
Jordan had given her now.

Part of her wondered why Jordan had been willing to give her the mica square—what conclusion she'd wanted Nadia to draw. It wasn't like her to give knowledge away so willingly. Did she want Nadia to unmask the Flame agents behind the constructs, so the Ice could neutralize the source? Retribution, perhaps, for their threats against Bar Vodnář. Or maybe even a witch as stubborn as Jordan realized she could be neutral no longer.

With a crunch of pebbles underfoot, the construct lumbered into the alleyway. Nadia stood stock-still on the lip of the roof, looking down at the creature. It would have seemed almost comical, if she hadn't known its purpose: long rectangles of stone strung on wiring to give it joints, like a stone scarecrow; white phosphorous eyes glowing in a lopsided face. Those eyes scanned upward, searching. Homing. And then it began to climb.

Steady. Relentless. Stone crunching against stone as it continued along the straightest path toward Nadia.

Nadia swallowed and braced herself. The construct was four meters down, now. Three. Two. Nadia gripped a handful of twigs bound in grass where it rested inside her satchel and uttered a protective word.

The construct's arm swung up and over the lip of the roof. Its face followed, studied her for a moment, head rotating slightly in a quizzical, almost canine expression.

Opened its mouth.

And every bone in Nadia's body vibrated, struck by the same bass tone.

The strap on Tanya's rhinestone-studded pumps snapped somewhere on the third flight of stairs. She kicked the broken pump aside and hop-unbuckled the other as she ran from the Lichtenštejnský Palace, trying to catch up to the fleet of ambulances and boxy VB cars. Fortunately, the guards were working in her favor for once, more interested in keeping people out of the palace than in; no one tried to stop her as she ran barefoot onto the street, empty save for the ambulances.

Metal on metal ricocheted through the cobblestones as a paramedic slammed the last ambulance door shut.

"Wait." Tanya hiked up a fistful of sequined gown and padded toward the ambulance. "Wait!"

The ambulance's engine turned over with a sputter, then it started down the road with a sharp wail.

A thousand curses ran through Tanya's mind. Charms, talismans—she had to have something. Her hairpins were embedded with bits of crystal; cheap copper wire bound the fake stones to the posts in her ears. She glanced down at the dirt wedged between the cobblestones. Well, at least she knew it was Czech soil.

Tanya ripped an earring free with one hand while the other pulled one hairpin loose. After twisting the earring wire around the hairpin, she jammed the hairpin's end into the gap between cobbles and uttered an ancient word.

A column of dirt and stone shot up a few hundred meters ahead of her as the force of her spell knocked her backward. Tires screeched against stone, and something heavy thudded against the metal. Tanya scrambled to her feet, hands still tingling from the ley line energy that had passed through her. But the ambulance had withstood the dagger of earth that her spell had thrust upward. After a few precarious moments of swaying back and forth from the impact, it righted itself and sped on down the street.

Tanya whirled back toward the Lichtenštejnský Palace, ready

to claw Gabriel Pritchard's eyes out. But he was nowhere to be found. She sought the nearest phone booth and dashed inside, hoping she had enough korunas wedged inside her clutch. The coins settled in the phone's belly with a satisfying *clunk*. Her fingers shook as she spun the phone's dial and cast through her mind for the right code phrase.

So many code phrases. So many signals. For Ice and the KGB both. How had her grandfather managed it? How could anyone be expected to manage?

The weak ringing sound halted as someone answered. *"Slushayu."*

"I am looking for Danilov." Her voice wavered. "Danilov" indicated one of the highest levels of urgency. "He is supposed to meet me at the hospital."

"He should be arriving soon," the operator answered. *We will dispatch a team now.*

"I've already drunk four cups of coffee." *Four men.* "An American man in the canteen is looking at me strangely."

"What kind of flowers should Danilov bring?"

Tanya's knuckles went white around the phone's cord. She wedged herself into the far corner of the booth, out of the reach of the streetlamp, just as Gabriel Pritchard and his dark-haired younger friend passed along the other side of the street, strolling along, chatting as if they'd just watched a particularly experimental play.

They were headed in the opposite direction of the hospital.

"I—I'm very sorry." Tanya swallowed past the lump in her throat. "I am afraid I was confused. I was not calling for Danilov."

She didn't need a codebook to translate the operator's sigh: *You're really not following protocol here.* "Is that so."

"Y-yes. I meant to call for Grikovsky." Grikovsky—the *observe only* name.

"Well, I'm sure he'll be along soon."

"No flowers are necessary." Tanya hung up the phone before the operator could respond.

But if Gabe wasn't trying to rush the scientists to the hospital for easy access, then what the hell had that brawl been about?

As soon as Gabe had turned the corner, Tanya slipped out of the phone booth. In one direction, Pritchard and whatever he had planned next. In the other, the hospital, where three Soviet minders and one scientist were incapacitated and vulnerable to whatever nonsense the Westerners could concoct. She could tail Gabe, see where he led her, see what else—if anything else—he had planned for this evening. Or she could meet up with the observation team and defuse any threats at the hospital.

Tanya shifted her bare feet on the cobbles and headed south toward the hospital.

She had a feeling her long night had only begun.

Nadia scraped herself off the rooftop, blinking frantically. Gradually, the blur of dark around her settled into distinct shapes. Most important, however, was the shape that was missing.

The construct.

How long had she been unconscious? Where was the construct? What the hell had happened?

Her sensors were still chiming in her bag, but fainter now. The construct was moving away. It must have seen through her ruse and activated some sort of—defensive system, maybe. Shit. The Flame was clever; she'd give them that. But she wasn't done with their servant yet.

Nadia wrenched the rooftop access door open and pounded

down the staircase. Followed the fluctuations in the sensors west, drawing closer toward the river. Then she saw it, lumbering through the shadows. Each step dragging slower than the last. It started across the bridge that spanned the Vltava—

But then, the moment it passed above the rushing river, it ground to a halt.

"Jesus, how do you stand this weather?"

Radek ground his teeth together and refused to look at the American seated opposite him in the rowboat. He focused on the rhythmic *splish* and *whump* of the water as his oars entered it, pushed, and lifted free. He'd tolerated men like this before. He could tolerate many more. Certainly, for what they were paying him, he could listen to the usual derision. Just as he tolerated the rotting stench coming from the blanket-wrapped bulk, the size of a man, wedged between them in the rowboat.

The American's cigar puffed to life as he took another pull. "It's disgusting," he continued. "Like I'm perpetually getting sneezed on by Mother Nature. Jesus. And I thought the Washington humidity was bad."

Radek pretended he didn't understand. He wondered why, when the American had gone to all the trouble to clothe himself in black, a balaclava even, he insisted on lighting that stupid cigar.

"All right. Here we are. Pull up nice and slow."

"Yes, sir," Radek muttered. They were not supposed to use names—he never did, when he was working these side jobs for the Americans—but this man had introduced himself straight away as Dominic. He feared nothing, this Dominic. Let his country see the Soviet tanks roll in, and then he might learn the true meaning of fear.

Radek brought the boat alongside the steep windowless wall of the Vltava-facing side of the Lichtenštejnský Palace. They were positioned beneath the balconies that jutted from the ballroom. In the distance, Radek heard the retreating wail of sirens, and above them, the chatter of a particularly rambunctious party. And yet the party threw no lights onto the Vltava's surface. As if the power had been cut.

No matter. Radek was not paid extra to understand what was happening. If anything, he was paid *not* to notice.

So when something dark and heavy splashed into the water beside them from the balcony, Radek said nothing. He ignored the gasps of shock that spilled out of the ballroom. On Dominic's count, he hoisted his end of the blanket-wrapped object up, and together they dumped the contents overboard.

The cloud of rot and decay that rose from it burned through Radek like cheap vodka, but this, too, he could ignore.

All was silent for a few moments save the slow bubble as their package sank to the bottom of the shallow river. Then a new figure emerged, still safely hidden beneath the balcony's cover, gasping for breath.

Dominic held out a hand to help pull the man aboard. In his too-tight cheap suit, the newcomer slithered onto the rowboat's floor like a fish.

"How'd our friends do?" Dominic asked their new arrival.

The man gasped for breath. "All three minders headed to the hospital with a police escort. Another of my colleagues, too."

Dominic nodded. "That'll keep them busy for a while."

Radek stared at the dance of moonlight across the Vltava and did his best not to hear the conversation beside him. He needed only to wait for Dominic's command. But for now, the American looked content to bask in the glow of a job well done. He reached into his breast pocket and offered a fresh cigar to the man on the bottom of the boat.

"For when we get you to the safe house," Dominic explained. "Congratulations, Maks. You're officially dead."

64
39
77
35
95
65
65

EPISODE 11

KING'S GAMBIT ACCEPTED

Ian Tregillis

Smíchov, Prague
February 27, 1970

1.

Two twenty-seven in the morning, somewhere behind the Iron Curtain: Footsteps creaking on a wooden dock. Wispy tendrils of moonlit fog dancing on the river. A trench-coated figure lurking in the shadows. The muffled echo of a two-stroke marine engine, slowly growing louder.

Maybe I should light a cigarette, Josh thought. *Just to complete the tableau.*

Binoculars. Butterflies in the stomach. Beads of sweat on the brow.

Add a whiskey priest with a rotten tooth, and I could be in a Graham Greene novel.

Even the Vltava had gotten in the mood, shrouding itself much like Josh in his trench coat. At least the coat served a purpose; the fog was pure affectation. Half an hour ago he'd been able to see clear across the river. Now the dock was an island in a silvery sea.

Hell. They'd never discussed the possibility of pea soup. How would Dom find the dock? All their preparations, all their precautions to keep the Reds off balance, and then in the end the *river* decided to throw them a curveball.

It was as though the Vltava were patiently erasing everything beyond the dock, to make him forget the outside world. He imagined this was how it felt to stand upon the banks of Lethe.

Well. Maybe it worked both ways. Maybe it would shroud them from their adversaries, too. Dom had insisted on this extraction route, after all, and he was the expert.

Somewhere on the water, still dozens of yards out, the two-stroke cut off in midputter. It became the faint creak of oarlocks and the swish of oars. Dom was zeroing in, despite the fog. Josh suppressed a shiver of admiration. Guys like Dom and Alestair, guys who'd been around awhile, they knew their business. It made him eager for the day when *he* was the experienced partner—inspiring younger officers with his confidence, impressing them with his stories. Oh did Alestair have stories . . .

"Antlers," said a low voice on the water, closer than Josh had thought possible. Close enough to make him jump.

"Goggles." A single word. Low, controlled, confident. It pleased Josh to no end that his voice didn't crack. He sounded like he belonged here.

A pause for triangulation. The oarlocks changed their rhythm. The susurration of water against a wooden prow. The boat drew closer. Then, barely more than a whisper:

"Peabody."

"WABAC."

A creak. A splash. A boat hove into view, ghostly fingers of mist grasping at the gunwales. Dom stood in the prow like Charon himself.

The classicist in Josh wished he'd brought an obol to pay the ferryman. But, then again, how did it work when the ferryman *retrieved* somebody from the underworld? Ovid and Virgil were a little unclear on the matter of refunds. And anyway, Charon probably didn't wear cable-knit turtlenecks.

Dom gave a single nod. Terse. Josh returned the gesture, and then he caught the rope that came sailing through the fog. *Calm. Cool. Like you belong here.* Josh looped it around the bollards while Dom maneuvered the boat against the dock with barely a scrape. Then the senior officer crouched between the thwarts and pulled back a tarpaulin. His passenger sat up, blinking and looking more than a little uncomfortable.

ANCHISES: Maksim Sokolov.

"This is our stop, Doctor." Dom whispered around the cigar clamped in the corner of his mouth. Maybe the cigarette wasn't such a silly idea after all.

He ushered the defector toward the dock, steadying him against the sway of the boat. Josh offered a hand. (*Strong grip,* he coached himself. *Confident, steady, trustworthy.*) Then he hauled Sokolov onto dry land.

"Easy, Doc. I've got you," he said. And he did. Recognition dawned, softening the Russian's expression. Good. The more relaxed he remained, the better.

Dom said, "Vehicle?"

Josh tipped his head toward the shore, where a replica police car waited in the shadows. "All clear."

Dom nodded. But rather than disembark so that Josh could release the lines and send the boat drifting downriver, he plucked the cigar from his mouth and tapped a dusting of ash along the keel and across the thwarts. For some reason it reminded Josh of a priest thumbing a cross on the forehead of an Ash Wednesday congregant.

Sokolov frowned. "Why is he doing that?"

Good question. It wasn't part of the plan. "Dom?"

"Everyone has their superstitions. Gabe has his flask. This is mine." *Tap, tap, tap.* "Kinda like my trademark."

A board rattled underfoot. Josh caught himself fidgeting. *Relax,* he commanded himself. *We built an hour of slack into the timeline. We can afford thirty seconds.* Still . . .

As if reading Josh's anxiety, Dom said, "I once made the mistake of not doing this. It cost me." More quietly, he added, "Not just me."

"And thus a ritual was born."

Dom narrowed his eyes, shot Josh an unreadable glance. But it passed as quickly as it came. "Got it in one."

Then he was out of the boat, cat-quick. Together they unlooped the lines from the bollards and tossed the coils aboard. Josh pressed the heel of one shoe against the prow—*Don't fall in; professionals don't fall in*—and pushed. Eddies of fog swirled about the boat as it slid into the current.

They hustled Sokolov along the dock, across a narrow riverfront path, and into the alley where Josh had parked the car between a retaining wall and the shuttered doors of a vacant wool warehouse. Josh tossed the keys to Dom, then bundled the defector into the backseat.

Dom started the car and eased it into gear.

"Nice work, Toms."

It felt good.

Tanya ditched the car at sunrise, several blocks from the embassy.

Throughout the night she'd berated herself. The constant grind of dip-circuit functions had left her tired and distracted;

she'd neglected to load up on charms before attending yet another. Lazy. It was bad tradecraft. She'd had an inkling that Gabe and his comrades were up to something; she ought to have been proactive, prepared for anything. Like Nadia. Instead, she'd burned all of the charms on her person before departing the Lichtenštejnský Palace.

She'd had to do things the mundane way. When she finally caught up with the ambulance at its destination hospital, three minders and one conference attendee had received medical attention for the wounds and bruises they'd taken during the brawl. But surely more than four people had been injured? She was stippled with glass cuts herself, and she hadn't been one of those who'd lost their minds. Yet where were the rest? So she'd done the rounds of all the other hospitals and clinics in the city. Two had received emergency cases overnight, but both had arrived hours after the ambulance had pulled away from the palace. And neither of those patients could have been at the party, anyway. Tanya was confident she wasn't pursuing a six-year-old girl, nor was she on the trail of a seventy-five-year-old emphysemic Bulgarian man.

Clinics and hospitals, she checked them all, working straight through the wolf hours.

Foolish. Prague was too big for one woman, too full of places to hide an ambulance. Too full of places to change vehicles. Too full of places to stash somebody. (Somebody who didn't want to go home?)

But she'd wanted, needed, so desperately to find the defector's ambulance. If she'd found it, its driver, its cargo, its anything, she could have reported partial success to Sasha. But now she had to face him—the man who'd broken into her apartment, taken her grandfather's radio, and then played her and Gabe like pawns when they'd tried to retrieve it—empty-handed. She'd have to look him in the eye and report a possible defection-in-progress, right under their noses.

She was limping, she realized, and had been for a while. When she paused to re-collect herself, the cuts on her arms and chest made themselves known. They'd stopped bleeding, but they hadn't stopped hurting. Her ankles throbbed from sprinting across treacherously frost-slick cobbles. More than once, she'd nearly crippled herself. Bruises mottled her knees and shoulders thanks to several tumbles on those same cobbles.

She'd called ahead. Comrade Komyetski arrived at KGB Prague Station barely more than fifteen minutes after Tanya did, despite the hour. He found her at her desk with one unshod foot hiked atop an open drawer, wincing each time she dabbed at the cuts with alcohol and a bloody towel. That wasn't the reason for his double take, she knew. She was still in her formal clothes, one of her dip-circuit outfits. There'd been no time to retrieve her coat. Her wardrobe gave her few options for formal outings, and this one was tattered and bloodstained in a dozen places. A complete loss.

"Tatiana Mikhailovna Morozova. You've had a night."

He attempted the same light tone that she'd endured for hours on end during her failed gambit to retrieve the radio. The voice he'd used when he'd threatened, indirectly, to have her grand-father killed. But the early hour, not to mention the heaviness of lost sleep, weighted it down.

"Yes, sir."

"At least you're not soaking wet."

She blinked at him. *What?*

"You didn't fall in the river this time."

Oh. "Oh. No, I didn't."

She made to stand. Exhaustion and pain made her wobbly. Sasha noticed.

"Sit, sit. I insist. You're injured. Do you need a physician?"

She shook her head. "I've already been to a hospital tonight. All of them, in point of fact."

That got his attention. "Well, then. Tell me about this night of yours, and why you had to call me before even bakers and birds start their days."

Tanya shook her head. They were the only two in Prague Station. And yet: "We shouldn't talk here. Better if we speak privately in your office."

In the vault, in other words. Had she not been looking for it, she might have missed his momentary glance of pure calculation. But it was there, if only for a second. Face a blank mask, he went straight to his office and, after a moment spent jangling his key ring, unlocked it. She followed.

He didn't offer her a chair, didn't insist she take the weight from her poor abused legs. Instead, he spoke as soon as the door was locked, sealing them into the Faraday cage. "Tell me what happened." This wasn't the jovial uncle speaking; she'd awakened the guarded station chief. He dropped into the chair behind the desk hard enough to make the casters groan. Fingers steepled before thin colorless lips, he listened.

First she recapped her recent reports and the observations she'd documented regarding potentially unusual activity by certain suspected officers of the Western intelligence services. Then she described the party, the brawl, her suspicions about the ambulances, her failed attempt to follow them.

Quiet reigned for several long beats after she fell silent. His gaze strayed to one of the chessboards on the desk. Now the steeple peeled apart; he reached forward, gingerly, to lay a fingertip atop a rook. He held that gesture of contemplation for several seconds before withdrawing, leaving the rook undisturbed.

Careless indecision like that would have been penalized in a tournament match, she knew. But not, of course, in a correspondence game. A steadfast rule in one arena, pointless and unenforceable in another.

"It could be nothing. A misunderstanding," he said.

"It isn't."

Sasha nodded. That was the answer he'd expected. "They'll move quickly."

Yes, they would. Now that the Westerners had their defector in hand—and they did, she felt it in her bones—they'd smuggle him or her out of Czechoslovakia and the Party's reach as soon as possible.

"It's best if we work quietly. We could seal the borders, stop all trains, ground all flights, board all boats. But that would tip our hand."

What at first she'd thought was the weight of lost sleep, filling his voice with gravel, she now recognized as the legacy of a late night spent with a bottle of vodka. It colored his eyes ever so slightly pink and made him blink at her just a bit too frequently, as though she and the world around her were blurry. His breath didn't betray him, not at this distance, but there were ways to disguise a scent.

He looked her over again. Her current state didn't instill confidence, she knew. And he already had reasons to doubt her loyalty. "Can you handle this?"

"Of course, sir." What else could she say? "We'll do everything possible to stop this."

Again, he looked over the chess pieces. He didn't reach for the rook, but his eyes did. "I meant you personally."

"Sir?"

"If you, Tatiana Morozova, led a successful counter-operation, it would do great things for your career. I would take it as my personal mission to ensure you received the credit you deserved." What was he on about? "I've heard from Center." His gaze snapped away from the game, as if he'd chosen a move. "You impressed them when you completed your delivery despite Comrade Bykovsky's bungling," he lied. "Stop the defection and your star will rise. You'll be trusted to safeguard ever more sensitive items."

Translation: *Do this and maybe, just maybe, you'll get your radio back.*

The remarkable thing about chess, she reflected, was its openness. The board hid nothing; the pieces were there for all to see. Castles harbored no defectors; bishops heard no secret confessions.

So it was with this lie.

You still have my radio. And you know I know it. But I have to pretend that I believe otherwise, that together we delivered it according to fake orders from Moscow Center, even though we both know that was a sham. I'm still bound to that fiction. That skein of lies is the only thing between me and Siberia.

Even bleary-eyed and just a little bit tipsy, Comrade Komyetski was a grand master of manipulation. Tanya might have admired it, if it didn't frighten her so.

"My sole concern is my duty to the state."

He nodded, simultaneously pleased and grim. "Then I charge you with thwarting this defection. Use whatever or whomever you must. But act soon."

It wasn't until she departed the embassy that she realized she couldn't go home. The key to her flat was still in the pocket of her coat, and that was at the Lichtenštejnský Palace.

The construct fell apart at Nadia's feet. The nemesis and prey that had kept her busy through the night was now just so much rubbish.

Dammit.

A quick inspection confirmed her suspicions. The remains gave her no clue as to the construct's origin, nor its makers. She kicked the trash into the river, swearing.

She chewed on the problem all the way back to her flat. The night-long chase should have left her exhausted. Instead, her frustration was like fire under a teakettle; if she didn't let off the steam, she'd burst. To hell with it.

An hour of sparring, if she could find a partner, or even a workout with a punching bag, would be infinitely more productive than trying to break down this wall with her forehead.

She stuffed her slightly smelly workout clothes into a rucksack. Bundle slung over one shoulder, she walked the distance from her khrushchyovka to the embassy gym rather than take a tram—the more she moved her body, the more she could let her subconscious spin while her conscious mind slipped into the patterns etched into her brain by years of training. Watching for tails, scanning the street for anything out of the ordinary, keeping eyes and ears—and that indescribable sixth sense that any good spy understood but couldn't explain—alert to the usual threats. Nadezhda Ostrokhina, Ice operative, melted into the background, and in her stead stood Nadia the KGB officer. Both ladies arrived at the gym without incident. (Not even a clumsy pass from the handful of early risers she passed on the streets. That was vaguely disappointing. She had to learn not to scowl so fiercely when deep in thought. She would have welcomed a good scrap just then.)

She changed clothes and wrapped her fists. And then everything disappeared except the rhythm of her breathing, the sway of the bag, the crunch of sand beneath her fists, the bag's grudging absorption of each jab, the drip of sweat along the unscratchable expanse between her shoulder blades. The charms' behavior the previous night became a dull discomfort in the back of her mind. It was like having something stuck between her molars, something no toothpick could dislodge.

It wasn't until she felt the hand on her shoulder that she realized somebody had been calling her name. The unexpected touch of skin startled her. She whirled, fists raised and a scorching curse on her tongue.

Tanya retreated so quickly she tripped over a stool, meeting the floor in an undignified heap. They glared at each other for a beat. Nadia shook it off—the itch in her mind was making her cranky. This wasn't Tanya's fault. She offered a sweaty hand, hauled her partner back to her feet.

"Sorry."

"I thought you were going to break my nose." Tanya righted the stool and plopped down. She rubbed her hip, her elbow, her shin, moving gingerly, a Young Pioneer charting a course across a topographic map of pain. Her arms were stippled with fresh scabs.

"You disappeared last night," Nadia panted. Words would come more easily as her heart rate inched back down. But her mind already felt sharper; even an abbreviated workout had its therapeutic benefits. "We need to talk. Something very odd happened."

Tanya nodded, sighed. "I spent the entire night chasing it."

A flush of relief washed through Nadia. Tanya had sensed it too. They were on the same page. They were still partners, still a solid team. "And then I was in the vault, telling Sasha about it."

The momentary comfort dissipated. "Wait, why in the world—"

"And then I immediately went looking for you."

"—did you tell *Sasha*?"

Tanya looked at her as if she'd gone punch-drunk. "Of course I reported it. Why didn't *you*? If there really was a—" Here she stopped herself. She took a moment to scan the entire room, squinting into every dusty corner. They were alone. Still, she dropped her voice so low that Nadia had to read her lips. "—a *defection*, and I'm convinced there was . . ."

Nadia reeled as if slapped. No—as if the punching bag had snuck up and walloped her in the neck.

"What are you saying?"

Tanya blinked. Froze. "I— Wait. *You* said something strange happened last night."

"It did." Nadia chewed her lip. Tasting the metallic tang of blood, she concluded: "But now I have a nauseating suspicion that *my* strange thing is not *your* strange thing."

Tanya deflated like a burst balloon. Elbows on her knees, she raked fingers through her hair until her forehead rested on her palms. There she hunched in exhausted contemplation until Nadia thought she'd actually dozed off. Finally, her partner looked up. "You first," she said, looking like she'd aged years in a few moments. When had she last eaten?

Nadia shook her head. "Not here. Let's go to my place. We'll talk on the way, and then we'll make breakfast. We both could use it."

They didn't speak again until Nadia had packed her gear and

both women were bundled against the early springtime chill. Prague had yawned and stretched and come to life during Nadia's workout. They let the rattling of trams, the thrum of automobiles, the *click-clack* of their boot heels on the pavement, the dinging of bells over shop doors mask their conversation. Nadia augmented the audio camouflage with a trifle of sorcery; she feared what might happen if Tanya attempted even the simplest magic in her state.

"There's something in the city. I've been sensing it, off and on, for several days. But last night my charms went crazy. I spent half the night chasing a construct. A very powerful construct. It was on the hunt, but it petered out at the river around dawn." Nadia paused for emphasis. "I've been thinking about what the American, Pritchard, told us at the Vyšehrad."

"Last night?" Tanya frowned. And then, in a tone of unassailable certainty, she said, "The golem had nothing to do with it."

"I can think of only one other possibility." They put the conversation on momentary hiatus while passing a trio of policemen milling outside a café. Tanya's wounds received second glances. But then, in response to her partner's frown, Nadia said, "This construct . . . the only time I've seen anything like it was the night we made contact with Zlata."

Tanya slowed to a stop. "Wait. I need you to be very explicit. Are you saying what I think you're saying?"

"I'm saying I think another Host has arrived in Prague. And that someone—someone *who is not us*—has several powerful constructs scouring the city for it."

"Little wonder you were so confused when I said I reported to Sasha."

"Now what's all this about . . . that thing you said at the gym?"

Nadia's building came into view when they turned the corner.

Her stomach growled. They picked up the pace to cross ahead of a tram. Trailing clouds of steamy breath like conversational chaff, Tanya explained how she'd spent the night.

"And the Westerners?"

Tanya shrugged. "The British officer, Winthrop, I'm not certain about. But the Americans were definitely part of it. Pritchard started the brawl, I'm certain."

"Because they were extracting a defector."

"It's the only thing that makes sense. I'm telling you, that brawl was a distraction."

They didn't speak again until they were safely alone and warm in Nadia's apartment, chewing on eggs and toast and a very unwelcome conclusion. Nadia put voice to it first. Draining the dregs of her tea, she said, "I was wrong. Now I'm afraid our problems are related."

Tanya sighed. "The Americans are extracting a defector . . ."

". . . who just *happens* to have arrived around the same time a new Host appeared in Prague." Nadia slammed down her cup. *"Bozhe moi."*

Zerena knew something was wrong the moment she entered the bakery. Knew it so deeply, so automatically, that her conscious mind lagged several seconds behind her instincts. But she went through the usual motions for the benefit of the mundane customers, her body coasting through the formalities while her mind calculated.

With a peck of the lips on each of Komyetski's stubbly cheeks, she muttered pleasantries. As usual, he smelled ever so faintly of alcohol.

"So good to see you again, Sasha."

His response was heartier, more sincere. "The pleasure is *entirely* mine."

And that was the moment she caught up with herself.

His smile, she realized. Sasha's smile was *genuine.*

The bakery smelled of cinnamon and freshly risen bread. Normally that mélange would have made her stomach growl with longing. Instead, it curdled.

But she kept her mask in place. "I hadn't expected to see you again so soon." Translation: *We'd agreed not to contact each other.* She made to sit, but he laid a hand on her shoulder—dear God, now he was being positively familiar with her—and ushered her toward the gap in the counter.

Exchanging nods with the woman at the register, he said, "Nor I, you, honestly. But I just knew you'd want to see this."

Zerena let him guide her from the shop into the kitchen. "I've baked a few cakes in my day, you know. The process is no mystery to me."

He laughed. Truly laughed. Something was wrong.

She kept up a bright patter, distracting him while she twisted her wedding ring through a half circle. Every charm on her person—the garnets in her earrings, the ancient coin tucked inside her clutch, even the silver threads sewn into the hem of her coat—gave a single faint jerk, as if acknowledging their activation. Let him try to kill her. Her protective wards would burn his bones to ash. She'd render this bakery, this entire street, a howling firestorm before she'd allow a pudgy alcoholic like Aleksander Vadimovich Komyetski to believe he could best her.

He took her to the walk-in pantry. There, on a table, a long length of cheesecloth concealed a bundle the size of a bread basket. Karel and Vladimir leaned against the wall—her junior acolytes, now eyeing her as if they thought they were sizing up her throne for themselves. That gave her pause. Sasha alone, she could defeat. Karel and Vladimir, too, she'd outwitted before. But all three? Hoping the men would dismiss it as a nervous tic, she gave her wedding ring another twist. This time the confirmatory shake from her charms filled her mouth with the tongue-writhing foulness of moldy bread.

Sasha waited to speak until the door was closed and Karel had propped a chair under the knob. Zerena recognized the static electricity tingle of a protective ward snapping into place. Then Sasha strode to the table and laid a hand on the cheesecloth. She rolled her eyes. Perhaps she'd die of boredom with this tedious showmanship before he tried to kill her.

Frowning, he ran his tongue around the inside of his mouth. Zerena watched it bulge first one cheek, then the other. Damn. He tasted it too. She'd gone overboard.

"Are you tense? There's no need. I merely have information to share."

"This isn't how we do it."

"No, but this is urgent, and it affects us all."

She eyed the other two. The tension in the way they leaned against the shelves, the glances flicking back and forth between them. *Aha. You don't know what Komyetski is about either. Maybe I won't have to scorch this place to the ground.*

Sasha was many things, but no fool. *And he'd never be so foolish as to attack all three of us at once.*

She waited for one of the buffoons to rise to Sasha's bait. It took but a second.

Vladimir crossed his arms. "We're all here now. What is it?"

At least Sasha had the courtesy to dispense with preambles. "There's a defector in Prague. And the CIA already has him."

Zerena didn't have to feign surprise. "Then I'd say you have quite a problem on your hands. But I can't help you. This is your mess. What could I possibly do?"

"Why, nothing." With a yank of the cloth, Sasha added, "You've already done little enough."

The hidden item was a radio. A recent conversation—a conversation about a radio—came unbidden to mind. Zerena didn't like where this was going.

Karel jerked his chin toward the table. "Are we supposed to understand the significance of that?"

"Examine it." Sasha spread his arms. "Be my guest. Take a good, close look." He met Zerena's eyes. "It's perfectly safe, I assure you."

It was the work of moments to perceive the foreign magic lurking within. The radio was a construct. And a subtle one.

"This is the work of an Ice sorcerer. A very fine one. Where did you obtain this?"

"I found it hidden behind a secret panel in dear Tanya's apartment. Since that time, she has gone to great lengths to retrieve it. I, of course, have deflected such efforts."

It took superior willpower not to shiver visibly as a frisson of genuine alarm tickled her spine. Sasha had inquired about this very same radio. Acting on instinct—on the sense of great untapped potential within Tatiana Morozova—Zerena had recklessly improvised an excuse to help shield the young officer from suspicion. A foolish gamble, she knew, even as she had made it. But in the moment the potential dividends had looked so rich . . . Now that careless lie was laid bare. And it made it look as though Zerena had deliberately interceded to conceal an Ice operation being carried out by one of Sasha's own officers.

Though she doubted Karel and Vladimir understood the context, the implication was clear enough. This was a coup attempt.

Or worse. But she played along, spooled things out a little further. She needed the delay to regain her equilibrium.

"I do hope you intend to start making sense today."

"It was Tanya who identified the defection-in-progress. She's a very fine officer. But she's clearly an agent, wittingly or otherwise, of our enemies. She must go." His jowls shimmied when he shook his head. "I truly dislike this course of action, even more than I dislike having it thrust upon me."

Karel crossed his arms. "I'm sure you don't dislike it any more than we dislike being kept in the dark—"

"Wait your turn," said Zerena, "while the adults speak." She needed no charm to summon a tone of voice capable of knocking a disobedient cur into instant submission. Vladimir and Karel both bristled; nevertheless, the latter's teeth clicked together. In a tone infinitesimally less frosty, she added: "Thrust upon you? Do explain."

"We relied upon you. It was your job to monitor our adversaries and keep us informed of their disposition in Prague. We trusted you." Again, the jowls shimmied. Sasha, the hapless victim. "Instead, you allowed an enemy agent to infiltrate *my* station. Had I not uncovered the truth myself, the damage could have been incalculable." He turned to the others, pulling a charm from his trouser pocket as he did so. She knew without looking what it would be: a jade-green hummingbird feather threaded through a minute hole in a lodestone, all bound with silver wire. Hummingbird because truth was so light and fragile, silver to reflect the value of honesty. A beautiful, deadly thing. "I call upon you both to witness this. I vouch that Zerena Pulnoc did state Tatiana Morozova's ownership of this radio was harmless and of no concern to our efforts. I vouch that, to the best of my knowledge, Zerena knowingly concealed the Ice affiliation of a KGB officer under my command, and did so to the detriment of all our efforts in Prague."

He pressed the charm to his lips. He bit the feather, pulled it loose, and spit it on the floor. It didn't burst into flames. Neither did he. He'd spoken the truth, or if nothing else, the truth as he understood it.

"I submit that Zerena Pulnoc is not suited for her position."

Vladimir frowned at the emerald pinion. Karel frowned at Zerena. "Do you deny this?"

"I deny that my actions were taken in support of Ice. I have reasons for everything I do."

"Yet you never share them."

"You share very little with us," Vladimir added.

Under other circumstances, she would have rolled her eyes at his petulant tone. She quirked an eyebrow. "Such as?"

"We know a Host has recently arrived. This we discerned for ourselves. You never mentioned it."

Sasha flinched as if he'd just received a static shock. "Is this true?"

The look of scorn she tossed in his direction might have flayed a thinner man down to the skeleton. "I thought you no longer trusted my pronouncements? You'll move against Morozova soon, I assume."

"I must. This is a delicate time. With a defection in progress—and now apparently an uncollared *Host* roaming the city—the risks of keeping her under observation outweigh the benefits." Sasha straightened. The shift in his body language was subtle but deliberate. When he spoke next, his voice wasn't that of a jolly uncle, nor was it that of a mealymouthed sycophant. "I will lament the loss of her skills, but she must be removed. And so she will be."

You want her gone because you believe she's my creature. Well, then, perhaps I will make her so.

"I see," she said, in what she hoped was a convincingly meek tone. It wasn't one she practiced often. *Cling to your illusions, Aleksander Komyetski. They serve us both.* "May I make a suggestion, then?"

It was galling, honestly, how he managed to load a single nod with such condescending magnanimity. But she swallowed her distaste. "We already have the tools in place for dealing with Morozova." She didn't take her eyes—a supplicant's eyes, she hoped—from Sasha, but she jerked her head toward the other Flame men, who eyed the exchange like caged canaries watching a pair of hungry housecats tear at each other. "Use one of their constructs. Doing so will leave your hands clean."

Vladimir and Karel exchanged a guilty look. Artless idiots. "We don't have—"

"Oh please." She let the disdain fly free. She could play the supplicant to Sasha if she must, but she'd never bend a knee to these idiots. Karel squirmed as though the hoarfrost in her tone had glazed his spine. "Don't insult me. The very moment you suspected there might be a new Host in town, you tripped over yourselves to build constructs to hunt it. Your latest has roamed the town for several nights."

To Sasha, she added, "I'm not *entirely* uninformed about the goings on in Prague, you know."

He scratched his chin. "A construct. Yes, that might do."

2.

A floorboard creaked. Josh cocked his head, briefly splitting his attention between the window overlooking the street and the room behind him.

"How is he?"

"Sleeping like a newborn kitten at his mother's teat." Dominic's voice was a gravelly rasp in the dark. The door to the safe house's only bedroom closed behind him with a quiet *click*.

"I'd have thought Sokolov would be too keyed up to sleep. I guess the adrenaline rush wore off."

Not mine, though. Not yet.

"Guess so. Or maybe it was the knockout drops I spiked his water glass with after we arrived."

That stole all of Josh's attention. His chair scraped across the floor as he pushed away from the window to stare at Dom, who had taken a seat at the kitchen table. The room was small enough that a stage whisper carried.

"Chloral hydrate? That wasn't in the mission brief."

Dom shrugged. "I made a situational judgment call. We need

Sokolov clearheaded and calm. He's neither of those things as long as he's coasting on a sleep deficit."

"But what if we have to move him in a hurry?"

"I'm not worried. You're a good man in the field, Toms. I'm confident we'd make it work."

Josh blushed, grateful for the shadows. He tried not to let the compliment swell his chest or his head. "I suppose it does make sense that he rests sooner rather than later."

Dom nodded. "Mission briefs are all fine and good—hey, I wrote this one, after all—but fieldwork is always about thinking on your feet." He pulled a cigar from the inner pocket of his sport coat. He didn't light it, thank God, but he did hold it under his nose. A few sniffs later, he added, "Always have a contingency plan in your back pocket. And a contingency for your contingency." The cigar made its way to the corner of his mouth. Speaking past it, Dom concluded, "I mean contingencies that aren't laid out in the mission brief. Your own personal plans B, C, and D for when it all goes to hell."

"Has that ever happened to you? Everything gone to hell, I mean?"

"And then some."

Josh chewed on this. He tried not to look too eager for advice. "You can't plan for everything, but you might as well try, huh?"

Dom shrugged again. "Nothing you haven't heard from Pritchard a dozen times or more."

"Hm."

Josh turned his attention back to the approach to the safe house. If unfriendlies showed up, he and Dom would have to shove the disconnected oven aside and scramble out through the crawlspace. He was still trying to figure out how they'd manage to extricate an unconscious Maksim if that happened when Dom stood. Carrying his chair, he joined Josh's vigil at the window.

"Get some rest, Dom. I'll spell you." *I couldn't sleep if you gave me twice the dose you gave Maksim.*

"Sure. I appreciate it."

Yet Dom's gaze didn't waver from the street. The curtains hid them from outside eyes, yet up close in a dark room, the window offered a good view of the alley. He cleared his throat, as if hesitating.

"Hey, Josh. Before I turn in? I know I've been a little heavy-handed with you. About . . . well, about things that are none of my damn business." Josh tensed. A prickle took root between his shoulders, auguring an uncomfortable conversation. The cigar tapped against Dom's teeth, making a muted scrape as he rolled it from one corner of his mouth to the other. "You did fine work tonight. That's all I care about. You're okay by me."

A spot of motion on the street gave Josh an excuse to turn his head. There it was again. He stood, leaned closer to the window, catching his weight on the sill so that he didn't disturb the curtain. He craned his neck, hissing, "Did you see that?"

"Easy, cowboy." Dom pointed. "Newspaper."

The wind picked up. A dust devil carried a piece of paper down the alley—a scrap of newsprint, darker on one side than the other. It flickered in the streetlamp shine.

Josh returned to his seat, blushing again, but not from pride. At least he hadn't knocked over the chair.

As if reading his thoughts, the other man said, "Better safe than sorry."

They shared a silent vigil. Perhaps a quarter hour passed. Nobody entered the alley. Not even a stray dog, piddling on the corner lamppost. Dom yawned. Josh fought down a sympathetic yawn of his own. He was about to reiterate his offer to spell Dom when the other man broke the silence.

"Ask you something?"

Josh tried to emulate one of Dom's shrugs, that easy nonchalance. "Hit me."

Dom's meaty hand curled into a fist. "If you say so, chief." He reared back as if winding up for a haymaker. Josh flinched. Dom broke into a grin, slapped him on the back. "Nah, I'm just shitting you." He allowed himself a little chuckle. "This time of night, people get punky. Once the excitement passes, the crash is hard. Gotta keep it interesting."

Gabe wasn't wrong about Dom. The guy could be an obnoxious jingoist. But that didn't make him so terrible. Dom was all right, in his own blustery way.

"Did you actually have a question?"

The other man nodded. "Pritchard." Again, it was like he'd just read Josh's thoughts. "What's his deal?"

Josh tore his attention from the alley. It wasn't as difficult as it had been half an hour ago.

"I don't understand the question."

"Does he make everybody work hard to get on his good side, or just me?"

"I don't . . . that's not my experience with Gabe."

"Just me, then." Dom pursed his lips. The cigar made another circuit of his mouth. Josh wouldn't have pegged him for the kind of guy with easily hurt feelings, but then again, how well could you really know somebody? Appearances were deceiving. Josh chastised himself; of all people, he should carry that truth deep in his marrow. Every part of his work, every part of his life, rested upon it.

Dom honestly looked put out. Josh sought a comforting word. But before he found it, Dom's blustery mask fell back in place.

"Don't get me wrong. He's good. I've got no problem with his work. I'm just trying to figure his angles."

"Honestly, you're overthinking it. Gabe doesn't have a lot of angles."

"Everybody has angles, son."

Well. There was that strangeness earlier this winter. But that had passed. If anything, as ANCHISES prep moved into high gear, Gabe had been more solid than at any time since Josh had known—

"How long have you known him?"

Josh reeled. This was getting downright uncanny.

"How the hell do you do that?"

"Do what?"

"It's like you're reading my mind."

"If I could do that, I wouldn't bother asking questions."

Josh flipped through the pages of a mental calendar. "I've worked with Gabe for about a year, I suppose."

"There you go, then. He's known you long enough to feel comfortable. But I'm the new guy—he's gotta keep me at arm's length. I get it. I'd do the same thing in his shoes." Dom took the cigar from his mouth and frowned at it. Shaking his head, as though ruing the fundamental injustice of the world, he added more quietly, "I'll tell you this much. It's a load of BS that the company quacks have so much power to derail a guy's career over nothing. Especially a solid guy like Pritchard."

Josh's antennae went up. His stifled yawn took a backseat to sudden alertness. He rubbed his eyes. Partially because they stung, but partially to give himself a few extra moments to parse Dom's meaning.

"Quacks. You mean doctors?"

"The Langley breed."

Josh chewed on this while the last stars disappeared from the sky. Somewhere, a municipal electrical timer registered the diurnal cycle and triggered a relay, and a split second later the electric streetlamp blinked off. Josh wondered how long it had been since an ancient city like this had actual lamplighters roaming the streets every dusk and dawn. Idle speculations like these were more comfortable than unraveling Dom's insinuations. The silence stretched under its own weight until, like an unwieldy glob of salt-water taffy, it snapped free of its hook and plopped on the floor.

"Aw, shit, Toms. Please tell me I ain't telling tales outside of school."

"Don't worry about it." The perfunctory reassurance sounded particularly brittle to Josh's own ears.

"Damn, man. I mean, you're his partner, for Chrissakes. I figured if he confided in anybody, it'd be you." Dom fished a handkerchief from the inner pocket of his coat. One corner was slightly browned with tobacco juice. Wrapping it around the cigar, he said, "I really stepped in it, didn't I? I'm gonna slink away now and give myself a solid sock in the jaw. I'll spell you in a few."

He turned to go. Meanwhile, Josh's memory revisited a hit parade of Gabe's greatest moments: Fallout from the Drahomir bungle. The fiasco with the cops that cold morning on the Staré Město. Strange interactions with that bartender at the Vodnář, not to mention with that honey-blond *KaGeBeznik* and her Amazonian pal . . .

Over his shoulder he said, "Dom. Hold up a sec."

Then again. Alestair seemed to know Gabe a bit. He would have warned Josh if he perceived a problem with his partner.

Wouldn't he? Not only because they were allies against the Iron Curtain, but also because of their connection. They had a connection, didn't they?

Dom hovered on the boundary between the kitchen and sleep. Josh deliberated.

The other officer yawned so widely the hinge of his jaw popped like an arthritic knuckle. Josh made his choice.

"I, uh . . . I didn't know doctors were involved." Which was true. He phrased it to imply that he knew stuff, oh, sure, he knew stuff. Just not, you know, the doctor part.

Arms crossed, leaning against the window frame, Dom pursed his lips, as though choosing his words carefully. "I suppose you have a right to know. It affects your career as long as you two are attached at the hip." He shrugged. "Everyone, really."

"I know he had a rough patch this winter. But he's only human. We all have those."

"Of course. I'm not pointing any fingers, okay? But on an op like this"—Dom cocked his head toward the closed bedroom door, from which emanated a faint snoring—"I have to be extra careful. I gotta know my team inside and out. I take my job and its responsibilities seriously. Seriously as cancer. So if I'd seen anything that made me doubt his, or your, or anybody's abilities, I'd have scotched the whole thing. I didn't, and that should tell you what I think of Drummond's team at Prague Station. But when I caught wind of Pritchard's 'rough patch,' I dug around. I know some guys. I got a copy of his file."

You know "some guys"? Guys who could get you a classified personnel file like it was no big deal?

"And?"

"You've heard he was stationed in Cairo before this, right?"

"He doesn't talk about it much, but yeah. I gather it was pretty dull."

"Uh-huh. That's the party line. I'm sure he wants everybody to think that. Drummond knows it's a bullshit smoke screen. Don't you buy it either. You know why his tour in Egypt ended?"

"Never asked."

"Try it sometime, and watch how he answers." Dom leaned closer, dropped his voice to a true whisper. "He doesn't know either."

"That's crazy."

"You tell me. Pritchard's trailing a guy. Everything's normal. Doing his thing, doing it well. Until right there on the street, bam! Blacks out." Dom punctuated the story with a snap of his fingers. The report echoed like a gunshot. Both officers waited, listening, until the low drone of Maksim's snoring resumed its rhythm. "Wakes up some time later raving like a loon. No memory of what happened. Cairo ships him home for observation. For the most part he seems okay, except every once in a while . . . But Pritchard twists a few arms, calls in a few favors, wheedles another posting in the field. He's not a hundred percent, though, is he?"

"Not always." A simple statement. It wasn't like he was revealing a secret. Everybody knew about the incident with the cops. So why did it feel like he was betraying a trust? "But like I said, everybody hits a rough patch."

"Everybody gets a nosebleed once in a while. Not everybody bleeds from the friggin' *eyes*, pal."

"Holy shit. Really? When did that happen?"

"A little while ago. To his credit, he shrugged it off like it was a mosquito bite. Not before I just about had a heart attack, though. You've never seen that?"

"I, uh . . . I've seen Gabe have . . . I don't know. I thought maybe it was a seizure. I knew he'd been in 'Nam. I just assumed he'd picked up something in the jungle. A parasite, maybe."

"These seizures. They getting worse?"

"No, actually. He's been in better shape recently than practically any time since I've known him."

"Well, that's something. You've noticed the flask?"

Oh, that. Josh chuckled in relief. "That's not what you think. He's not a drunk."

"I know. I confronted him about it. But that's just it. I could understand a guy who drinks under the table. You think he'd be the first tippler in the clandestine service? Kid, you ever get sent on a tour of the real backwaters—and I hope you don't—you'll see seasoned officers behaving in ways that'll curl your toes." He shook his head. "You gotta admit, even for a superstition, it's a strange one."

Before his weary mind could catch up and rein in his mouth, Josh heard himself say, "Alestair Winthrop carries a flask." He flinched.

But Dom conceded the point. "True. Those two do spend a lot of time together."

That wasn't what Josh meant. But Dom wasn't wrong, come to think of it.

Outside, the first car of the day blurred past the alley. Prague was waking up. Josh clenched his jaw, fighting to keep a traitorous yawn penned in solitary. "What do you think happened to Gabe?"

"Couldn't say." Dom shrugged. "Not my place, either. But hey, like I said. He's a good officer. Solid guy. If he chose not to bring you inside on it, I'm sure he had a good reason."

"I'm sure."

But if you're not trusting me with this, Gabe, what else might you be keeping from me? Why do you always look like a kid caught with his hand in the cookie jar every time you find yourself in the same room with that KGB chippy? Where do you go when I can't find you?

Dom yawned again. "I gotta hit the hay. You're okay out here for a couple more hours?"

"Sure. I'll make some coffee."

"I'll spell you in two." Dom went straight to the couch. The springs creaked. His eyelids fell like a boom. But then he cracked them again, briefly. "Hey, Toms. This was just between you and me, right? I like Prague. I'm not the type to crap where I eat, you know?"

"Sure. I know."

If not for the curtains in the window, the flat on the ragged edge of an industrial zone might have been empty. From the street, it appeared dark. If anybody sat at that window—and someone ought to be sitting there—they didn't twitch the curtain, didn't do anything to reveal themselves when Gabe strolled up the alley.

He knocked twice. Paused. Twice more.

Footsteps behind the door. Then Josh's voice: "Whiplash."

"Fenwick." *I'm unharmed,* it meant, *and our trail is clean.* Had he said *Do-Right,* Josh would have double-bolted the door, grabbed Maksim, and scrammed out through the emergency exit while Gabe tried to distract or confuse the adversaries converging on the safe house. So far, though, ANCHISES was proving itself more of a Nell than a Dudley. Gabe hoped it would stay that way.

A dead bolt clacked. A chain rattled. The door opened just widely enough for Gabe to duck inside.

"Morning, pal." He opened his overcoat, revealing the waxed-paper bag he'd held cradled to his chest. He hadn't wanted to look like he was meeting somebody for breakfast. "I brought koláče."

Josh bit his lip. "Hmm. Thanks."

His eyes were pink, and the skin beneath them dark and papery. "Have you been on watch since you got here? Where's Dom?"

"I let him sleep. I had a lot to think about."

Gabe put the bag on the card table just outside the tiny kitchen. The hitchhiker stirred, like a napping cat flicking one ear, when he focused on the bedroom door. Sokolov was in there, all right. He could sense the Host. Sense the negative space, the elemental-shaped metaphysical void, within the man.

"Any nibbles from our friends?"

"Quiet night." Josh rubbed his eyes. "Speaking of, you were gone quite a while."

"I back-traced the entire overland route. No signs of activity." He pointed to the table. "And then I picked up breakfast, in case you missed that part." He opened the bag, inhaled. "Got your favorite. Apricot, right? I figured you deserved an *attaboy* after the way you handled things last night." He stuck out his hand. "Nice work, by the way."

Josh looked at Gabe's outstretched hand, then the bag of pastries. He took the latter and disregarded the former. "I'll see if Maksim's hungry." The curled top of the paper sack crinkled in his fist. He knocked on the bedroom door and stepped inside without waiting for a response.

Dom tossed off the flannel blanket under which he'd been quietly snoring. He sat up, stretched hard enough to coax a creak from the springs. Sniffed. "Did I hear the magic word? Koláče?"

But Gabe was still frowning at the closed door. "What the hell got into you?" he muttered to himself.

"Aw, don't mind Toms. He's been up all night."

The conference agenda was canceled and the attendees confined—discreetly, but firmly—to the hotel. Immediately following Tanya's conversation with Sasha, he had made half a dozen telephone calls, including one to his superiors in Moscow. Within an hour, the StB had stationed extra plainclothes officers in the lobby, the kitchen, and at every egress.

Two of the scientists' original minders were still in the hospital, recuperating from injuries they'd sustained during the brawl. Neither could tell Tanya just how the fight had started, or why, or why they'd been so relentlessly determined to injure themselves and anybody around them.

Of course they couldn't. They'd been enchanted by a CIA officer. Tanya knew it in her bones.

And to think I'd actually begun to trust you, Gabriel Pritchard. What if Sasha hadn't tricked us? Would you have stolen Grandfather's construct for yourself? For America? *Perhaps your story about the "hitchhiker" was nothing but air. A ruse to gain my cooperation. In this, I should have heeded Nadia.*

And worse yet . . . if Gabe had learned how to achieve a spell like this, it was entirely due to Alestair's tutelage. Like a frozen lake in late spring, the Ice was starting to crack.

The third minder had been discharged with only superficial bruises, but she couldn't speak with him. At some point during that long night he'd been "recruited for special duty." Which meant that even now he was probably on a fast train to someplace very distant and quite cold.

So that left it up to Tanya and Nadia to manually account for each and every member of the conference. Per Sasha's orders that the defection be known to a bare minimum of officers, they had to do so under the guise of delivering complimentary toiletries from the hotel. They split up, lest the census take all morning.

More than one of the male scientists clearly hoped Tanya was a prostitute in disguise. Pigs. But only a few of those earned a hyperextended thumb thanks to a mislaid hand or a poor choice of words.

Indeed, she discovered that most of the conference attendees were desperately eager to resume the meeting, to an extent that was almost endearing. Nobody could admit outright that the great scientific farce known as Lysenkoism had stunted Soviet agriculture and put botanical science decades behind the West. She imagined it took a certain kind of bravery to devote oneself to a study that had been taboo, a bourgeois pseudoscience, less than a decade ago. Thirty years ago, the title "geneticist" had been a death sentence. Literally.

She was crossing door number eleven from her list—Piotr Medvedev, a bespectacled expert on wheat rust—when the news came down: Somebody had found a body in the Vltava, a bit downriver of the Lichtenštejnský Palace. The palace, she recalled, featured a balcony overlooking the river. Perhaps somebody had fallen during the brawl.

Or perhaps it was meant to appear that way.

Yet at every door on her list, Tanya found a bored and confused scientist right where she or he was supposed to be.

Not so for her partner. When they met three hours later to compare notes, Nadia reported that nobody had answered the second door on her list. Not the first time she knocked, not after she completed the remainder of the list and returned.

She circled the name.

"Well, well, well, Comrade Sokolov," said Tanya. "I wonder if our friend Mr. Pritchard knows you're a Host?"

3.

Karel wouldn't take a cup of tea. He wouldn't even take a seat. He stood by the French windows, arms crossed, scowling. As if he found Zerena's company distasteful. How quickly they forget. Vladimir hadn't even bothered to answer her summons, the insolent little rat.

Well, no. Not a summons. A polite request for a conversation. To confer with her . . . equals.

But Zerena disregarded the slight. As long as the men believed she'd been bested, that Sasha had somehow chastened her and thereby assumed control of Flame operations in the city, she could take advantage of their foolishness. She could still get what she wanted. It was merely a matter of making them believe that she served Sasha's agenda now, and thus their own.

So she flashed her best smile—tainting it with a hint of disappointment at the corners, just large enough to let Karel glimpse the chinks in her armor, to see how the fall from grace rankled her, deep in her private heart of hearts—and, with a minute shrug, poured herself a cup. Karel's cup, an LFZ original sporting a cobalt net pattern like the rest of the tea service, went untouched.

Brightly, but with a hint of cloud, she said, "I trust you and your absent partner haven't broken your new toy?"

He inspected his fingernails. "I told Vladimir that you wanted a meeting so that you could try to wrest a construct from us. I'm not going to do that."

"Oh, Karel. Truly? You truly think I'd summ—" She caught herself, and did it slowly so he'd notice. "—I'd request a meeting just to ask for a share of your own efforts? To beg for table scraps?"

He shifted. Zerena hoped she was better at projecting the meekness of a broken spirit than he was at hiding genuine unease. "If you try to wrest it from me, you'll fail," he said. Full points for bravado; he spoke as if he believed it, even though they both knew it to be a transparent lie. "And then you'll incur Komyetski's displeasure."

Zerena lowered her eyes, lest he see just how laughable she found this threat. Gaze downcast, she held her cup before her lips. It warmed her fingers. She inhaled wisps of steam, rolled a ghostly hint of citrus and pekoe across her tongue. She counted to ten before responding in what she gauged to be the right combination of indignation and regret.

"I know we've had our conflicts. Which is why I requested this meeting, so that we could put that behind us and start working together."

He picked at a fingernail with his teeth, grooming himself like an animal. "Together?"

She nodded. Laying one hand on a lacquered box alongside the tea service, she said, "Your construct. Has it found the Host yet?"

Karel gave her his best attempt at a blank stare. Bless his foolish heart, he actually believed she couldn't read him as easily as a samizdat Bible. Sasha's gambit had emboldened them all.

Of course it hasn't found the Host yet. You'd be crowing it from the rooftops and lording it over me if it had.

Finally, he shook his head. "It definitely had the trail, but lost it at the river."

It took two sips of very hot, very expensive tea before she trusted herself to speak again. She set down the cup and opened the box. It contained a brooch of pounded silver braided with copper and a smaller, matching pendant on a tarnished chain the color of an old bruise. Karel stepped away from the window for a closer look.

She took the pendant. "It would take very little for me to earn a modicum of trust from Morozova. Perhaps a token of affection. A gift." She slid a finger across the brooch. Then she offered the pendant to Karel and chose her words carefully, reminding herself not to phrase things as a command or edict. "I propose you let Morozova do your work for you. Let her find the Host. If you install this in your construct, it will be drawn to her jewelry, and thus your quarry. Sasha wants the woman gone; let the construct do as its nature demands." When he didn't immediately move to accept the pendant, she shrugged. "You'll get the Host plus credit for eliminating Morozova in a way that keeps Sasha's hands completely clean."

"And what do you get, Zerena?"

"I get a pat on the head. I get to live. I get to keep serving our cause." This time, the look on his face truly was unreadable. In response, she said, "If you think my ego is so great that I'd rather die than live with a bruise, you've never understood me."

Reluctantly he took the pendant. Even then, however, he wouldn't take a cup of tea with her.

She breathed in and suppressed a smile.

His loss, the petty fool. It was excellent.

By evening, it was official: Maksim Sokolov was nowhere to be found.

But the body pulled from the Vltava was a rough match for his size, coloring, and body type. Unfortunately, the poor bastard who'd fallen into the river had also fallen afoul of a marine propeller, which just happened to mangle his face beyond simple identification.

Strange, how perfectly inconvenient that was. Almost as if somebody had planned it so. Tanya and Nadia couldn't prove that the dead man and the missing man were the same person. Nor could they prove they weren't.

They couldn't home in directly on the Host without animating their own construct, much like the one Nadia had tried to distract. But that was difficult and time-consuming, and the spellwork would set Prague's ley lines vibrating like a pair of plucked harp strings. If Gabe sensed that—or if Alestair did, assuming he was part of this—he'd take countermeasures. Ordinarily Tanya wouldn't spare a second thought for the pointless efforts of a hatchling sorcerer. But the hitchhiker—if it existed—made Gabe unpredictable, unknowable.

Furthermore, the existence of the roaming construct indicated that at least some of the local Flame acolytes were already hunting the Host; a major magical work by the Ice would put every Flame magician in Prague on alert.

But maybe, just maybe, they could track the Host without resorting to the brute force of a hunter construct. Hosts left faint magical footprints everywhere they went. If they acted quickly, before those ripples faded, they could follow Sokolov's trail. Parts of it, anyway. Doing so put far less stress on the ley lines, especially when they augmented their search with traditional spycraft. They started at the river's edge, at the very spot to which Nadia had chased the construct when the hulking mass of braided trash and magic lost its quarry.

Chill water lapping at the toes of her boots, Tanya unlimbered the tripod slung over her shoulder. Its legs locked into place with a quiet *snick*, and then, with a heave, she pressed the points into mud made squelchy by an early spring thaw. Nadia stood watch while Tanya readied the magical theodolite; both women wore jackets identifying them as city workers and kept their hair tucked under their helmets. To any casual passersby, they might have been surveyors assessing the old wooden quay at the abandoned wool warehouse.

From the apex of the tripod Tanya hung an elaborate swirl of green glass. Obtaining the sixty-year-old wine had been an expensive and cumbersome chore; immediately dumping the contents down the sink as if it were worthless plonk had been an oenophile's nightmare. But the mineral content of the glass and the contours of its punt made for a unique confluence of magical potentials. Girded in copper wire and hung from a thread of—*Forgive me, you poor girl*—Andula Zlata's hair, it became a combination compass and telescope.

It swung freely, aimlessly. When Tanya peered through the glass, it offered a murky view of the opposing shoreline and nothing else.

The sorcerers each laid a hand atop the tripod. The charm quivered as if anticipating the chant taking shape in their minds.

A shared nod, a sharp intake of breath, and then as one they spit complementary chains of ancient syllables at the glass. Tanya's half filled her mouth with the taste of rancid butter. The glass slammed to a stop at the nadir of its swing and began to swivel like a light-house' lens.

Tanya crouched. Now, when viewed through the bottom of the wine bottle, the ground at their feet evidenced a faint shimmer, as though somebody had sprinkled a razor-thin trail of luminescent dust down the alley straight to the river. The line stopped abruptly at the water. This was the Host's trail as sensed by the construct. No wonder it had lost the scent. Nadia uncoiled the copper wire wrapped around one tripod leg. Tanya kept watching through the glass, directing her—"Left. Right. A little more. A few millimeters toward me. There."—until the frayed end of the wire went into the stinking mud astraddle the luminous trail. The theodolite emitted a faint hum; Tanya's fillings tasted like ozone.

She glanced at the almost-invisible thread of Host hair; weeks ago it had powered Nadia's brief impersonation of Andula Zlata, and now, without it, their magical theodolite would have been impossible. It was entirely due to Tanya and Nadia's efforts that the local Flame acolytes lacked access to such a resource and, thus, subtler magics than the brute force of a construct. But where was Andula now? What of the barge and its comatose passengers? What ends had Tanya's hard-earned success advanced?

The magicked punt swept back and forth like a compass needle. Each oscillation covered a narrower arc until the charm locked on the trail. Tanya crouched again to peer through the murky glass. She'd expected the charm to zero in on a landing spot somewhere on the opposing bank; Pritchard knew enough to be aware that moving a Host across the river would dampen its trail. Instead, the thumb-shaped swell of glass pointed upriver, to a building barely visible in the far distance: the Lichtenštejnský Palace.

The river beneath the balconies, innocuous to the naked eye, shimmered faintly when viewed through the punt. Sure enough, the Host had fallen—deliberately or accidentally—into the river *there* . . . and disembarked on dry land *here*. Almost undoubtedly straight into the welcoming arms of a CIA extraction team. Right here, on this spot.

This wasn't the end of the Host's trail through the city. It was the beginning. And as long as it didn't breach the river again, they could track it easily.

Nice try, Gabriel Pritchard.

Nadia kept stealing sidelong glances at her while they reoriented the charm to begin the laborious process of backtracking through the city. The third time, Tanya called her on it.

"What?"

"I will go in your place, when it comes time to retrieve the defector."

Tanya shook her head. "You will not. Our mutual superior ordered me to lead the team. And as the senior officer among the two of us, I forbid you from participating in the operation."

"In this matter, I am *your* superior." Nadia pricked her thumb with a frayed strand of copper, sacrificing a drop of blood to reenergize the charm. "The Host takes precedence over the defector. Once the Westerners remove Sokolov from Prague, we can't protect him." In response to the flash of irritation that Tanya failed to hide, Nadia quickly added, "Try to put the barge aside for a moment. I'm right and you know it."

Tanya sighed. "Yes, I want to keep Sokolov out of the Flame's reach. But our only avenue for doing that is as intelligence officers.

In order to save the Host, we must capture the defector. That makes our priority the intelligence work."

"And what will you do once we've found where the Westerners have hidden Sokolov? With no time to plan and mount a proper operation, will you stroll up to the front door like a good little *KaGeBeznik*? Or will you arm yourself with charms and wards?"

"Of course I will. I'm not a fool."

"Then you will be acting as an Ice sorcerer when you retrieve Sokolov . . ."

And so they went, around and around and around, twirling like a broken compass.

"He's here."

Tanya pressed a thumbtack into the map pinned on Sasha's office wall, marking a spot on the edge of an industrial district. Her voice was scratchy; she and Nadia had bickered themselves hoarse, trying to unravel the jurisdictional Gordian knot while crisscrossing the city to triangulate the Host's location.

Her KGB superior frowned at his fingernails, then tucked them under his chin. He squinted at the map. Frowned again.

"We believe it's a CIA safe house," she added.

He didn't blink. "You know this how?"

"We don't," she admitted. "It's our best, most educated guess." She explained her hunch that the embassy brawl had been a diversion enabling one man to "fall" unnoticed from a balcony, and that the body found in the river was a rough match for the missing Sokolov. She'd concocted a trail of invented witnesses in lieu of magical triangulation, and then finished with a summary of the surveillance she and Nadia had conducted to confirm the likely presence of a foreign intelligence service at the site.

In reality, no fortuitous sequence of witnesses, no matter how observant, could have led them to the spot. This was magical tradecraft, through and through. But what did Komyetski make of it?

He kept his silence long enough for exhaustion to reclaim her. She leaned against a filing cabinet, easing the weight from her knees until they no longer threatened to collapse like a house of cards.

Finally, he spoke. "You're a very fine officer, Tatiana Morozova."

"Thank you, sir."

"The next forty-eight hours will determine our futures. Yours and mine."

She could practically hear the ratcheting as he reeled in the line. She stiffened, waiting for the yank and the sting of a barbed hook.

"Moscow Center is monitoring us closely through this crisis. You have shown exceptional judgment and initiative in the face of this unprovoked incursion from the West. In light of that, our superiors trust that you will apply those same qualities toward the immediate recovery of our wayward countryman from the Americans."

"Immediate" left no room for subtlety. No room for preparations, no room for clandestine operations, no room for patience. Those took time. "Immediate" meant frontal assault.

If she dodged an urgent order from Moscow, she'd be a traitor. If she went, she'd walk straight into the Americans' security precautions.

Nadia was right. This was indeed a trap. One that Tanya wasn't meant to survive.

56
38
60
75
43
86
35
47

EPISODE 12

SHE'LL LIE DOWN IN THE SNOW

Cassandra Rose Clarke

Prague, Czechoslovak Socialist Republic
March 1, 1970

1.

The waitress dropped off a coffee, but Dom left it untouched, just let it steam in the cool air of the café. He kept his eye on the door. He didn't know this place. His contact had suggested it, told him it was out of the way. And *charming*, like he'd care about that sort of thing. He pulled a cigar out of his coat pocket and ran it under his nose, then stuck it in his mouth without lighting it. His contact wouldn't want the scent of cigar smoke seeping into her clothes.

A clock on the far wall started to chime the hour, and as if she'd been waiting outside for the sound, his contact breezed through the door. She threw off sunlight like a diamond. She barely seemed to look at him as she glided across the room, slipping her sunglasses off with one hand. He leaned back in his chair, braced the cigar between his teeth.

"Hello, Zerena," he said.

"Dominic." She sank into her chair and gestured at the waitress, who darted over, notepad in hand. Zerena ordered a coffee—black, the same as his.

"How are you enjoying our lovely city?" she said. "Have you visited the Charles Bridge yet?"

"Haven't exactly had the time." He grinned at her around his cigar. She shook her head in fake disgust.

"I don't know how you can stand those things."

"Hey, at least I didn't light it."

"I'm sure everyone here thanks you for it." Zerena stirred her coffee once and took a sip. She gazed at him over the lip, her eyes gleaming. Dom still hadn't touched his own cup. He wasn't planning on staying long. Although he had to admit, he was enjoying the small talk.

Zerena set her cup down. "Really, though, it would be such a shame if you were to miss the Charles Bridge. How many Westerners are able to see such a thing, these days?"

"I'm not here as a tourist." Dom set his cigar on one of the table's napkins. "As you well know."

"That I do." Her demeanor changed; she hardened, and Dom saw it happen, the glossy facade falling away. Here was the Zerena who had sent word to him through the usual channels: *I must speak with you immediately.* He'd never seen her before that party during his first days in Prague, and yet she was already proving herself a useful ally.

"I spoke to our mutual acquaintance last night," Zerena said. "And I learned something I think you'll want to hear."

He leaned forward, shoving the coffee out of the way.

"Which acquaintance?"

Zerena's mouth curled into a sly smile. "I think you know."

Dom didn't say anything. He did know. Sasha Komyetski. Not a true acquaintance, of course, but rather someone he—and the CIA—was interested in keeping tabs on. And Zerena was the perfect bridge between Dominic Alvarez and the KGB chief of station.

A contact with whom he could be seen speaking without raising *too* many questions.

"I'd heard whispers," Zerena said, "and confirmed it with him as soon as I could. His office knows you have the scientist."

Dom's heart jolted.

"And not only that, but his office knows where that scientist is staying, where your people have him tucked away in safety."

Dom picked up his cigar again. He fought the urge to light it up anyway, Zerena be damned.

"He's sending one of his officers to this location tonight. I thought you should be made aware."

"What time tonight?" Dom stared across the table at Zerena. "You're gonna have to give me more than that to go on."

She frowned. It turned the sharp angles of her face dangerous and cruel. "I don't know, Dominic. He didn't tell me. But you can still prepare."

"This is a pretty flashy move, even for the KGB," Dom said. "Sending an officer right to our front door."

Zerena shrugged, her slim shoulders brushing the ends of her hair. "It's what our mutual acquaintance wants. I simply thought I should warn you."

"I thank you for it." Dom bit down hard on the cigar. The pungent flavor of tobacco flooded over his tongue. He stood up. Zerena just watched him.

"I haven't finished my coffee," she said sweetly.

"You know I shouldn't stick around."

Her eyes glittered; she only smiled at him and then took a sip.

"I appreciate your help," he said.

"Oh, I know." She smoothed a hand down one side of her sleek, pale hair.

Dom nodded, satisfied. Then he turned and strode out of the café, into the bright morning.

Nadia banged on the apartment door, pounding out her frustrations with her fists. She knew it was risky, being here, risky and stupid and in its own way hypocritical. She hated having to come to this apartment—to seek out this man—for help. But she was desperate.

She knocked again, so hard that the cuts on her knuckles split open again and left little dots of blood on the apartment door. "Open up!" she shouted.

As if someone had been waiting for the cue, the door sprang open. Alestair peered down at her, looking as unruffled as always. Her anger flared at the sight of him, but she pressed it down— there were more important forces in the world than this modern divide between capitalism and socialism.

"What are you doing?" Alestair sounded pleasant enough, but Nadia heard the chill beneath his words. "Do you want the whole floor to know you're here?"

Nadia squeezed past him into the apartment. She wasn't going to be intimidated by Alestair Winthrop. "Close the door," she snapped. "We need to talk."

Alestair raised an eyebrow but did as she asked. He slid the lock into place too, and crossed his arms over his chest, studying her. He almost seemed to be smiling, like this was all some delightful prank. Nadia took a deep breath, trying to calm herself. *Don't let him see your panic,* she thought, and then she realized how absurd that was—panic was exactly what she needed for him to understand the gravity of the situation.

"I'm here on Ice business," she said.

"Oh, well, in that case, shall I make you some tea?"

Nadia glared at him. "No. No tea. This is important, Mr. Winthrop. Life-and-death kind of important." She drew herself up, clenched her hands into fists. "That weasel Sasha Komyetski is trying to kill Tanya. *Our* Tanya."

Alestair did not let his face betray his emotions, but he said, "My dear, I think tea is almost certainly in order. Have a seat."

Nadia wanted to scream. She had crossed lines of loyalty for Alestair's help, and he was nattering on about *tea*? But he had already whisked out of the room, and she could hear him in the kitchen, running water and opening cupboards. She stalked toward the sounds.

"Did you hear me?" she asked from the kitchen doorway. "The Ice is in danger of losing one of its best sorcerers."

"I heard you, yes." Alestair did not turn away from the kitchen counter. "And it's terribly troubling. Hence: tea." He set a kettle on the stove and then, finally, looked over at her.

"I don't want to be here," she said. "But I'm—" She closed her eyes. Her heart was pounding; her chest was tight. And she kept seeing Tanya's face, so impassive in her insistence that she must do what was necessary to serve her country, that if she had to die, then she had to die, and that was the end of it.

"You don't need to say it," Alestair murmured.

Nadia looked at him, and for the first time she was grateful to have come here.

"Is Tanya in immediate danger?"

Nadia hesitated, then shook her head. "Tonight. She's going to her death tonight."

"Then we have time."

"No, we don't! Not if we're going to craft a protection spell that could actually help her."

Alestair scooped tea into a wire-mesh tea ball. "A protection spell of that caliber would take more than the two of us, and more than the few hours we have."

Nadia scowled. "Someone as high-ranking in the Ice as you should have access to that kind of magic. Why do you think I'm here?"

"I think you're here because you're afraid for Tanya. Go sit on the sofa. I'll bring the tea in a moment, and we can talk this through." Alestair paused, watching her. "Ice to Ice."

Nadia relented, feeling drained. She knew Alestair was right about the protection charms; for a good one, they would have had to have cast the spell weeks ago. But there was still a chance that Alestair had a prepared charm tucked away somewhere.

Nadia trudged back into the living room and sank into the couch. She studied a blank spot on the wall across from her. Alestair emerged from the kitchen, carrying two teacups that released wisps of steam into the air. He set them down on the coffee table and then sat beside Nadia on the sofa. For a moment they stared at each other. Ice and Ice, Russian and English. Then Alestair plucked up his tea and took a sip.

"Tell me what you know." That light mocking lilt had gone out of his voice; he was serious now. They were colleagues.

Nadia told him. She told him about her conversation with Tanya, that Sasha—"You're certain it was Sasha?" Alestair asked, and Nadia glowered, which he took for affirmation—had ordered Tanya to raid the safe house where the defector was being kept by the Americans, even though it would violate a thousand treaties and she would be exposed, and vulnerable, and better off dead—

Alestair held up one hand. "I see, yes. This is a delicate situation."

"'Delicate' is not the word I would use," Nadia said.

"Drink your tea, dear. It will help calm you."

Nadia grabbed her cup and drank just so he would stop talking about the damned tea. The warmth spread through her—was she actually calming down? She hoped not. She needed Alestair's help, but she didn't want to prove him *right*.

"Now," Alestair said. "About those protection charms."

"Do you have one prepared?" Nadia asked. "I heard you old-timers always have one or two tucked away for safekeeping."

"You heard incorrectly, I'm afraid." Alestair watched her with his glacial-blue eyes. "As we already established, the kind of charm you want is extremely difficult to produce—"

Nadia sighed in frustration.

"—and tends to lose its potency if not used immediately. The kind of power to stop death? It's not easy to come by."

"But it's not impossible," Nadia said. "And Tanya's worth it."

"I don't disagree. I'm merely saying that we don't have the time or the resources to make such a charm before tonight." Alestair paused and sipped at his tea. "Not even *I* have the resources to make such a charm. Believe me, Nadia, I would if it were at all possible."

Nadia slumped back on the couch. She stared down at her tea. This had been her last chance. She wondered if Alestair was lying, if she could trash the place and see what turned up. But she took one look at him, at his worried expression, and she knew he was telling the truth. He might be MI6, but he wouldn't let an Ice sorcerer die for no reason.

"However," Alestair said, "I do believe I can help in another way."

Nadia sat up, alert. "What? How?" She felt a thrill of relief. Maybe Tanya could be safe after all.

"Tanya is lucky in that she has an . . . ally, of sorts, with connections to the defector."

"What are you talking about?" Nadia demanded, her relief vanishing. What was he playing at? "Tanya has no connections to the CIA."

Alestair looked pointedly at her, and Nadia realized to whom he was referring. *Pritchard.* She cursed in Russian.

"So you do know him."

"Stupid capitalist schlub," Nadia snapped. "And as we aren't in need of a golem tonight, I don't see how he's going to help us."

Alestair chuckled. "Yes, that was a rather ill-informed decision on his part. But he can still be useful. I'm not sure how much Tanya has told you—"

Not much, Nadia thought, although she said nothing

"—but she has been assisting him as of late. Solely on Ice business, of course, but it's still enough that he, as the Americans say, owes her one."

"What are you getting at?" Tanya was too entangled with Pritchard as it was. If she owed her life to him—that would be a dangerous thing.

"I can pass word along that Tanya will be coming to the safe house tonight." Alestair sipped at his tea. "If he could have his countrymen, let's say, *move* the defector to another location, and the safe house is empty when Tanya arrives . . ." Alestair shrugged. "What international incident could that incite? A KGB officer breaks down the door to an empty house? It might be an embarrassment to her, yes, but at least she won't be dead."

Nadia studied him. He seemed sincere. He was Ice. They were not complete enemies.

"Is this Pritchard to be convinced?" She still wished they could use magic to protect Tanya. Magic was more trustworthy than an American.

Alestair smiled. "Leave the convincing to me. I've been helping him with his troubles these last few weeks, and I believe he'll listen to an MI6 man, if not to reason. I assure you this plan is better than any charm we could cook up in the time we have."

Nadia set her tea down and looked over at the window. The curtains were drawn, but not tightly; a sliver of sunlight fell through the crack and into a bright line across the floor. A line of energy, although a different sort, a more mundane sort, than the ley lines that were the source of all her troubles.

"If she dies," Nadia said, "I will hold you accountable." She turned to Alestair one last time, so that he would know she was serious.

"I understand," Alestair said.

Nadia stood and studied Alestair for a moment, long enough to decide she trusted him. And then she marched out of the apartment, away from the West, back to her side of the war.

Tanya stared down at her typewriter, fingers poised over the keys. She was supposed to be typing a report, a run-of-the-mill thing, something she did every day. But her thoughts were too cloudy to concentrate. She kept seeing Sasha in her head. Sasha leaning over her desk, the radio, *her* radio, the one thing she had left of her grandfather, sitting in his office as if it belonged there. Sasha flashing her a knowing look as he passed her in the hallway. Sasha informing her that she was to raid the Americans' safe house, to bring the defector back to Russia. And then Nadia, uncharacteristically worried about the danger, commanding Tanya not to go.

But she *had* to go. Nadia should understand that, but Nadia's brains had apparently been rattled from all her boxing. This was a hopeless situation that could only turn more hopeless if Tanya failed to act. Doing nothing would be a betrayal of Russia, and Russia was the one loyalty she could still cling to. She had the Ice, yes, but when it came to defectors—

Tanya closed her eyes. There was another reason she had to go, a reason she couldn't tell Nadia. If the defector, the Host, left Prague, his fate would rest heavy on her conscience. Either he would be usurped by international Flame operatives, or the American Ice would collect him and freeze him for his own safety. Imperfect options, both of them, and some small part of her thought maybe, *maybe*, she could find another way. Even if she died tonight. Even if the defector died tonight. Sometimes, death was the better choice.

Tanya shoved away from her desk. She looked up at the clock on the wall. The hands were inching toward afternoon, evening, nightfall. The embassy bustled around her, the voices of the secretaries a faint chatter in the background, and she couldn't stand it. In these last hours, she needed silence and sunlight and the light touch of the breeze outside. Not this dead, fluorescent office air.

She grabbed her coat and scarf and slipped out. Did she avoid Sasha's watchful gaze? At this point, she wasn't sure it mattered anymore. He already had her radio, already knew he was sending her to die.

The day was surprisingly bright, the still-bare trees stark against the brilliant blue sky. Tanya tightened her scarf around her throat and tucked her hands into her pockets as she made her way down the embassy steps. The air stung at her cheeks, made her eyes water. It might look like spring was nigh, but they were still in the depths of winter.

"Tatiana? Tatiana Morozova?"

The voice rang out like a bell, but it took Tanya a moment to place it. She wasn't used to hearing it here, but rather at parties, with soft music tinkling all around. She glanced over and found Zerena Pulnoc walking toward her, one hand clasping her tasteful wool coat closed at her throat.

"Hello, Zerena." She looked around the empty steps, trying to find a way to excuse herself.

"It's a lovely day, don't you think?" Zerena floated closer. "I can feel spring moving in."

Tanya could feel no such thing, only that shivering, biting cold, strong enough to drown out the heat of the sun. But it didn't surprise her that Zerena felt in her element out here.

"In fact," Zerena said, "if you aren't busy—and, forgive me, it seems you aren't, if you're leaving the embassy so early—perhaps we could go for a walk. To enjoy the spring air." Here, she gestured toward the lifeless trees.

Tanya studied Zerena's bright smile; Zerena, of course, gave nothing away.

"Yes," she said finally. "A walk."

"Wonderful!" Zerena tucked her arm into Tanya's as if they were schoolgirls, and together they made their way down the steps and onto the path that wove through the line of trees. "Nothing like a walk to clear your head in times of difficulty, don't you think, Tanya?"

Tanya stiffened. What did Zerena *know*?

Zerena laughed. "Oh, I'm not blaming *you* for the Americans' capture of Maksim Sokolov. Don't worry. But these things can make for tense times at the embassy, yes?"

Tanya pulled her arm away from the crook of Zerena's elbow. Her chest was tight. "Yes," she said. "It can."

"Such troublesome times we live in," Zerena went on, speaking airily, looking toward the trees as if discussing quotidian frivolities and not the KGB's deepest failures. "That's why I think my parties are so important. They're a distraction from the difficulties of your job. I see the toll it can take on my husband. Poor thing. Always so sick."

"I'm managing well, thank you," Tanya mumbled. Zerena had never shown her any real kindness, much less made overtures of friendship. She had always been distant and untouchable. Unimportant, really, in Tanya's day-to-day life. And yet here they were, their boots clacking out of sync on the stone path while the cold wind whipped around them.

"Are you? You seem rather pale." Zerena stopped and turned toward Tanya, who stumbled, unsure what to do next. Zerena studied her for a moment, her eyes burning across Tanya's skin.

"I'm fine," Tanya snapped, and then she continued walking. Get this bizarre stroll over with, and then she could find a place to be alone, to think, to accept her fate.

"You may be a professional liar," Zerena purred, falling into step alongside her, "but we both know you're not telling the truth."

Tanya said nothing. Her heart pumped. She stared at the path ahead, curving around into the trees.

Zerena leaned in close, her breath warm on Tanya's ear. "I know what Sashenka has asked you to do."

Tanya froze. Her throat closed up. A stupid move, a rookie

move, one that gave everything away, and yet she was distracted, she was not herself—

Zerena laughed. It sounded like icicles clinking together. Tanya's face flushed with heat. It was one thing for the ambassador's wife to know about the defector, but for her to know that in less than eight hours' time Tanya would be breaking international treaties—

Zerena linked arms with Tanya again and pulled her forward. "You look like a deer caught in a hunter's scope," she said. "Don't be so frightened! I'm not here to hurt you. Quite the contrary."

And then she reached into the pocket of her coat and pulled out a linen handkerchief folded into a neat square. She picked up Tanya's hand and placed the handkerchief in her palm, then curled Tanya's fingers around it.

"A gift," she said. "For a new friend. You can open it here, in the privacy of the trees, but you'll see that it's perhaps something to keep secret."

Tanya glanced up at Zerena, trying to find some guidance in her inscrutable features. The object was light, a barely noticeable weight in her palm.

"Go on," Zerena said. "It won't hurt you."

And so Tanya unfolded the linen, hands trembling. When she saw what was wrapped inside, her breath stuck in her throat. She almost dropped the object to the ground and ran.

It was a charm, although it looked like a piece of jewelry— silver pounded into a flat triangle, copper wires wrapped around it in byzantine patterns. It was beautiful. And not of Ice design.

"I made it myself," Zerena said. "You can wear it as a brooch, if you desire, or keep it tucked away out of sight." She leaned in close, pitching her voice low. "It's for *protection*."

"Why are you giving this to me?" Tanya stared down at the charm. It gleamed in the sunlight.

"I want you to take it to the safe house with you tonight."

Tanya whipped her gaze around to Zerena. "What? Why?"

Zerena flicked her hand dismissively. "Is that your concern? Let's just say that I don't always agree with Sasha's motivations. Please, Tatiana, promise me you'll take it with you."

"Only if you tell me why you're helping me."

Zerena laughed. She took Tanya's hand in hers and pulled her along the path. "What reasons are there? I could say patriotism, that I don't want Russia to suffer such a terrible embarrassment. Or I could say kindness—perhaps you are my charity case for the season." Zerena looked over at Tanya. "Only know that I feel some people are better alive than dead. Surely that's enough?"

It wasn't. But Tanya looked down at the charm again. If she were closer to a ley line, she wondered if she would be able to feel its power, to get a sense of what it would do to protect her.

"You think this is a trap." Zerena smiled and shook her head. "Sashenka has you paranoid. We aren't all as cruel as he."

"We?" Tanya said.

Zerena didn't look over at Tanya, but her mouth curved up into a teasing smile. "Oh, Tatiana, don't pretend you don't recognize the origin of that charm's magic."

Tanya stopped. The charm pressed against her palm. Zerena strode a few steps farther, and then she stopped as well and glanced over her shoulder.

"You're Flame," Tanya whispered. Her head buzzed. The charm seemed to burn against her skin.

"Maybe. Maybe not." Zerena slinked back toward her, her movements as graceful and easy as if she were dancing. "But if we're to be friends, I will tell you this." Zerena leaned in close, the tips of her hair grazing against Tanya's cheek. Tanya stood very still, afraid that if she moved, Zerena would lash out with Flame magic. "I know the names of all the Flame operatives in Prague," Zerena whispered. "And as a show of faith, I'll tell you one now."

"Why?" snapped Tanya.

"Shhh. Listen." A pause. Tanya could barely breathe. What did it mean for Russia, that the ambassador's wife belonged to the Flame? And why was she helping Tanya? Tanya curled her fingers over the charm. A trap. It had to be a trap.

"Sasha Komyetski," Zerena said.

Tanya jerked away, stunned. She blinked at Zerena, who was watching her with a calm, appraising expression.

"What did you say?" Tanya hissed.

"Sasha Komyetski, head of KGB Prague Station, is an Acolyte of Flame." Zerena waved one hand dismissively in the direction of the embassy. "Now you know why he was so insistent on sending you to your death. But as I said"—and here she smiled her dazzling party smile—"I don't agree with his choice of actions."

Zerena began walking again, and Tanya followed, taking deep breaths, trying to calm herself. She didn't want to believe Zerena, but this revelation made an unsettling sort of sense. No wonder her grandfather's radio held such a fascination for Sasha. He'd never thought she was a traitor to Russia—he was only a Flame operative, trying to get at the Ice. Tanya closed her eyes. She wondered if he'd spoken to her grandfather's construct. What he said, what he asked.

"What's in it for you, telling me this?" Tanya asked, although she didn't expect an answer.

Zerena smiled. "Such a good little spy. You won't stop digging until you get that intel, will you?"

Tanya didn't respond.

"Fine. I'll divulge one more secret: Sasha . . . *upset* me yesterday. He behaved inappropriately. I won't say more than that. Perhaps we may soon become true friends, and I will elaborate."

They had reached the end of the path. The embassy appeared up ahead, windows shining in the sunlight. Tanya considered it. She thought of her grandfather's radio, sitting in Sasha's office, and her stomach turned.

Tanya didn't know if she trusted Zerena. But in that moment, she made a decision. She shoved the charm into her pocket. Handed the handkerchief back to Zerena.

Zerena brushed it away. "Keep it," she said. "Perhaps, when you are alive tomorrow morning, it will serve as a reminder as to who helped you in this dark time, and who wanted to see you dead."

2.

The longer Alestair talked, the less Gabe liked what he had to say.

"Wait," Gabe interrupted, pinching the bridge of his nose. They sat on a bench in one of the parks near the US embassy; Gabe had just gotten off defector duty, and this was, in fact, supposed to be his break, a chance for him to catch up on sleep and food until he had to return the next day. But then he'd gotten waylaid by Alestair, and now he saw his day falling into ruin. "I don't understand—are you asking me to commit *treason*?"

"Of course not!" Alestair at least had the decency to look aghast. "I'm merely asking you to aid the Ice."

"By doing what, exactly? Handing Maksim Sokolov over to the KGB?" Gabe shook his head, gave a sharp, bitter laugh. "I don't think so."

"I'm asking you to do no such thing. Surely there can be a mutually beneficial solution to our problem? A way for you to whisk the defector off somewhere so Tanya doesn't find herself in a position to sacrifice all for Mother Russia?"

Gabe tilted his head back and blinked up at the bright blue sky. They knew. The KGB. They had tracked Sokolov to the safe house somehow. All his team's careful planning hadn't been worth shit. And Tanya, *of course* she was the one who had to be involved, because her mere presence was enough to complicate—

Gabe went cold all over. His heart thudded.

It wasn't a coincidence that Tanya was the one heading for the safe house, was it? She'd probably been the one to locate Sokolov in the first place. The one to figure out he was more than just a defector. After all, she and that partner of hers had found that other one, that girl—Andula. Sent magic out into the city to find her, isolate her, drag her to that frozen death barge.

Alestair was still chattering along, drawing up plans to keep Tanya alive, although now his words seemed to drip with menace. Maybe this wasn't about Tanya at all. Maybe Alestair *knew* Sokolov was a Host, and this was some way of getting his Ice hands on him.

But no, that didn't make sense. If Alestair wanted Sokolov for the Ice, he'd have easier ways of getting at him, more direct ways, without having to involve the KGB. This really was about Ice solidarity—Gabe even thought he could see a trace of affectionate concern in Alestair's features as he talked about keeping Tanya safe.

Gabe hunkered down in his coat, contemplating his options. Alestair was stressing the importance of keeping Tanya alive—"I know she's KGB, but she has the sort of magical talent of which most of us only dream. A maestro, really, and the Ice can't lose her if they want any hope of defeating the Flame. Do you understand, Gabriel? We mustn't let the Flame win."

"You keep saying that," Gabe said. *But at what costs should the Flame lose?* Gabe understood they were dangerous. Alestair and

Tanya had both stressed that enough. But was it worth it, to add another person to that row of bodies in a magic-infused barge, drifting lazily down the Vltava?

"Because it's true." Alestair's voice sharpened. "I don't think you understand the severity of this situation. You're too blinded by your own nationalism."

Icy river water, his breath condensing in clouds on the air. A row of bodies, each one lying unmoving in the cold. The stink of magic everywhere.

Gabe understood the severity of the situation just fine.

"I don't want her to die either," Gabe finally said. "But I don't know what you expect me to do." He looked over at Alestair. "How did the Russians find out about Sokolov, anyway?"

"I don't know." Alestair looked like he was telling the truth. "Nadezhda didn't tell me."

Nadezhda. Tanya's partner. Not just in the KGB, but in the Ice, too. They had to know Sokolov was a Host but hadn't appeared to tell Alestair. Gabe wasn't sure what to make of that. He fiddled with his coat buttons.

"Gabe," Alestair said softly. "There are stronger and more dangerous forces than the KGB."

Gabe thought back to Cairo, back to the ritual he had interrupted. Dry heat and watering eyes. It couldn't have been more different from the barge, and yet—

"The Ice is trying to protect you," Alestair said fiercely. Gabe stared at the trees, Alestair's voice like an insect whine in his ear. "They're trying to protect everyone. The Flame only cares about their own. If we lose Tanya, that makes it that much easier for the Flame to burn the world down."

"The Ice doesn't want to protect everyone," Gabe muttered.

"Pardon?"

Gabe stood up. He needed to take this to Dom, let him know the Russians were coming. He wanted to leave Alestair sitting in the cold. Let him deal with his world of magic.

"I'll remind you," Alestair said, "that it's the Ice who has helped you with your hitchhiker. The Flame would never have done so."

Gabe's hands curled into fists. He whirled around to face Alestair, who was regarding him with the kind of stony stare that reminded you he really was a spy. It sizzled on the tip of Gabe's tongue, the confession that he'd seen the barge. But he kept it close to his chest. This was not the place. Not the time.

He knew that Alestair was, in some ways, right. The Flame were dangerous. Gabe had a hitchhiker shoved into his thoughts because of the Flame.

But the Ice weren't exactly paragons of virtue either. And if anyone was being blinded by loyalties, it was Alestair—not loyalty to Britain, but to the Ice. He trusted Nadezhda Ostrokhina, a fucking KGB officer, over Gabe, solely because she was Ice.

And maybe Gabe could use that against him. Make him see the Russian Ice weren't being as forthright as he thought. It required a sacrifice, sure, but what didn't these days, in this kind of war?

"Ostrokhina didn't tell you the whole story," Gabe said.

Alestair stared at him, his face dispassionate.

"It wasn't the KGB that found Sokolov. It was the Ice."

"What in God's name are you talking about?" Alestair said.

Gabe shifted his weight from foot to foot, a little dance to help him warm up in the cold. He stopped before he spoke.

"Maksim Sokolov is a Host," Gabe said.

Alestair's eyes widened, and for a moment he lost his

composure. He was genuinely shocked. *Good,* Gabe thought, even if he couldn't rid himself of that dull aching guilt that he'd condemned Sokolov to a fairy-tale curse.

"Are you certain?" Alestair said. "How do you know?"

Gabe tapped the side of his head. "The hitchhiker. Sokolov set it clanging around the minute I saw him. Morozova and Ostrokhina must have sent one of those—things they use to track Hosts. . . ."

"Constructs," Alestair murmured.

"Yeah, constructs. That's how they knew where he was."

"The Ice doesn't use constructs," Alestair said. "Not for this. But we have ways of tracking." He closed his eyes, rubbed at his head. "You're sure the defector is a Host?"

Gabe nodded. "I told you Ostrokhina was keeping information from you."

"Not just her! You knew Sokolov was a Host, and you kept it a secret?"

Gabe stared at him.

"Why on earth would you do such a thing?"

A second of silence passed between them.

"The same reason Ostrokhina did," Gabe said. "Because I'm a spy." Revealing the truth about Sokolov didn't make Gabe feel better about the situation—if anything, it ignited the frustration he should have felt from the beginning, that this magic nonsense was going to screw him. Alestair was worried about Tanya, but Gabe was worried about keeping ANCHISES from going belly-up.

"Nadia had her reasons for keeping the identity of the Host from me," Alestair said softly. "Ice reasons."

Gabe jolted at the diminutive. What the hell was he dealing with here?

"This only complicates things, Gabriel. It only makes it even more imperative that we protect Tanya. And now we have to protect the Host, as well."

Gabe snorted. "Up until you freeze the poor bastard."

Alestair's eyes narrowed. "What did you say?"

"You heard me. I know what you do to those Hosts." Gabe shoved his hands into his pockets. Anger flushed in his cheeks. He couldn't believe Alestair didn't seem to give a shit that *Nadia* had kept the Host's identity from him. "I found your barge. Climbed right on board. Found the cargo." He spit out the last word.

Alestair lifted his chin, his expression unreadable. He said nothing.

"My job comes before the Ice. Always has." Gabe looked up at the spiderweb of bare tree branches. "We've got to protect Sokolov, Al. That's how it is. And shoving a Sokolov Popsicle into a barge isn't succeeding." He looked back down at Alestair. "The West needs him. You know that. What's the Ice going to do with him? Put him on ice like he's somebody's dinner? I'm not saying I want Tanya to die, but right now, my job is to help Maksim Sokolov."

"I see," Alestair said.

Gabe pushed his hands into his pockets. Turned to leave. He didn't have anything else to say. He'd already endangered Sokolov's life on a gamble that didn't pay out.

"The Ice has saved your life," Alestair called out. "You and I both know this. I've already *clearly* said that no one, not even Nadia, expects you to betray your country. And the barge is . . . a complicated matter, and I understand your concern. Someday I hope I can explain its reasons to your satisfaction."

Gabe scoffed. Kept walking.

"Gabriel, I didn't come to you about a Host. I came to you about Tanya."

At that, Gabe stopped. He didn't say anything. He didn't look at Alestair. But he was listening.

"At this point, I don't see how you can pretend that Tanya is simply your enemy. You've worked alongside her. You've aided her. She is Ice, and whether you want to admit it or not, you are an Ice ally, in your own way."

Gabe gazed out at the dead, empty park again. Still no sign of green. Still no sign of spring.

"If you let this happen—if you let her storm your safe house and sacrifice herself to ensure this defector doesn't defect—then the Ice will have lost a powerful sorcerer. One whose power, I'll add, has gotten you out of a tight spot or two."

"Jordan," Gabe muttered. "She's the one who helped me. And you. Not Tanya."

"Bollocks. You don't believe that."

It was true. Gabe didn't. He remembered the way he and Tanya had combined their strength to take down that golem. He sighed and turned around to face Alestair. Pressed his head into his hands. He missed the world as it had been before Cairo, when a woman like Tanya would have only been his enemy, when a defector was only threatened by the Russians.

"What do you say?" Alestair's voice was a low murmur, calm like a nurse consoling a dying man. "Will you do this favor for the Ice? Find a way to stop your boys from killing our girl?"

An enemy and an ally. Ice and KGB. Gabe could just see the lines of the US embassy building through the trees.

"I'll see if I can move Sokolov," he finally said. "But that's all I can promise."

"You're shitting me."

Gabe shook his head. Across the table, Dom leaned back in his chair, his arms crossed over his chest. He gave a short, barking laugh.

"What the hell do they think they'll accomplish?" he asked. "Busting in on us like that?"

"I don't know." Gabe hadn't, of course, told Dom the entire story. He'd carefully stripped away any mention of magic, of Hosts, of barges filled with frozen bodies. But he'd told him enough. Gabe had left Alestair and come straight to the embassy, where he sat down with Dom in one of the spare meeting rooms and laid out everything nonmagical that he knew.

"Well, I say that if they want to embarrass themselves, let 'em." Dom smirked. "We've got the firepower to show 'em that they've made a mistake."

Gabe knew he should have seen this coming, this American machismo grandstanding. "We still need to move the defector," he said. "As quickly as we can." *Hope that's good enough for you, Al.*

Dom considered this. "Think that's such a good idea, though? They're probably watching the safe house as we speak."

Damn it, Dom was probably right. Even if Ostrokhina didn't actually want Tanya to attack, the KGB themselves were still going to have eyes on the place.

"So we—what?" Gabe said. "Let the Russians blow a hole in Sokolov? We really can't afford to be flippant about this."

Dom laughed, slapped one hand down on the table. "I like that spirit, Pritchard. Obviously we'll start working up a getaway plan. While the Russkies are bum-rushing through the front door, we'll be escorting Sokolov out the back." He grinned. "Perfect plan, really. Sokolov gets away, but the Russians can still embarrass the hell out of themselves."

Gabe shifted his weight in his seat. Glanced over to the window that gave a view of the hallway. Dom had closed the blinds when they came in, but Gabe could see a flicker of movement in the place where the blinds had gotten shoved aside. People walking past.

"You're putting our men at risk," Gabe said, still looking at the window. "Unnecessarily."

"Not unnecessarily at all. And you know it."

Gabe looked back at Dom, who was sitting up straighter now, acting more serious.

"It could be a disaster if we try to move Sokolov before the Russians show up," Dom went on. "If we let them attack us, we've got the upper hand. We'll be ready for them. I'll bring in reinforcements." He grinned, although there was no real mirth behind it. "You saying our guys aren't up for the challenge?"

Gabe scowled. "No one should have to die over this." He saw a flash of Tanya's face as he spoke. "But yeah, you're right. Moving early could be a problem."

"So it's settled." Dom stood up, smoothed out his jacket. "I'll get the ball rolling on that escape plan. I'll let Sokolov know too. Get me the location of some alternate safe houses within the hour so we can have them prepped."

Gabe nodded, although he didn't move to get up. He knew damn well he'd done the right thing for the US, bringing the information to Dom. But now he wasn't sure he'd done the right thing for Alestair, for Tanya. Not if Dom was going to have their men playing shoot-'em-up with the Russians.

"Within the hour," Dom repeated as he pushed the door open, letting in the yellow light from the hallway.

"Will do," Gabe said, and he decided in that moment that he would be at the safe house tonight too.

The Americans' safe house was a ramshackle brick building tucked away in a narrow alley. Tanya slipped through the darkness, her little Makarov pistol held low, Zerena's protection charm pinned inside her coat. Yes, she'd brought it. Maybe it was a stupid idea. But she hadn't sensed any danger from it, and with this situation, her whole career and her whole life about to be blown open, she didn't think it could do any more harm.

Tanya was aware of Nadia slinking alongside her—she'd insisted on coming, said she'd be damned if she was going to let her best Ice operative blink out in such an absurd, pointless way. And Tanya hadn't fought it. She knew it was useless, that Nadia was going to try to protect her. Somehow.

They lurched to a stop at the edge of the alley. Three other KGB officers took their positions in the darkness up ahead, and Tanya could only see the faint glint of their guns in the moonlight. She felt sorry for them, angry that Sasha was willing to let others die just to carry out this absurd plan. But they were all low-ranked and loyal to the Party, willing to do something desperate if it meant glory. They wanted to be here as much as she didn't.

All the windows of the safe house were dark save for one on the second floor, its glow thin and muted behind a curtain. No one was standing guard outside, but that didn't mean a damn thing. Tanya glanced over at Nadia, her eyes fixed straight ahead, her hands gripped tight around her gun.

"Are you ready?" Tanya asked in a low voice.

"It's not too late to turn around." Nadia didn't look away from the safe house. "We can knock out the others and leave town. You know the Ice will protect us both."

"You'd betray our country?" The safe house loomed up ahead. The other operatives were inching closer, ready for a fight, ready to die.

"Maybe some things are more important," Nadia said.

Tanya closed her eyes and took a deep breath. She didn't know if she agreed or not. All her life she had been trained to do as the Party asked, to do as the Ice asked. The Ice had lied to her. Perhaps the Party had lied to her as well. But she'd never *caught* them in a lie, and her loyalties to Russia felt stronger in this moment, as she crept toward the house. And it would be easy, to make sure the Host was caught in the crossfire. Zerena's charm didn't have to extend to him.

Surely a quick death was a better fate than the alternative.

Tanya looked at the house. She could hear Nadia breathing beside her.

"Let's move," she said.

She darted forward, her shoulders hunched, her muscles tight with anxiety. The other operatives skittered over the cold cement. Was Nadia following? Did it matter?

Tanya stopped at the door. Lifted her gun. The operatives fanned out behind her—and then Nadia was at her side, smiling bitterly, her gun up.

"You won't get away from me that easily, Tanushka," she murmured.

Tanya nodded at the largest of the operatives, Ilia, and he returned the nod, acknowledging, then stepped forward and kicked the door in.

The world exploded into noise and light.

Tanya ran inside. Her heart beat so fast she could only hear the blood in her ears, a sound like the ocean. Nothing else. She didn't hear the Americans screaming in English as they swarmed into the hallway, three of them, all carrying M16s. She didn't hear the rattle of bullets. She didn't hear Nadia laughing as she fired her weapon and ducked into a darkened room on Tanya's left. She didn't hear the blast of her own pistol, only felt it, the way it jerked her arms back over her head.

The Americans had terrible aim. Their bullets shredded the wall behind her, but she was able to drop to the floor and roll out of the way, firing off shots as she did so. One of the operatives, Sergei—a kid, really, just out of school—slammed hard onto the floor beside her. His eyes were glassy and blank.

The sight of those empty eyes filled Tanya with a sudden, all-encompassing rage. *Damn you, Sasha.* She slid up along the wall and fired at the Americans until her clip ran out and the Americans, all three of them, were lying in a tangle on the blood-soaked floor. The third operative, Yuri, was slumped in a corner, bleeding from his stomach. Ilia and Nadia were gone, vanished into the back of the house, and Tanya could hear shouting, feet pounding overhead.

The Host. She had to find the Host.

She skirted around the edge of the room, avoiding the bodies splayed out on the floor, and knelt beside Yuri. He peered up at her, blood glistening on his lips, and smiled.

"You're a lucky one," he mumbled. "Their bullets didn't even graze you."

Tanya suddenly felt the weight of Zerena's charm pressing against her rib cage.

"Yes," she murmured. "Lucky. You need to get out. Find help for your wounds. Nadia and Ilia and I can find the defector."

Yuri coughed. Blood gushed from the hole in his stomach. Tanya wasn't sure he could even walk.

"Find help," she said, feeling hopeless, and then she stood up and reloaded her gun before she followed the sounds of the shouts she had heard earlier. The house was silent again: a bad sign. Nadia could be dead. The Host could be gone, all this madness for nothing.

Before she got to the stairs, a figure darted out of one of the darkened doorways and raced down the hallway.

"Stop!" Tanya shouted in English, and then she followed, careening around the hallway corner, ready to fire. A door slammed. Tanya ran up to it, wriggled the handle. Locked. She pointed her gun, turned her head away, fired—

Something slammed into her, flinging her into the far wall. Her vision flashed black and white. She fired again, wildly.

"What the hell do you think you're doing?" A hand was on her throat; the voice was rough in her ear. She struggled against the grip, and it took her a moment to realize that her assailant spoke Russian, his American accent turning the vowels to mush. "Are you Reds crazy? You think this is actually going to work?"

He flung her to the floor. Tanya rolled onto her back and fired her gun. There was a flash of light and a sudden eruption of noise, like a thunderstorm. Her assailant dropped to the floor, blood pooling over the floorboards. Tanya got shakily to her feet. She had shot him in the forehead and now she couldn't see his face, only a black mess of blood and bone, and she didn't know who it was. She jogged back over to the door, pulled on the handle. It fell off in her hand and the door swung open, revealing a long line of stairs plummeting into the earth. A single bare lightbulb burned down below, the string still swinging back and forth.

Would the Host be stupid enough, frightened enough, to run into the basement?

Tanya descended. A sense of dread swarmed over her, and with each step it pulled tighter, choking the breath out of her.

"Maksim," she sang out, as if calling a reluctant cat. "Maksim, I only want to speak with you."

The lie rolled off her tongue and disappeared into the dark space surrounding the lightbulb's glow. Tanya stopped at the bottom step and peered around the basement. Was that a flicker of movement? She hoisted her gun. Something was wrong, not with the basement, but with *her*—

And then, with a gasp, she pressed one hand against her coat, where Zerena's charm should have been. But it was gone. The air rushed out of her. The charm had protected her from the gunfire upstairs; she was certain of that. She must have lost it in the fight. No matter. She just needed to find the Host, to complete her mission. His death was the easiest way out.

"Maksim!" she called out again. She stepped off the stairs and onto the packed-dirt floor. She swung her head around, then stepped past the line of light. She blinked twice, waiting for her eyes to adjust.

"I only want to help you," she said softly, and Andula's face flickered in her head. Andula terrified on the street after the construct attacked; Andula frowning in her apartment, about to say yes; Andula lying cold and still and only half-alive on an Ice barge in the middle of the Vltava.

"It's the only thing that can help you," she whispered, more to herself.

Something clicked in the darkness.

Tanya tensed. She recognized the sound of a round being chambered into place.

"Drop your weapon."

She recognized that voice, too.

"Gabe," breathed Tanya.

"Drop it, Miss Morozova."

"There's no need to be so formal." She was still looking into the darkness. She thought she could feel Gabe's breath on the back of her neck.

"Tanya." A pause. "Please."

Maybe it was the "please," that tiny hint of politeness. Tanya laid her gun on the ground and lifted her hands into the air. And then she turned around, slowly, her heart pounding in her throat. Had the Host ever been down here? Had it been Gabe all along?

He stood with his feet planted apart, his gun pointed at her chest. The light from the bare bulb haloed around him, smudging his features into unreadable shadows. Tanya stared at him. Nadia and Alestair and the Ice be damned; she was ready to die. The moment Ilia kicked that door down, she had assured her humiliation and the humiliation of the KGB.

And for all that, the Host was still alive. Still at risk from the Ice and the Flame.

"What the hell does the KGB think it's doing?" Gabe asked. The muzzle of his gun yawned at her.

"Stopping a defection."

They stared at each other.

"Like this?" Gabe said. "Really?"

"Shoot me," Tanya said. "I know you're only doing your job."

Gabe frowned. Tanya watched his finger tap against the gun, her calm like an anesthetic. She felt nothing.

But then he let out a long exhalation, and the gun dropped away, out of sight. He squeezed his eyes shut and ran his free hand over his face, mussing his hair. Tanya felt a lightness that she realized was relief.

Maybe she hadn't been so ready to die, after all.

"He's not here," Gabe said. His hand fell to his side. "Sokolov. We had a plan in place, and we got him out of here before the gunfire started. Did the KGB brass seriously think this was worth it?" Gabe let out a sharp, disbelieving laugh. "You kick our door down, start firing guns—it's practically an act of war."

"It was an act of desperation," Tanya said. But of course it was more than that. This wasn't just about stopping a defection, and it wasn't just about the KGB, either. That was merely a convenient side effect. At its core, this was the Flame sending an Ice sorcerer to her death.

"You have to bring him back to me," Tanya said in a low, dangerous voice. "This is bigger than you think—"

"Why? Because he's a Host?"

Tanya gasped, took a step backward. Her heel knocked into her gun and sent it clattering away.

"Yeah, I figured it out."

"*How?*" Tanya stared at Gabe, trying to work through this revelation. In the dim light his eyes were sunk into shadows, and he looked eerie, like he was capable of real magic, after all. "Was it Jordan? That woman, she doesn't understand—"

"No, it wasn't Jordan." Gabe stepped toward her. His gun glinted at his side. Tanya curled her fingers, wishing she hadn't capitulated so easily. "My goddamned hitchhiker let me in on it. Went off like a warning bell." His voice was tight with anger. "That's the real reason you're here, isn't it? So you can lock him up in that nightmare barge?"

Tanya recoiled as if she'd been slapped. Had he seen in the

darkness? She hoped not. "You don't understand what's at stake," she hissed. "If the Flame got hold of him—" *Or the Ice.*

"I'm not handing him over to you," Gabe snapped. "He'll be safer in America."

"You don't know that. The Flame operates everywhere. Don't be blind, Gabriel. Give him to me. *I* can keep him safe." She stressed the "I," a bit of desperation. Maybe he'd see he didn't have to give the Host to the Ice, only to her, and that she might find some other way.

"Give it up, Morozova." Gabe jerked his chin toward the stairs. "Now get the hell out of here before you make the KGB look any worse." A dark expression flared over his features. "Not that I give a shit."

"You don't understand what you're doing."

"I understand fine." Gabe stepped away from her. She didn't move, didn't reach for her gun. His gun stayed hanging at his side.

He hesitated at the base of the stairs, and for a moment Tanya thought he'd changed his mind, that he'd seen reason, that he couldn't protect the Host from the Flame *or* the Ice.

"Good luck," he said.

Tanya glared at him.

He bounded up the stairs, disappearing into the light above. For a moment Tanya stood in the darkness, and then, as if a switch had been flipped, she followed him, just in time to see him sprint out the front door of the house. Tanya stood at the top of the basement stairs, her heart hammering. She knew she should tail him to the Host's new location and continue with her mission. But he'd be watching for her. He certainly wouldn't let her kill the Host; he would never see that was the only way. And that made her realize she was too tired to follow through with her plan. Too defeated. She was starting to hear things too—she was certain someone was calling her name, a distant voice like a dream. *Grandfather,* she thought stupidly, and then she realized, no, it was a woman's voice. Nadia. It was Nadia calling her.

"Tanya! Are you clear?" A pause. "You better not be dead!"

There it was again. Relief. Relief that Nadia wasn't dead either.

"Clear!" she called back. "Where are you?"

"In the kitchen!" Nadia shouted, and Tanya wove her way through the back of the house. The kitchen was small and bathed in yellow light, the floor tiles cracked and dirty. Nadia was slouched at a rickety kitchen table, her gun resting beside her. She smiled when she saw Tanya.

"Not dead," she said. "That's a relief."

"The defector's gone." Tanya almost said *Host,* but Ilia was in the kitchen too, leaning up against the far wall. "They knew we were coming somehow. They probably took him away before we even got here." She didn't say anything about Gabe. The thought of him sent anger seething inside her. Didn't he understand what he was doing, how he was putting the Host at risk? At least Tanya had found a way to serve both her country and the Ice. Gabe only cared about his country, about getting that brilliant mind to American science. All he'd seen and he still didn't recognize the real threat.

"I assumed as much." Nadia gestured at Ilia, who straightened, ready to do as a superior officer asked. "Go look for clues," she told him. "See if you can find where the Americans took the defector."

Ilia nodded and ducked out of the kitchen. Tanya and Nadia stared at each other.

"We got lucky," Nadia murmured. "The Host not being here."

"Don't say that."

"It's true." Nadia swung her legs in an arc as she stood up. She grabbed her gun off the table. "I don't think we should go after him, either, but we need to make it seem as if we tried. For Sasha's sake."

Tanya whirled away and marched out of the kitchen. She had no right to be angry, not when she had let Gabe run off without following. But she also didn't agree with Nadia. Not really.

"I'm going to see what I can find," she said, and she stalked into the hallway. If she couldn't find the defector, then at the very least she could find Gabe, to try one more time to make him understand the urgency of this situation. That it wasn't just about the KGB. And yet he was so blind in his patriotism that he couldn't see it.

Tanya ducked into one of the doorways halfway down the hall and switched on the lamp. It was a living room, with a shabby, threadbare couch, a beat-up old table. Someone's mug of coffee was still resting next to a chess game. Tanya sighed. Always the chess games.

She walked over to the table. The game had been interrupted by their raid; one of the white pawns lay on its side, askew. She reached over and set it back up. Then she stopped, her hand hovering in midair. Something about the arrangement of the board struck her as—*familiar.*

But that was nonsensical. She did not have time to play chess these days. The only time she ever even saw chessboards was in Sasha's office. All those boards set up like this one, games frozen in time as he waited for his opponent to write him with the next move.

And then Tanya's whole body went cold.

"No," she whispered. She pushed the chessboard around so she could get a better look at the positions of the pieces. *"No."*

She had seen this board before. She had looked at the pieces without looking at them, and yet now she saw them for the first time. In a different place, a different situation.

Tanya's throat was dry. She backed away from the board, one hand out to steady herself.

Sasha and his correspondence chess. All this time, he had been playing with an *American*. The KGB chief of station did not socialize with Americans outside the diplomatic circuit, even if it was just a game of chess. But if he was thinking as a Flame operative, perhaps he did not see his opponent as an enemy.

Tanya had to find Gabe. Now.

3.

The phone jangled through the silent apartment. Gabe rolled over onto his side; he'd been lying in bed but hadn't been sleeping. He couldn't sleep. He kept seeing goddamned Tanya, standing there in the yellow light of the safe house's basement. He'd lured her down there during the firefight, after Dom had whisked Sokolov out to safety. Maybe he'd been trying to keep his word to Alestair, to keep her safe. Maybe not.

Gabe kept thinking about how terrified Sokolov had looked when they told him they were moving him again, that there was a chance the Russians knew where he was. Terrified and *betrayed*, like it was their fault the Russians were acting like maniacs. The hitchhiker had throbbed in Gabe's head, a slow, steady pulse, as Sokolov pulled on his coat and Dom whispered to Gabe, "Don't you worry—I'm taking him to the most secure location I know."

The phone was still ringing. Gabe pushed off the bed and ambled toward it, his chest tight. He wondered what message waited for him on the other end. Something encoded, no doubt, an unknown voice asking a nonsense question. Maybe they'd be telling him Sokolov was secure. Or maybe they'd be telling him Sokolov was dead.

Either way, Gabe knew he had to pick up the phone.

"Hello?" he said. He leaned up against the wall and waited.

"Gabe?"

"Jordan?" The last person he had expected. But hearing her voice stirred up a whole new storm of fears—had Tanya gotten ahold of Sokolov somehow, dragged him off to the Ice? Had she followed him when he left the safe house? He'd taken the necessary precautions and was sure she hadn't.

"Oh good, you picked up." Jordan's voice was fuzzy through the phone lines. "Your little *KaGeBeznik* friend is here. She needs to talk to you. Says it's urgent."

Gabe stiffened. "She just fucking attacked us. She's not my friend."

At least she hadn't followed him.

A pause. Muffled voices on the other end. Then Jordan came back on the line: "She insists it's not about that."

Gabe clenched the phone and considered hanging up. "Bullshit."

Jordan dropped her voice to a low whisper. "She looks *terrified*, Gabe. Something's not right. I think you need to talk to her. I'll be here the whole time."

"It's her job to look terrified," Gabe snapped. "When she wants to."

"And it's my job to know when people are lying. You want my advice? You need to come down here. See what's going on. She won't tell me anything." And then Jordan hung up the phone. Had to make sure she got the last word in.

Gabe stared down at the receiver, the dial tone whining in the distance. He sighed and set the phone down. He wouldn't say he was convinced, exactly, but he also knew Jordan wouldn't jerk him around. He could give a shit if Tanya looked terrified. But Jordan sounded scared, and that had him nervous.

He pulled on a clean sweater, his boots, and a coat, and stepped out into the cold night.

A figure stepped out of Gabe's apartment building, and Josh sat up in the seat of his car and peered through his binoculars to get a better look. Even in the gloomy light of the streetlamps, he'd recognize Gabe's broad frame anywhere.

Josh tensed his fingers against the binoculars. "Don't do this to me," he murmured, and he told himself that this wasn't what it looked like, that Gabe probably just needed to walk off the extra adrenaline from the firefight at the safe house earlier. Except—

Except Josh had *seen* him. Seen him in the basement. After helping Dom escort Sokolov outside to safety, he'd come back inside through the basement entrance, hoping to get the jump on the KGB upstairs. But instead he saw Tatiana Morozova. And he saw Gabe, lowering his weapon and telling this known KGB officer that the defector was gone.

Josh had felt the world tightening around him when he saw that.

Gabe made his way quickly down the street, hands tucked in his pockets, head tilted down. Josh almost considered turning on the car's engine and driving away. Gabe was his partner. He had to trust that his partner was doing the right thing.

But the doubt still lingered in his chest like the last vestiges of a bad flu.

Josh slid out of the car, careful to avoid making noise. Gabe was far enough ahead of him that it probably didn't matter. Still, he was a seasoned professional—he knew the same tailing techniques Josh did. But Josh wasn't about to let himself get caught.

He followed several paces behind Gabe, keeping his steps soft and quick. Gabe, for his part, didn't hesitate, didn't make any sudden turns and disappear down some convoluted path. In fact, it didn't take long for Josh to realize where Gabe was headed: Bar Vodnář. He recognized the buildings around here, even in the dark, and sure enough, the bar materialized up ahead, the windows glowing golden in the darkness.

Was this it? Just Gabe going out for a late drink after a nightmare of an exfiltration op?

Gabe banged on the door, and Jordan answered like she was expecting him. Gabe disappeared inside. Josh slipped forward. He just wanted to confirm that his suspicion was only paranoia, absurd and unfounded. He sidled up alongside the bar, breezed past the windows without stopping. It was easy to peek inside, with the lights turned on, and the night so dark.

But what Josh saw inside turned him as hard and cold as stone. Gabe wasn't the only one looking for a late-night drink.

Tatiana Morozova was waiting for him.

Bar Vodnář's windows were lit up like Jordan had kept the place open late. The door was locked, though, and Gabe banged on it, then tucked his hands into his coat to keep them warm. A few seconds later, the door swung open, and Jordan sighed when she saw him.

"She's waiting for you."

She stepped aside and Gabe went in. The floor gleamed; the chairs were all sitting on top of the tables, legs up. Tanya waited in a booth at the far end of the room, sipping from a glass of beer. She peered up at him, her eyes huge and haunted in the golden light.

"What the hell do you want?" he asked.

"You're *Flame*."

This was the last thing Gabe had expected. He looked over his shoulder to find Jordan, ready to see what she thought about this madness. But Jordan had vanished. *I'll be here the whole time,* his ass.

"She promised she'd let us talk alone."

Gabe turned back to Tanya, who was peering at him over the top of her beer.

"I'm not doing this with you," Gabe snapped, and for a moment he was back in the basement of the safe house, ready to shoot through Tanya's heart. He couldn't bring himself to do it. Not after the conversation with Alestair, and not with her watching him the way she had. *Christ.* He'd never been one to let sentimentality get in the way of his work.

"You lied." Tanya's voice pitched into a mocking singsong. "Oh, my headaches; oh, let's call up a golem." She paused. "You knew all along."

"I have no goddamned idea what you're talking about." Gabe stomped across the room. Tanya didn't take her eyes off him. He slid into the booth across from her. "I hate this magic shit. Why the hell would I be Flame?"

Tanya's frightened expression wavered. "Then you're stupid," she told him, "and can't see the Flame man under your own nose."

Gabe rolled his eyes and slouched back against the seat. "My men are loyal," he said. "I don't have any spies on my team. Sorry you don't have that kind of assurance in the KGB." He paused. "And sorry you didn't get your man," he added sarcastically. "Sokolov is safe, and this magic nonsense isn't going to get me to give him up."

Tanya's eyes glimmered. "I didn't say there was a Russian spy on your team, you idiot. One of your men is Flame. This is not about getting Sokolov back for the Russians, but for the Ice. Are you listening to me at all?" She took a long drink of her beer. Gabe suddenly didn't feel so sure of himself.

"This is not about Russia and the West," she hissed. "You know the defector is a Host. I am not going to deny that it was the KGB who ordered me to raid your safe house. But I am asking for your help now. Not as a spy, but as a sorcerer for the Ice."

The room spun around. Gabe grabbed Tanya's half-empty beer and took a long drink. Tanya didn't protest.

"Fuck," he said when he had finished.

No, no one on his team was a traitor. He could be sure of that. But could he be so sure none of them were Flame? He didn't know enough about magic to be certain.

"Fuck," he said again, more softly this time.

"Yes," said Tanya.

They eyed each other across the table.

"You want to turn him into an icicle, don't you?" Gabe finally said.

Tanya looked down at the top of her beer. There was that haunted quality again. "I don't want him to fall into the hands of the Flame. The Ice's methods are—" Her voice faded away, and she closed her eyes and shook her head. "It doesn't matter. I won't let the Flame have him. I don't care about the Americans anymore. But the Host cannot go over to the Flame."

Gabe sat unmoving. Tanya's cheeks were flushed; her chest

rose and fell with her quickened breath. She didn't like the idea of the barge either, he realized with a jolt. She wasn't going to come out and say it, but he could tell, the way she hadn't looked at him when he'd brought up the frozen bodies.

"You know what the Flame is capable of, don't you?" she asked in a hard voice.

He hesitated, then nodded. Alestair had told him about the Flame, about what they wanted to do to the world. Burn it down and start over.

"We can't be on opposite sides anymore," Tanya whispered.

Gabe knew she was right.

Josh bolted around to Bar Vodnář's back door—he remembered Gabe mentioning it once or twice, and was grateful to discover that it actually existed. Unfortunately, it was locked, but the lock was old, and Josh was sure he could pick it. He slipped his set of picks out of his pocket and jammed them in the keyhole, then rattled them around.

The door sprang open.

Josh leaped back. His picks clattered to the ground. Jordan Rhemes stared at him.

"Let me in," Josh said. "I need to know what Gabe is doing."

"Gabe's talking to an acquaintance."

"He's talking to the KGB!"

Jordan sighed. Fiddled with her bracelets. "You don't know what you're dealing with, Mr. Toms."

"I know enough to know that you are interfering with business of interest to the US government. If you don't let me in, there could be consequences."

Jordan rolled her eyes. Josh felt a flash of irritation.

"I'm serious, Miss Rhemes."

She sighed, and Josh was prepared to push the matter further, to flash his credentials and make veiled threats. But then she sighed again and pushed the door open.

"I know you're not going to give up," she said. "So just come in. Listen away. It doesn't matter."

A trap? Maybe, but he was going to have to take the risk.

"Thank you," he said as he walked in, but she just shook her head.

"You won't understand."

He didn't know what to make of that. But he could hear the low murmur of Gabe's and Tanya's voices in the next room. He crept up the stairs, onto the balcony. The lights were off up there, and it was easy for him to sink into the shadows.

Josh pressed himself against the wall and turned toward the balcony to listen.

Gabe's voice drifted up from below: *I'm not doing this with you.* Then Morozova's: *You lied.* And did she say something about a golem?

Josh frowned. He leaned closer to the balcony, trying to make sense of this senseless conversation. *Ice. Flame. Magic.* It had to be some kind of code. And Jordan had warned him: *You won't understand.*

Part of him hoped that Gabe had just been grooming Morozova on the side, that this wasn't what it looked like. But why would they need this ridiculous code, if that were the case?

The voices fell silent. Josh pushed himself closer to the balcony's edge and peered down. He could barely make out the booth where they were sitting. Gabe took a swig of Morozova's beer. Friendly, casual, like they'd known each other for years.

Josh jerked his head away and pressed against the wall. His heart pumped. *He's just grooming her,* he told himself, over and over, but those weird code words jangled around in his thoughts. *I won't let the Flame have him. . . . The Host cannot go over to the Flame.* Who was the Host? The Flame? Was Ice Russia? It made sense, in an obvious sort of way. Was the United States Flame? But no, she had said *the Americans,* as if they were separate.

Gabe's and Tanya's voices murmured together, too low for Josh to hear now. A dark anger churned inside his chest. He wanted to leap over the balcony, pull his gun on both of them. Demand answers. But of course he didn't. He wasn't stupid. He just sat in the darkness, listening.

"This way, Mr. Sokolov. Watch your step, now." The American pointed at a place where the sidewalk had crumbled away, leaving a jagged hole in the cement. "Wouldn't want you tripping and hitting your head." He grinned and winked. Maksim gave a thin smile in return. The American was a friendly man, gregarious and charming. He'd been the one to pull Maksim out of the safe house before the KGB arrived, and in the car ride over, he'd even offered Maksim one of his cigars. "It'll help calm your nerves," he said.

It hadn't, but Maksim still appreciated the gesture.

"We're in the city," Maksim said, a stupid observation. But after the horror of tonight, he only had room in his head for stupid observations. "Is that wise, moving me so close to the KGB offices?"

"You'll be fine, Mr. Sokolov. You have my word." They were at the front door, and the American—*Dom, his name was Dom;* Maksim knew he needed to remember the names of his protectors—reached into his pocket and extracted a key, a big, brass, old-fashioned thing. The lock let out a click and a hiss when the key turned. *Odd,* thought Maksim.

"This is a neutral safe house," Dom said as he pushed the door open. "That's why it's safer. The KGB doesn't know about it."

Dom stepped inside, blending into the shadows. Maksim hesitated—what did he mean, a neutral safe house? Wasn't the whole point of any American safe house that the KGB not know of it?—but only for a second, because he did not like being out in the open. When he crossed the threshold, a knot of tension formed at the back of his head. He rubbed it. He was so tired.

Dom swung the door closed, locked it—there was that strange click-and-hiss again—and flipped on the lights to reveal a sparse living room. Maksim wrinkled his nose. The air inside had a strange, metallic odor to it, as if they stood in a machine shop and not a house. Maksim rubbed at the growing ache at the back of his head.

Dom glanced over at him and gave a small smile.

"Let's get you set up in one of the bedrooms," he said. "Make sure you're nice and comfortable."

Maksim nodded. The metallic scent strengthened. It wasn't unpleasant, exactly—just unnerving. He couldn't place where it was coming from.

Dom led Maksim down the hall and into a small bedroom. No furniture except for a mattress in the corner.

"I know it's not exactly the Ritz," Dom said, "but you'll be safe here."

Maksim nodded. The pain in his head was spreading down his spine. He needed to rest. Lie down. Try to sleep.

He moved across the bedroom and sank into the mattress. Dom watched him from the doorway, leaning up against the frame.

"It's been a long night," Maksim said apologetically.

"That it has." Dom grinned, pulled out his half-smoked cigar. "I know just the thing to help you unwind."

Maksim looked up. Was the lock on the door *glowing*? No, it was only the moonlight. Only his imagination.

"Tell me, Mr. Sokolov," Dom said, chomping down hard on his cigar. "Do you play chess?"

58
86
76
53
62
66
69
79
37
48

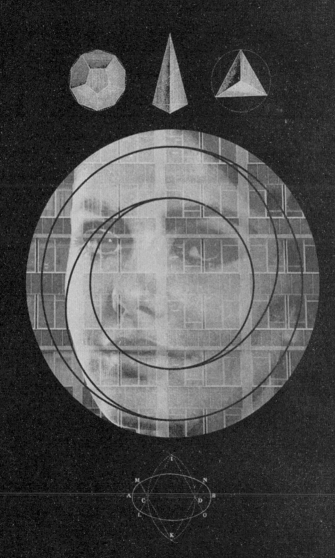

EPISODE 13

COMPANY TIME

Max Gladstone and Lindsay Smith

Prague, Czechoslovak Socialist Republic
March 2, 1970

1.

The CIA pilot readied his plane in the cold before dawn.

Whatever you're imagining, he didn't quite look like that. Higher-ups in his line of work frowned upon people who looked like anything in particular, and he conducted himself so as to minimize any form of notice, including frowns. He took no risks. He turned in early. He smoked, but never more than three a day. He did not drink outside his home. He last had a hangover in 1959. Whatever derring-do was, he daring didn't.

The pilot walked slow circles and reviewed his checklist. No ice on the wings. Wheel well: free of detritus. No rivets loose. He reviewed two checklists—the one on his clipboard, and the one in his head. The checklist in his head featured a few select, secret, Langley-mandated items the one in his hand did not. For most people, this would defeat the purpose of a checklist. The pilot was not most people.

The fuel truck came. He exchanged nods and broad gestures with the crew; when they needed to speak, they used broken German. The pilot's German was perfect, as was his Czech, but he did not want the crew to know he spoke either language well. He waved thank you to them. They waved back. Any description the flight crew later offered would be muddled by his gloves and hat and scarf and coat.

The sky above the airfield blued.

Prague winter morning cold crystallized the air. The pilot's breath sparkled with ice. He stood before his plane's nose, stared up at the featureless glass curve of the cockpit windshield, hands in his pockets. He rose onto his toes and settled back down again.

He relished waiting. He liked the pause, the tension like a coiled spring. Everyone the pilot knew thought about flight differently. For him, its magic consisted of suspension: the coyote magic of moving through air unfallen, so long as you kept to the plan and didn't think too much. So long as you did what needed doing, when it needed doing.

The sun threatened the horizon. The pilot checked his watch. Not late. Not yet.

Gabe Pritchard ran a stop sign, skidded over a dusting of snow, and slammed the brakes, bringing the Moskvich to a sudden stop by the steps of a gray apartment building. Alestair Winthrop, smoking on the sidewalk and so swathed in slick fur and black wool against the cold that he looked like a pomaded werewolf, turned toward Gabe with the disdain of a man roused far too early for far too little cause. "Gabriel. I was about to leave. Surely your emergency can wait until morning."

"I need your help, Alestair." Gabe climbed the four front steps in a jump, tried the door—locked, of course—took a knee, and pulled lockpicks from his inside jacket pocket. Hands shaking. That would be the heartbeat. He closed his eyes, took a deep breath, and tried not being furious, without much success. Not enough time.

"Apparently, if you're willing to do that in full public view." The Brit ran up the steps and spread his jacket wide like wings to shelter Gabe.

Gabe doubted the sail of Alestair's coat would help them *avoid* attracting attention, though maybe well-dressed men flashed closed front doors in Prague on a regular basis. He'd run into weirder local customs in his travels. Distraction. That was the adrenaline, messing with him.

"What, pray tell, brought you to such a state?"

Gabe's second attempt almost broke the pick. Adrenaline, again. No one on the street, no open windows. Maybe talking would help. "Dom's cover's blown." Alestair said nothing—he was monumental and impassive, playing out the beat for more information. "The Flame had someone in the safe house before the Soviet raid. They know Dom's fallback plan—they could jump him and snatch the target before they reach the plane." So exposed, saying this stuff out loud. Hell. No time. Focus. Exhale. Tension, rotate, rake. The lock slipped, the knob turned, the door opened, and he ran inside, Alestair following.

"Your man won't be home." Running upstairs after Gabe didn't seem to hurt Alestair's composure any. His voice barely shook. "Not after what happened last night." Not after the raid, he didn't say. Not after an all-out KGB attack broke a CIA safe house that should have been impregnable, not to mention a secret. Not after a months-long plan to run a defector came to fuck-all because of what looked like the machinations of a cabal of—Christ—cultists. Because in spite of their precautions against the KGB, they hadn't guarded against bedtime stories.

It was Gabe's fault, again. His fault Dom was on the run. His fault Dom might already be dead, from magic or from a more prosaic bullet, and Maksim Sokolov, defector and elemental Host, in the hands of the Flame.

"You can help me find him." Gabe turned a circle on the fourth floor, scratched wood floors sandy with snowmelt grit, walls long grayed from their former white. Dom's apartment lay behind the stairwell, facing the street. Gabe ran to the door, which was, of goddamned course, locked. "With—" Even now, even after the madness of the last few months, his voice hooked when he said, "With magic. If we can find something of his, maybe you can do that whatsit, synecdoche thing—"

"Sympathy."

"Whatever." The door fit poorly in the jamb. He knelt, checked the light that filtered through. "Dead bolt. Dammit."

"Stand back," Alestair said.

The Brit spent so much time affecting the fop that even Gabe, who knew better, tended to forget what he really was: an intelligence veteran of decades' service, an old-school cowboy James Bond son of a bitch, and a sorcerer.

Gabe stood back.

Alestair drew his hands from his pockets and removed his gloves by the tips. He rolled his shoulders, then swirled his hands through two perfect circles in the air. Gabe saw—no, he couldn't have seen, he knew magic didn't work that way—arcs of light trail the man's tapering fingers. Alestair and the world stood perfectly still together.

Then Alestair kicked the door down.

The jamb splintered; the door swung open. Gabe rushed through the door, hands raised and out, ready to put them over his head (in case Dom was here and sleeping with a gun), or tackle whoever was waiting here, armed, for some dumb grunt like Gabe to pull exactly this maneuver.

On the ride over, he'd thought all the angles through. Dom would be here and alive, in which case he'd explain as fast as he could; Dom would be here and dead, in which case, if the assassin remained, disable him or her and interrogate, and if the assassin had gone, search for clues; most likely Dom would be gone, in which case search his personal effects for something Alestair could use to track him.

Gabe was ready for anything but a room that looked like no one had ever lived there.

"You got no idea how good you're gonna have it in the West, Doc." Dom cornered hard onto the airfield. Maksim Sokolov jerked against his seat belt and let out a breath of air. "Sorry about that."

"In Leningrad, drivers worse," Sokolov said, slowly, in English. "Also in the war."

"You're doing great, Doc. Just great. You'll fit in fine. And we have absolutely everything, you'll see. Freedom. Good booze. And the women! Nothing quite like an American woman. Just a few more hours."

"If we escape." Sokolov glanced over his shoulder for the eightieth or three hundredth time this ride—conservative estimates, both. Maybe he wasn't used to being shot at, maybe the raid on the safe house hit him hard, maybe a lot of things. But for the love of Pete, you'd think having a timeless elemental locked up inside your skull would make a body less skittish. *Jaysis H. Christ.*

Still, no sense teasing the Host, so Dom said: "I get it, I really do, all that old-country pessimism. It's a good reflex, especially where you come from. But you're on your way to a better place, my friend." Dom plucked the cigar from his mouth with his gloved hand, and pointed its ember across the airfield to a cargo prop warming itself on the runway. "See? There's our ride."

Empty didn't begin to cover it. Empty was how you were supposed to leave a safe house when you shipped out. Dom's one-room apartment, on the other hand, had been scoured. The floors shone. Not a speck of dust lingered in the corners. The bare mattress stank of bleach. No pictures hung on the walls. No clothes lay in the drawers. The acrid stench of burned hair filled the place. Gabe traced that smell to the glistening white bathroom. Toothbrush, shaving kit—all gone, if they were ever here. Shower curtain, ditto. Charred ash coated the bottom of the bathtub; a few embers still smoldered there. Gabe poked through the ashes with the toe of his shoe: scraps of cloth from the bedsheets. A camelhair suit he remembered Dom wearing. Everything that couldn't be taken.

The fire should have cracked the tub but hadn't. Blackened flame tracks rose to a height of one foot all around the inside of the tub and stopped clean, as if they'd met a wall that wasn't there.

Gabe backed up slowly from the tub, out into the main room, past the untouched stove.

"He's left us a gift, at least." Alestair lifted a wrapped cigar from the windowsill, as if it might bite him. "Not his brand, unless I am very much mistaken. A joke of sorts, I do not doubt, considering the thoroughness displayed elsewhere."

"This isn't normal," Gabe said, "is it."

"Define normal." Alestair rolled the cigar between his fingertips.

"This is how I would proceed, if I wanted to keep an acolyte from tracing me. Clean thoroughly. Remove any trace that might be used to establish a sympathetic or"—with a trace of humor Gabe didn't share at the moment—"*synecdochial* link, as you would have it."

"They burned the sheets in the bathroom." He couldn't quite bring himself to say *he*—but the cigar was a message, wasn't it? "Nothing else caught."

"The Flame does enjoy its cheap tricks." Alestair sighed and pocketed the cigar.

For all his shaking earlier, for all the adrenaline and urgency, Gabe was still now, and cold. He saw Dom in his mind's eye as clearly as if the man stood right in front of him, smoking that damn cigar in this cast-off shell of an apartment, a shell within a shell. "He's—" He stopped.

"There are many explanations," Alestair said. He sniffed the bed. His face wrinkled briefly at the smell of bleach. "If the Acolytes of Flame seized your man, they might have returned to his apartment to ensure we could not trace him through mystical means."

But the Dom in Gabe's mind's eye just grinned around the cigar stub and shook his head. Gabe agreed with him. "If they snatched Dom, they wouldn't have left him alive—if he's dead, they don't have to worry about us tracking him. One bullet in the brain, one body in the river—that's a lot less risky than scouring his apartment. For all they knew, his place was under surveillance. And even if they had some use for him: Why leave the cigar? It's a taunt. This is magic. Dom's magic. He's not one of ours, is he?"

Alestair turned on Gabe. "Ours?"

Dammit. He hated saying it: "Ice."

Alestair's left eyebrow twitched up so small an increment Gabe might have believed it unintentional, had he not lowered it again just as gradually. Gabe waited for the Brit to push it—to point out that Gabe was calling himself Ice now, what an interesting development *that* was, how droll, fantastical, indeed. Waited for the other man to rub it in.

Alestair wasn't a kind man, Gabe knew. But he was kinder than that, at least. "No," he said. "I'm afraid not."

Dom set the chessboard on a spare crate in the hold. Sokolov, strapped in across from him, wrung his hands and glanced left and right: up toward the cabin and out toward the runway. He awkwardly tugged the sleeves of his heavy coat, fixing an invisible crease.

"You're safe, Doc. Nothing's going to stop us now."

"I will never see Leningrad again. Saint Petersburg," Sokolov said, testing the old name as if deciding whether he liked it. "My son, they will investigate him, to be certain he did not attempt to hide the details of my escape. He knows nothing. I have not spoken to him in years."

"He'll be fine." Dom wouldn't have lasted in this line of work if he didn't know how to keep uncertainty out of his voice. He reviewed, by reflex, the many ways to hurt a man. Bamboo under the fingernails. Just take the fingernails off. The thing with the arms behind the back, dislocating the shoulders, what did they call that again? Was that strappado, or was strappado the thing with the feet? Fire, of course. Fire had a lot of advantages. Phantom pains, for example.

He slid a new cigar from his pocket and offered it to Sokolov, who didn't notice. Dom cut the cigar tip off with his belt knife—he always carried a knife on assignment, never knew when you might need a blade. The blade curved through tobacco leaf and dimpled the pad of his thumb.

He lit the cigar with a long match, held the smoke in his mouth. In the cockpit, the pilot raised his hand.

"See, Doc? That's the all clear. We're good to go." He pointed his ember to the chessboard. "Would you like to play white or black?"

"Stop the plane!" Gabe sprinted into the CIA comms station, trailing Alestair and a wake of perplexed embassy staff. "Get the pilot on the horn, contact Langley if you have to, but we need Sokolov's plane grounded."

"Sir?" *Roslin* was the comms officer's name. Gabe's brain produced it just in time—cooperating at last. Where had it been all these months when he needed it?

"Do it, Keith. The operation's been compromised. Sokolov's in danger. We need him on the ground."

Roslin hesitated, hand on the radio. Transistors hummed and whirred. The marine who'd been chasing Gabe caught his arm, but didn't pull him away. A tight line ran from his eyes to Roslin's. Gabe's skull felt tense, his head hurt, and he wondered if that was the elemental inside him, or his native mix of exhaustion, fury, and caffeine. He made himself cold and earnest. This was part of the job too. You could offer, you could trade, you could build trust all day long, but sometimes you had no resources left but your own authority.

Roslin picked up the receiver.

A phone rang in the CIA pilot's cockpit. He frowned. That phone was not supposed to ring. He dropped his hand from the overhead instrument panel, lifted the receiver. "Hello?" No call signs, no identifying handshake. No one had this number. He did not have the number that was calling him.

He wasn't angry, because he did not get angry. But he was frustrated.

Distortion squawked into his ear. A mess of voices tangled one another, crushing meaning.

"Repeat. You're not clear."

The competing voices stilled. One spoke into his ear.

Off to his left, a small cargo plane lifted off.

"I don't understand."

A repeated question.

"I have not received the package. Your delivery boy is late. I had to forfeit my slot in line to a cargo prop." He leaned over to starboard and squinted. "Though the prop didn't load any cargo that I saw. Just two passengers."

Takeoff was so gentle on this clear, cold day that the chess pieces barely slid on their board during ascent. "Good move," Dom said as Sokolov drew back his hand. Bishop forking bishop and knight. Whichever way Dom played, he'd lose one, though if he sacked the bishop, he could retake with the rook's pawn and open the rook—though then he'd have doubled up his pawns, and he'd dropped a pawn already in a dumb fast-tempo play early on and shouldn't be trading now in any event. This was why Dom preferred correspondence chess. His grandfather had taught him how to play in summers of long, slow games, days-long sometimes, hot south Florida afternoons spent drinking sweet, strong coffee on the back porch overlooking the creek. The old man was patient, calm. Sitting across from him, you didn't feel bad taking an hour to puzzle out a move. Grandpa smoked, and waited, and sometimes hummed. He wasn't going anywhere.

Until he did.

Which was the point of all this fucking around with Hosts and magic, after all. Cancer. Death. Bad ideas. Dom wanted nothing to do with them.

At any rate, ever since the old man went, Dom had lost his patience for face-to-face games. He wanted to be moving, to take control, to rush in and slaughter enemy pieces, positional advantage be damned. The pressure of his opponent's presence made him want to scream. *There's no cooperation here, buddy. There's just you and me in this world. And I'm going to win.*

So he made stupid moves, sometimes, and got himself into trouble.

"Good move, Doc. I need to think a bit." He worked the cigar between his teeth. "Think I'll head up and talk to the pilot."

"Of course," Sokolov said. He clasped his hands, each set of knuckles white.

One hand always on the plane wall, Dom worked his way forward to the cockpit and settled down beside his man. Dom didn't know the guy—another acolyte the Flame had found, a pilot pledged to the cause. That was fine. Everything worked better that way: No need for names. No need to know what precious cargo he carried.

Their flight plan circled them back over the airfield. Prague's steeples and rooftops spread below, half medieval winter paradise and half Communist hellhole. And somewhere down there on the airfield, Dom thought he could see the speck of plane he was supposed to have boarded with Sokolov not half an hour ago.

Farewell, Prague Station. Farewell, CIA. I'll see you when I see you.

He tossed them all a salute that he would never have admitted wasn't mocking, and walked back to the chessboard. He sat and started humming, like the old man. After he lost the bishop, he realized he was humming "As Time Goes By."

"Fuck." Gabe slammed the receiver down. He'd torn it from Roslin's hands as soon as the call had gone through. He stood in the radio closet, breathing hard. Roslin stared. Alestair watched, betraying nothing.

The operation was blown. Dom was Flame. Dom had Sokolov.

Gabe tore his arm free from the marine's grip and straightened the lapels of his coat. He marched from the closet, down the narrow, windowless hall toward a dead end, head down, thinking nothing.

Footsteps behind: He recognized Alestair's step before the Brit spoke. "Gabriel." Conciliatory. Calming. Cocksucker.

"Don't start." Gabe dragged in a hot, hard breath. "They have Sokolov."

"That seems to be the case."

Gabe hit the wall, hard. His fist hurt. He knew how to hit, knew it on a deep, reflexive level, and good thing too, or else he would have broken his wrist. "What can they do with that? What can they do with him?"

"A great many things."

Gabe heard the hesitation—Alestair was a good agent runner. Knowledge was power. You have something the agent wants. Don't give it up for free. He remembered Cairo: dust and sun and silver in shadow, a knife and a fire behind his eyes. He remembered

Sokolov entering the hotel, quiet and scared and surer than he had any right to be. "Tell me some."

"They want to break the world open, to burn it and build something—no doubt they would call it beautiful—from the ashes. They need Hosts for that, as we need Hosts to stop them. Sokolov can fuel their workings."

"He wouldn't do that. The guy is a scientist."

"Science, Gabriel, is a way of knowing, not a set of beliefs. If they show Sokolov their powers, he will believe them."

"He was leaving the Russians. No way he'd fall for the Flame's line."

"Perhaps. Then again, perhaps not. The Flame has ways to encourage cooperation, as have we. Bribery of all sorts, subtle and grand. Of course, they also have ways to compel allegiance. And failing both—we have no idea to what extent they have developed the ceremony that embedded that elemental in your head. If Sokolov resists, a possibility on which I would not wish to wager, they may be able to rip his elemental from him, and grant it to a creature more firmly theirs. Failing this, we suspect that if they control the conditions of a Host's death, they can direct the elemental to an infant of their choosing."

"If. May. Suspect."

"You've always known our fields were not entirely dissimilar, Gabriel. That's the reason so many of us operate . . . amphibiously, if you will. In both worlds of hidden knowledge at once. We know what we know—or what they want us to believe. We are reasonably certain we can tell truth from falsehood. But only reasonably."

"With him, will they have enough to do—whatever it is they want?"

"We don't know how many is enough. They'll have more power, certainly. And any one Host could be the one they need."

The rage that had seized Gabe cooled. He turned. Alestair was staring at the blank yellow wall as if into a crystal ball that showed him a future he didn't like. "We won't be able to catch him," Gabe said. "We don't know where that plane's going. It could change call signs a dozen times before it goes to ground. They could land it forty miles from here, or four hundred. Fly it under radar."

Alestair nodded.

"Could we stop it? With—" Gabe breathed in and out. "Witchcraft?"

"Sorcery, please."

"I'm American, Alestair. For us, magic is witches."

Down the hall, Roslin shouted in Czech at the aircraft control tower. *Need more information*, Gabe caught. Yeah. Good luck with that.

"We have no Hosts in Prague," Alestair said. "I am a . . . witch, as you say. But we lack a Host."

"The barge on the Vltava—"

"Has moved on, taking with it the Hosts and their elementals."

He might be telling the truth. Or he might be lying through his teeth, backing Gabe against the wall, forcing him to say now: "What about me, Alestair?"

If Alestair felt triumph, he was too careful to show it. "We would need ley line control."

"Jordan's bar. She'll let us use it."

"And we need acolytes." Alestair closed his eyes. "I'm sorry. Witches, if you prefer."

"You can't do it alone?"

"No."

"So we bring them in," he said.

"Them?"

Gabe lowered his voice. Made it vicious. "Tanya Morozova. Nadia Ostrokhina. We need their help."

2.

Tanya dragged herself up the stairs of the apartment building, moving against the flow of the early morning workers headed to their factories and desks. The world felt far too normal, after everything she'd endured. How could these people carry on, unmarred by fear of the chaos to come? How could they smile and laugh and trade little barbs as if they were not living on borrowed time under the threat of the Flame's terrible plans?

Nadia opened the door before Tanya even knocked. "*Bozhe moi.*" Nadia scrunched up her nose. "You look like—"

"—shit. Yes, I know."

"No. I've seen you look like shit before." Nadia stood back to let her enter. "This . . . this is something else entirely."

Tanya glanced at Nadia's sofa, a threadbare floral life raft. Her every joint ached, screamed at her to sit, but she feared that if she sat, she'd never be able to get back up again. "Before you say that you told me so . . ."

"*Tikho.* I don't care about that." Nadia gripped her by her shoulders. "You are here."

"For now." Tanya sucked in a ragged breath and closed her eyes. "They have the defector. The Host. The *Flame* has him."

"Wait—" Nadia had been picking up a mug of coffee; she slowly set it back down. "The CIA is Flame?"

"Yes. No. One of them is." Tanya pinched the bridge of her nose. "Someone in the safe house—he's been in contact with Sasha. I saw a chessboard that was exactly the same as the one Sasha's been playing, and the magic that was used—" Tanya took a deep breath. "One of the Americans is working with the Flame. This wasn't an exfiltration op for the Westerners. It was the Flame, seizing a Host for themselves."

Nadia had been wound in a tight ball, but as she listened to Tanya's exhaustion-tinged raving, she slowly unfurled, focused and ready for battle. Tanya locked eyes with her and leaned forward, desperate, her body pointed like an arrow. Nadia had to believe her. Tanya couldn't prove her claims at all, not with hard evidence and carefully sourced intelligence reports. All she had was her operator's intuition. But keeping a Host out of the Flame's grasp was too important to leave to chance.

"And what," Nadia said very carefully, "do you think the Ice should do about this?"

Tanya exhaled. "We must stop them from leaving with the Host."

"Leaving?" Nadia asked.

Tanya nodded. "The safe house was a waiting room. They were prepping for exfiltration. Maybe they'll take the Host back to America, maybe not, but wherever they mean to take him, we can be sure what they mean to do with him there."

Nadia pressed her lips into a thin line. The fact was, they weren't entirely sure *how* the Flame was using the Hosts, only that they *were*. Thirty-six Hosts in the world at a time, representing the thirty-six elements, no more, no less. And the more of them the Flame had at their disposal, the more Hosts they placed along the confluences that crisscrossed the globe, the more power they could draw on to fuel their rituals. These were the facts under which the Ice operated, ever since whispers of the Flame and their dark goals had begun to crackle in recent decades.

Then there were the rumors. Tanya was quite certain Nadia did not wish her to hear about them, and every time Tanya had tried to ask her grandfather's construct in the radio, before Sasha had stolen it from her, he'd behaved as if it were beyond his scope. But Tanya knew better. Nadia had told her about the wild eyes of Ice operatives who'd witnessed things they wished they hadn't. She'd heard the tight whispers in Bar Vodnář. That the Flame was finding a way to harvest the elementals from their human vessels. Plant them into people of their own. It made for a great scary story to tell Hosts, to convince them to give themselves over to Ice custody. But as a reality . . . the thought made Tanya's stomach wring itself dry.

Tanya rested a hand on Nadia's forearm. Her partner had height on her, and a boxer's easy confidence, but Tanya knew the force behind her chilly stare. "I must ask you something, knowing full well that as your subordinate, you need not answer me."

A vein throbbed along Nadia's throat.

"How many Hosts does the Ice have in custody?" Tanya asked. "Not just in the barge, here in Prague. How many, total?"

Nadia shrank from Tanya's grip. "Not enough." She squeezed her eyes shut. "Not nearly enough."

"Then we cannot let the Flame have even one more."

"No." Nadia's voice was tiny, high pitched. It occurred to Tanya that she'd never seen her friend, her superior and subordinate, without her masks before. Had never even noticed that the easy bluffer, the insouciant seducer of men and women alike, the boxer and jazz aficionado and condemner of all things capitalist even *was* a mask. But she saw past it now, and it sent a chill worming straight to her heart.

Tanya relaxed her fingers, and her hand fell from Nadia's arm. "Then I have an idea."

Nadia's living room offered few obvious hiding places, but Tanya was a veteran at rooting out dead drops. She kicked up the threadbare Kazakh rug and began tapping the edges of floorboards with her toe. One popped up easily, and Tanya knelt to scoop out the contents of the hollow beneath the board. Tangled copper wires; crystals; a collection of vials tightly rubber-banded together, all of them sloshing with muddy water and labeled in Nadia's loose script.

"That's not my best stash. Not by far." Nadia loomed over her. "Tell me this plan."

"You won't like it." Tanya shoved the whole collection of vials into her coat pocket. "It requires the American."

Nadia swore. "You can't be serious."

"So he's capitalist swine. You think I don't know that? You think I don't wish to strangle him myself for snatching the scientist out from right under our noses?" Tanya groaned. "We need the power of his elemental if we want a chance of succeeding. We have to try. He hates the Flame as much as any of the Ice's faithful—perhaps more so, for what they have done to him. You read Winthrop's report, as I did. Pritchard has every reason to want the Flame to fail."

Nadia worked her jaw back and forth. "Fine. So we enlist Mr.

Pritchard's assistance, and more importantly, the aid of his little elemental friend. But then what? We storm the airfield? I'm sure they are already well on their way to Washington, or whatever Flame depot they're redirecting to."

Tanya smiled sweetly. "So we stop the plane."

Nadia flinched as if slapped. "Pritchard will never agree. And the sort of spell it would require—I mean, you've seen the effort it took for us to work the Ostankino protocols a few years ago, and that wasn't nearly as life-or-death as this could be. . . ."

"Please. We have to try. Get in touch with Winthrop; let him be the one to persuade Gabe. I'll start gathering components."

"Winthrop has already pushed counter to the Ice's wishes as far as he dares for me. He's too cautious. After what he's done, he wouldn't empower a charm without orders in triplicate from his Ice superiors." Nadia barked a dry laugh. "Even if we can convince him that the American—"

She stopped abruptly at the sound of a knock on her apartment door.

Tanya carefully fastened the cover of her satchel closed, her gaze locked on Nadia's. Should she hide? Should they both hide? The Americans could have agents anywhere, after all. Someone in the KGB. Someone like Sasha, sent to stop them.

Nadia held up a hand, then wedged the other behind her shabby couch. When she pulled it back out, she was clutching a Makarov pistol. "Who is it?" she called, her voice pinched and high.

Tanya shifted the weight of the satchel to her shoulder and rose silently. Adrenaline burned off all of her exhaustion in an instant. She leaned forward, weight on the balls of her feet, an ancient language on her lips—

THE WITCH WHO CAME IN FROM THE COLD

"A friend." British accent. Tanya exhaled, and the exhaustion came roaring back. Winthrop. "I, ah, I'm afraid I might require your help."

Nadia returned the Makarov to its hiding place, then moved toward the door. "I'm afraid you do."

Zerena had been battling a monster of a headache for the better part of the morning, and Aleksander Komyetski was not helping matters.

"You may embarrass me in front of those imbeciles from the university all you like, but this office"—Sasha jammed a meaty finger onto his desk—"is mine. You have no authority here. None. Even your *ublyudok vanyuchii* husband, should he ever deign to visit the embassy again, is not welcome beyond the doors of this vault. I am the chief of the rezidentura. And I will not have you or anybody else meddling in my operations!"

Zerena popped an aspirin into her mouth and bit down hard. Relished the bitter, chalky taste. It tasted no worse than Sasha's grating voice felt. "I would never dream of interfering in the KGB's business, Sashenka. I am a diplomat, after all. I have no place in the affairs of spies."

Sasha barked a laugh at her, the sound so crisp she nearly flinched. "If you are a diplomat, then I am Andrew fucking Carnegie. What did you do, Zerena? The miraculous return of my operative reeks of your meddling."

"You have kept your star operative and have not humiliated this entire office with your foolish bid to send good men to their deaths over a perceived slight by the Americans. I would say you are sitting quite nicely at the moment," Zerena countered.

Sasha ripped a sheet of paper from his typewriter. "Flash cable to Moscow Station. 'It is with great sadness that I must report the death of Tatiana Mikhailovna Morozova, who perished attempting to recover a Soviet person or persons who we believe may have been forcibly taken into American custody for their extensive knowledge of the Soviet Union's superior engineering techniques. I authorized no such course of action, fearing for Comrade Morozova's life, and instead cautioned her to develop an alternative means to recover the abducted scientist. Sadly, she took it upon herself—'"

Sasha snarled and began to mutilate the sheet of paper. Zerena frowned as the snow of the draft sprinkled down upon her.

"I needed this. *We* needed this. The KGB would not have appeared remiss in its efforts to recover the scientist, our colleagues would have still acquired the *component* we need, and we'd have rid ourselves of this lying bitch, all at once."

Zerena held up her palm—smooth, lightly scented with Parisian lotion. "Sashenka."

He exhaled through his nose like a bull, but at least he stopped shouting. Zerena felt her pulse throbbing through the pain of her headache and waited a few moments before she continued.

"You look at our dear Tanushka, and you see nothing but one of *them*. An adversary. Someone opposite you on your little boards, yes?"

Sasha glanced at one of his chessboards. Zerena followed his gaze and, after a moment studying the board, saw he was stuck in that particular game. Any move he could make would guarantee a loss.

"But she has other uses to us. Knowledge. Power. A position of some importance. The chance to be a conduit for us, a puppet. And, given her heritage, I am sure she is not without some skill in our arts." Zerena allowed a brief smile to flicker on her lips. "It wouldn't do to waste the resources we have at our disposal, now would it? Leave that to the bourgeois capitalists."

"You know nothing of the workers' struggle," Sasha said, his tone low. "Ever since you married *him* you've been bathed in the blood of the exploited—"

Zerena's anger and rage narrowed into a single point that burned hot inside her. The metal in her blood was on fire. The gold on her wrists was molten. She was incandescent, her fury liquid and rippling. For one brief moment, she imagined letting Sasha drown in it.

Then she drew a slow breath and eased back.

"I know everything," she said carefully, "of what it is to struggle. To strive."

Sasha's arms remained folded, but now they appeared more as a shield.

"I can reshape her. Make far better use of her as she is than as a line item on your cable." Zerena rolled her shoulders back with a satisfying crack. "I will leave you to your work. But you must leave me to mine."

Sasha stared at her for a long moment, then nodded wearily. All the fight seemed to have left him, for now. Zerena knew better than to hope it would last for long. His gaze drifted toward a scroll hanging from his wall, a Japanese landscape of misty mountains and delicate tree branches.

"One more acquired," he intoned.

Zerena smiled. Her headache was lifting. "One more acquired."

She dissolved the auditory charm protecting the office from eavesdroppers and entered the main rezidentura vault.

Then froze. Nadia Ostrokhina was at her desk ten meters away, digging through her drawers, but with the lazy aspect of someone less interested in locating some treasure than in looking busy. It wasn't so early in the morning that she had no business being here, and yet . . . a flash of gold in Nadia's hand snagged Zerena's attention.

"Rather early for you, is it not, Comrade?" Zerena asked, sidling toward her with a dagger-sharp smile. "I shall have to tell the French ambassador his parties are getting too dull."

Nadia returned the smile a little too readily. "I'm afraid I missed the French party. Wasn't feeling well. Still not, in fact." She bumped her drawer shut with her hip. "I was just getting a few things before I returned home."

Nadia's hand was still clutched tight around whatever it was that Zerena had glimpsed. The woman was a junior officer, but she spent an awful lot of time around Morozova, Zerena knew, and the possibility couldn't be ignored . . .

Zerena darted forward and snatched Nadia by the wrist. Her thumb found the soft patch between the woman's wrist bones and dug in. Nadia yelped and jerked her arm back, but Zerena's grip stayed firm.

"Comrade—" Nadia looked at her with wide eyes. "Please—"

Zerena continued to press. Nadia's fingers popped open in surrender. But no—no ritual components, nothing remotely useful at all. Only the nub of a worn-down yellow pencil rested in her palm.

"We have had a problem with the theft of office supplies in the embassy," Zerena said, keeping her tone sharp. "I would hate to think any of Sashenka's officers were responsible."

Nadia's brows furrowed, and, for a moment, Zerena feared she might see through the lie. Might know precisely what she'd really been looking for. But the moment passed, and some of the tension in Zerena's skull eased. She released Nadia with another smile.

"I apologize for the roughness, but I am sure you understand the importance of protocol." Zerena slipped into her jacket. "Do feel better, Comrade."

"Thank you," Nadia murmured, still flustered.

Zerena didn't glance back. She had work to do.

3.

Prague Station convulsed around Gabe. He hunkered in the records vault, thumbing through files with a flashlight between his teeth, while the usually quiet machine of the CIA station outside broke into a clamor of clicking heels and growling voices and grinding organizational gears. His hands sweated, and he fumbled file tabs. His heart had its own rhythm for assignments: a quick light patter like a child's sprint. He forced himself to slow and focus and listen. Panic tightened nerves, spring-loaded the engines of blame. If his colleagues found him here, and his half-baked excuse—wanting to check a lead in Sokolov's file—didn't stick, the best he could hope for was to be held under supervision until long after all chance to stop Dom had passed. Most of the other options involved a bullet in his brain.

Somewhere in the world outside the records vault, Frank screamed at Emily. Frank never raised his voice, he didn't need to, but the moment—the whole goddamned op—had gone exceptional. Questions jumped between unwary minds. Spies treasure gossip like caviar—and for once everyone could talk about their fears, everyone but Gabe. They asked: Had Dominic betrayed them? Had he then been betrayed in turn? Was he sitting pretty in some tropical paradise, laughing around his cigar? Or lying silent in the mud beneath the Vltava's cold waters?

Gabe alone knew the truth, but he couldn't say; nobody else knew, and they compensated by saying everything they suspected at the top of their lungs. This wasn't Gabe's mess, though no doubt someone back at Langley would try to hang it on him—anything to avoid tainting Dom, and by association every asset he ever handled, every higher-up who ever tagged him for promotion. Maybe they'd settle on the truth, or a version they could accept without having to understand elementals and Hosts and the whole fucked-up witchcraft world—Dom had turned, or started sour. But Gabe wasn't optimistic. He'd been in the service too long. His neck was furthest out; he'd get the knife when the time came, whether they thought they were killing him for treason or gross incompetence.

Fine. Let them. He hadn't expected to die in bed since Cairo.

But he had to catch Dom and Sokolov, stop them while there was still time. For that, Alestair said, for their ritual, they needed information. *Everything we can get on Sokolov, especially the details of his birth. Date, time, location—precise as possible, my dear man. The more we know, the more certain a fix we'll have on our target, and the greater our assurance the ritual will work.*

Not Dominic? Gabe had asked.

Well, no. Your man's an operator. He will have obscured the key details in his file. Stick to Sokolov.

Gabe found the file under *S*, propped it open, and copied the key details into a notebook from his pocket: city of birth, address, date, time. Nice and clear. Hopefully it would help. Every little bit, right? He closed the file cabinet, locked it, tore the notebook page free, folded it small, and slipped it under his watchband.

He turned off the lights in the vault before he emerged into the hallway. So far, so good. Look busy. Walk fast. Quick steps, hands in pockets, head down. Turn right to leave the station. Down the front steps. The rest of the world waits past those street-level doors: a chance to make this whole damn mess right. Beyond, Prague sidewalks lay cold and caked with snow and soot.

"Gabe!"

Far enough away for him to have plausibly misheard. Just a few more steps. He pushed through the double doors into the chill, and measured his pace as he walked. The steam of his own breath wreathed him. *Stay calm. Don't draw attention to yourself.*

Someone caught his arm. He turned, too sharply for innocence.

Josh Toms stood behind him, panting and purple from the run.

"Josh. You'll get cold without a coat."

The kid shook: cold, exertion, and nerves. "What are you doing, Gabe?"

"Taking a walk." He stilled his heart, counted time for his breath, kept his eyes on the young man's eyes. He could act normal, when needed. "I have to clear my head. This thing with Dom, I can't believe he'd betray us."

"You were in the records vault. I saw you come out. And you headed straight for the street." *Damn.* Gabe had been right—the kid was wasted behind a desk. "Are you working Sokolov for Morozova? For the Flame, and the Ice?"

And because Gabe was a professional, he didn't slip, didn't flee, didn't slug Josh in the face. He considered, for the slightest of instants, palming the notepad page, eating it on the way back to the station. Calculation took the drawing of a breath: Josh was scared, and desperate, like the rest of them. He knew—too much. Where had he learned those names? What had Gabe let slip during his argument with Alestair earlier? But Josh had mentioned Morozova in connection with the Ice, which meant, shit, he'd been in the Vodnář. Gabe stepped toward him. Spoke low. "I'm not working for Morozova," he said. "She's working for me. There's a deep game here, Josh. An iceberg game. You only know the tip of it."

"You're a traitor."

"I'm not the traitor here. Dom is, and maybe others. I think I can stop him. But I can't do it through official channels."

"God damn it, Gabe, if Dom's soured, if you have proof, Langley has to know. Frank has to know." Josh caught Gabe's wrist and pulled him back toward the embassy.

Gabe didn't move. Josh stumbled; Gabe caught his lapel and dragged him closer, face to face, nose to nose. Hair-thin wrinkles crossed the kid's forehead. Gabe had never noticed them before. "You think Langley doesn't know? Who sent Dom in the first damn place?"

"Tell me what's going on, Gabe." Pleading. "Give me something."

He almost did. Damn him, he almost did. What would relief feel like? To tell this kid about the witches and the weird, about the truths Gabe wished he didn't know? *Pain shared is halved,* Ma used to say. But Gabe had traveled farther, done more, and learned some pains don't halve by the sharing.

"I can't," he said finally. "This isn't your game. But—I can fix everything, if you let me."

Josh said nothing.

Gabe let him go. "I'm going down that street. You don't have to stop me."

Sometimes authority is all you have.

He turned, walked away.

Josh didn't chase him.

Tanya wasn't sure what she was expecting when she reached the Vodnář, but the air of the mundane unnerved her. It was business as usual. Witches nursed their drinks over the usual animated arguments about pharmacopoeia, while men in stiff-collared jackets sank into the shadows of the booths. She shifted the satchel on her shoulder, letting its weight against her hip ground her. Normalcy was good. Normalcy was the goal. If they could pull this ritual off, if she could really trust the American—and the Ice, for that matter—then no one ever needed to be the wiser.

Jordan caught her eye from the doorway leading toward the back rooms. Toward the chamber that rested atop the confluence of the ley lines. Tanya could almost feel it, vibrating beneath her feet, threading through the components in her bag. She smiled wearily. Jordan pressed her lips together in response, and jerked her head toward the darkened corridor.

It was time.

"He's not here yet," Jordan warned her, as they made their way into the bowels of the Vodnář. She didn't need to say who.

"Will he really come?" Tanya's own voice sounded faint to her ears.

Jordan's teeth clicked together. "Depends."

Tanya understood. It depended on which Gabe valued more—being a good little patriot, allergic to any collusion with the Soviets, or saving the world. Well, most Westerners she'd met believed them to be the same thing. Tanya's task was to untwine the two.

And now for the holding of breath: to find out if all her

developmental work had been for naught. This time, it had been more than just a spy game. She'd meant every word of warning about the Flame. Whether Gabe believed her or not was on him.

Nadia already sat cross-legged against one wall of the curved chamber. Candlelight cut sharp shadows across her face as she studied Alestair across the room. Alestair, for his part, was making a good show of calm, his hands propped atop his umbrella handle and his posture relaxed, but Tanya saw the taut muscles of his neck.

"Well, then," he said, as Tanya and Jordan entered. "I suppose we'd best begin."

"What about Pritchard?" Fear coiled tight in Tanya's belly. Without his elemental attunement, the ritual wouldn't be nearly as strong.

Alestair exhaled through his nose. "I believe he is willing, but the choice is ultimately his. Unlike some, we are not in the business of coercion." He smiled thinly. "Now, if you'll kindly prepare the instruments, I think I've found an appropriate passage—"

"You mean to lead the ritual, then?" Nadia asked.

"Well, I hardly think it appropriate for a Russki to be leading a ritual designed to halt a CIA operative from carrying out an exfiltration operation." Alestair snapped the tip of his umbrella against the stone floor. "It's a matter of propriety."

Jordan sighed. "I don't give a shit about your stupid Western propriety. Let's just get on with it."

"Wait. I'm here."

Tanya's attention snapped to the doorway. Gabe wedged his way past Jordan, his face ruddy, a sheen of perspiration slicking his hair to his brow. The knot in Tanya's stomach went slack.

The candlelight shimmered as Gabe made his way into the

room and spread out an aeronautical map in the center of the circle. Tanya padded toward him and bit her lower lip. The red classified markings on the paper, the hasty pencil scratches copied from encrypted sources . . . She'd just persuaded Gabe to turn over state secrets. She should feel elated. But all she felt instead was the grim weight of the task before them. The more Hosts the Flame collected, the closer they came to realizing their horrible plans.

"Now," Alestair said, "we were just discussing who ought to be leading us here today."

Gabe nodded at Alestair, then scanned the gathered crowd. He set his jaw and met Tanya's gaze. "Maybe Tanya should lead."

All heads whipped toward her. Tanya's whole body quivered. Grandfather had never prepared her to do something so massive as this. Ice magic was a subtle nudge here and there, a steady hand guiding one's path. It was not a fist, decisive and difficult to contest.

But that's just what they meant to do here.

Tanya let the satchel in her hands sag to the floor with a clank of crystals and stones. Her gaze fell on Nadia, but the woman's expression offered no comfort. They were close, but they'd never been in the business of comfort. And neither, Tanya supposed, had the Ice.

"This is everything we were able to recover," Nadia said, gesturing to the heap before them. Chunks and hinges of the construct scattered across Gabe's map, copper wiring and quartz and ashed herbs arranged in a miniature, roughly human shape. Jordan mashed a still-smoldering clump of papers and herbs in her mortar and pestle, then scattered it atop the construct's remains while Tanya watched.

Tanya's skin felt too tight for her body. The pulse of the ley lines beat against her like a drum. Already, the energy was pouring into the crystals. Now the task fell to her to bring it to life. Give it direction.

And hope that Gabe's own elemental—hell, that Gabe himself—would cooperate.

"The map shows the original flight plan the CIA charted for Dominic, but he'll likely have chosen his own path," Gabe explained. The words were rushing out of him all at once, as if someone had pulled his plug free. "Still, it's a good chart of the wind currents. I thought it might—might help us guide the way."

"It's good," Tanya said. "It is a starting point."

Gabe grimaced, somewhere between smiling at her approval and cringing at it. Tanya supposed it was the best she could hope for from him. "One last thing from the embassy's trash," he said, then pulled a chewed-up stub of a cigar from his pocket and tossed it onto the heap of components. "To help us focus on Dominic."

Tanya nodded. She linked hands with Nadia, who linked with Alestair, who linked with Jordan. Then she held her hand out toward Gabe.

"Once we join hands," Tanya told him, "you can't let go."

Incense clogged his lungs, and the shadows of Jordan's basement wadded thick and cloying as wet cotton around him. He swam, or drowned, in the dimness. The construct twitched in the circle, a spidery Tinkertoy twist of broken metal. He wasn't supposed to be here. This wasn't what Gabe Pritchard did. He served his country. He fought. He killed. He betrayed, sometimes. But this—this was Cairo and worse.

He had to stop Dom. He couldn't, without Tanya's help. All the other screwing around with Ice and Flame, that had all been spy work, or close to it. This was something different. He glanced to Jordan for help, but Jordan's eyes were closed. She was part of this ceremony, now. This ritual. They needed him.

Tanya's hand glowed in the dark.

Sokolov pondered the board, and Dom wondered if he'd see the trap. Dom had lost the first game, and won the second on a fluke misplay he blamed on Sokolov's exhaustion, but he'd have liked to win this game on his own merits. *Never count on your enemy's mistake,* Grandpa had taught him. Dom wondered, waiting, if he'd ever go back to Florida. Didn't matter one way or the other. He'd never liked the state much. Everyone had to grow up somewhere— no sense letting nostalgia bog you down.

He thought he'd set the Russian up proper this time, baiting the trap with a knight apparently exposed to Sokolov's bishop and rook. Dom's own rook guarded the knight, but Sokolov might accept the trade, maintaining his material lead—if Sokolov didn't notice that, by moving his rook, he would place himself in check. If Sokolov attacked with the bishop, Dom could take the bishop with his own rook, and then Sokolov's pinned rook as well; if he tried rook takes knight, the trap wouldn't spring, but at least Dom would gain tempo.

Sokolov reached for the bishop, and Dom tried not to look as if he cared. The scientist's fingers closed around the piece, and he twisted it in place. His lips thinned.

Then a fist of wind struck the plane.

Chess pieces scattered. Dom slid, rolled, and rose into a fighting crouch, hand to his knife. Sokolov sprawled on the floor among rolling bishops.

Dom staggered toward the Host, kicking pawns out from

underfoot. Sokolov caught his wrist, levered himself upright. The man didn't look hurt. Dom helped him to a seat and strapped him in. "How about a little warning next time?" he shouted up to the pilot.

"Turbulence." The pilot sounded tense. "Weather's getting strange up here. Sudden clouds, weren't on any of the forecasts."

"Strange how?" No answer. Sokolov reached for Dom's jacket, but Dom stepped back. "It's fine. You'll be fine. We got this under control." He smiled. Sokolov did not seem to calm.

The airplane jerked again. The Russian cried out. Fuck it. Dom ran for the cockpit.

Dom barreled into the cockpit. "What the hell is going—" The sky silenced him.

Black clouds—not gray, but the color of volcanic ash—boiled up against either side of the plane; ahead, they bubbled into new, twisted curves, spitting out columns of smoke. Weird, sick, green-and-purple lightning crackled from their depths. The plane was flying into a sky like a closed fist.

The pilot was talking. "—never seen anything like—"

Neither had Dom, but he recognized it all the same. This wasn't weather. This was a weapon.

"Turn around," he said.

The pilot twisted the yoke. The plane rattled, but didn't turn. "It's not responding."

Sparks played over the instrument panel.

"Get down," Dom said. He felt—nothing. Wooden. Locked inside himself, frozen in the face of the sky.

"It's fine. We can weather it. The plane's insulated."

"Get down, dammit!" There was the anger; there was the sweat. "Low as you can go."

Sokolov babbled in Russian, some kind of prayer Dom couldn't follow through the engine noise.

"Down!"

"Gabriel." Tanya's voice sounded so childish to her ears. No, not childish—exposed. There were no more games or roles or covers to maintain. She hated it.

But if her most honest self was what she needed to convince Gabe Pritchard to help, then that was what she'd be.

Gabe looked at her as he sucked in an incense-choked breath. Orange sparks danced in the gleam of his eyes. "I . . ."

The construct—what was left of it—surged to life with a rattle of quartz and wire. And those crystal eyes—those orbs that had hunted for a Host, a very specific Host—began to glow.

Gabe's fingers laced in Tanya's.

"—down, God damn it, get us down, get—"

And then there was light.

The construct hung in the center of the circle of people with the limpness of a marionette. Only there was no hand holding it up— just their chanting. Tanya didn't need to be told the words or the language; she felt them, strumming inside her like a chord, and all she needed was to open her mouth and let them pour out.

Gabe's hand was like fire against hers, searing away dead skin, spreading through her limbs and on to Nadia on her other side. His elemental tasted of metal and intoxication, like a thick, silvery alcohol in her blood. It oozed, quicksilver, through her senses, plating her words in mercury.

Threads of gold spun from the chanters' mouths. Stitched themselves around the hovering construct, its quartz joints, crystal eyes, even the nub of cigar. A fierce wind circled them, picking up speed. Whipping at their clothes and hair. Pressing in on them in the eye of the storm.

The construct rose higher as the wind howled against the chamber's roof. Its limbs twitched and fought; its crystal eyes rotated, giving the impression of a spooked horse.

Gabe's hand became Tanya's, and his elemental became all of them, knitting a fine web of magic over everything. Two ley lines and an elemental to power the spell—Tanya wondered, dimly, if that raw energy might tear her apart. Too late. She was mercury and air, quartz and crystal and ash, she was the pinprick on the map that linked all these things together and the cool alpine air on the other side. She could almost see it, in the gaps between her words—the aluminum frame of the plane. The chess pieces flying around in its cabin. And then the sudden crush of pressure as the storm converged—

The world whirled and returned. Some small, feverish beast screamed in Dom's ears. He was Dom, still. He was alive. Spinning, collapsed against the instrument panel, but alive.

He blinked tears from his eyes and pushed himself upright. The pilot slumped against his harness, neck broken. Vomit and spit and blood leaked from his mouth. Poor bastard must have bitten through his tongue, along with everything else.

"Fuck," Dom said, but he couldn't hear his own voice.

Clouds swirled and burned outside the plane. He didn't look into them. He didn't want to see the things he knew were there. This storm wasn't natural. The goddamned Ice again. Pushing. Always pushing. Jealous fuckers. They'd called things in the night, monsters in the storm, great quivering snakes of shadow in the sky.

And the plane was going down.

Dom shoved the dead pilot off his yoke. His stomach lurched as he moved. The plane swirled. *God damn it, God damn it.* He tugged the yoke, twisted—no control at all. Couldn't even guide the spin. Stalled. He risked a glance out the window, fine so long as he didn't stare into the clouds: The plane was miles up and falling fast, nose to ground, rolling on its axis.

No way to save the plane, not now. Fine. Fine. *Repeat that enough times and you'll convince yourself it's . . . What's done's done. Get a parachute.*

He felt curiously weightless as he climbed onto the back of the pilot's chair, jumped, then caught the cockpit doorframe and pulled himself up, legs flailing. He panted and surged onto the bulkhead, collapsed. Seconds left, if that.

The parachutes hung toward the rear of the aircraft, near the seats. To reach them he'd have to climb straight up, fifteen feet in this whirling coffin. He couldn't make it in time. The plane would pancake into Ass-End, West Germany, with him inside.

Then the emergency exit door behind him blew. He heard that, even over the small, high screaming of the beast. *Don't give up. Turn.* Sokolov stood by the open door, parachute on his back, tensing. Of course. He'd been strapped in, near the parachutes. He wouldn't have blacked out. Plenty of time to grab a chute and go.

The Flame needed this poor bastard: a perfect Host, tractable, timid. They knew Dom's flight path, they'd be along before the CIA could mobilize the local authorities.

Your duty's clear. Be the pawn. Sacrifice yourself.

But Sokolov trembled at the door. Dom had seen it before: afraid to jump, even if staying meant death.

Dom forced himself to his feet, worked his way along the bulkhead to Sokolov, wrapped one arm around his shoulders, and slit the old man's throat with his knife.

Blood sprayed across Dom's hands and shirt. It burned. Magic? Guilt? No time to worry. Sokolov gaped at him with both mouths. Dom tore off the old man's parachute, adjusted the straps, and dove out into the magic-mad sky.

Something had changed around Tanya. With a blink, she realized it was the room. It was crooked. No—she was. Her cheek throbbed something fierce where it rested on the cold concrete floor. A thousand specks stung her face; when she wiped at it, her hand came away with pulverized stone and blood.

"Tanya." Gabe was crouched over her, nudging her shoulder. Sweat crept down his temples.

Everything was brighter now, but hadn't the candles gone out? She tried to glance around for the light source. It hurt her eyes too much to move them. She squeezed them shut with a groan.

"Tanya." Nadia, now. *"Tanushka. Otveti mne."*

"She's fine." Jordan's voice, smoky and cracked. "Nothing a shot of vodka can't fix."

Tanya rolled onto her stomach and forced herself into a crouch. Gabe's hand on her shoulder fell away as he scrambled back from her.

Tanya rocked onto her heels, still curled in a ball, and forced herself to open her eyes once more.

What was left of the map smoldered in the center of the ritual floor. And on top of it—she squinted. The construct. Lifeless and shattered beyond repair.

Tanya swallowed down the lump in her throat. Her mouth still tasted of toxic metal. "Maksim Sokolov is dead."

Zerena tapped away the ash from her cigarette and pressed the transmit button on the radio with one lacquered fingernail. "Wraith requesting status update."

"Nothing to report, Wraith." The American voice on the other end was taut. "I'll have to go dark soon."

"Nothing?" Karel snapped, hovering over Zerena's shoulder. "They should have landed two hours ago!"

Zerena regarded him with narrowed eyes as she took a sip of her bourbon.

"This is unacceptable. Your contact at the air base is lying to us." Karel shoved his hands into his pockets. "He is leading you on. They want the Host for themselves."

"My contact and his Flame sponsor are not . . . pleasant men," Zerena conceded. She wrinkled her nose, remembering Dominic and his awful cigars. "But they are loyal to our cause."

"How can you know? Honestly. How can you be sure? With you and Sasha constantly stabbing each other in the back, and then that disaster in Cairo—we're falling to shit." Karel shoved his hands into his hair and left them there. "It's unacceptable, Zerena. At this rate, the bloody Ice will acquire more Hosts than we will."

"They did not capture the Host," Zerena said. "I am confident of that."

"Does it matter, at this stage? They've captured many more. We're falling behind."

"But they have no courage to kill them." Zerena smiled. "To kill a Host is to lose the elemental—set it free into the world once more. Then it must find a newborn Host. It could latch on to anyone, and we'd have to find them anew. But look, Karel, at the favor they have done us. With their cowardice, their reluctance to kill, they have instead collected all of these Hosts for us, their elementals neatly contained."

"Collected," Karel echoed. "You are certain."

"Reasonably." Zerena stared at the ash collecting on her cigarette and tapped it away again. "I *am* quite certain who does know for sure."

Karel exhaled loudly. "And I don't suppose you'll be sharing that information with me anytime soon."

"Of course not. Look what happens when I do." She pressed the transmit button once more. "Wraith going dark. Report any further information through the usual channels."

"Copy."

She switched the radio off with a snap, then looked back at Karel. His rumpled suit, his stubble, the oily tint to his face. Such disarray, over one little piece of a much larger machine.

"Make sure you hide that radio somewhere less obvious this time," Zerena told him. "Even I can't control when the StB will conduct searches."

Karel shot her a withering stare. "Yes, well, what *can* you control these days?"

Zerena's fingers were around his throat in a flash. Ruby lacquer pressing into fish-belly-pale flesh. Karel's lips pulled back, swollen and slimy, to reveal mossy teeth.

Somewhere in the room around them, a flame crackled, hungry.

"Stay out of my way." Zerena's Czech turned into a hiss. "Soon, I'll have more Hosts than your tiny mind will even know what to do with."

Karel's muscles slackened, though only by a fraction. "I know precisely what to do with them."

Zerena tilted her head to one side, arching one brow. "Then you'd better start finding me acceptable vessels."

She released him and spun on her heel to fetch her jacket from its hook.

Karel rubbed at his throat, watching her, something like fear or irritation dancing across his features. "From the ashes," he whispered.

"From the ashes," Zerena echoed. "Very soon."

And then she was gone.

4.

An unseasonable warmth held Prague in a gentle embrace. Tanya shucked off her jacket and paused on the Charles Bridge, watching the workers pass her by, as a soft orange sunset spread like egg yolk in the west. Exhaustion pulled at her bones, but it was a good exhaustion. The weight of a job well done. The weight of being alive.

After the past few days, she'd gladly bear that weight.

By the time she reached the embassy, it had emptied out for the day. She'd missed a full day of work. No matter. Tanya smiled wearily as she made her way down the concrete steps to the vault. She still had a report to write.

Frank stared out his narrow office window into the embassy courtyard. Steam drifted from his coffee mug.

"I can't say I'm happy to hear any of this."

A file lay open on his desk: close-typed pages stamped TOP

SECRET and a black-and-white photograph of a wreck only a professional could identify as a crashed cargo plane.

"They found the plane in West Germany, which wasn't on the flight plan." Frank set his coffee on the windowsill and pulled a cigarette from the pack in his shirt pocket. He lit the cigarette and drew a breath. "Nobody knows why Dom turned. Langley says he was a model agent. Impeccable credentials. No one knows how he got this far down the road. No one even knows why. Sokolov was a fine asset for us, a nice grab, but he wouldn't have won us the war. From a Soviet perspective, Dom was a much higher-value asset. So: Sokolov was more valuable than we knew. Or Dom had overplayed himself somehow, would have been found out soon, wanted to take as high-value a play as he could get. Or he wasn't working for the Soviets, and planned to go solo. Too damn many questions, and I don't like any of the answers the eggheads back home keep pushing my way." He tipped ash into an ashtray. "And then there's Gabe."

The overhead light painted the bare walls green. Somewhere in the world outside Frank's office, typewriter keys hammered against paper.

Frank shook his head. "I can't believe any of it. He's a sharp agent. He's had his knocks, sure. Cairo hit him hard, and I've been riding him even harder to get him to shape up. But he's a clean, good worker, and he's had a thousand chances to betray us if he's had one. So. I don't like your tale. I don't like hearing it so soon after Dom. I feel like there's another game running next to ours, or on top of it—which I wouldn't mind if it hadn't suddenly started moving pieces that matter to me, and to the United States of America. I don't like being pulled into games I don't play." He turned from the window. "Thank you for coming to me with this, Toms."

Josh kept still. He'd spent all his conviction telling the story. Now, having spoken, he felt alone. "I didn't know where else to turn, sir," Josh said.

Tanya had already fed a fresh sheet of paper into her typewriter when she noticed the thin strip of light beneath Chief Komyetski's office door. Her fingers froze, hovering over the keys, as panic clenched around her heart. He'd sent her to her death. Whether he knew of her connection to the Ice or not, he'd tried to murder her. And he'd been working with the American Flame man all along.

But she was done with hiding. From the KGB chief, and from the Flame.

Tanya squeezed the crystal paperweight on her desk, then stood. Her stool gave a faint metal groan as she tucked it away.

Sasha's back was to her; he was resetting a chessboard to its starting position in one corner of the room. Several of his games had been reset, in fact. She tucked that little detail away for later.

"Tanya. My dear girl." Sasha turned toward her with a hideous smile pressed firmly in place. He was no happier about this than she was. "I was horrified to learn that those capitalist fiends shot at you. And poor Sergei, Yuri . . ." His whole face sagged with sorrow, as subtle as a Kabuki mask.

"Do not be sad, Comrade. We will find a way to make the Americans pay."

"Indeed we shall." His gaze sparkled in the harsh fluorescent light. "I am working with Lubyanka on several ideas this very moment, in fact. But you!" He wagged one finger at her. "You should not be working so hard. Take a week off, Tanushka. I insist on it. Rest. Clear your mind of this dreadful ordeal."

"But, sir—the paperwork."

"Bah, the paperwork can wait." He waved her toward the door. "Go. Rest."

Tanya had no doubt there was some ulterior motive in his desire to send her away, but she was too weary to puzzle it out just now. She could use the rest. Rest . . . and time to regroup and plan. How she wished she could speak to her grandfather again, or even his construct in the radio. Someone who could guide her through whatever came next.

Open warfare with the Acolytes of Flame? No—Prague was not a place for open battle. They would continue as they had been, with feints and stabs in the shadows. But Tanya had no doubt that there were far greater dangers lurking right around the corner. There was a larger web being spun around her, and Chief Komyetski was only one spider waiting for her to be caught.

But at least she saw the web now. Now she could begin to tear it down.

"Actually, Comrade . . ."

She gestured toward the chessboard that Sasha had just arranged, then sank into the chair before it. White. In spells, it was a purifying color. In some cultures, though, it was the color of death. She plucked up a pawn and rubbed it between her fingers.

"I think I'd like to play a game."

Acknowledgments

LINDSAY: First and foremost, I have to thank Julian Yap and Max Gladstone, who somehow said, "We need a Soviet witchy espionage-y showrunner," and came up with my name. I'm humbled and thrilled! The entire Serial Box team has been phenomenal to work with—Leah Withers, Caitlin Burns, and Molly Barton in particular have gone above and beyond to get *Witch* out into the world.

I cannot say enough about our incredible writers, Max, Ian Tregillis, and Cassandra Rose Clarke, who make my job as painless as can be with their clever plotting and gorgeous prose. My agent, Ammi-Joan Paquette, is ever patient and brilliant as I pinball through my genres and projects. And the entire *Witch* editing team has helped us put all the clockwork together with great finesse: Juliet Ulman, Noa Wheeler, and Navah Wolfe. Thank you, all!

MAX: Thanks first to Ian, Cassie, and Lindsay, intrepid and inventive partners in fake spy shenanigans, and to Juliet, for always pushing us to take that next big step along the road. Without the tireless efforts of Julian, Molly, and Leah at Serial Box, and Navah and team at Saga Press, there's no way you'd have this volume in your hands today. And, as always, thanks to Steph, most excellent and beloved, and ontologically prior to all this.

IAN: I'm honored that Julian, Lindsay, Max, and Cassie invited me to play in their mystical sandbox, and grateful for their willingness to listen to my absurd ideas with such equanimity and grace.

Juliet Ulman's eagle-eyed editing has been crucial to this effort, as has Noa Wheeler's meticulous copyediting. Julian Yap, Caitlin Burns, Molly Barton, and Leah Withers not only made the project a reality but also made the outside world know and care about it.

CASSANDRA: Thank you to Julian Yap for giving me the chance to work on *Witch* in the first place, and as well to my fellow *Witch* writers Lindsay Smith, Max Gladstone, Ian Tregillis, and Michael Swanwick—I'm so pleased with what we've done together! In addition, thanks to my agent, Stacia Decker; the *Witch* editors Juliet Ulman, Noa Wheeler, and Navah Wolfe; and the entire team at Serial Box: Leah Withers, Caitlin Burns, and Molly Barton. We couldn't have done it without you!

MICHAEL: My thanks to everybody at Serial Box, my fellow writers in particular, for letting me play in their sandbox. You're a great batch of people.

THE
WITCH
WHO CAME
IN FROM
THE
COLD